Wesley North is a husband and father. He lives in the south eastern most part of Ireland. Coming armed with a vivid imagination and a passion for world building, he launches his *Kingdom of Heroes* series as his first adventure. He aims to develop a long lasting career in developing memorable characters and exciting story-telling.

He enjoys reading, writing, woodland walks and spending time with his family.

I want to dedicate this book to my friends and family – thank you for believing in me when so many didn't.

Wesley North

KINGDOM OF HEROES

AUSTIN MACAULEY PUBLISHERS™

LONDON * CAMBRIDGE * NEW YORK * SHARJAH

Copyright © Wesley North 2024

The right of Wesley North to be identified as author of this work has been asserted by the author in accordance with sections 77 and 78 of the Copyright, Designs and Patents Act 1988.

All rights reserved. No part of this publication may be reproduced, stored in a retrieval system, or transmitted in any form or by any means, electronic, mechanical, photocopying, recording, or otherwise, without the prior permission of the publishers.

Any person who commits any unauthorised act in relation to this publication may be liable to criminal prosecution and civil claims for damages.

This is a work of fiction. Names, characters, businesses, places, events, locales, and incidents are either the products of the author's imagination or used in a fictitious manner. Any resemblance to actual persons, living or dead, or actual events is purely coincidental.

A CIP catalogue record for this title is available from the British Library.

ISBN 9781035843305 (Paperback)
ISBN 9781035843312 (ePub e-book)

www.austinmacauley.com

First Published 2024
Austin Macauley Publishers Ltd®
1 Canada Square
Canary Wharf
London
E14 5AA

A special mention to my sister Rosa, without whom this book would forever be a dream, you made it a reality – thank you.

To influencers Lisa Ferland and Aylssa Matesic; you have both given me so much help during the writing and development of my work, your positivity and guidance has been inspiring and motivational – thank you.

And of course, to all the good people at Austin Macauley Publishers form taking a chance on a nobody with a dream and a laptop – thank you.

Table of Contents

Chapter 1: Sparrowhawk's Last Job — 12

Chapter 2: An Uneasy Alliance — 22

Chapter 3: Unwelcomed Visitors — 29

Chapter 4: Gormley's Kidnapping — 40

Chapter 5: The Whistling Woods — 52

Chapter 6: Perfect Strangers — 62

Chapter 7: War Studies — 68

Chapter 8: The Evergreen Massacre — 76

Chapter 9: Long-Tooth Goes Back to Sleep — 86

Chapter 10: Into the Unknown — 92

Chapter 11: A Sour Deal — 99

Chapter 12: Dimator's Promotion — 110

Chapter 13: Theo'dor Meets the Prince — 119

Chapter 14: Sparrowhawk's Plan — 126

Chapter 15: An Important Discovery — 131

Chapter 16: The Great Escape — 137

Chapter 17: The Not-So-Great Escape — 144

Chapter 18: Home to Rose — 148

Chapter 19: A Wealth of Knowledge — 165

Chapter 20: Sparrowhawk Meets His Match — 176

Chapter 21: A Breath of Fresh Air	190
Chapter 22: Man of the Mountains	200
Chapter 23: Stranger in the Night	206
Chapter 24: Meadow's Home	212
Chapter 25: Enemy at the Gates	224
Chapter 26: The Third Army	232
Chapter 27: Attack of the City	235
Chapter 28: The Aftermath	255
Stars of the Story	263
Chapter 1: Gormley Learns to Fly	266

We begin promptly, amidst the great war that has been raging for over a decade. Lands have been destroyed, homes burned to smouldering rubble and countless hundreds of sons and fathers lost to the earth never to smile or laugh again, lay in its path.

With no clear end in sight, the usurper King of Kor' dor; Balltimor, has decided to hold his position on the western banks of the Blacksnake River, his united force of Kor' Cali rebels sitting at his back. The uncrowned boy-King Armando's troops remain camped on the eastern banks, the capital city of Whiterock, sitting proudly at his rear. A stalemate has begun.

Neither side willing to retreat, as it would be a solid sign of weakness, and to advance into an enemy that has been so well 'dug-in' for so long, would result in the unnecessary depletion of already dwindling troops on either front. With both sides near to breaking point, resources at an all-time low and the common people beginning to feel the full weight of the cost of war, one side has taken drastic steps to end it once and for all.

Chapter 1
Sparrowhawk's Last Job

The howling wind thrust white sand into his already stinging eyes as he buried his half-covered face into his elbow to lessen the assault. The ragged black shemagh scarf, which he had traded his last piece of salted beef roll to obtain, helped his mouth and nose to stay clear, but did little to protect his eyes as he squeezed them tightly shut.

'*Bloody sand*,' he muttered silently to himself, shaking his head and rubbing his eyes gently in an unsuccessful bid to ease the blistering pain.

It was to be a simple two-week bounty trek, 'Easy Owls…' Markos had told him, '…just ride south-west through the Hindlands into Marshaven, go to "The Golden Axe" tavern and bag the outlaw known only as Long-tooth, you'll be back in two weeks,' and finished with a heartly deep laugh that only a man of Markos's size can achieve.

That had been years ago now and, in that time, old Sparrowhawk had been through the ringer. Even though he was no spring chicken anymore, and hadn't been for quite some time, he felt he could handle just one more 'Job,' before hanging up his 'girls' for good.

However, things on the trek had changed somewhat since his last contract, and none to his liking either.

Men in the south had lost what little honour they had to begin with. A fair fight was a thing of the past, gone were the days of the glorious duel, when one man could call another out and the two fought until one had put down his weapon. Loss of life was extremely rare in the good old days, but of course, there were many ways to make a killing blow look completely accidental, if the notion fell upon the wrong person.

Now however, it was a case of whoever had the most loyal friends nearby, or owls in their purse to hire some on-the-spot loyal friends that usually came out the victor. And right there was where good old Sparrowhawk had made his first mistake; assumption was never a friend of those in his line of profession.

It was late in the evening on a cloudless night and it had seemed a reasonable enough proposal in his own mind, simply stroll into the tavern and call out the outlaw. With his short-horned jackal-bow concealed under his rugged brown journeyman cloak, not to invite any unwanted attention, along with his girls who were always close to hand in case things should turn sour quickly, he entered the foul smelling, dark and gloomy drinking house and glanced around.

He knew little of 'Long-tooth' when he took the contract and felt there was probably no need to ask, it was after all a simple bounty for easy owls, how dangerous could he possibly be, that was probably his second mistake.

But, did they have to laugh at him, that's what weighed the heaviest. The entire room turned and burst their sides at his declaration for the arrest of one Long-tooth second name unknown. To add insult to injury, after a moment, most of them candidly turned their attention back to their tankards of mead and games of Rublo; a dice game he had yet to learn the rules, paying him no more attention.

Needless to say, the bearded giant, that answered to the name on that arrest warrant who was seated at a round table near the rear of the "Golden Axe" and encompassed by a multitude of other bearded giants, neither laughed or turned away.

They were in fact in the middle of counting out the gold they had just robbed from a caravan travelling east, blood still wet on their weapons. He stared blanky at the odd newcomer, who was standing alone in an unfriendly situation, with neither friend nor brains to back him up, Long-tooth had quickly assessed.

'I said, I have come to…' Sparrowhawk deemed it wise to repeat the reason for his presence, just in case there was a misunderstanding, a loss in translation perhaps… his third mistake.

'We 'eard what ye said ye old pig trot, ain't nobody 'ere care too much,' came a voice at the table Long-tooth was house at, not letting the Ranger finish his second attempt to bring them into submission with his words.

Of course, Sparrowhawk had no idea what his target looked like, so he approached the table of gents. He singled out the man who had spoken and focused his gaze upon him, ignoring the rest. He felt it best to show no fear, outlaws respected that.

'I've come to take you back to Whiterock for trial, Long-tooth…' he spoke in a matter-of-fact tone '…who knows, they might go easy on you if you come peacefully, I may even put in a good word for you myself, how about that?' Sparrowhawk had bagged his last three deserters in like manner, no reason for bloodshed and no reason he shouldn't have the same results now.

The table of men looked up at him, they were at a loss for words. But it wasn't confusion built on a foundation of fear, instead he saw amusement there, some were even smiling. His quick eyes drifted naturally to the table, hundreds of owls sat there staring back at him, in great stacks. An equal amount before each man, except the man at the back of the table, the furthest from him, he had almost double the rest. He wore a bandana around his neck, it had illegible red writing on it, more like scribbles than actual words.

The gold glistened in the candlelight, flickering in the cool breeze as the mini towers of owls cast dancing shadows on the table. The man to his left's gold was covered in a bright crimson substance, a dagger lying motionless beside his take, the sharp steel blade also covered in the same vivid colour.

There was a strange silence coming from the table, the rest of the occupants of the tavern were laughing and shouting, insulting each other in a friendly manner, but not these men, none of them moved, they simply looked at him. Just then Sparrowhawk remembered something, a key ingredient in his last couple of successful arrests, he forgot to mention his name, when they knew who they were dealing with, they would give him respect. They would fear him then.

'Long-tooth,' he commanded, addressing the same man.

The man he assumed was Long-tooth looked to the man with the largest stack of owls.

'Aye?' the man with the bandana replied, a deep low voice that spoke of too many tankards of mead and not enough cups of chamomile tea.

'The furthest from the door, the largest stack of booty, of course,' he had found Long-tooth.

'Name's Sparrowhawk,' he said loudly enough for the whole room to hear. He said it confidently and he scanned the room to noticed that nobody cared.

The table erupted with another howl of laughter as he turned back to face them, more so this time than the last. He stood there, mystified at the outburst. One outlaw was wiping tears from his eyes with his sleeve, mouth gaping open as if trying to catch his breath.

After a few moments the guffawing subsided and he had their attention again.

'Get ye outta 'ere quickly, lawman,' it was the booming voice of an annoyed Long-tooth that was speaking to him now.

'I am no lawman,' Sparrowhawk spat, insulted at the insinuation. Sparrowhawk waited for a moment, if he was expecting an apology, he was sorely mistaken.

The man who was closest to him was on his feet before Sparrowhawk could react. The blow to his face sent him whirling back across the floor and onto a small table behind him, he slid across the table, legs in the air and ended with a thump onto the filthy floor as the aging timber gave way under his weight. Another bout of laughter, the entire establishment was in on the jest.

'Now, fly 'way little sparrow, afore I git' over there to pluck an' skin ye,' someone shouted to another wave of hysterics.

'Dat' a way to show 'em, Silver-tongue,' cheered someone from another table.

He lay on the floor for a moment, his head spinning and his mind somewhere in the middle of next week. The floor was hard, much harder than it looked from a standing position, the feet as it turns out were ill advised in the process of determining whether or not solid floorboards were easy on the bones. And it was dirty too, much dirtier than one might realise, had one not had their face thump against the cold wet boards that stank of vomit and years old stale mead baked into the very grains of the wood. He considered his options, they were only a few, granted, but as far as he could count, which wasn't easy right now, he landed on three possible outcomes to his present predicament.

One was to take the advice he had just received, stagger to his feet, bid farewell to the gentlemen at the table, apologise for the intrusion, pay for the broken table and leave alive, his pride shattered for life, his name ruined when word of the day's events spread, but alive.

The second option was to reason with Long-tooth and his band of uneducated misfits, surely, they would see things his way after a few rounds of mead and riveting games of Rublo, no time like the present to find out why the game was so popular.

Then there was option three, he checked his right front pocket of his leather pants to see if the third option was even in play. His fingers found what there were scrambling for, he didn't know if he wanted to find it, might have been better if it wasn't there at all. But it was there and his daughter was dying. He needed, more than wanted the bounty.

No, there was only one true option for him. He took out the tiny little bottle and drank about half of the dark green slimy liquid. It was time to bag the outlaw Long-tooth, second name unknown.

Silver-tongue was re-enacting the wonderful sucker punch he had inflicted on Sparrowhawk's jaw, sound effects and all added in for good measure to the enjoyment of his comrades. He performed a mock stagger backwards into a table and threw himself onto the floor, legs flailing and landing with an unexpectedly heavy bang on his rear end. Sore backside he might have, but he also won over the crowd. He stood slowly and bowed to all.

The wanted men had forgotten their unfortunate visitor for a few moments, and that was their mistake.

Sparrowhawk was on his feet in one swift movement, his bow was drawn and two shining and extremely pointy metal arrow heads were trained in the general direction of Silver-tongue's back, his brown journeyman cloak was floating through the still breeze.

They all darted their eyes to where Sparrowhawk now stood, mouths catching flies. The men at the back of the table stood up to get a better vantage point, craning their necks to see past the man soaking up the applause in front.

Silver-tongue froze, confused he stared at them staring past him, something was going on behind him, he frowned and turned slowly. His legs were stationary, but his head spun a full one-hundred-and-eighty-degrees, he never saw the two arrows, but felt the air on either side of his cheeks disappear behind him. Two simultaneous shouts came from behind, more of a double whimper to be precise, he spun his head back again, another one-hundred-and-eighty-degrees exactly.

Two of his gang had arrow shafts sticking out of their chests, right where their hearts used to beat. It was time to turn again, his last one-hundred-and-eighty-degree turn was met with a squelchy thud, he looked down to see the horror of a third arrow shaft, almost feathers deep, ploughed into his own chest, he didn't feel any pain however, his legs immediately collapsed from under him and he was gone.

Sparrowhawk had notched, aimed and loosed five more single arrow shafts in the time it took his cloak to land on the floor at his feet, and the table was now seated by seven bearded giants with seven arrow shafts bulging from their chests.

The laughter had stopped suddenly in the Golden Axe then, the only sound was the now slowly advancing footsteps of a man who was tired and needed money to save his sick daughter, adrenaline racing through his veins and he would not be denied his due. He was Sparrowhawk and his name commanded respect, now they would fear the name, now they would not forget the name.

'Eh, who in the Seven Kingdoms do ye think ye are?' the buffalo sized woman behind the counter called.

It was the day that was in it.

'Sparrowhawk,' he replied deflated 'My name is Sparrowhawk.'

Another howling whistle of a gust came from nowhere, almost sending the old Ranger unceremoniously to the sand below, a fall in his now battered state would surely leave him for the Scorpions. Long-tooth shifted on the back of the horse to find a new uncomfortable position, lying hog-tied across Rogue. The horse was a Thoroughbred, a Winning Brew.

With a beautiful tanned coat and four black stockings pulled up to the tip of the knee on each leg, she was his most valuable asset. Her beauty was a welcomed bonus, but not the object of her purchase, he procured her for one reason only, her speed. Rogue could outrun most animals in the known world and probably most in the unmapped regions of the north and beyond. Both horse and rider had been together many years, she had seen him through many scrapes and she was the only living creature that he trusted with his life.

Rogue would never double cross him like so many others had during his time on the job. She was as close to him as a man could become to an animal, in truth he preferred Rogue's company to any man he knew.

'Let me go, pig trot,' demanded the heavily tied Long-tooth from behind.

Sure enough, the outlaw had not come quietly, after the fine display of archery performed by Sparrowhawk at the Golden Axe, Long-tooth had gone for his Khopesh.

The huge piece of steel cut through the air with lightning speed, such was the strength and anger of its wielder. Sparrowhawk had made another mistake after he had downed Long-tooth's posse, he got too close. He should have kept his distance to where a swinging crescent-shaped sword could not separate his head from his shoulders.

The giant lunged forward with all his might, sweeping the round table, chairs and dead men sitting in those chairs to one side. He came far too quickly that his size and physical attributes should allow, swinging that weapon like a toothpick and moved forward like a spring chicken. Long-tooth it seemed had no knowledge of the laws of physics. Sparrowhawk did not have the luxury of time to evaluate his opponents lack of respect for such laws, he simply allowed himself to react with his natural ability, training and reflexes now taking control of his movements.

Long-tooth swung high, then low in great arching blows, a successful chop would dismember any man in its path. Luckily for Sparrowhawk, Long-tooth had let his rage become his driving tool and not his brain. Although, the man was swinging with a terrible force, the efforts were easily sidestepped. Sparrowhawk was moving backwards, he calculated he had another ten to twelve steps before he was against the door. He just swivelled in time to evade a surprise low backhanded attempt to take off his left leg.

He hit the door in four steps, unexpectedly.

Long-tooth lunged with all his force, full charge attack, he rushed forward in a huge bounce and rocketed through the main door and into the mud outside the tavern as Sparrowhawk ducked and rolled to the right.

'Eh, ye goin' to settle up for that, are ye?' the hefty barwoman bellowed, none too impressed with him at this stage, and to be fair he was more or less responsible for the breaking of a table, now the dismantling of her front door and not to mention the fact he had killed half of her customer base.

Long-tooth rolled off the remains of the door, timber shattered and pieces of metal studs scattered everywhere.

'*Surely the man has had enough,*' thought Sparrowhawk as he rounded the corner of the doorframe to stand half-in half-out of the Golden Axe.

Long-tooth raised himself to his feet, grunting angrily at something. He was unsure of where to look at first, he turned around a few times to find his target. He was holding his left side with his right hand; a small stream of blood was slowly running out through his fingers as he tried to apply some pressure to the wound. Sparrowhawk spied a piece of black iron sticking out between his red fingers, it was about three inches in length.

If there was three inches on the outside there must be about three more inside, or the weight of the iron with the help of gravity would outweigh itself and plummet to the mud. It was one of the bolts that used to hold the door together, for some reason the carpenter had not allowed for the event of a bearded giant crashing straight into it, shoddy workmanship to say the least.

Long-tooth was breathing heavily as he found the cause of his torment, standing meters away, still inside the dark of the tavern.

'Yooooou,' he roared.

It was a roar that said, 'I'm not quite finished.'

Sparrowhawk stepped outside as Long-tooth stepped backward off the timber under his feet. Sparrowhawk's hand slowly swung around to his quiver that was strapped to the lower back position, allowing for the concealment when he first entered the tavern. He had fashioned the straps himself, punching extra holes in the over-hanging length to generate a stable lower position where the arrows remained upright but lower down his back, for such occasions like this evening.

The hollow quiver itself was separated into three different sections on the inside, giving him the opportunity to divide his different arrow classes into different sections, allowing for him to choose which arrow was most desirable for unique situations, like now. He carefully dismissed the bottom section, which held his normal everyday run-of-the-mill shafts like the ones he had used to clear the tavern, instead he chose an arrow from the middle compartment. He brought up his bow and notched the arrow.

'Hah, wat ye think ye be doin' with that?' the tactless outlaw called and smiled a smile that only a mother could see and not feel queasy.

Sparrowhawk knew what the injured man was referring to at once. The arrows in the middle section did not take the form of a regular arrowhead, instead they were blunt and coloured green. A hollow egg was secured to the tip of the arrow, where the sharp pointy head should be in usual circumstances.

'Come along quietly now Long-tooth, I can't promise to put in that good word for you with the King's Guard, not after this. But at least you won't have to suffer any longer, let's get that fixed up for you, eh?' Sparrowhawk nodded towards the blood coming steadily from Long-tooth's side. Make no mistake about Sparrowhawk, he was a killer, nobody could say otherwise with a straight face, but he was not a cold-blooded assassin.

He always looked for another safer, more civilised route other than violence where possible, although sometimes, they chose the latter.

'Yooou… will… die…' the criminal cried.

Sparrowhawk frowned, 'So be it.'

Long-tooth thought about going for the small blade tucked into his left boot, but his right hand was busy trying to keep him alive, long enough to die it seemed. Without a weapon and without warning he was moving for Sparrowhawk, a lot slower this time, but he was coming, he was not going to let a solid piece of iron sticking into his gut take his glory from him.

Sparrowhawk let loose the green arrow. It took no more than a split second to reach its target, square in the chest.

A cloud of green smoke exploded on Long-tooth's chest; it covered his whole upper body for a moment. He stopped his advance and felled like a great old oak.

The people who had gathered to watch the incident from the tavern were taken aback. They had formed a semi-circle around the fallen outlaw. The barwoman approached the downed bandit and kicked him roughly to see whether he was still alive, maybe he was a friend or maybe he owed her money, who knew.

'Where would I find a healer?' Sparrowhawk questioned the group.

'Healer?' someone started. 'What's wrong wit ye?' someone else finished.

'Aye, ye don't look half bad,' called another man, with long blonde hair tied back and braided, he carried a huge wooden shield strapped to his back, a warrior from the north-west, he assumed. The man carried no sword on his person, that was a good sign, strange but good.

'I mean for him, he needs herds and rest,' Sparrowhawk replied calmly, he was still not sure about these people.

A skinny whip of a man came scuttling over and started to rummage through Long-tooth's pants, looking for anything valuable. He was quicky clattered about the head with a club, fell atop of Long-tooth and was out cold.

'A healer, is there a healer near here?' Sparrowhawk questioned them again.

There was silence. Were they thinking of where the healer lived, trying to figure out the quickest way to his house perhaps or was thinking a step too far for these people?

'Ye… got coin?' someone asked nervously after another few minutes. They all looked slowly at Sparrowhawk, some even scanned his waist, looking for a bulging sack of gold.

'No, but I do have these,' Sparrowhawk replied calmly, slapping his quiver.

The crowd scattered in all directions, some ducked back into the tavern, some ran up the road, some ran down.

It was a small backwater town that Long-tooth had made his final stand in, a town that Sparrowhawk didn't care to remember, he couldn't even pronounce the local name without his tongue getting all tied up in a knot. There were few houses, a blacksmith, a bakery, what looked like a sewing ring in the centre and of course the good old Golden Axe to finish it off. The road was not a road, it was a stretch of land from one end to the other, the weather of the day determined if it was useable or not.

Sparrowhawk watched them go, the only one who remained was the blonde warrior. He stood there looking at the two men unconscious on the ground. He had decades old scars across his arms, some newer, fresher ones across his cheeks. This was a man who stood death in the face and laughed, Sparrowhawk respected that.

'Healer lives at the last shack outta town, that way,' he said without looking at Sparrowhawk, pointed up the road and was turning back towards the tavern.

'You have my thanks, here take it,' Sparrowhawk replied and tossed an owl in his direction, the coin arched perfectly into his waiting hand.

He said nothing, but gave the Ranger a nod of appreciation.

Sparrowhawk was now faced with a slight dilemma. There was no way to carry the heavy man all the way up the road, not without Rogue, whom he had hidden in the bush a mile or so away. He also couldn't leave his captive here alone, who knew what the locals might do to him. The thought had crossed his mind about asking the northern warrior for his help, but rested on not involving the man any further. Even if he wanted to help, there was a chance that the others in town might not take to kindly to him helping Sparrowhawk.

He thought about using a whistling arrow, they made up the third and final compartment in his quiver. Specially crafted arrows used for calling Rogue to his position. But, after a quick glance at Long-tooth's steady flow of blood, he calculated that there may not be enough time to wait for Rogue to arrive, he'd have to use Rogue as plan B.

'*The last shack at the end of town*,' he thought. He could see the building from where he stood. He could make out a dim light coming from the east facing window, but more importantly he saw the vague outline of a door.

Notching an arrow from the bottom compartment, he took aim at the healer's house, said a prayer that the man didn't open the door to come outside to answer the call of nature and loosed.

Chapter 2
An Uneasy Alliance

The old man was busy grinding down thyme, ginger-root and valerian in a small rounded stone bowl using a thick piece of granite. His back ached as he bent over the bench, so to relieve the pain he shuffled his feet over to fetch the stool that was stationed close to the hearth. The dwindling fire was but a meek orange glow on the blackened embers, too weak to give any real heat to his poorly insulated abode.

With some effort and a sigh of annoyance he leaned on the stool and pushed it simultaneously towards his work space. Sitting down with the bowl in his lap, he continued at his task, he ground and ground the three herbs into a paste, satisfied that the consistency was just right, he poured in some alcohol, one hundred per cent alcohol to be exact. He spilled a good amount across his workbench with his shaking hands, the strong-smelling liquid seeping into the timber causing his already wrinkled forehead to produce a few more hard lines to their number.

It had cost him everything he had, for buying illegal substances was not cheap, but it was necessary to make the best elixirs and salves in the southern realm. Only the chief stuff would do his clients, and they did not accept anything but the best. He need only squint down at the cocktail sausage shaped stumps where the tops of his missing pinkie fingers used to be, if he ever needed reminding of that.

Two months of waiting for the shipment of alcohol from that ragged lot, most probably out of their feeble minds at Greta's tavern by now. It was a sheer phenomenon that they hadn't opened the crate to see what was inside, if they had there was little doubt that they would have smelled the substance and drank the whole lot. He despised having to deal with the likes of them, but it was an unfortunate occupational hazard, a means to an end.

It was not too long before his lower back was now complaining, there was always some part of his body moaning against another, each muscle or ligament in a constant competition to see which could cause him the most discomfort. In his youth he had been as agile as a honey badger, strong as an ox and fit as a mountain lion, but that had been a long time ago, old age crept up on him unawares while he was busying himself with his medicines and it came with more cons than pros, but surely, he was due at least a little relief once in a while.

It had taken weeks of extensive foraging through the overgrown swamps in Marshaven to locate and harvest enough Moonglow that would finish off the latest batch of his special tonic. Weeks of crawling through the deadly floor of the Forgotten Bogs, had rewarded him with a plentiful harvest, but it had taken its toll on his withering bones.

He had also lost all three of his loyal apprentices to the Bog. One was bitten by an Orange-pin-tailed-bulltoad, the only known species of toad that had teeth, unlucky for poor Wilhelm that he managed to step right on its colourful tail. The boy had screamed in pain and within a few minutes the poison was taking full effect.

Firstly, the eyes start to cloud and the pupils burst causing the victim to go completely blind, then the internal organs start to implode one by one, foaming from the mouth is a usual side effect, but not mandatory and finally the skin turns a deathly white as all the blood cells erupt. It was not a pretty sight and the youth died in his mentor's arms before the moon was high.

The second and somewhat clumsy apprentice died in the name of love. In truth it was a fine state he had gotten himself into, one that could have been easily avoided if he had paid more attention to his tutor and his studies. It all started when a female member from one of the more civilised tribes in the area had approached them and handed each man a flower, it was a custom of her tribe to greet strangers with a single yellow goldcup. It symbolised a safe return from the many dangers of the Bog.

She was a timid thing, but Alistair decided there and then that there might be a chance of winning himself a bride. So, without further instruction on the local foliage, he set about to surprise his future fiancée with a bunch of flowers and cast his eyes to the bushes. As they were walking away, he spotted his chance growing on the ground just off the track. He quickly filled his hands with the plant, ran back to her and rammed it into her face.

Her eyes went wide with horror, in his defence it was a dark green leaf set with beautiful sapphire flowers. Although his chosen bouquet was a grand idea based on sight alone, gladeweed is also as poisonous as a box jellyfish. The girl's small frame hit the mud with a barely noticeable flop, Alistair looked around at his companions, they froze when they saw what was in his hands. Alistair dropped the plant, suddenly realising his err.

'They're poisonous' Fedrick had called to him in dismay.

He stood there looking at them, shaking involuntary.

'Just walk over to us…' the healer cautioned. '…get away from the picked gladeweed.'

'Right,' Alistair replied without having to be told twice.

He walked slowly back to the group, glancing back at the body lying lifeless on the dirt.

'Why did I not die?' He called to them.

'Because ye had the good sense not to smell it… me thinks,' his tutor replied, trying to encourage the boy, and make him think he was not a complete buffoon, not believing his words for a moment.

'Right…' he said. '…I didn't know the smell was that strong, I mean, I didn't smell a thing as I was picking them,' he finished by sticking his fingers to his nose and took a huge sniff.

'Noooo…' Fedrick shouted. Alistair had time to look up before he fell down.

The third to fall prey to the Bog, was the youngest of the three and far more advanced in the trade, he was the clear runner destined to take the old healers place in the coming years. Alas, Fedrick had placed a foot wrong while crossing the swamp, he unknowingly stepped into what the bizarre inhabitants of the area called a 'Dead-man's hole.'

Fedrick was to learn first-hand of the awful circumstances he had found himself in. It was a slow sucking sink-hole, if it had of been one of the faster varieties, he may have stood a chance. Although it dragged its victims down to a muddy grave quite slowly, it was the strength of the grip it took on you that posed the problem.

Crushing your bones and limbs as you sank deeper and deeper into the abyss below, helpless to win your freedom. The faster sink holes were rather easy to free oneself from as the hold was far less intense. Fedrick spend half a day struggling before he disappeared.

He was on the verge of finishing a full load, it was what his clients requested, or rather demanded. A shack rattling thud came from the door, it was if someone had kicked it with a heavy boot. It broke the top hinge clean off, luckily the bottom hinge held firm, for now. He almost fell off his stool with the fright, but luckily his outstretched arm grabbed onto the bench to steady himself.

'Who can be bothering me at this hour?' he complained.

Slowly he slid his aching body off the side of the stool and made is way to the door. He was surprised to be greeted by about an inch of metal looking coldly at him, sticking through the timbers, splinter's surrounding the pointy visitor.

'Now… what?' he grumbled, looking at the tip of the arrowhead. Had he been anybody else he may have deliberated that his little home was under siege and to crack open the door meant certain death by another well-placed shaft, but he was not anybody else.

He opened the door and let in the chill of the still night, and he shivered against it, pulling his coat closer around his scrawny shoulders, he shivered.

He stood there for a moment, still as a cattle-rod, narrowing his eyes to focus and holding his breath to hear more clearly. He looked at the motionless town and the motionless town looked back at him, neither given the other much signs of life, it was a standoff.

Satisfied there was nobody there he went to shut the door, when he heard something, off in the distance, faint enough, but it was there.

'Ooooou,' it seemed to call. Was it the wind, the old b'uwak that came from the north. But, how can the wind howl so, on this a windless night. He strained again.

'Eyyy oooou,' it got louder. He was full sure there was a noise coming from down the road and it was not a noise made by the elements of nature. And if it was an unnatural noise, which he was sure it was, it must have been made by man, the most unnatural creature of them all.

'Whaaaaaat?' he called back, not sure exactly to who or where, his head nodding up and down.

'Eeeedeeeelp,' he heard.

It was a cold night and he was so close to completing his order that more than likely meant his death if it was late and he cared little for the woes of men he could not see. But nonetheless, he was a man of medicine and he had taken an oath to always help others in their time of peril. It was an oath he had made up himself however, and on closer reflection he thought he should have added in some kind of loop hole to release him from emergencies such as this.

He closed the door, the new addition sticking out some two feet on the outside almost taking his head off as he swung it shut. He set off at a tortoise pace to find more mischief, no doubt, for himself.

The path towards the tavern was lit by the few buildings as he shuffled along. It hadn't rained in a couple of days so the road was passable, for that much at least he was thankful.

'Eeeed eeeelp, indeed,' he complained, shaking his head back and forth.

Now he saw the reason for his unscheduled journey in the middle of the night, a bar fight.

'*Great*,' he complained to himself.

Sparrowhawk had to kneel down beside Long-tooth and apply pressure to the man's wound to stop or at least slow down the flow of blood. He had been watching the small man from this position making his way down the road, he was as slow as a king's funeral. Long-tooth could have bled out twice at this rate.

He looked up as the man, who's years were easily time and a half again as his own, came close to investigate the scene.

'Ah, in a spot of bother are we… me thinks?' he asked cheerfully nodding in agreement with himself. He was looking down at the two unconscious men, and Sparrowhawk kneeling beside one, his hands covered in blood.

'My name is Sparrowhawk… are you the town healer?' Sparrowhawk pleaded.

'I don't care much for names, but aye, I am the only healer this side of the Hindlands, well the only one that won't experiment on ye with leaches an' tape maggots,' he replied coolly.

Sparrowhawk didn't even know what a tape maggot was, but it sounded like something that he would be quite happy to never find out about.

'This man needs an iron bolt removed from his gut; can you perform such an operation?' Sparrowhawk asked the timid man.

'A bolt, now what's eh' doing with an iron bolt in his gut, he should know better,' the healer revealed some serious words of wisdom, bobbing his head up and down.

Sparrowhawk was a kind man and could enjoy a good well-timed joke as good as the next, but now was not good timing. His last chance to collect the number of owls needed to save his daughter was dripping out of Long-tooth, drop by precious drop.

'Of course, I can heal him,' the old man shot out more seriously as he noticed Sparrowhawk frowning at him.

'And what's about 'im?' the old man pointed down to the second man who had set about to pickpocket Long-tooth.

'What about him?' Sparrowhawk answered blankly.

Their attention was back on the prize without another mention of the thief.

'You keep the pressure 'ere, good… good. We can't move 'em, might cause internal bleeding, that would kill 'em straight off. I'll just pop back to me…' the man stopped speaking as he saw who it was that he was about to save, his face dropped.

Sparrowhawk's face twitched to a look of confusion.

'*Did the healer know Long-tooth?*' he thought to himself.

The healer looked at Sparrowhawk, old as he might be he was not blind. He was a well learned man and well-travelled too. He had much experience within the Seven Kingdoms over the years and he had seen it all. He spotted the quiver on the Rangers back. He took in the no-nonsense tone in his voice, the Ranger wanted Long-tooth alive, of that there was little discussion to be had. '*But, why… ah, a bounty*,' he hit the nail on the battered head now.

'Let 'em die, be doing everyone a turn,' the old healer announced and spun around to make the journey home, he was nearly finished his order after all.

'*So… he does know Long-tooth*,' Sparrowhawk concluded.

'Wait… healer, please…' Sparrowhawk began.

The healer ignored him and slowly shuffled his feet back up the road.

Sparrowhawk released his hold on Long-tooth and quickly notched a whistling arrow, he was running out of options, the arrow went rocketing up into the sky.

The old man thought he heard something, a whizzing sound.

'Must be the wind… me thinks,' he decided, his head nodding rapidly.

He arrived at his door after the long walk, he took some time to admire the Ranger's arrow, planted an inch below the small copper doorbell, its thin string sitting casually on the shaft. It was a beautiful arrow too; the smoothness was uncanny. Someone had sanded down the length of the shaft to a warm soft texture, such the like he had never seen before. The feathers were placed perfectly apart at equal distance for maximum effect which would have generated a more accurate course, if fired by the right bow and dedicated archer. The feathers were tied in with cat hairs and not the favoured method of the troop in the King's Guard who use twine. This arrow was crafted by a master.

He heard the wind again coming from behind him, this time it was neither a whizz or an 'Eeed eeelp,' but more of a light thumping sound. He turned around annoyed.

'I did say please…' Sparrowhawk was sitting on Rogue, Long-tooth was lying still as a dead badger on the horses back and one of those beautiful arrows with the smooth shaft and well-placed feathers was aimed at the healer's chest.

Chapter 3
Unwelcomed Visitors

The dark morning glow as the sun was gradually making its ascent to cast the shadows back from where they came, was her favourite time of the day. It was the waking of the forest.

The navy light was turning bluer, soon it would grow brighter and brighter, until the dark greens of the forest melted into the descending sky blue of the heavens.

Sitting high on the rock, she could see across the valley, her view blocked only by the enormous purple rises and green fields nestled below the Royal Mountains.

The morning mist was turning into droplets of moisture, blanketing the entire valley like a good morning kiss, she loved to watch it all taking place before her eyes.

But her morning could not be spent sitting and watching the world stir out of its slumber, there was work to be done and it was hers to do.

She set off at a running pace, down treacherously steep slopes, she skipped and jumped, each footfall was guided by concentration and years of practice, for no one, man nor beast knew the forest as she did. It was a narrow path she now navigated down, a forty-foot drop onto jagged rocks below to her left and a cool dip in the white-water currents of the racing river to her right should she put a toe out of place. The loose stones chased after her as she ran, the wind blowing through her hair, the rush of exhilaration was her daily dose of excitement. It wasn't long however that she had reached the bottom, uninjured.

A bright smile on her face as she panted, the adrenalin pumped through her body, she was ready to go forward again, so she did.

Her bare feet cooled as she splashed through the shallowest part of the river, even at full sprint, she was a full thirty seconds getting to the other shore. She had always tried to race across without getting her ragged clothes wet, it seemed impossible, but she was up for the challenge. Today she was not successful, tomorrow she would try again.

She paused here for a moment, just before she entered the trees. She needed all her energy to get through the most dangerous part of the forest.

Visibility was poor inside, the trees were so tight together in places, it was difficult to gather up much speed.

'Wild beast hunt in those woods Mea'dow, best you don't enter,' her mother had told her when she was a pup.

'Yes Mama,' she had always obeyed her parents, they had raised her right, taught her the ways of the forest and the ways of man. Taught her that they were two much different ways of life, but must walk together, if all were to survive. They taught her not to fear either way, but to respect both.

She fingered the small pendant as she remembered them now, hanging loosely around her neck, raising it to her mouth she kissed the metal circle with the embossed shape of a wolfs head. It was given to her by her mother not long before her parents were taken from her, it was her most cherished possession in the world.

His 'White wolf,' her father had called her mother, and only ever by that name had she known her. She could not remember his name, it had been difficult to pronounce for her young tongue but, she liked to call him, 'Papa Wolf,' her mother had said he came from a tribe of ferocious wolves to the far north and was a great warrior among his people.

But she had lost her parents, long ago. And she felt when her mother had died, her warning about the forest died with her, for she was now all that was left and she would not fear, what she did not know.

Convinced she was ready, she took off into the darkness, alone but unafraid.

She had always used the same path as she moved through the scattered trees, the pin needle carpet soft and bouncy underfoot.

Her movement was paced at about fifty percent, she liked to keep a little in reserve in case of emergencies. Just last week a pack of wolves, well two if she was being honest, had picked up her scent. Their howls were not far off as she reached the tree line on the far side and she spotted them as she made it to the water that was waiting on the far side of the forest, wolves did not like to get their paws wet, apparently.

She thought about changing her route mid-run, but decided that the two strays had probably wandered from the main pack and that her current course was probably the safest if she didn't want to get caught, if she altered it now, she might land herself nose first into the entire pack.

The run was going well so far, she was enjoying the freedom that nature provided. Her honed senses picked up only the stale warm air prisoned beneath the blackout cover of leaves on the tall trees surrounding her, the eerie sound of the grinding wood against wood as the trees swayed leisurely back and forth in the higher up branches.

She was now approaching the denser section of the forest; the trees were thicker here and grew much closer together. Huge roots revealing themselves to the open air and disappearing back underground as soon as they had risen, not staying long enough to be part of the forest. They did however pose a serious tripping hazard, if one was not accustomed to the area. The lack of a major light source also didn't help the casual Sunday morning jogger, Meadow on the other hand was not a casual anything, she was always all or nothing.

As she was about halfway through the darkest part of her morning run, she heard something. It was faint, but it was definite.

She continued on, pressing herself a little more, she pushed herself to run as fast and as quietly as possible without risking a collision with an unforgiving trunk of a pine tree. Ducking and weaving between the spiky low-lying branches she went as she listened and watched all around her, keeping her breathing steady.

It was a perfect ambush point for any bandits or desperate men on the bounce from the authorities. Secluded and far enough from the sophisticated world, where there would be nobody to hear the screams of a lone girl been attacked, nobody close enough to make it in time that was for sure, she kept on running.

Another sound reached her prickled ears, a sort of growl and some heavy scratching, she would not have to wait long to find out what they were planning.

A huge tree lay dead ahead, an ideal hiding place to lay in wait for an unsuspecting victim lost in the woods. She got closer, her speed was clocking in at eight feet per second, she counted the steps in her mind, and figured the tree she was focused on was precisely ten seconds away. She placed her right hand into her belt, she found the bound hilt of her bone dagger waiting, she was ready. Five… four… three.

Meadow never got to the tree; a huge eight-hundred-pound bear roared around the trunk to block her path. Baring his incredible set of pearly white razor-sharp teeth, he bellowed out a tree shaking roar of disapproval in the direction of the miniature creature before him.

'Well at least you're not a band of low-life thieves,' she announced to the monster before her.

He growled again and lifted himself upon his back legs to show his full height, she had to look up, tilting her head backwards a few degrees to meet his eyes.

He dropped to all fours, making a mini earthquake ripple through the forest floor, shaking a few of the thinner trees nearby.

Her knowledge of bears was quite vast, so her mind quickly scanned over her options. She was in the bears natural habitat; this was his backyard and she had stumbled into it. A chance meeting with the wolves would have been a more desirable outcome for her early morning exercise.

The first and most natural course of action would be to run, but she knew the beast would be on her in no time with those powerful strong legs propelling it forward, it was a claw/foot race she was never going to win, running was out.

Next, her mind thought about climbing a tree, but alas this too was futile as bears were better climbers than humans, another idea not worth thinking about.

Her next option was the river, get to the river and swim downstream with all her might. Unfortunately, bears were expert swimmers, they were just at home in the water as they were among the trees. The thing would probably drag her tiny frame under the surface of the water and drown her under its immense weight, if it didn't crush her to death with his brawny paws first.

With no other options of escape available, it was time to consider damage control.

Quickly, she stopped looking at the bear, casting her gaze to the ground, eye contact was a sign of challenge and she did not have an effective method to challenge a creature so above her weight class. Slowly she lowered herself to the soft, dry ground.

The bear grunted and snorted as it beat the ground a few times, throwing moss and shovelfuls of dead pine needles into the air. He scratched at the roots in front of him and marched from side to side, studying his breakfast with a keen eye. After a short period of time for the bear, but an age for Meadow, he came forward at a trot.

She rolled herself into position, dragging her knees up to her chest and her hands wrapped around them, she lay on the ground. Her life was now at the mercy of an animal that could kill her in an instant or ragdoll her into oblivion.

She heard the bear coming and she tried to control her breathing, tried to keep her nerve and trusted in her training. He grabbed her leg and dragged her forward with a speed her body had never been subject to before. The ground in which she had consider to be soft and warm as she lay there just seconds ago, had transformed momentarily in a rough hard bed of sharp rocks and protruding roots, as she felt every bump and unseen solid object hitting into her back and legs.

The huge bear suddenly let her go, climbing onto his back legs he growled ferociously into the trees as a steam of hot breath jetted out from his maws, sending warm spittle all over her clothes and exposed skin. He landed back on top of her in a flash, both front legs almost burying her into the earth, luckily, they had landed alongside her shoulders and not on top of them, the ground beneath her shaking. He looked around for a split second and bellowed again, bears do a lot of that.

Now was her moment, with all her might she dug her hands into the soil and pushed herself forward, allowing her to slide across the surface of the ground quickly and under the body of the annoyed bear. She slapped his hairy knees as she went past with her hands, not to hard, but just enough so he would feel it. When she was out the other side she was swiftly on her feet, the bear was turning slowly, somewhat dismayed as to where she had disappeared to, she presently let him know.

With an effortless leap she was on his back, grabbing tightly onto his course hairs, and there she remained, holding on for dear life.

The bear was back standing upright once more, he swung his mighty paws this way and that, he roared in frustration, he tried to grab at her, but she was too small to get a grip on, dodging the attempts by moving her hips out of harm's way. He howled and grunted, releasing more hot steam into the trees, he snorted and spat, but could not shift her.

Deflated, he landed back down to his more natural position, seeming to weigh his options.

She did not give him much time, she quickly released her right-hand grip and poked his belly, roughly but not with too much force, at this he roared his loudest since the battle had begun.

Another attempt to loosen her grip came as he ran a few feet and stopped abruptly, if he was hoping she would fly over his head, he was mistaken. She was expecting it and had prepared for the sudden stop. Her grip was iron, the bear panted, and was breathing heavily, frustrated at being out witted by this small pest.

She released her left hand and poked him in like manner as before, this time on the left side. Again, none to impressed he grunted, this time he performed a new tactic, he shook like a dog drying himself after being stuck out in the rain too long.

He paused for a moment, and scratched at the ground vigorously, rubbing his face into whatever he had found and was looking to occupy himself with something else, apparently forgetting all about her.

As soon as she released her right hand, aiming for another poke at his weak spot, he shifted rapidly to the opposite side shaking violently, she was not expecting such a manoeuvre and flew through the air, she landed upside down on her back.

She was up again with a backflip summersault, facing the infuriated brute. He slowly advanced, steam coming from his black nostrils, menace in his fiery eyes. He looked ready to rip her apart, chew the flesh off her bones and bury her body in three unmarked graves so she would never bother him again, slowly he came, hungry and mad.

'Now Koda, what have we learnt here today?' Meadow called quizzingly.

Koda stopped his momentum, looked at her and lowered his head.

'That's right, isn't it. You were too busy shouting and hollering for whatever reason, that I was easily able to take your knees. And then, and this is the embarrassing part for you Koda, then you allowed me to get up on your back,' she stopped and shook her head in disgust.

'Your baaaaaack!' she emphasised by getting down on all fours herself and patting her back while looking at Koda. Koda was embarrassed, she could tell.

'If I had a bigger weapon on me, you would more than likely be skinned, sliced and barbequed. How would you like that, Koda? I don't want to eat you, but I will, just to teach you a lesson,' she said.

Koda let out a whine. 'Oh no, no… no… no. They'll be none of that, thank you very much,' she said sternly and walked over to console the crestfallen beast.

She threw her arms around him, and gave him a little human size cuddle, he snorted a huge bear size booger on top of her head.

She backed away and stared an unenthusiastic gaze at him, slowly she put her hand to her head and came back down with a sticky, green-yellow handful of bear mucus. She looked at her hand and she looked at Koda, mouth thin-lined.

'A ruse…' she cried cheerfully, '…you stinking overgrown cub,' she jested, darting in for another bear hug.

Koda rose to his back legs, Meadow not expecting the quick movement fell backwards onto the again soft ground, landing on her rear-end she looked up at all his towering eight-foot frame, he raised his two front paws in the air as a sign of victory. She laughed heartly.

'Good ambush, Koda,' she exclaimed when he had finished his celebrations.

Koda nodded his big heavy head a couple times and grunted, agreeing completely with her.

They spent a few minutes going over what they had both done wrong during the encounter, before Meadow had to leave. Meadow decided it was mainly Koda who had made the errors in the attack and Koda decided Meadow was at fault on more than one occasion, it was probably for the best that there was a slight language barrier between the two or they would spend all day arguing rather than training.

Meadow had reached her home in the forest not long after departing from Koda. As she came down the side of the incline, she checked the perimeter for watching eyes and all was quiet. It was a one room hut concealed underground, buried deep into the forest floor, hidden from the outside world.

The roof was in need of some major repairs, as the leaves and branches she had used were starting to fall off and break, this had left more than a few fist-sized holes. It wasn't the rainwater getting in that was the issue, it was the fact that anyone walking past could see in from the outside, and there were but a few living creatures that knew where she slept, she wanted to keep it that way.

So, she felt it best to gather some moss from the rocks close-by. It wasn't long when she had the roof patched up, she would need some wet mud to use as an adhesive to finish the job, but that could wait till later.

She glanced about her, checking the tree line and listening. She heard nothing, she saw no movements, although the sun was getting higher, it was still quite early so there was usually neither beast nor fowl anywhere close. Her parents had chosen this spot for the advantage of its seclusion.

Assured she was alone, she rolled the large rounded stone from the front of the fallen tree, just enough. Behind the stone lay a narrow tunnel made from the trunk of a fallen tree, a hole that a regular sized man would have difficulty negotiating through, but a skinny athletic girl would have little trouble.

She clambered inside the tunnel that led into her hut, and pulled the ivy rope she had attached to the stone back across the entrance. It was a short shimmy up the trunk of the tree and each time she crawled up it, she practiced holding her breath as she moved. At first, she had raced to get to the end quicker, but realised that a steadier pace allowed her to concentrate on her breathing, or lack of, and she made it further in each time.

She reached the end of the trunk and the entrance to the hut, not successful this time, but she was getting so close, it would be merely a matter of time before she had perfected the craft.

The dank smell is always the first thing that assaults her as she enters into the underground hut. The contrast from the crisp fresh morning air was off-putting to say the least, but she had been gone longer than she had anticipated, due to Koda's surprise attack. Checking in on Twitcher was essential.

The only light source in the roof now shutdown, the room was a pitch black. She moved across the room to her table, a large stone that was stationary in the centre of the room. She avoided putting her mucky feet on her animal hide bedclothes as she passed by.

She reached out her hands to find Twitcher, he was gone. Instinctively she looked around, resulting in finding only darkness looking back at her, she made a soft sucking sound with her lips. Nothing answered her, she tried again.

'Twitcher,' she whispered, not wanting to raise her voice too loud. She stooped down to her knees, and called again, soft and low.

Within moments, he came to her.

'Aww, good morning,' she crooned.

'I was beginning to think you had left me, little one,' she said fondly.

The small rabbit sniffed and licked at her face as she went in for a kiss. His minuscule whiskers tickling her cheeks as she showed him much affection.

'How's the ear, today?' she asked.

Running her fingers delicately over the area that had been bitten by a wild fox after a life threating scrap two days ago, he whimpered at her touch. The cloth bandage had come off, but that was expected and necessary. She had tended the wound with a poultice and given the rabbit some herbs and plenty of clear fresh water, a rarity in these parts; the nearest river was a good twenty-minute run east. Now the air was adding its own unique healing powers to the wound.

'Sorry, little fella, truly I am,' she apologised.

He flinched, trying to escape her clutches, but he calmed down after she rubbed his grey furry little head and held him close against her chest, rocking from side to side gently as a mother does lovingly to a new-born.

'Better?' she asked, not seeing his twitching nose as a sign of his forgiveness. She lowered him gently to the ground, and he hopped back into whichever hidden corner he had sprung from.

In all the excitement of the mornings events she had forgotten to eat, her tiny belly was rumbling and calling for breakfast. She knelt down to where the wooden wicker basket was usually located, she found it sitting patiently for her and removed the lit.

With no light in the room to aid her, she carefully extended her hand in to fish out some local juicy cuisine, she felt the small grubs tickle her skin as she pulled out a handful. Some escaped to safety as she lifted her hand to her open saliva filled mouth, teeth separated and ready. In they dropped into her mouth, wriggling and squirming helplessly as her teeth came down and up and down again. There is not much chewing involved in the process of grub eating so the little guys were quickly swallowed. As Koda had taken much of her energy this morning, to fill herself until dinner she decided to go for another handful. Drop, chew, swallow, lovely.

It was late morning when she heard them coming. Her daily routine of collecting elderberries and sorrel had to be cut short when she spotted a flock of white-tailed geese flying overhead, it was far too early for white-tailed geese to be flying anywhere, let alone this far east, she knew something was amiss straight away and went to investigate.

A family of deer bounced and hurried past just a couple of meters away from her as she travelled west, they were looking all around with prickled ears, something had scared them.

More floor creatures were running about in a haphazard fashion to secure a familiar hole or find a new hiding spot. Some ran aimlessly around, unaware of what was happening. She had witnessed a scene like this only once before, so long ago now. It had happened when her parents were alive, when it was over, they were dead.

Most of the animals seemed to be coming from the direction that the deer had been fleeing from, it was there she must go.

After a short time stalking the forest as she moved to meet whatever was coming her way, she noticed that all the animals big and small had disappeared, then she felt it. Lowering herself to the ground she placed both hands down, palms first, fingers spread like the roots of a large oak.

It was faint, but it was definite. A very slight vibration sent her body shaking, not for its strength, but the realisation that there were few things that could cause such a strange ripple in the soil. One was a herd of buffalo; however, buffalo were never this far into the woods, something had either scared them or they had come free of their masters. The beast-men kept buffalo for meat, but had other uses for them also, uses that she did not like to think about, for beast-men were cruel.

Scared as she was, she was far more curious, so on she went, slower but more vigilant. She concentrated on her other senses to aid her, sight was useless for now, but she had other ones that would be more functional at this time.

She listened, held her breath and focused all her might on the sounds of the forest. The swaying trees, the rustle of leaves scraping off each other on the ground, the low howl of the eastern breeze passing gently through the trees. All this she could disregard without trying, all the accustomed noises did not register any longer, she was listening for the noises that the forest did not make.

And there they were, off in the distance.

'No buffalo… beast-man come,' she whispered to herself and grimaced.

They were shouting and laughing to one another, she had picked up many voices, more than she could count in fact, which led her to believe it was a hunting party. Her father had told her of such things, it was sport for the beast-men. Barbaric and vicious, they would come east to the great woods, that they believed was theirs. They would come and kill the animals of the land, even though her father had said that they did not need it for nourishment as they herded their own meat, they still came to bring their ways of destruction.

They had come back, after all these years they were here once more to steal, to burn and to kill. Nothing would be safe this day in her peaceful home.

She reached into the tiny pocket she had sewn into the front of her tunic, and came out with her wooden blow-stick. When she blew into it, she knew there would not be much time. The beast-men would hear it and come searching, but the animals would hear it also and they would know what it meant too. It had to be done to save them, even if it cost her dearly.

She placed the small wooden whistle to her lips and she let out three ear-piercing shrills, every animal for miles around would hear it, they would know danger was coming. But right now, the invaders would be coming for her.

She turned and fled back to her hut; it was the only place that she had to hide in. She ran and ran with all her might, even though the sounds of the invaders had been a while off, she panicked. A bear she can handle, fight and even reason with, but these brutes, they were of another nature completely, her parents had found that out first-hand.

She had zigzagged her way back to the hut, running up and down through the trees to throw them off her trail, she knew the forest better than most of the animals that lived there, it should not be much trouble to evade a bunch of monsters that are new to the area, or so she believed.

The round stone was rolled back, the smaller creatures of the forest should be after leaving this part of the forest and she was under the ground, hiding also. It had never been so dark in the hut as it was then, she tried to find Twitcher for comfort, but blindly walked into the mud wall, poking herself in the face with a thick root that stuck into her subversive home.

All was quiet, very quiet. But that was good she thought, as now she would hear them coming from a way off, say one thing for the beast-men, say they are noisy.

She considered it best to sit down and wait it out, she had few options available at such short notice, the beast-men had somehow snuck up on her, she had become complacent and was annoyed at herself.

She made the sucking noise to call Twitcher, she needed some companionship right now, she didn't want to face whatever was coming alone. Twitcher did not come to her, maybe he was hiding too, maybe he had found a new way out, he was a resourceful and practiced underground burrow digger after all.

Her head sprung up as she heard voices, rough deep voices calling to each other, they were spread out judging by the time it took for each one to answer the last. They gave off an echo, as if they were close, but walking away. But the sounds were getting louder, they were fanning out, checking everywhere, any hope that she had thrown them off her trail was sinking fast.

Chapter 4
Gormley's Kidnapping

The tavern erupted to the final course of 'The Maiden's tale.'

Gormley took his bow from the stage; a wooden upturned box in the centre of the crowded room and he waved his hands in the air for more applause, the crowd obliged him and another deafening cheer went up.

The waitresses were struggling to keep the ale flowing as the largest tavern in Winters Peak was packed to capacity, even the mice were finding it difficult to squeeze in.

'Friends… it is good to be here among such fine, honourable folk such as yourselves,' the bard announced and the small people of the mountains were in agreement as they cheered on their entertainer for the evening.

'I've travelled many lands over the past two seasons and let me assure you, I've seen it all…' he started, shaking his head, '…war, oh I've seen war… enough to last a hundred lifetimes, more than any one man should ever see in fact,' he said sadly. Someone shouted at the back, something about smashing Balltimor's skull with his hammer and freeing the continent from the chains of slavery, Gormley didn't quite hear his comment properly over the noise.

'Exactly, couldn't have said it better my brave blacksmith,' Gormley did not know the man was a blacksmith, but he was in Winters Peak and with a soot ridded face like that, plus the man said he owned a hammer that could smash a skull, it was a good guess. The man held up his drink, Gormley knew to hold his tongue for a moment as the inhabitants of the tavern joined the man.

'To de crushing of Balltimor's skull,' he roared.

'To de crushing of Balltimor's skull,' the course of voices echoed in unison at his call and they all crashed their big tankards together with the closest tankard they could find, some went around crashing their cup into many more, spilling their precious ale all over the sawdust covered floor, making a slippery slush underfoot.

Gormley waited until the men had finished and settled down again before he continued. It was safer that way, best not to interrupt a D'warfen toast.

'Indeed, Balltimor's skull is not worthy of your mighty hammers my friends, not worthy at all. But where was I… ah yes, my travels. Let me tell ye a tale of a forest so dark and troubling that the wild beasts fear its haunting dim. A place where only the unlawful go to practice their unlawful ways… where the towering trees scrape the clouds and the sun has no place among… its… thick… black… shadows,' he spoke low and slowly, encompassing the room with his voice, he had everyone at the edge of their seats, the scene was prepared perfectly.

Without further explanation he started into his tale in a deep voice.

'Twaaas on that niiiiiiight… that I… was born,
A loooooonleeeey moon… lit up… the morn.
The hoooooowling wolves… caaaaalled out… my name.
As maaaaarching men… through treeeees they came.
They broke the will of men once free… they came that night… to… capture… me.

Aneeeeath the skies o' crimsoooon red,
They took it all… as neighbooours fled.
With axe and boooow and swoooord and flame,
Tooo their deeeeeds… they aaadded shame.
As they left away with me… a slave for life I… was… to… be.

Through whip I learnt… an' whip I knew,
My heart twas weeeak… but something grew.
With yeeeears came strength… and man I came,
I would shooooow these men… the same.
I would break these chains on me… a day would come to… see… me… free.

To waaar… t'was time to send me to,
With axe in haaand… to capture you.
Among those treeees… where I was born,
As flames licked high in freezing morn.

They took a babe just like me… I knew now how to… set… me… free.
With axe nooooow raised… above my head,
It fell aaand fell till all… were dead.
I slayed my caaaaaptors… where they stood,
Among my burninnnng home of wood.
An arrow through my baaack pierced me… t'was on that day that… I… be… free.'

    The bard paused for a moment as the patrons of the tavern finished his tale.
    'T'was on that day that… I… be… free,' they all roared together and shouted their appreciation.
    'Gentlemen…' the bard started again after the rowdy crowd of half drunken men quietened down a bit '… 'tis a song about slavery and freedom, written by an unknown source about an unknown man, nonetheless I consider it a fair-tale in kind to many a man's story here in Gala' Mor. One in which any struggle can be overturned, if you are hungry enough to want it,' he finished.
    There was a silence among his audience as they were thinking.
    'But, didn't te wee buggar get pinned be an arrow,' shouted a voice.
    'He did, yes,' Gormley replied.
    'So, he died, did he?' the man shouted, somewhat confused.
    'Yes, he dies in the end of the tale,' the bard answered, trying to assure the man that the song was supposed to be sung that way, there were no mistakes on his behalf.
    The man looked around him, not quite standing in the same field as the bard.
    'But, ye said he's free… he cannabe free an' ded,' the man said baffled.
    'Well, you see he's no longer a slave…' Gormley tried again.
    'Aye… so he's a free dedman, is tat what yer telling us?' the poor man frowned, seemingly preferring that the man in the tale to be a live slave rather than a dead freeman.
    'Well, I guess so. You see it's better to be dead than to live your life working for somebody else's benefit without any thanks whatsoever,' he replied before realising he was in a room full with D'warfen, people who worked all their lives for the benefit of the Kingdom without any thanks whatsoever.
    There was such a dead silence that you could hear a mouse squeak, and one did.

'But, let's not dwell on tales of slaves...' Gormley was reaching for straws at the moment '...here's one about a certain Hero of the North... Hurin the Unifier,' he finished as the crowd went back to their wild shouting and cheering, his accidental insult already long in the past and forgotten. If ever in doubt about what to sing while in a tavern in the middle of the Forever Mountains surrounded by an uneasy crowd of over intoxicated D'warfen, sing about Hurin.

'Hurin the Unifier,' called the same man who had made the first toast before the last song, raising his tankard high in the air.

'Hurin the Unifier,' came the response from the mob. Again, the same clanging of metal on metal and the customary spilling of half their drinks on the floor, Gormley watched as the barkeep smiled at the sight, he wondered if maybe the short-legged man grinning behind the counter had come up with the tradition himself to sell more ale.

'Right, a song about the great hero himself... Hurin the Unifier, of course, any requests?' he mistakenly asked. Now to the average sized man this might seem like a normal request of your spectators; to choose the next song, but to the vertically challenged D'warfen, who were famous for their short temper and arguing, it was not such a productive idea.

'Te Battle o' Inish' mire,' called somebody from the back of the room.

'I know that one, an excellent choice,' the bard replied, happy the focus was no longer on him.

'Te wind tat rocks te mountain' another man bellowed from somewhere.

'Alright, alright... we'll do that one too,' Gormley replied.

'No... te' anvil sings when te 'ammer falls,' came another request.

'Well, come now, one at a time...' Gormley looked around nervously as men were starting to picks sides as to which song should be sung first.

'Ye bunch o' snow lickers... let te man sing, can't ye?' called one man with a braided beard up the front, nodding to Gormley. Gormley looked back and gave a half smile as a tankard came hurling through the air and bounced off the top of his head, landing in front of Gormley's wooden box stage.

The man with the braided beard promptly turned around and thumped an innocent man sitting directly behind him square in the nose, which resulted in that man's friend jumping over the table he was sitting at and landing on top of the braided man, to which of course, his friend jumped on top of that man and so on and so forth until there was a huge mosh in the centre of the floor right in front of the stage.

The men at the back had started their own pile up, seemingly trying to outdo the other one near the front. Fists were flying and cups were thrown, blood was flowing and ale was spilling, men were shouting insults and calling names, others were running and jumping on downed companions, it was a free for all.

Gormley stood on the box looking at the carnage in bewilderment.

'Best ye head on wit yerself,' came a voice from the floor, Gormley turned to see the barkeep standing there looking up.

'Alright,' Gormley replied nervously, amazed at how calm the small man was at the riot now in full swing on his premises.

The barkeep handed him a small pouch of coin, Gormley took it with thanks.

'Amm, will you be alright?' he asked, concerned for the barkeep as a chair landed a few inches to the right of his foot, shattering in a mess of splinters and small bolts.

'Me, o' aye. Just blowing off a wee bit o' steam, the lads are… 'appens more tat ye might guess,' he replied calmy and laughed a little, before taking a small run and launching himself into the nearest pile up, his short arms and legs flaying in all directions. Gormley quietly headed for the door.

'Tat strange long-legged one in the gable room has requested a morning wake-up call, Belinda' called her father as she was preparing the oatcakes for breakfast over the piping hot stove.

'Aye, I'll give 'em a shout now in a wee minute,' she answered as she slid the dozen or so cakes off the long-handled oven tray onto the hot wire rack, over the open flames.

'Just need to finish up 'ere first,' she added, not wanting to leave the food unattended.

They did not take long to brown up and the outer layer of sugared oats turned crispy and hard in the intense heat. She quickly slid the tray back underneath the cake and removed them from the flames, she placed them on a waiting shelve to cool.

She was whistling as she worked, some tune her father taught her when she was knee high. Removing a small wooden bowl from the cupboard she filled it with ice cold water from the outside barrel and made her way back down the hall towards the guest rooms. She greeted a few of the other guests with a smile and a quick 'Stay ye' well.'

The gable room was at the end of the hallway, built into the gable wall, hence its name. She gave a quick rap on the door, but there was no answer, she slowly lifted the latch and peeked inside, she saw the strange tall man sleeping soundly on the bed, the blankets rising and falling in unison with his breathing, she entered the room quietly.

She was approaching the bed when she spotted some peculiar items in the room. An instrument of sorts sat on the floor beside the bed and there were many pieces of papayus scattered about the room. She also spotted a small coin pouch sitting on the small locker beside the bed, she frowned at his carelessness, the whole point of the locker was to lock his valuables inside, not to leave them sitting on top for all the world to see, who knows who might sneak in and take it, she shook her head.

Nevertheless, she came right up to the side of the bed and looked at the man. He was handsome, in a strange kind of way, with long golden curls and a three-day old beard, he looked rugged and young.

Not thinking any more about it, she threw the water from the bowl right on top of him.

The man got such a fright he twisted this way and back that way a few times with lightning speed and only stopped because he threw himself out of the bed and onto the cold flagstone floor.

'Arrrrrgh,' he shouted and jumped to his feet with his back to Belinda, britches and shirt peppered with splotches of wet. He stood there for a moment shaking the water off his head like a wet dog.

'Burrrr, what in the…' he started to study the timbers over his head, looking for a hole, there was in fact nothing wrong with the roof '…arrragh,' he finished, reaching for the tunic swung over the wardrobe at the other side of the room.

'Having breakfast… Ser?' Belinda called.

Gormley swung around and he stopped suddenly in surprise as he saw the tiny head peeking up over the bedclothes on the other side of the room, two big blue eyes blinking at him.

'What are you… I mean who… who are you?' he said forgetting where he was for a moment.

She shook her head dramatically.

'Name's Belinda, Fillame is me father… do ye be taking… in… breakfast?' she spoke slowly as if the man did not understand her language.

'Breakfast… yes, of course,' he replied, finally coming to the land of the living again.

'Of course, ye do,' she replied and was making her way towards the door.

'Did em…' he began and waited for her to turn around.

'Yes,' she replied impatiently.

'Did you em… wet… me?' he asked slowly not quite believing she would do such a thing, but he was wet and she did have a dripping bowl in her hands.

'Yes,' she replied casually.

There was a pause as he waited for an explanation or heaven's forbid even an apology.

She blinked her eyes rapidly waiting for him to ask another question, he was just standing there looking at her, he was a strange one.

'Right…' he announced. '…breakfast, I'll be right along,' he said and clasped his hands together.

'Right, I'll announce ye as ye enter the breakfast hall… shall I?' she said and offered a slight bow.

He smiled widely and nodded back.

'Well now, there really is no need to go to such measures, I mean…' he was being too modest.

'I'll not be announcing ye, or anybody else for that matter,' she said flatly not taking her eyes off him.

He stared at her, then realised she was having a joke at his expense and she didn't even seem to be enjoying it.

'Right' was all he could muster looking around the room.

She turned her back towards him and left the room without another word, and he was glad to see the back of her, she was a strange one.

At breakfast he didn't see the girl anywhere, he was glad of that for sure. The circular wooden table was finely crafted and keenly polished, there were no tools for eating with, save a tiny wooden spoon in front of him that looked about a century old, all cracked and dented, ready to fall apart to the point he was afraid to pick it up.

The room was open and warm due to the roaring fire built neatly into the side wall. He smelled the morning food cooking on the stove the second he entered the room, it was a mix of breads, tarts and other wonderful aromas he couldn't account for.

The décor was simple, but pleasant. Many pictures of charcoal decorated the walls, mostly capturing the images of mines and hammers. Old tools and equipment hung from the rafters, well used and long since retired.

Gormley was thinking about his journey back to his home in 'The Two Glens' and the long cold trek back was no mean feat, what with a war raging and everyone in the mountains panicking about the news of something unusual happening at the trench, when his thoughts were disrupted by a familiar voice.

''ave ye got another wee song for us bard… 'afore we head off to do the Kings work for 'em without the befitting recognition?' it came from his left and he turned to see who was talking to him, unless there was another bard in the inn that had called the entire D'warfen people slaves. The man was actually speaking in a welcoming tone, it appears he had not been too offended by Gormley's comments.

He turned to meet the face of the braided man who had been sitting up front, along with his fancy beard, he now had a black eye, some cuts on his cheek and a bruised eyebrow. There were other men at his table, clearly present at the tavern last night also, judging by their faces.

'Good morning,' Gormley called back to the men's table cheerfully, '…interesting evening we had last night, I see you survived the battle of White Peaks intact,' he joked.

'Oh, tat was no battle… just a wee bit o' fun with the locals… they love a good old dance, so they do,' he laughed.

'Ah, so you're not from around here either?' Gormley replied to be nice, not really inviting the man to join him, but not really refusing either as the battered man got up from his own table and sat down in a chair beside Gormley.

'Oh, em…' Gormley startled at the sudden attempted conquest of his personal space.

'When is it yer heading south and how far exactly?' the intruder asked bluntly, staring Gormley down with his beady little eyes.

'What… how did you know where I'm travelling to… and more frighteningly, why do you ask?' the bard questioned the small stocky man, who was leaning in too close for comfort.

'Sure, yer in the north laddie, ye must be heading south. Unless yer going west into Halti country, in which case yer a fool. Of course, ye could be heading east, right into the blasted trench, in which case yer a fool again. Then again ye could be heading north over the mountains, in which case yer a bugger of a fool,' the man slapped Gormley between the shoulder blades, nearly sending the surprised bard forward onto the table, Gormley's hands caught the side of the table as he went forward saving his embarrassing collision with the fine-dining cutlery.

'True, true... your process of elimination is commendable, I must say,' Gormley conceded.

'Aye, it is tat, laddie,' the man replied.

'Gormley, my name is Gormley,' he offered as the girl was back with his breakfast. She presented him with the reason he had only a spoon in front of him, a bowl of piping hot oatflakes, mixed with, what he assumed was goats' milk and a tiny handful of raisins.

'Thank you... Belinda,' he forced a smile and checked the bottom of the bowl with his spoon, looking for stones or something even worse, he did not trust that one, not at all.

'You're welcome, Wormley... sorry, Gormley,' she forced her own smile and walked away.

He watched her leave and his companion slapped him roughly again on the back, another struggle to remain in his chair followed, the man laughed.

'A right wee lassey tat one, but between ye and me... she's as stubborn as a pack mule,' he sniggered.

'I can certainly agree with you on that point,' he replied quickly, blew on a spoonful of sloppy oat flakes and tasted the food, it was hot, nourishing and delicious.

'Zaltan... call me Zaltan,' the man said after he allowed Gormley to swallow his mouthful.

'Ah, it's a pleasure, Zaltan,' Gormley replied and waited for the braided man to excuse himself, his food would have turned ice cold if he was just going to sit there and wait.

'So...' Zaltan asked.

'So...?' Gormley repeated, after a moment.

'South, when are ye leaving, laddie?' Zaltan asked, completely ignoring Gormley's request to use his actual name.

Gormley looked down at the man, he had a serious face and was waiting patiently for an answer.

'I'm leaving right after breakfast,' he replied nervously, looking directly at Zaltan.

'Right...,' Zaltan stood up and called over to his friends '...he's leaving after breakfast.'

Gormley turned around and was horrified as the men at the other table quickly finished their food and got ready to leave, Gormley faced Zaltan.

'We're coming with ye,' he confirmed and walked back to his companions who were now up, with their bags, which just appeared from thin air, in their hands and ready to move out. They had a slight huddle, with arms around each other to make a small circle in the middle of the breakfast hall, while peeking out at Gormley from time to time, as they discussed something of the utmost secrecy.

Gormley sat there watching the strange sight holding the spoon in his hand, confused.

'We'll meet ye outside, when yer done,' Zaltan called towards Gormley's table, then in military precision, they walked single file out of the room.

Gormley looked at them leave, his mouth gaping open.

'Something wrong with me cooking… Ser?' Gormley turned to see an angry looking Belinda staring at him at eye level and pointing to the floor, her foot tapping the floorboards. Gormley looked down to see he had dropped a blob of milky oat flakes right where she was pointing.

'Oh, excuse me, it must have fallen off my spoon… I'll clean it up, right away,' Gormley apologised.

'See tat ye do,' she replied and marched off back to the kitchen at her father's bequest.

Floor and plates clean, he headed outside to see if the small man was serious or was just having a bet with his mates to make a fool of him.

Unfortunately, he was not the butt of a strange prank, he immediately spotted the men waiting for him as he stepped outside into the snow. The cool morning air circulating inside his lungs, now freezing him from the inside as well as the outside. His breath was visible as he inhaled and exhaled the new day, whatever it might bring his way, he had no idea yet.

'Be headin' soon… will ye?' one of the other men shouted toward him, a long-haired man who was clearly the oldest of the group.

Gormley ignored the question for he knew it was a rhetorical jibe at him for keeping them waiting while he finished his much-needed breakfast.

'Amm, where is my horse?' Gormley asked, surprised that it was not tied to the post where he had left it the previous day.

'Has it been stolen? Oh dear, I must report this to the guards,' he was speaking to no one in particular, which suited the D'warfen, as they were not particularly interested in his early morning dilemma. They were checking their packs and making sure the knots on their carry bags were tight and secure.

'Sold it for ye,' Zaltan called to him.

'Sold what… my horse?' Gormley had started with a smile and even chuckled a trifle, but it rapidly trailed off to a concrete frown as he realised his newest friend was not kidding.

'D'warfen don't ride horses, laddie,' he said almost laughing at the tallest man in Winters Peaks ignorance.

'We walk,' a different man shouted, he looked much younger than the rest of the unit, by a very good margin in fact.

'Walk… to the south?' Gormley almost collapsed at the thought of it.

'It's hundreds of miles before "The Two Glens" …you can't be genuine?' he asked, both feet rooted in the freezing snow.

'Bout four hundred an' fifty, I believe,' the youngest man replied with a wink.

Gormley stood in the road as the men started off, he looked around for help, but all he could do was look. He was in their land now and he would have to play by their rules. They could take a notion to leave him behind with a few bumps on his head, then what would he do. No, it was better to follow and keep quiet, for now.

The freshly fallen snow crunched lightly underfoot as he shaped new imprints into the perfectly even surface, enjoying the sound, it reminded him of that first visit he had made into the Forever Mountains many years ago as a boy, if he had known the outcome of this trip beforehand, he might well have stayed in The Two Glens.

The landscape was truly beautiful, as far as the eye could see there was an enormous carpet of white covering the entire land. Trees trying in vain to poke out through the high drifts, birds fluttering their feathers to keep warm and single trails of smoke meandering sky bound from houses dotted across the valley.

A few hundred meters down the snow-covered valley he realised that they were going the wrong way.

'This way will take us further from The Two Glens, if I am not mistaken,' he announced as he caught up.

'Ye are not mistaken, bard. Got a good head on them shoulders,' Zaltan slowed down to walk in step with him, patting himself on his own square shaped head.

'So, it will take us even longer to reach the south then, you are aware of that,' Gormley noted.

'Well, we have a slight change in plans,' Zaltan spoke like the newest member to his squad didn't really need to know.

'A change in plans, really?' Gormley replied, amazed at the morning he was having.

'Aye, we're heading east,' Zaltan announced, without so much as a glance at him as if Gormley shouldn't mind the complete forced altercation to his life.

Chapter 5
The Whistling Woods

A wide clearing in the outskirts of the forest was playing host to a large group of soldiers, it was rocky terrain with clumps of overgrowth every couple of yards. They stood in a loose formation column, young men all. Around them stood their officers and a captain of many hard-earned years in the King's Guard keeping his men in tow.

The full regiment starting from the top down; consisted of a Captain, eight seasoned officers, two hundred and fifty fighting men, or rather fighting boys, eighteen hunters; unregistered men employed by the King's Guard to catch the four-legged food and one tracker, not even considered human, he was a slave from the eastern tribes of Gala' less, a land not many had travelled, but without the tracker, they all might as well of stayed at home.

'What are you talking about, Daxos here is the fastest drainer you've ever seen,' the man leaning on his spear claimed. He wore the uniform of the King's Guard, a red tunic, covered with silver frails and a huge lion crest in the centre, roaring from his chest.

'Fastest? he may in truth be the ugliest, but the fastest, I think not,' replied his friend leaning on a shield, a rather plump young man with a balding head and a full ginger beard, no one knew his actual name, so they all called him, 'Down-side up' or Down-side for short.

'Ugly is it…' Daxos started his protest, thinking for a moment '…well sure, I'm ugly… but I'd beat any man in this regiment in a challenge of Downing Four and anytime too' after a second or two he gladly conceded his lack of good looks for his skill at the drinking game.

'You musta' knocked your head with that big chicken bone you got there if you think you could beat Halard the Blagard in a challenge of Downing Four Daxos,' Down-side laughed.

'First of all, this…' Daxos patted his heavy mace hanging on his hip like he was petting the family dog, '…is no chicken bone, it's a finely crafted killing machine. Secondly, I've a raven here, says I'll beat the Blagard when we get back from this bloody hunt,' he announced proudly.

'A raven, eh?' Down-side gasped, Daxos was from a wealthy family, with more coin than sense he liked to flash his good fortune around. The man with the spear shook his head, amazed at the considerable wager his companion was willing to bet.

'Halard mate, you up for a challenge when we get outta this wretched forest, there's two owls in it when you win, all expenses paid?' Down-side bellowed to the rear of the troops. Of course, he did it on purpose to stir the men, he was looking to make a few coins on this one for his own pocket.

There was a mummer of chatter within the ranks, some laughed, others were looking to get in on the action as it had been a boring slog in the forest while others didn't care a fig.

Word came back through the throng that Halard had accepted the challenge, he was after all getting a free drink and when he won, he would be two owls the heavier. Even if he was beaten, which was as unlikely as a field of mushrooms, he still got a free drink.

'It's settled then, this blooming march wasn't a complete waste of time after all,' Down-side said pleased with the turn around.

The hunt was a century's old custom in Gala' Mor, when the old king had died and the new king was about to be sworn in. It was a celebration of sorts, that an entire regiment of his troop should hunt the Evergreen Forest that swept from the western banks of the Blacksnake to the Purple Mountains and all the way west to the colossal walled city of Whiterock, homestead of the King and capital of the continent.

They were expected to return with a good-days catch, draining the forest of any and all wildlife they came across. The day had been bountiful so far, with over forty downed deer and so many rabbits it would keep the city fed for days. They were sure to receive high honours from the boy-king himself.

'Get your lazy, sorry, good for nothing behinds up front you two Milk-Suckers,' the officer with the long back cloak called to Down-side and Daxos.

'Right, Captain. On our way,' Daxos roared back.

'Cap-tin, more like Tin-Cap,' Down-side said in what he felt was low enough for those only within close proximity to catch, forgetting how deep his voice could be.

The Captain watched the two sorry excuses for soldiers advance towards the front of the column, sitting atop a fine grey mare, blanketed in a warm cotton shawl, a dire scowl plastered across his hard features. He was a veteran in the King's Guard, a man who has seen more 'Time' than all the new recruits he was now in command of, put together.

He had been given the role as a reward for his services, for all the years of combat and his recent victory against the 'turnip heads' at the battle of 'The Second Charge.'

Daxos and Down-side knew what they were being called for, and they spotted the dead animal as soon as they came to the fore.

'Get it back to the cart, now,' thundered the Captain.

'Yes, Ser. Back to the cart to the rear of the troop, Ser,' Daxos called loudly.

It was the job of the new recruits to follow the hunters close-by, along by the trees, but staying back at a safe distance as not to warn off the fowl of the forest. The expert hunters would spread out in among the trees and shoot down the animals, carry it back out of the forest, dump it on the ground for the soldiers to sort out and continue on, looking for their next kill. The Milk-Suckers; the name given to Daxos and Bottom-side's regiment, would follow behind and carry the unlucky animals to a waiting cart.

'No,' shouted the Captain.

The two 'Milk-Suckers' were just bending down to pick up the fresh deer, when they stopped and looked at each other as they heard the Captain. After a look of confusion towards each other, they turned their attention to the silver-helmet wearing Captain.

'No?' they both replied in unison.

There was a pause between the three men and a strange grin appeared on the Captain's face. Captain Titus was not known for his grinning abilities; this would not be good.

'No… not to the cart at the rear,' he paused seemingly delighted with himself as he looked around to the men within earshot.

'Take this doe to the cart in the barracks,' he finished to a stunned silence from all. The birds flying high overhead in the skies held their breath, the wind ceased to blow and the full weight of his words hit their brains like a battering ram.

'Sorry Ser, but I think we may have misheard you there, did you say you want this doe carried back to the barracks?' Daxos said slowly, he ventured maybe the Captain had misspoken, it had been a long morning after all and he was quite old, it could be he was a little confused himself and forgot that they were a full day's trek out from the city.

'That is what I said, ferret,' he growled.

Down-side up and Daxos smiled and were almost close to laughing, expecting the whole army to shout 'got-cha' at any moment, but the look on Captain Titus's face told them otherwise and that there was no well organised skit being pulled on them. Their smiles disappeared with the realisation of their task.

'Now get a move on it, Tin-Cap has spoken,' the Captain demanded and finished with a mock laugh.

'Ser, yes Ser, of course Ser,' Daxos replied and threw Down-side a look of disapproval, the Captain had heard his insult and that was the reason for their punishment.

Down-side was the bigger of the two so Daxos allocated his 'friend' to the tail side of the beast, as a thank you for landing them in this mess, while he circled around to the lighter head end of the deer.

With some effort they started to drag the deer away, it was heavy to move but manageable. It wasn't so bad pulling it down the slope of the forest, but they knew the whole way back to the barracks would not be all downhill, there were plenty of steep climbs and even a few rivers to cross.

As they tugged at the deer, they spotted more than a few of their fellow recruits and an odd officer greatly entertained at their misfortune.

'You buffoon,' Daxos called to his partner under his breath.

'You lemon, why should I be the one to carry the…' Down-side did not finish, but dropped the legs of the deer and looked in the direction where the sound had come from.

The entire regiment was now standing still and facing east, the face of a thousand trees were standing still and facing the regiment.

It had been three long loud whistle shrills, not like anything they had heard before, most certainly not a horn, so they knew it wasn't a battle call from some enemy, anyway they were too far from the Blacksnake, there was surely no enemy this far west, but you never knew.

They all stood, unknowing the best course of action to take, standing dumbfound seemed to be working so far, luckily old Tin-Cap was not as stationary as his men.

'Hold the line,' he bellowed. The troops turned around to look at him, dumb-faced and disorganised.

'Into position men, form a line, front facing, shields and spears at the ready,' he called again, they stared back at him, unfortunately he assumed he had been given men who had the basic level of combat training for the King's Guard, he had been mistaken.

The officers were running down the lines of the regiment, arranging the clueless trainee troops into a defensive position, just in case. It took a while, but eventually they were ready.

'Congratulations men, a fine display on how to get your officers, your beloved Captain and yourselves, all killed. I have never seen such a poor response time in all my life in this troop and should I live another sixty-seven years, please don't let it be so…' he shook his head in dismay '…I am most likely never to see the likes again,' Captain Titus was far from amused at them.

They waited for a time to see would anyone or anything emerge from the towering trees.

The Captain sat on his mare and commended the non-existent enemy force for its cunning and tactical prowess. I mean they had managed to sneak past all the hunters that were distributed out among the woods, they had taken up an excellent position on the tree line, giving them cover from his own archers while catching their enemy out in the open. He could not have planned such a more perfect ambush himself.

Suddenly there was movement coming from the trees they were facing, the phalanx tightened closer together at the command of one of the darkly dressed officers. A lone figure materialised from a backdrop of browns and dark greens.

There was complete silence as the Captain squinted at the figure, the officers were likewise trying to assess the new developments. A twang sound came from the rear of the troop. They all watched as a single arrow arched across the sky with wonder. It sailed unchallenged across the open space and landed with an unheard thump, just three meters in front of the tracker.

'Is aye,' shouted the strangely dressed man as he called at them.

Now fully aware of who the visitor happened to be, the most valuable person on the hunt, the Captain sat up on his horse and spun around.

'Who did that?' he said calmly, unsurprised at the incredible insult to common sense.

There was more silence from the troop, most men took it upon themselves to study the nearest stone at his feet, as if there had been no other stone like it in the universe.

The Captain paused, took in a deep breath through his mouth and released it slowly through his nostrils, tickling the hairs on his scruffy beard.

'Is aye,' the tracker roared at them again, waving his hands in the air, unaffected by the attempt on his life.

'I said who did that, who almost killed Yogi,' the Captain scanned them, looking for a sign.

'Now grant it, I do not like Yogi much, he's a creature of extreme savagery. Eats his own toenails he does… I know because I've seen him. He smells like a lower city latrine and I cannot for the life of me understand a single word that sprays out of his vile mouth, will someone please try to translate what he is saying…' the Captain had started peacefully enough, but finished by losing his temper and almost falling off his mare with sheer frustration.

An officer sent one of the troops up to ask Yogi what was happening as a hand went slowly up at the back of the phalanx.

Quickly an officer barged into the mass of men, grabbed the suspect without a word and dragged him back to the waiting Captain.

He was a clean-shaven youth with long brown hair to his shoulders, handsome and had the look of someone who might have been a charismatic leader full of confidence with that square jaw and high cheekbones, but at this moment he was not too confident or charismatic. He looked up at the Captain sheepishly.

'Brought a bow with you eh, lad?' the Captain said smiling.

'Yes… Ser, thought it might come in handy,' he replied, his self-confidence creeping back.

'Handy? He thought a bow might come in handy, Dimator. What do you think of that?' Captain Titus was addressing his senior officer.

'Well, we are on a hunt, Ser,' Dimator replied, showing no emotion.

'Exactly,' the Captain agreed, surprisingly cheerfully.

'Exactly,' the boy was smiling, joining in on the entertainment. He was beginning to deliberate as to why he was so shy about owning up right away, it was a simple mistake after all.

'Then we shall have a hunt of our own…' the Captain called joyfully, '…whoever brought a bow with them, why I have no idea, please step forward and make a line, if possible, just behind our newest champion archer,' he finished.

It took a few minutes to get the new want to be hunters to form up a straight line facing the waving Yogi.

'How many?' Captain Titus asked the officer.

'Thirty-five, Ser,' Dimator replied immediately.

'You there…' the Captain gestured to the lad who had fired the arrow, not bothering to ask his name '…you will be the deer and these fine, highly trained archers here, will be our hunters…' the Captain nodded, '…begin,' he shouted.

Unsurprisingly, nobody moved.

'Ah… Ser?' the youth replied nervously.

'Oh, I must apologise my young man, I forgot to explain the rules, how silly of me. It's relatively easy, you are the deer, these men behind you will be the archers. You run to where Yogi is, and they will hunt you. If you make it, you live, if you don't, then, well you don't,' the Captain smiled and seemed pretty proud of himself at his powers of invention.

'Eh… Ser?' it was the turn of one of the new archers to voice his unrequested opinion.

'Oh dear, I just thought of a new rule, we are having fun, aren't we, Dimator?' He said looking to Dimator, ignoring the concerned archer.

'I know I am,' Dimator responded blankly.

'Excellent, where was I… oh yes, a new rule. If the deer makes it to Yogi, all the archers will face the block, along with their families, neighbours and all their pets,' the Captain laughed dryly.

The boy looked at the Captain for confirmation of his seriousness, he saw no sign that the man was jesting. He looked at Dimator, who just frowned back at him, the picture of sombre. And finally, he looked to the archers, his last dwindling hope of salvation, his comrades just moments prior, to his horror they were all notching arrows to their bows.

There was silence then as they all looked to the Captain for the signal.

'I already said begin,' he called impatiently, throwing his arms up in the air.

The lad took off like a deer in the hunt, looking behind him for a glance at his would-be attackers. The last thing he saw was thirty-five deathly sharp arrow shafts coming straight for him. Although not all of them hit their target, twenty plus did, and that was enough to secure the lives of the families, their neighbours and pets of the archers.

The boy who had been sent up to Yogi returned to the officer.

'Well, what does he want?' Dimator asked.

'Is aye,' the boy replied.

'What in all the swamps of Marshaven does that mean?' the Captain called as he heard the message.

Yogi was pointed towards the trees.

'This way, Ser. Yogi wants us to follow him,' Dimator answered coolly.

Yogi led them to an area where many large trees had been felled, they had been cut down and had been laying on the ground a long time. All the hunters had gathered there and were waiting for Yogi and the rest of the troop to arrive.

'Yogi says whoever blew that whistle is close-by,' one of the hunters approached the Captain and relayed his assessment to Dimator.

'How close?' the Captain said.

'Yogi,' the hunter called and made some hand signals to the tracker as he came over. Yogi made a few strange signals back and the hunter looked around. He pointed to the trees and Yogi shook his head, pointing to the ground.

'Strange,' the hunter said, scratching his chin and looking around again.

Knowing that the Captain had the patience of a billy goat with three legs he was about to quickly inform him of the news, but left it a moment too long.

'What… what is strange?' Captain Titus commanded to be educated in the secret arts of hand signals and chin scratching.

'Well, it's just Yogi says he tracked the smell of something human to where he found footprints, over in that direction,' the hunter pointed to where Meadow had come from. 'Then he followed the footprints to this spot. He says the footprints disappear here, but the smell lingers,' the hunter explained to the Captain.

Captain Titus sniffed the air, he smelled nothing unusual, he looked at the ground, again nothing.

'So… they vanished, great. Dimator pin a medal on everyone present here today when we get back to Whiterock,' the Captain shouted sarcastically.

Yogi walked slowly about, looking around, he was now kneeling down low, feeling the ground, he paused. He sniffed the air and waved over to the hunter who was able to understand him. After a long discussion with many more hand signals, lots of pointing and both shaking their heads a number of times, he returned to where the Captain and the officers were waiting.

'Amm…' the hunter began, clearly not wanting to translate the trackers message.

'What is it Condon… or Condin… or, oh never mind your name, what did the savage say now?' the Captain bellowed.

'Yogi said… people walk below us,' the hunter offered, unconvinced.

The Captain was ready to leave, he was ready to pack up the rest of the deer and just leave the forest and head for home, never to return. But he was in charge, a charge he ill wanted, nonetheless he had received the job so he must see it through.

'Ghosts, Yogi, that's what you found… ghosts,' the Captain called as Yogi frowned at him. Yogi was the only man in the troop that did not care what the Captain thought of him, he welcomed the block, it would mean a quick release from his imbecilic captors.

Just at that instant a small rabbit came out of the ground right where Yogi was standing, it came up and rubbed at his feet, trying to climb his leg.

The Captain saw it, and sat up in his saddle to get a better look.

'Looks like a rabbit Yogi, some tracker you turned out to be,' the Captain frowned.

Yogi scoffed at the insult he didn't understand and he looked back at the ground where the rabbit had appeared from. There was fresh evergreen moss growing on the felled branches before him, not a common sight. A large rounded rock sat unexpectedly where no other similar rocks were in the vicinity. The ground to an untrained eye looked out of place, to a tracker it looked like a rose in a bunch of thistles.

The troop were starting to disperse, as Yogi bend down and slowly touched the moss, he realised it was not growing there at all, it slid off easily and without much effort on his part, then he saw the hole and he looked in. It was dark, but it was hollow. Then he saw her, she was looking right into his yellowish eyes.

Yogi stood up and called to the hunter, as the hunter turned to face him, Yogi crossed both arms across his chest, the signal that he had spotted an enemy.

'Yogi has found them,' the hunter called to the Captain.

'Where?' Dimator shouted back.

Yogi was pointing to where he had spied the girl.

The officers shaped their men into a defensive position in front of the Captain.

'Protect the Captain,' Dimator bellowed to a few recruits as he advanced to the front of the gathering troops.

The Captain's hand instinctively reached for his sword and was ready to fight, he wanted to leap off Bella and join Dimator. But nowadays it took him a full three minutes with the aid of two men to help him reach the ground, there would be no leaping today, or ever again, so he sat back and released his weapon.

Captain Titus, eight seasoned officers, two hundred and forty-nine fighting boys, eighteen hunters, and Yogi were ready. They formed a phalanx of twenty abreast that was twenty-five deep. Their shields sporting the lion crest of Gala' Mor were locked at the front of the lines, the trainee spearmen just behind them with their weapons coming out over the shields to face the enemy, each man had a short Xavier sword for close quarters combat.

Those standing in the third and fourth lines readied themselves to take the places of the men in front as they fell. The officers were spread out evenly among the recruits to give orders and encouragement as the fight went on, the Captain sat looking over the Gala' Mor war machine in action. True, his troop were young and inexperienced, they were also a bunch of half-wits, most of them, but the Captain believed in the training exercises of the Kingdom and he was certain he had more numbers than the enemy.

'Ready, men,' Dimator called. 'We stand as one, we face the enemy with a knowledge of our superior weapons, our superior strength and our superior leadership. We hold fast, we hold strong, but above all, whatever comes out of that hole this day… we hoooooooold,' he roared. The troops roared with him, the Captain roared as did his bodyguard of ten fighting boys.

There was a pause as the sounds of silence deafened every man.

All eyes were on the small hole in the ground, then without a sound the large rock started to move. Fingers tightened around lances, men braced themselves for the end, thinking of their loved ones they might never see again as a little girl came out from behind the fallen oak tree and stood in front of them.

Chapter 6
Perfect Strangers

The old healer had just finished washing the blood off his shaking hands. He had removed the bolt, stitched the gaping hole in Long-tooth's stomach and patched up the wound with a large bandage he had torn from a cotton sheet.

'You would have left him in the mud to bleed out, healer… why?' Sparrowhawk asked as he sat on the rocky stool, filing the steel on the arrowhead he had removed from the door back to its former pointy glory.

'Bah… begone Ranger, it's far from 'ere ye should be… me thinks,' the old man replied coldly, and Sparrowhawk sensed the tone, 'Not your place… down 'ere, so it ain't,' he added, shaking his head.

Sparrowhawk agreed whole heartedly with the healer, he stuck out like a sore thumb this far south. But it had been a necessary trip, one he hoped would be his last.

He sat in silence, taking in his surroundings and pondering over his next move. The shack itself was in dire straits, it was on the verge of crumbling at any moment. He was thankful that his arrow had not collapsed the structure on impact. Killing the old healer and all his chances of getting back to Marcus with his prisoner.

He would need to stop in a town on his return trek to obtain some essential supplies. How would that look, he thought, riding into the streets with a wanted outlaw tied to Rogue, depending on the town he had entered the locals would either cheer him on arrival or hang him from the nearest tree. Most towns up north had a garrison stationed there, since the war began it was a priority to keep a watchful eye on the commoners and quash any and all signs of rebellion before they gained any traction.

But down this far south, the war had not affected the people to the extent it did in the north and east, there was simply no strategic advantage to either side to control the swamps and outlaw hideouts. Sure, the land was not fit for tillage or breeding herds on, but there was an untapped medical goldmine down here, fortunately for the locals, nobody was aware of it.

Sparrowhawk looked around the healer's shack, it was covered from roof to floor with hundreds of different shapes and sized bottles, full to the brim with potions and elixirs. There were white bags and nets hanging from the ceiling, containing brown and green flaky herds that were dying out. The Kings physicians would have a field-day if they saw this place.

'*But, then again, maybe that's why you work out here, alone,*' Sparrowhawk thought for a moment looking at the old healer.

Long-tooth let out a moan as the healer was clearing away the pieces of blood-soaked cloths and his small metal instruments he had used from his workbench.

'Whaaaat… the…' Long-tooth had begun, the slits of his eyes showing some colour.

The healer whacked the patient over the head with an old heavy iron pot, adding another dent to the collection.

'Hey?' Sparrowhawk rose to his feet and advanced towards the healer, who immediately dropped the weapon/cooking utensil, it nearly went through the rotting floorboards as it landed with a clatter.

'You better not have killed him?' Sparrowhawk went to check on Long-tooth, feeling for a pulse, he felt the blood flow throb back against his thumb.

'Are you crazy? Do you know the damage that thing could have done, I need this man alive,' Sparrowhawk barked.

'Ye mean I didn't kill 'em…' the healer shook his head, disappointed that his assassination attempt had failed. '…move ye aside Ranger, I will give 'em another one… me thinks,' the old man stooped down, grabbed the abused pot and came up ready for round two.

'Give me that,' Sparrowhawk took the pot easily from the healer.

'Now go over there and calm down,' Sparrowhawk ordered. He hadn't given anyone a command like that in a while, but the healer obeyed it right away.

'Awww…' was all the old man had to say for himself.

'You repair his wounds, then you try to turn his brain into cabbage soup?' Sparrowhawk asked puzzled by the old man's actions.

The old man held up his two hands, his fingers spread wide. Sparrowhawk had noticed the missing pinkie fingers before now, but thought it best not to bring up the unusual handicap.

Now the healer was throwing it out into the open, wanting Sparrowhawk to notice it, and it didn't take the Ranger long to figure it out.

'I see, Long-tooth did that to you?' Sparrowhawk asked sincerely.

'Yes…' the old man spat, looking at the unconscious outlaw '…and 'is posse of water-wags,' the healer finished with a mouthful of phlegm rocketing to the floor, splashing out in all directions. Sparrowhawk frowned, '*why would a man spit on his own floor*,' the thought almost revolted him.

'Better for us all, if 'em never wakes up again, cause of too many 'ardship that one,' the healer was shaking.

'Fair enough, to that I can't protest. But I need to take him to Whiterock, there he will sit trial before the King,' Sparrowhawk spoke slowly and clearly, so the healer could understand.

The healer understood perfectly well what a trial before the King would mean for Long-tooth. Trials were called to order only once or possibly twice a season; it was a big deal in the capital. It was a special sitting of the most wanted men in the Kingdom, brought before the King and his court for trial, records state that no man or woman on trial has ever been freed. Some are hung on the spot, while others are sent to the mines in the mountains, a quick hanging was preferred to the mines, the old healer was hoping Long-tooth would be sentenced to the latter.

'Trial afore the King… yes, yes… a fitting end to the rat-bag, me thinks,' the healer replied blissfully, smiling at this new development.

'Ah, we are in agreement then. You stop scrambling his brains and I'll take him for his trial, agreed?' Sparrowhawk was starting to loosen up a little. An understanding between the two men was close.

'Agreed, yes yes, of course. Will ye be 'aveing some tea?' his tune had finally turned, to the delight of Sparrowhawk.

'Tea, yes please. A mouthful of some warm tea would be perfect before I head back,' Sparrowhawk checked on Long-tooth's pulse one more time, satisfied he rested his bones on the stool again.

The healer was back with the tea in a few minutes, the crane attached to the fireplace was a worn-down piece of metal that swung in and out over the flames. The kettle just to tie in with the rest of the shack, was also in great need of replacement.

It took some time for the water to heat up as the fire was almost extinguished and the healer was not wasting good logs on a stranger who broke his door.

'Ah… 'ere we are,' the old man replied and handed the Ranger a wooden bowl, carved from the trunk of a resident ash.

The smell hit him like a charging herd of wild buffalo before he even had the homemade bowl in his waiting hands. It was an overpowering twang that made his eyes water slightly. He took the bowl with a nod of appreciation.

He looked into the bowl and saw a swamp of twigs and petals; it was a mish mash of all sorts of colours and strange looking plants. With the dim light in the room, he was unsure what else could be inside the bowl.

The healer joined him and sat on the floor, gesturing for Sparrowhawk to remain where he was as the Ranger was getting up to return the stool to the old man.

The healer held his own bowl in his hands and was sipping the tar-like liquid with great satisfaction from time to time.

Sparrowhawk was feeling like he was being rude, so with an effort he raised the bowl to his mouth, he was saved by the healer's voice.

'Good, drink all, we must leave soon…' the old man said.

Sparrowhawk thought he heard the old man say *'we must leave soon… we?'* but it was probably the strong odour from the tea causing his senses to falter.

'Did you say… we?' Sparrowhawk probed the healer.

'Of course… we. The bag of dung 'ere…' the healer snorted in the general direction of Long-tooth '…will need constant attention on the journey. Do you know how the internal organs react to such an injury, are ye familiar with the signs the body makes should 'em go into shock and can you supress such an incident… me thinks not?' The healer had the Ranger there. Sparrowhawk kicked himself for not having thought of it, he prided himself on having a great ability to calculate every possible outcome on one of his jobs. His daughter had told him he was getting old before he left, he decided she was over exaggerating, but the old man had just confirmed his daughter's allegations.

He thought for a moment on these new developments, unfortunately his choices were quite limited. It was an imaginary owl toss between taking the healer with him and giving Long-tooth the best percentage rate of survival, or head off on his own with the outlaw and risk missing out on his final payday and losing his one and only child, the invisible owl had landed 'take the healer' side up.

Looking down at his tea, a bug with at least a hundred legs came crawling out from behind some of the twigs, glanced up at him and scurried back into his warm timber frame house.

'We leave now,' Sparrowhawk said while he stood, setting his bowl of wholesome tea on the workbench.

'Oh, I see, I see,' the healer replied hastily.

'But we must deliver this 'ere crate to Narrow's Crossing first,' the old man nodded as he walked away to fetch his travel essentials, he had spoken as more of an order and not a request.

Sparrowhawk looked at the crate that was the size of a large canine, he wondered how the healer was planning on carrying the container.

'I can finish it on the way… plenty o' time… me thinks,' he muttered to nobody, bobbing his head while busying himself with bottles and small nets full with herbs. He hurried about the place with a quickness that betrayed his old frame, he then disappeared outside while Sparrowhawk was thinking about his next course of action.

The chill of the night air was cool, but not cold, he had been blessed with warm weather all trek, for that at least he was thankful. He had calculated that he would need to stop along the way back to Whiterock to top up on supplies, so Narrow's Crossing would do nicely. It was however a short distance out of the way, but he had little choice. The old shaky man popped his head back in through the open door a few moments later.

'We leave now?' he asked.

Without a word Sparrowhawk checked outside to see a large cart pulled by two fine black work horses, he had not seen the transport when he had arrived, but then it was dark, the cart and the horses could have been sitting right outside the front door and he would most likely have missed them.

'We leave now,' Sparrowhawk assured him.

Sparrowhawk picked up Long-tooth by the armpits and dragged him out to the cart, with a heave and a hoe he had the outlaw inside. The old man had placed a number of bags of herbs and some blankets in the rear of the cart.

Sparrowhawk tied the bearded man to one of the iron railings, the cart was sporting four lengths of iron on each side, Sparrowhawk was an expert knotsman, so he was positive the man would not roll off the end and make his escape. As an extra precaution he removed the small bell at the door of the shack and tied it to Long-tooth's left leg, with his hands tightly tied behind his back, there was little chance of him going anywhere or doing anything without him alerting the Ranger or the old healer.

'He will sleep most of the journey… me thinks,' the old man said confidently and slapped Long-tooth on the head as if he was swatting a fly.

Sparrowhawk ducked inside the shack for a moment and returned with the healer's crate, the fourth and final member of the group. Despite its size it was rather light, it rattled with bottles as he moved it. He quickly had it tucked safely in the corner opposite Long-tooth and near the front of the cart close to the healer, the crate was also tied down to the railing.

'On to Narrow's Crossing,' the healer shouted from the seat with the reigns in his hands, cowboy style.

Sparrowhawk walked over to Rogue and rooted in the saddle bag, he produced a handful of nuts and allowed Rogue to feast before he mounted his trusted steed. Sparrowhawk rubbed her neck, and had a man to mount conversation. Rogue neighed and shook her big head from side to side, as if she disapproved. Sparrowhawk did his best to calm the horse down, talking to her in calm, measured tones, rubbing her gently on the neck.

The healer looked on amazed.

Soon Rogue's outburst subsided and Sparrowhawk glanced over to the old man, shifting impatiently in the cart.

'Are ye two… ok?' the healer inquired.

'Rogue is a little disgruntled at our unscheduled stop at Narrow's Crossing, that is all,' Sparrowhawk answered, a little disgruntled himself.

The healer stared at Sparrowhawk and then at Rogue, his face a blank picture of confusion.

'On to Narrow's Crossing,' Sparrowhawk called and kicked Rogue into gear, she neighed, snorted and shook her head again. Rogue soon set off at a slow walk. The healers cart followed closely behind, his own horses not making a sound.

Chapter 7
War Studies

The towering stack of books sat dangerously close to the edge of his table, any accidental knock against a leg or uncalculated tap on the surface of the old wood might send the volumes of "The Art of Mining" crashing to the hardwood floorboards below. It would not be the first time he had disturbed the whole class with his carelessness on the first day of his "War Studies" lessons.

The room had many portraits of former masters dotted around the four walls, in great big golden framed rectangles, he was sure they were sketched by expert artists, the faces looked almost lifelike staring back at him.

His tutor at the front of the room was talking about what possible outcomes could result in multiplying the wind speed by the weight of the arrow shaft, and allowing for distance and air pockets caused by atmospheric pressure. Theodor did not hear a single word, he had more important things on his mind.

'Well… Theo'dor. Can you give us your evaluation?' the tutor called to the back of the room. His face chiselled with frowns, no doubt a result of years of stress and hardship caused by his students. He wore an odd little hat with a bobble on top, even in warmer weather when he would dress to suit the climate, the hat remained. The only remarkable feature about him was his ridiculously bushy eyebrows, like two fluffy grey caterpillars motionlessly sitting just above his dark eyes. There was silence in the hall.

Theo'dor was busy with his ink-feather, his hand was moving habitually across a piece of papayus taking notes, his eyes glued to chapter eighteen of the volume open in front of him.

'Theo'dor… are you with us today?' the tutor called again, this time he sounded a little irked.

Many of the other students swivelled on their stools to glance back to check, the squeaks of the timber on timber shook him out of his stupor.

'No… Master,' he called to the tutor, looking up. The tutor's face remained a picture of disapproval, red as a whipped mule.

'Yes… Master,' he tried, still no change from the aging man at the head of the class, if anything his eyebrows seemed to grow longer and meet in the middle.

'What… Master?' he called; a titter of laughter sounded around the room.

'I see,' the tutor replied irritably an let out an exaggerated puff of air, his face as pink as a sow.

'Well, we are sorry to interrupt the great Theo'dor D'Souza, from his important daydream,' he began. All of the students were now standing on the first or second rungs on their stool to get a clearer look at a D'Souza, a mummer of chatter erupted from the class.

He was used to this behaviour, it never got enjoyable, but he got used to it.

'Settle down,' the tutor roared over the noise and was abruptly obeyed as each student sat backside down on their stools and faced forward immediately. Nobody wanted to be removed from the most sought-after class in the Kingdom, to do so on the first day would bring shame to their family, and that would not do.

'Yes… yes, boys and… girl…' he paused to glance over at the only girl in the class. She was not just the only female to gain entry into his hall this season, but she would be the first female to ever be trained at Command School, '…we have a distinguished guest with us for the remainder of the season…' he spoke like a circus master, arms spread wide for full effect '…he will be here to woe us with his impeccable knowledge on the arts of combat, tactical siege warfare and if we are fortunate enough, he will even share his in-dept wisdom regarding the previous question,' the circus announcement was over.

There was utter silence within the four walls, a pin could be heard, if anyone was brave enough to drop it, they were not.

Theo'dor had no clue what the master was referring to, he had not been listening at all to what was going on during class. He had found some books in the library earlier that morning and was in a hurry to read them. He decided he better act fast and glanced up to the front of the hall. There he found the huge black slate at the top of the room, nailed to the front wall beside the door. It was covered in small animations of a battle.

There was what looked like a collection of shapes split into two separate groups and numbers on the slate, *'battle formations,'* he thought. The letters G and B were written over each group respectively. He had to squint slightly to see everything correctly, war-table tutor his Master may be, but he was no artist.

At the front of each force were small squares, he deducted that *'these were the shield troops.'* Next each force had rectangles, vertical in position, *'these must be the advancing spearmen,'* and finally the rear most position was taken up by triangles, *'who else but the archers should be at the back and shaped like an arrowhead,'* he concluded.

There were numbers written on the board also, but there were not digits that would represent the number of troops. One number was up high on the board, directly over the impending battle of two-dimensional shapes, it had an arrow underneath it… *'ah, wind speed and direction,'* he thought.

Next the number beside the archers had a tiny circle after it, it was high and almost touching the second digit on each side of the board *'the angle of the archers flight course.'* His mind did a rapid calculation, it was all too easy.

'Who will win the battle, the answer is group G,' came a soft low whisper from beside him. It was a girl's voice, he did not look at her as the tutor was glaring directly at him, she was trying to help.

'Group B will win the battle and comfortably too,' he replied to the tutor with sheer confidence.

The class gasped.

'Group B, as you like to call it Theo'dor, are the barbarians to the north. Vicious tribe of baby killers, the lot of 'em. While group G, represents the glorious troops of Gala' Mor, Theo'dor. We would never lose a fight to those rotten vermin,' the tutor scoffed at the mere thought of them.

'So, why do they win?' Theo'dor asked.

'They don't win…' the tutor began, but was cut off.

'But it seems that the trajectory of the archers is off by two point five degrees,' he replied.

The tutor looked back at his work of art on the slate for a moment, then turned back to Theo'dor.

'The archers in group G will miss their target, which I assume is the spearmen, by approximately six to seven meters,' Theo'dor finish his evaluation.

'What…?' the tutor marched like a general back towards the slate. He worked for a few minutes frantically, chalk squeaking and dust flying in all directions as he erased parts of his masterpiece, adding new numbers and decimal points here and there.

Theo'dor took a moment to look towards the girl who had whispered to him. When he looked over, she was concentrating on watching the tutor work. She glanced down at her own work from time to time and was trying to figure it out, she looked puzzled.

He scanned around the room, almost everybody was doing likewise, some even discussed it with their neighbours, they all looked like they were having the same problems. He knew where they were making their mistake, he turned back to the girl.

'The wind is too weak, not too strong,' he said quietly enough for just her to hear.

She stopped for a second, looked at him and looked back at her papayus, confused.

'No, it isn't?' she replied.

'Yes, it is,' he said.

'How so?' she asked quickly and checked the tutor was still working on the issue, he was.

'The weight of the shafts is too heavy to allow its course to set, the wind will take it off course as the shafts rise, before they can reach maximum velocity, changing the shafts course by two point five degrees,' he announced in a hushed whisper.

She wrote it all down as he spoke, she took a moment to study it as it stared back at her, she looked at Theo'dore and grinned.

'It is,' she whispered.

'Ink down,' the tutor shouted, startling the two of them.

The class did as instructed without delay.

'It would appear Ser D'Souza here, has corrected me, this is not a wise move…' the class froze in place. Master Calcus continued, '…unless of course, you are one thousand per cent sure in your correction and it is justified to be true…' everyone held their breath as the Master was continuing '…on this occasion… it is justified,' he finished and nodded his head.

'We are all here to learn, including I, yes you may think this a strife ridiculous but, I too can make mistakes like any man… or woman,' he corrected himself and acknowledged the young lady sitting close to Theo'dor.

Theo'dor was surprised at the Master's prompt acceptance of his mistake, he had thought the famous ex-Commander in the King's Guard would not appreciate being called out like that.

'Did anybody else come to the same detections as our new class genius here?' the Master announced. Nobody answered him.

'I should think not,' Master Calcus agreed more to himself than anybody. He picked up a handful of sheets of papayus from his huge timber desk, it was the size of a large timber door set horizontal on four hefty legs, the weight of such a thing was immense.

'Alright, class dismissed for today…' he called.

The students started to move, but stopped as the Master continued, looking back towards him, '…I want the whole class to review this manuscript this evening and come back with an evaluation for the beginning of class in the morrow. It refers to the battle of Watersdeep, three decades ago, I'm sure you've heard of it. As I have made an unforgivable err in today's lesson, I wish not to repeat the same blunder in tomorrow's class,' he spoke menacingly.

As the first student received the waiting manuscript he frowned.

'Master, this will take us all evening,' he complained.

The master looked horrified.

'It will?' he gasped in mock horror, putting the back of his hand to his forehead, looking up in surprise.

'Well, I think you should make haste to get working on it then, Ser Musi,' Master Calcus announced, enjoying his display.

The class was taken back to say the least, then it all became clear as to what was happening.

'Of course, should anybody have trouble with their assignment, please feel free to contact Theo'dor, I'm sure he will enjoy correcting his peers as much as he does his tutors' Master Calcus announced grinning widely. Everyone turned to face Theo'dor and they were not showing the same enthusiasm as their Master.

Theo'dor sighed, so there it was. It appeared the Master was not so understanding at his correction earlier.

He did it every year, the Master, it was a simple marker for the class, I am right and you are just a simple child who will not question my authority under any circumstances. This year it was Theo'dor D'Souza's turn to be the example, D'Souza or not, nobody makes a show of ex-Commander Calcus.

It wasn't long before some of the other members of the class made their feelings known to Theo'dor how they felt about loud-mouthed know-it-all's getting them extra assessments on warm sunny evenings, where their time was more valuably spent rowing on the lake or chatting with the students of the first season embroidery classes. And like always, it was always the larger boys built like small houses who were the most vocal with their fists, that came forward to voice their disapproval.

It didn't help his situation that Theo'dor had told the boys that maybe if they had of paid more attention to their lessons than that of stuffing their big mouths with Alsan the bakers cream rolls, they might have been able to solve the question on the Master's slate.

In truth it wasn't the worst beating he had taken over the years that his brain was responsible for, though it was right up there. They had cornered him in the common room just after leaving Master Calcus's hall, it was a good time to deal out a thrashing to be fair, classes were over for the day and the common room was free of witnesses, you have to take your opportunities when they come.

As he lay on the floor hunched against the far wall, nursing his wounds he didn't blame his attackers, he knew before coming to the academy that he would not fit in like the other students. He was after all a D'Souza, and that meant a certain level of jealously came with the baggage, his father was the richest merchant in Gala' Mor, and that would draw some unwanted attention where ever he found himself.

After a quick poke with his hand, he assessed that although extremely painful, his nose was not broken, maybe a bit out of shape, but still fully functional. His left eye was almost closed, he was squinting through the bottom eyelid coming up to meet the upper eyelid that was coming down, again painful, but no permanent damage he thought. He was on his feet in moments, the pain was more than enough for most boys his age to keep himself down and feel sorry for themselves for another while. But his father had bought the best tutors in the Kingdom to prepare his only son for the ways of the world, and one of those tutors was Alsamat.

He was walking through the main door, and was immediately blinded by the beautiful white of the sun, trying to adjust his one good eye as it hit him, he focused painfully. As he was looking around, many people were looking at him, blood still fresh on his face, running down from the left corner of his purple lip.

'Theo'dor, were you fighting, with whom?' came the sweet voice that he recognised from class not long before his thumping.

'Ah, you should see the other four brigands,' he answered into her concerned face, eyes big and bright.

'We need to report this…' she pleaded, '…you can't let thugs get away with their… their…' she was visibly angry at the incident; this made the pain a little easier to bear.

'Their… thug-a-ry,' Theo'dor finished her stumbling attempt to find the correct word with a smile, a very unattractive smile it must be stated, his swollen bottom lip not thankful for his effort.

'Hmm,' she replied sensing his tone, her excitement about bringing the entire Kingdom to a standstill while the culprits were captured and imprisoned, somewhat deflated.

'I guess we should leave it be,' she said, realising any tattle-tailing on her part would more than likely result in his other eye receiving the same treatment as the first, it was hard enough to see as it is.

'Well, I'm taking you to the medical officer, she will have a look at those bruises,' the girl offered.

'There's a medical officer? You learn something new every day,' Theo'dor said surprised.

She led him slowly across the Grand Everglade Gardens, where the students lingered on their time off, lying on the fresh grass and enjoying the beautiful plants and many fountains scattered about the area. No doubt discussing the topics of the day's lessons and the ongoing war, it was difficult to find somebody who did not have an opinion on who would win or what the best tactic was to use in the newest developments of the conflict.

Many watched them go past, pointing and peering to get a better look at his broken features, others ignored them completely, engaged in conversation with their equals.

As they were coming close to a building that Theo'dor had not seen before, perhaps because it was rather out of his way as he was new to the academy, she picked up the courage to ask him the question that had been desperate to get out ever since she had started walking him to get treatment for his wounds.

'How did you figure out that Master Calcus had the wrong calculations, I saw your papayus, it was blank of any equations. How could you figure it out so quickly?' she asked and realised she had maybe spoken out of turn.

'Of course, it's really none of my business… if you would rather not talk…' she quickly added, but he cut her off.

'I did it in my head,' he responded.

'No… no you didn't, it was too complicated to not write the problem down. You cannot calculate all those different allowances, I mean wind speed, weight of the arrow shafts, positioning of the opposing armies, in your head that quickly, nobody can,' she raced all her words together, trying to get them out before they arrived at the door of the sickbay.

They arrived at the sickbay.

Theo'dor gave her a sideways smile and said nothing.

She looked back dumbfounded, confused *'No no he didn't, he couldn't have,'* she thought.

The door opened in front of them with a mean sour-faced bulky frame of a woman standing there glaring down at them. She had obviously thought that they had been eavesdropping outside her station, but quickly realised the reason for their visit with one look at Theo'dor.

'Oh dear, what in the "Plains of Solitude" have you been up to, young Ser?' she said compassionately and swung the door open wide for him to come inside.

'You should see the other four boys,' the girl answered for him. He smiled sorely.

'Oh dear, I'll wager you left them in a fettle of a mess, to be sure,' the big woman joked.

As he was being escorted into the room, he realised something, so he turned around and faced his new friend, who was waiting outside watching him and the nurse.

'I don't even know your name?' he called as she put her hand on the door to close it.

'Neadielo, my name is Neadielo,' she answered and closed the door as he disappeared inside.

Chapter 8
The Evergreen Massacre

Dimator gazed all around him, sure there was an ambush coming, but all his senses told him otherwise. There was no movement from the treeline in any direction, there was no sound of men shouting orders to each other in the distance, no horses braying or neighing over the sound of hooves and feet marching towards them, all was quiet.

'What's this?' the Captain called to the hunters.

Yogi made signs to his hunter, rapid motions and hand signals.

'It appears to be a girl, Captain. Yogi says he's never seen one before, heard only rumours about them,' he replied to a snort of laughter from the troops.

'I can see that, you half-brained-court-jester, what is it doing here?' the Captain bellowed.

Yogi sprang into action again, he was a man on a mission, his hands swinging up and down, back and forward, he even preformed a two-foot-high jump into the air and landed with a thump. The men close to him looked on in wonder, the hunter beside him nodded knowingly.

'Yogi says, she's lost… Ser,' the hunter relayed the message to the Captain.

'Well, but of course she is lost, you do not expect me to believe she lives out here all alone, do you?' the Captain replied, getting irritated by the men in his care.

'Dimator, take the brat into chains, we shall bring her back with us, she won't get much at market, but we can't leave her here to perish, that would be un-captain-like,' he called to his senior officer.

Dimator nodded and called two of the nearest boys to him, spoke to them in a hushed tone and they nodded to confirm his orders.

The Captain was satisfied with that, then he took one last look at the girl and was about to turn his horse and thoughts back to the hunt, but he spotted something.

'What is that you have there, brat,' he called to the girl as he saw a small wooden item in her hands.

'Dimator, what does she hold there,' the Captain shouted at him.

Dimator looked at her just as she was lifting the small unknown device to her lips. He focused in on it as she blew two long loud shrills.

The men who were approaching her slowly clapped their hands to their ears as if they were on fire. Most of the remaining troop did likewise, the shrill echoed and bounced all around them for a few seconds, shaking their heads to get the sound out of their ears.

'It appears to be a whistle of some kind,' Dimator called back to the Captain.

'Thank you Dimator, I'm glad you're here to confirm that for us, what would we do without your powers of evaluation?' the Captain shouted.

'Ok girl, no more of that now, you hear,' Dimator instructed her with his arm held towards her palm up, expecting her to hand over the whistle.

As the men were getting close, Meadow didn't move. They were about six meters from her when a call came from behind.

'Beaaaar,' somebody roared.

The entire throng of men turned to see what the commotion was about, and true to the roar, there was a large black bear slowly making its way down from the trees, it was heading straight for them. None of the boys had ever seen such an animal before, they were amazed by its size and ignorance, just simply strolling down to so many armed men, was not a wise course of action after all.

'Hold your positions, form ranks, face the enemy… I mean bear,' an officer called; the troops were quick to obey this time. Even the two soldiers who were told to capture Meadow left her be and re-joined their unit.

The Captain sat high on his horse taking in the rare sight. He immediately thought of his trophy wall, that big grizzly's head would sit perfectly beside his mountain lion, his troops had killed years ago while on campaign in the Purple Mountains.

'Kill it men, but do not harm the head,' he called.

'You heard the Captain, take it down,' Dimator roared and the men cheered confidently.

The bear was approaching, meandering down through the overgrowth, he was low to the ground and was disappearing and reappearing as he came in and out of the thick bushes.

'Another beaaaar, to the south,' a shout when out.

The Captain spun in his saddle, almost falling over, the reigns saving him from an embarrassing and painful tumble. He saw the second animal and gasped, it was larger than the first one and it was coming towards them also.

The officers looked at one another, the boys of the King's Guard regiment were flabbergasted. Luckily, Dimator had many hardened years under his belt.

'Split the phalanx, half facing the bear to the south, the other half remain where you are, move quick men,' he directed them from the front, standing before them pointing and pushing them into position.

As the first bear was bearing down on them, he stopped, almost within spears reach.

The boys at the front of the line were brave, but with no way of knowing what to expect they were still nervous, their officers looking on, encouraging them to hold the line.

The second phalanx was now in position, facing the oncoming bear from the south, they too held the line as the bear approached slowly, the second bear moving exactly the same as the first had done, avoiding the heavier bushes and coming on to meet them at a leisurely pace. They had been trained to ignore the screams of a charging foe coming for them, not a calmly placid bear going for what looked like a morning stroll. What they failed to realise was that the bears were conserving their energy, for they too had been trained.

The first bear now sat down; the troops more confused now than anything.

'Hooold,' an officer called; in case anyone was getting any funny ideas about relaxing his position.

The south bear was now the same distance from the second phalanx as the other bear was from the first.

'Beeeeeaaar, to the east,' a call from the first phalanx.

'What…?' the Captain shouted, beside himself with uncertainty as he spotted another bear coming from the east this time. To see one bear was a one in a million find, but three, something was very wrong. He looked all around him, another officer was leading a third column of men who had broken off from the rear lines of the other two, to face the third invasion. He was losing control of the situation and fast, his men hurried about as best they could, but could they keep their composure against these bizarre circumstances.

An army of bandits would have been a much more enjoyable foe to face, but an army of wild bears, that was unheard of, there was no playbook for what was about to happen.

'Hold the lines, do not engage, they may be just curious to our presence, no sudden movements,' Dimator was commanding his troop like a proper commander, the Captain nodded to his officer and was glad to have the man by his side. He remembered the days when he was on the ground, barking at his men in the field, days long ago.

The three bears now sat in front of their respective groups of men, about eighty or so in each phalanx, forward facing, spears glistening in the rising mid-morning sun.

Dimator looked at the situation like a commander, he was secretly in agreement with his Captain, something was wrong here. One bear wondering out of the trees to investigate the occupation of its home by a foreign species was one for the campfire, but three at the same time, and all sitting patiently, seemingly waiting for something, but for what.

Then it hit him like a kick from a foaling mule in the behind, an incident which had actually happened to him as a young boy, '*why would wild animals be waiting, unless they were not, in fact, wild. The bears had appeared right after the girl had blown her whistle, not before,*' the flow of events passed in his mind.

Dimator flew his gaze back to where he had left the girl, he had forgotten all about her. He was sure she had made her escape while the bears had strolled up to his units, but when he looked back to locate her, she was still there, smiling fondly at the large animals as if she had some kind of connection with them.

Then like another kick from the same mule, it hit him, '*it wasn't the bears that were waiting, it was her.*' The brightness from the sky drained away slowly, a strange darkness rolled in without any breeze in the still air. The soldiers looked up instinctively and a fog of fear came upon them. The young men were muttering to each other in fearful whispers, Dimator looked up, then he saw that there were no clouds above them, the blackness had been caused by a massive flock of birds coming over the trees and stopping their flight right above their position.

There was a strange calm as they circled the troops, after a moment of nervous glances to the skies the birds called out an ear-piercing squawk from above. The men were beginning to show signs of anxiety, some looking around for the nearest exit.

Yogi ran off to the side, calling something inaudible in his native language back to his hunter translator, pointed to the birds and took off without any additional hand's signals. The hunter raised his arms wide, clearly clueless to the tracker's strange actions.

'What… in the great trench?' the Captain bellowed with all his might over the noise of the birds towards Dimator.

Dimator looked at the Captain, unsure of what he had said but the look in his Captain's eyes gave him an idea, he looked at the tracker getting smaller by the second and looked at the girl, the only person in the wide clearing that looked comfortable.

'It's the girl,' he called back.

The Captain frowned, his officer's words lost to the squealing of the black birds hovering high in the sky.

Meadow raised the whistle to her lips again.

Dimator saw her movement, he called to the nearest men to seize her, but with all the noise nobody heard his cries. He watched as the whistle connected with her lips, her cheeks puffed out and then she blew.

A single shrill sounded, high but very short.

The hovering birds dove straight down upon the now terrified soldiers, causing chaos among the ranks as the new recruits focused their attention on the aerial assault. The lucky ones who had a shield had some protection against the bombardment, the spearmen soon realised that their eight-foot-long prodding weapons were useless to counter such an attack, they dropped their weapons and unsheathed their short swords and swung wildly in the air, swatting at the angry birds.

As none of the recruits had been issued any sort of head gear, they were an easy target for the dropping feathered missiles, they soon started to feel the full weight of such a storm. Many soldiers dropped to the ground holding their heads as birds pecked, clawed and flew straight into their unprotected scalps. Some were seriously injured, others simply went down to the safety of the ground, hoping the birds would hit into someone standing and not them, while others hit the ground and remained still as boulders, gaping wounds in their skulls.

Dimator was in the thick of it, he kept low to avoid the surprise battering, calling orders for his men to protect the phalanx with their shields by holding them up and horizontal, while the rest of the troop got underneath the metal wall, it was working for now.

The birds came thumping into the shields at thundering speed and bounced off the protective cover. The other phalanx's saw the success of Dimator's group and followed suit.

With a defensive wall in effect the soldiers gained a bit of hope. Dimator ordered the men on the edges to swing their swords out around the shields and hit the birds on the flanks. They discovered their efforts were not in vain as many swords cut through the birds like hot honey, they had generated an effective effort.

Just as quickly as the birds had attacked, they stopped and ascended into the sky again and flew back over the trees.

The skyward shield wall was ordered to cease and as they came down the blue sky was once again painted high above them, the huge flock of birds escaping back from the direction whence they had come, the blitz was over.

A huge cheer went up from the survivors, although it did not last long. As the soldiers looked around them, they noticed to their horror a number of their forces were killed in the attack. Many were injured and would be unable to perform fully should the killer birds return.

Dimator scanned the scene with his experienced eyes, the men were disheartened, confused and tired from such a frantic attack. It was then he spotted the bears, in all the excitement with the birds he had forgotten all about them, they remained sitting where they had always been. The rest of his troops seemed to have forgotten about them also, no one seemed to be paying the creatures any heed, dazed from the ludicrous onslaught they had just witnessed.

He quickly shot his gaze in the direction of the girl, but in all the panic his phalanx had moved eastwards a hundred metres, trying to avoid the birds and get themselves into position for a counter offensive. She too, like the bears had not moved an inch, the birds had not laid a claw upon her.

She was looking directly at him, she frowned and breathed heavily, her chest heaving as she lifted the whistle.

His eyes widened and his mouth opened to shout something to his men, he was not sure what he was going to roar, and never got the chance to find out as another shrill came from the girl. The whole force glanced back towards the sound.

They heard the bears before they saw them coming. With a howl from each monster, and a running start they were heading straight for the waiting troops.

'Shields front, spears level, hooooold,' Dimator roared to his men. The shield bearers were quick to react, they had just seen what damage a few birds can do first-hand, they did not want to find out the devastation a bunch of bears can bring to the party.

The shields locked into position, but the spearmen had no spears, they had been ordered to discard them in the battle with the birds, and they were scattered all around them on the ground, the men in front standing on them. Some managed to grab one and try to get into position, but it was not enough.

The bears broke through the shield walls with the first charge, shields broke, men fell back and the bears were in the middle of the phalanxes in a matter of seconds, swinging their bone-crushing arms at the outsiders. Claws cut into flesh with ease, men were dropping and running away. The bears took no prisoners, maiming and slashing in fits of rage. They mauled and bit, roaring loudly at their prey as they cut through the recruits with remarkable simplicity.

The troops panicked, they were making no worthy efforts to subdue the huge beasts of the forest, the best they could muster was to circle around the bears. When someone found the courage to go in for a slash at the bears thick fur, the bear took the brave soldier down, causing the rest of the men to gasp in horror, morale was sinking like a rock in a puddle.

Dimator was busy ordering his men to strike at the bear that had attacked his group, but it was no good. Maybe if he had veterans alongside him, they might have stood a chance, but the boys were inexperienced and not prepared either mentally or physically for such a fight.

The bear charged directly for him, he braced himself with his small buckler shield, the bear struck him with a power he had never felt before, with his shield taking the blunt of the blow, he was sent sprawling across the open ground. Luckily a brave young man sprang in between him and the bear, receiving a claw to the back for his troubles.

Dimator was getting up and he saw the girl, '*she got them to attack, she can bloody well get them to stop.*'

'Get the girl,' he called to the men closest to her, they lost no time in obeying, almost delighted to be told to get out of harm's way.

Dimator ran also to join them, as soon as they dragged the girl to him, he put his sword to her throat. She was not smiling anymore as she looked into his maddening eyes.

'Call them off,' he roared at her, the three soldiers looked at the officer, unsure as to what he was talking about.

A huge eagle came out of nowhere and attacked the men holding the girl, one of the men took a talon to the head and was screaming in pain, blood gushing from the wound. The eagle flapped its wings and downed another man. Dimator swung he sword, but missed. The bird came at him and he barely managed to get his shield into a defensive position in time. The swift eagle bounced off the metal plate and landed a few feet away. It looked dazed, its beak had been slightly twisted in the attack and one of its legs looked injured.

More men had come in to aid the officer and the bird was severely outnumbered, with a scream it flapped its great wings and took to the skies once more.

Dimator shook off the attack and concentrated his attention back to the girl.

'Sha woe a mor,' she spat at him.

Another problem had just presented itself, as if the day couldn't get any worse. '*The brat doesn't speak our tongue,*' he thought, looking hopelessly for the runaway tracker for assistance, if he knew how to communicate with her, he was long gone and useless now.

He was a resourceful man and quickly came up with a way of communication that she would understand.

He pressed his blade slowly into her neck, a sliver of blood ran free, she refused to give him any ground, small tears gathering in the corner of her eyes.

'Call them off or I'll take your head this minute,' he roared, spittle landing everywhere.

She leaned her head to the side and shouted towards the bears, who were slaughtering the recruits, one scared boy at a time.

'Koda,' she roared past the men towering over her.

The bears stopped their rampage, the shaking men stood still and the bears turned on their heels and ran full speed back to the trees without so much as a goodbye.

Dimator exhaled loudly, scanning the battlefield his eyes took in the disaster that had just befallen them. Men were screaming in pain with deep cuts into the bellies, sides and faces. Men lay face down in the dirt never to see another sun rise in a cloudless sky again.

In all his years on campaign, Dimator had never seen such destruction in such a short period of time. He turned back to the girl and held out his hand.

'Give me that whistle, brat,' he shouted.

Meadow knew what he was talking about straight away, she stared at him defiantly. Her parents had died for such defiance right before her eyes many years ago. It was not going to do her or her forest any good for her to die now, she handed him her blow-stick.

Dimator turned it over in his hand, examining the craftmanship of the small timber whistle.

'Take her…' he called to the soldiers, '…whatever you do, do not let her out of your sight,' he finished and turned to get a full report from his men.

'Captain?' Dimator called, looking frantically around for him, stepping over dead bodies as he walked across the clearing to the last place he remembered seeing the Captain.

'Over here, Ser,' a soldier shouted back, Dimator made his way to where a bunch of soldiers were gathered in a small circle looking down at the ground.

'Damage report?' Dimator called to an officer as he reached the soldiers, lying there motionless beside his horse was the Captain. His wounds were covering his face and upper body. Dimator frowned, as the soldiers said nothing, looking to him for leadership.

'Fifty-seven dead, eighty-six wounded and as far as we can tell, Ser… twelve deserters,' an officer said as he came up beside Dimator.

'That's about half our regiment, either dead or inefficient,' he said in disbelief.

The officer just nodded, much in shock himself.

Dimator took the reins of the dead Captain's horse, and patted the animal gently on the neck, rubbing her up and down to calm her, the smell of blood fresh in her nostrils making her eyes flare.

'Easy girl,' he said softly.

The officers had gathered around him, looking to him for instructions.

Dimator climbed upon the horse, it was his place to lead now and his men would follow him.

'We leave the field,' he called to everyone.

'The dead, Ser?' the closest officer asked.

'We leave them, for now. I'll not risk losing another man in this forest to bears, birds or whatever else is hiding beyond those trees. Take only what you can carry,' Dimator ordered, it was his first order as their official commander and it was an order of retreat. He frowned to himself, but he knew the safety of his men took priority, it was the right decision, enough lives have been lost this day.

Chapter 9
Long-Tooth Goes Back to Sleep

They had been riding for two long, exhausting days, the detour to Narrow's Crossing in the updated schedule was causing more of a delay than he had originally realised. The slowly moving healer in his slowly moving cart were certainly proving to be less useful than their worth.

Long-tooth in the rear of the cart had moaned and groaned a little, but had not woken once since they had set off from the shabby little town in Marshaven.

The old man was in good temperament the whole journey, he appeared to be none to disappointed for leaving the town at his back, who could blame him.

They had camped under the stars on both nights, the old man remained in his cart beside the felon, while Sparrowhawk had used the ground as his bed and his long cape as his pillow. Cold as it was, Sparrowhawk was content to have captured Long-tooth and was now on his return course to meet with the jailer, get paid and purchase a vial of swallow, the medicine for his daughter. The hard part was behind him, or so he thought.

It was midday when boredom overtook him and he reined in beside the noisy cart, the wheels groaning at each full turn while the healer was humming unapologetically loudly to the entire countryside, if there were bandits in the area, they would probably kill them both just to get a bit of peace and quiet.

'So, healer, what did you do to deserve that?' Sparrowhawk nodded towards the healer's missing fingers.

'I dun's nothing Ranger, nothing at all,' the old man called over to him, almost shouting to be heard over the noise of the moaning cart.

Sparrowhawk sensed a little discontent in his tone, it wasn't anger or resentment at the question, rather a revulsion towards Long-tooth.

'I see, so they fell off did they,' Sparrowhawk chanced a lighter tone, maybe bring the old man around that way.

The healer scoffed and looked off in the distance for a moment as if thinking.

'It be that brigand in the rear, well one of em's cronies to be fair, that did's it. T'was a warning from me employer,' he spat.

'A kind of, do what we ask or you'll lose the other eight, kind of warning?' Sparrowhawk understood the tactic, fear was used far and wide to subdue men to bend to the will of the tyrant, sometimes mentally employed, in the healers case it had been a physical message.

'That's right, Ranger. Sent this here log-head down from Narrow's Crossing to dispatch the word. Course, I was happy to oblige with all ten fingers, but ye know how things be around 'ere,' the healer replied.

Sparrowhawk knew how things were around anywhere, this backwards little part of the world was no different, the strong take from the weak by any means possible.

'So, what was the word… the job?' Sparrowhawk asked, enjoying the conversation, it beat the silence, at least for a short time.

'The word was…' the healer checked all around him, making sure there was nobody within earshot, who he was expecting to find was a mystery, as he had to shout so the man right beside him could hear, satisfied he continued, '…they wanted tonics made, special tonics that Whiterock palace might not be too ecstatic about… me thinks,' he finished by tapping his finger on the side of his nose.

Sparrowhawk had no idea what he was talking about, what kind of tonic's would the authorities disapprove of, although he accepted that he did not know much in that line of expertise and nodded his head.

The healer said no more on the subject and Sparrowhawk did not press for more information, a man's business is his own, illegal or otherwise.

They rode on for another couple of hours with the thumping of the cart and the out-of-tune humming of the healer, before they stopped for something to eat and to rub down the horses.

As the healer was cooking the rabbit Sparrowhawk had caught, the Ranger fetched a brush from his bag and started rubbing Rogue with both hands as the healer started into a different tune, the melody still all over the place, but at least it was a change. Sparrowhawk thought he heard a jingle sound, but assumed it was the healers singing.

'Shut ye that racket up, old timer,' a voice came from behind Sparrowhawk, he turned to see the ugly face of Long-tooth glaring at the old man, holding a six-inch shank in his hand.

'You, away from tat horse,' he turned and called to Sparrowhawk.

Long-tooth stumbled forward, but he managed to regain his balance after a moment. He was looking around, clueless to where he was and what had happened.

'Where's the boys, what have ye' done with 'em?' he called.

The healer was sitting down by the fire with the rabbit stewing in his favourite pot, legs hanging out over the side, almost kicking the licking flames.

Sparrowhawk was about to reach for his bow, but then he saw it sitting by the side of the cart, he had taken it off to rub down the horses, moments before. He had his girls waiting for a chance to cause some destruction on his back, but with no bow to fire them, he stood still, thinking.

'The boys… eh?' Long-tooth roared.

'They be back in Shallow Water… me thinks,' the healer answered.

'*Shallow Water… so that's what it's called,*' the Ranger thought, he would probably forget that name by the morrow.

Long-tooth was disorientated, he looked around confused. He held his head and found a huge bump and yelped at the pain as his fingers made contact.

The old man looked at the pot and then at Sparrowhawk, and back to the pot again, then to Long-tooth's bump, could the confused man make the connection, it was highly unlikely, the healer hoped not.

'Careful with that knife, now,' Sparrowhawk called.

Long-tooth glared at the Ranger, his head was heavy and his vision was somewhat blurred, he came forward, getting closer to the Ranger. The small bell tied to his foot distracted him for a moment and he raised his leg shaking it wildly, sending the bell into overdrive, he looked down at the bell and then at Sparrowhawk.

'What… in… the… Northern Realms be this?' he shouted loudly.

'It… um… be a bell,' Sparrowhawk answered calmly as if it was common practiced to tie bells to people while they slept in the back of a cart.

Long-tooth ignored the ringing as soon as he realised what he was doing and kept course for Sparrowhawk.

'You… I know me that face… where do I know ye' from?' Long-tooth was squinting in the bright sunshine. He was now within stabbing distance,

Sparrowhawk had the speed to reach the knife, but Long-tooth was the size of a young buffalo, his strength would be too much for the Ranger, it would be a fifty-fifty gamble and those odds were just not agreeable enough.

'I have travelled many lands and towns, each a new adventure…' Sparrowhawk was riding on luck for now, hoping the man with the ability to break him in half did not come fully around and remembered the brawl a few nights before.

Long-tooth shook his head, trying to remember, but it was gone. The pain in his side made him stagger back, Sparrowhawk moved forward instinctively, but Long-tooth shouted for him to go back.

'Stay where ye' be, now move ye back,' he called. Sparrowhawk complied with the commands and stepped back a foot, bumping into Rogue.

'I'm back… you need medical attention, that wound may fester if you don't relax,' Sparrowhawk tried to calm him down.

Long-tooth looked down at his stomach, the large white bandage wrapped around his back and covering the injury, he grunted with pain. He looked again into Sparrowhawk's eyes and a hint of recognition sparked, he seemed to be remembering something.

'How did I…' he said no more and landed with a thump on the ground at Sparrowhawk's feet.

'Hey?' Sparrowhawk shouted as the healer stood over the downed Long-tooth, black pot in his right hand.

'I had too 'em was going a make you,' the old man said defensively.

Sparrowhawk looked at Long-tooth, then he looked at the healer.

'Alright, you're right…' Sparrowhawk acknowledged '…I shouldn't have left my bow down, you did good,' the Ranger nodded his approval, the healer smiled.

'Is 'em dead?' the old man said, none too worryingly.

'You better hope he isn't,' Sparrowhawk answered.

He reached down and felt for a pulse, with a sigh of relief he stood back up and nodded.

'He's still with us, for now, anyway,' Sparrowhawk announced.

'That's wonderful news,' the healer returned, with as little concern as he could muster and made his way back to the fire.

Looking over the old mans shoulder, Sparrowhawk called after him, 'Hey, what did you do with the meat?'

'Don't fettle, it's on that rock over yonder, see, perfectly safe,' he replied pointing to a large grey rock sitting immobile on the ground.

'Right, let's get him back to the cart, you grab his legs,' Sparrowhawk called.

The healer looked at him as if the Ranger had just slapped him in the face.

'You must be pullin' me leg, I can't lift that sack of rotten turnips, I'll break my back, the size of 'em,' the healer replied nodding and turned back to the fire, pot in hand with another indentation on the bottom, it's a wonder the thing still had the ability to cook anything at all.

As Sparrowhawk was dragging the sack of rotten turnips to the cart, he spotted another bump on top of Long-tooth's head, his head looked like the surface of the moon, the man was lucky to be still breathing.

When he arrived at the cart, he struggled to lift the oversized man into the back of it, even with the end door down it was a high distance from the ground. Eventually he got the heavy outlaw up and in, then he made sure to tie a tribble knot around his ankles and hands. This time Sparrowhawk checked Long-tooth for any more concealed weapons or surprises, when he found nothing that the man could use to free himself again, he jumped down from the back of the cart. The veteran Ranger picked up his bow and swung it around his left shoulder, the string tightly pressed against his chest, he was not letting his friend out of arms reach for the remainder of the trip.

'Stew fit for a king, boy or nay!' the old man called to him as Sparrowhawk joined him beside the fire, sitting uncomfortably on a hard grey rock.

'A king can go catch his own, this meat is for us,' Sparrowhawk answered and took the bowl the healer was handing to him, the bottom of the bowl heating his hands as he cupped it.

'Ha… a king who hunts for his own supper, now there be a sight I would pay to see,' the healer replied. A kind of uneasy friendship was slowly building between the two travellers, in any other circumstances they would have never got along together, two completely different men from two completely different parts of the Kingdom, but somehow a strange bond was starting to form.

'Sure, if you had the owls to pay for it,' the Ranger threw at him.

'Never ye be minding what's in me coffers, a sight more than a wayward man of the road such as ye'self might be hoarding, me thinks,' he finished with a nodding of his head.

'Can't argue with you there, old man,' Sparrowhawk agreed wholeheartedly.

'Sabat A'choo,' the healer said proudly.

The Ranger looked cautiously at the old man and moved slowly to the rock beside him, further away from the healer, careful not to spill his food.

'Where be ye going?' the old man asked between handfuls of food, a large piece of fat dripping from his mouth and landing safely back into his bowl with a splash.

'I don't want to catch whatever you're throwing,' the Ranger replied.

What are ye talking about?' the man frowned.

'You just said saaa choo, and you didn't even cover yourself adequately,' Sparrowhawk shot back in disgust.

'No no, ye bandit catching rabbit murderer, my name, it be Sabat A'choo, that is what I said,' he laughed.

'Your name is a sneeze, great parents you had Sabat,' Sparrowhawk joked back.

'Ye be one to be talking of unusual names…' he laughed before he could finish '…I mean, who name's their wee child after a bird,' he nodded uncontrollably.

'I chose that name myself,' Sparrowhawk was slightly offended.

'Oh… ho ho, whatever for?' Sabat asked unable to contain his glee.

'Ideally to cause fear in the men I hunted,' Sparrowhawk had believed it to be a good solid name, one worthy of his craft, Sabat did not agree in the least.

'You wished to cause fear…, then why didn't to pick a snake or a… I dunno birdman… a lion or something that is actually scary,' he finished with a hoot and lost his supper to the dirt below as he slid off his perch on the rock and landed on the ground.

It was now Sparrowhawk's turn to laugh, as Sabat thumped the wet ground in frustration, he did however manage to salvage some lumps of cooked meat, popping them into his mouth and smiling.

Chapter 10
Into the Unknown

He made his way briskly across the large open area that was generally used for target practice for the new archers of the King's Guard, today however they were off on some hunt to the east, catching deer for Armando's coronation in a few days. He wore the academy tunic, a white and blue robe which covered most of his front and back. It was extra heavy today as he had made a few altercations to the inside of the garment, he would need it later.

'Come to join the Archers Guild?' a young man said hopefully as he approached him. He was dressed in the official gear of the famous Gala' Mor Archers Guild from head to foot.

'Not today, I am sorry,' he replied casually and the young man with the strange pointy hat turned his attention to another possible prospect on the other side of the courtyard.

Theo'dor had more important things to do today, far more important.

The nurse had bandaged up his bruises and handed him a green coloured ointment that smelled like drain water, but he did as instructed and applied the thick sticky substance on his face whenever required. The swelling had subsided and a few cuts were all that remained of his previous day's trashing.

As he had been hoping, she also gave him the rest of the week off lessons, to rest up and relax, giving his injuries the best possible chance for a speedy recovery, but he had somewhere to be that morning, and rest and relaxation were not on the table.

He had planned the whole incursion in his small private room the week before, it helped to have a father who owned half the city. It was a matter of timing and simple distraction.

His first obstacle would be getting time off lessons… check.

He knew making a few enemies on the first day would be useful, insulting them was the icing on the cake, painful icing, but sweet.

Next, he would have to get past the gatehouse guards, the main gate separating the Upper Ring from the palace would be manned by three armed soldiers, no-nonsense types with short tempers. He carried two bottles of Gil'berg with him as he approached the gate.

'Ho there... sunshine, where do you think you are going there?' asked one of the bored looking guards.

'Delivery for the palace, milord,' Theo'dor answered politely, holding up the bottles of expensive strong whiskey.

'Two Gil'berg's, eh?' the guard noticed.

'Gil' berg?' one of the other guards said, walking over to investigate the unusual provisions being carried by a student of the academy. His eyes lit up upon closer inspection.

'By all the wolves in Halti, I haven't seen a Gil'berg in years, my old pa used to be partial to a slug on holidays and the like' the second man had said, remembering his father.

'Aye, had a bottle myself, some time ago... dowry from Marta's parents, it was. Best tasting shine I've ever had, too bad the stuff cost as much as a whole-years pay packet,' the first man put in.

The third guard was asleep leaning against the wall, he did not add to the conversation, which made things a little easier for Theo'dor.

'Well, the palace has only ordered one bottle, the trader at the market gave me two by mistake,' Theo'dor started, the guards were listening intensively at the mention of the oversight by the careless trader.

'So, I guess I could leave one of these bottles with you, nobody will ever miss it,' Theo'dor finished his rehearsed speech, the guards almost fell over with excitement at his words.

'Why, that's a splendid idea young man, what did you say your name was?' the second man replied smiling at the thought of getting his hands on the drink that he had never tasted before, but had heard so much about.

'Anton,' Theo'dor lied, he always used his father's first name in situations like this, no point in leaving a trail of bread crumbs that might lead back to Theo'dor D'Souza.

'Good lad,' the first guard said, taking one of the bottles from Theo'dor. Both guards left him there and headed into the small gatehouse that was built into the high surrounding walls, the door closed behind them and Theo'dor had passed the second part of his plan with ease… check.

He made his way up the main walkway of tiny loose stones, with a beautiful small box hedging running parallel, edging the path with green and white flowers dotted everywhere like stars on a cloudless night. At the other side of the hedging was a low-cut lawn, trees were scattered about the place with bushes and shrubs in full colour. The crunch of the stones underfoot gave him a satisfied feeling that he was doing the right thing.

Many posh looking people walked past him slowly, as if walking slow was a sign that you had a lot of money, they looked strangely at him, wondering no doubt *'why was a student among them, and a student with a black eye too… for shame.'* Theo'dor did not care to much about their disapproving glances, he knew what these people were like, having been around them all his life, and he was sick to the stomach of their pompous attitude and behaviour around people they believed to be lesser than themselves.

As he approached the main palace, he spotted two White Rhinos guarding the main entrance, he had expected this, so stepping over the perfectly trimmed hedging, he made a new path in the freshly cut grass to the side of the building.

Unlike the guards at the gate, he had just skipped past, the White Rhinos would not be so easily distracted. These guards were a special unit within the palace grounds, they were huge men, chosen for their size and sheer discipline, they never left the grounds and their sole purpose was to protect the royal family. They had full permission to act first if they felt something was not right, and ask questions later. Theo'dor needed to avoid these guards at all costs.

He strolled on the grass as he came alongside the tall building of the Grand Hall, it was the main area where the King hosted his parties and from time to time held a trial by the King.

He checked his surroundings, there was nobody watching him, he quickly removed his tunic declaring him a student, turned it inside out and put it back on again over his head, pulling the clothes into position and straightening out any creases. He now donned the tunic of a palace hand, dressed in the dark navy of the palace with black arms and a palace crest he had bought from the market for half an owl, placed perfectly over his heart.

Phase three… check.

He glanced up at the open top windowless windows, he counted from the end until he reached number twenty-four, the storage room. He had spent many hours and coin researching all the rooms in the top floor of the palace, the storage room was the safest to sneak into, it was the most likely place to be empty of people and it would be quiet.

It looked doable, but if he was caught scaling the walls of the palace, there would be no amount of Gil' berg that could save him, he wasn't even sure his father could get him out of this one, and that was if the Rhinos didn't skewer him with one of those enormous halberds they carried.

He had come this far, he was not going to let a minor setback like dying stand in his way, so he placed the second bottle of shine on the ground and lifted himself onto the stonework, his fingertips feeling for nooks and crannies, his feet balancing his weight and propelling his body upwards. He climbed and climbed.

About halfway up, he chanced a look down to make sure there was nobody watching his endeavour to scale the palace walls, it was a bad idea, his head started to spin and his legs started to wobble slightly, he closed his eyes tight. He allowed himself a few minutes to recover before opening them. He knew that if he had been seen, someone would call out, a bell would sound and every sword wielding soldier within the city would come running, there was no need for him to check, they'd let him know pretty fast.

On he ascended, the stones were not as closely compacted the higher he went, the gaps were considerably wider, making it easier as he climbed. The wind however, was getting blusterier at this altitude, although not causing him to be swept away, it was remarkably cooler.

He reached the hole in the wall that pretended to be a window, he listened for voices and footfalls, he heard nothing. He lifted himself up, just as his chin was level with the sill, he spotted a moving shadow, quickly he lowered himself back down out of sight. He listened again.

Very faint footfalls could be heard on the hardwood timber inside as they passed, he shot up again and caught the back of a maid walking down the hallway.

'*Hallway, where's the storage room?*' He thought to himself. Had he calculated wrong, had he misjudged the size of the room. No, he couldn't have, he checked and checked a hundred times, and when he was finished checking, he checked another hundred times, just to be sure. But all was not right, he would have to improvise, and that was not the strongest card in his deck, but what other choice had he, to go back down… 'Nah.'

Slowly he checked both up and down the hallway, it was empty, he was on the top floor after all, there shouldn't be too much traffic up here. He swung one leg over the sill and then the other, he was inside. With both feet safely on solid ground he looked back out the window to admire his victorious climb, he was so high up that he could not make out the bottle of Gil' berg he had set down directly underneath him, thinking back now maybe he'd be safer to try bribe the White Rhinos at the palace door next time he visited.

'And what do ye think ye are doing 'ere?' a shrill voice came roaring from behind him. '*The game was up, Theo'dor old chap… prepare for execution,*' the voice inside his head told him.

He turned quickly around to face his captor. To his surprise it was a tiny little woman of about four foot nothing, she looked up at him with both hands on her hips, her mouth a crooked line of unforgiving malice.

'Me?' Theo'dor called back, looking down at her.

'Yes, yeeeeee,' she answered, shaking her tiny little head from side to side.

She was clearly one of the Minefolk, they lived up in the Forever Mountains and were keepers of the Kingdoms minerals, such as steel, copper, tin and of course white and yellow gold, the precious metal that was used to craft the owls, ravens and eagles, the currency of the Gala' Mor Kingdom.

Theo'dor thought for a moment, he had not calculated on meeting one of the Minefolk in the palace, he was taken aback.

'Just checking ta see of de Kingdom was still there, were ye?' the little woman said and looked out the window, seeing only blue sky as she was too small to see the city from her low vantage point.

'Ah yes, I mean no… what?' Theo'dor was at a loss for words.

'I've a good mind to 'ave ye taken to the pillar,' she said, still frowning.

It was then that Theo'dore realised that she thought he was a palace hand, they had been known for the harsh punishment for disobeying an order from a superior. So, he had now learnt two important factors, firstly; his disguise worked a treat, plus this little woman before him was in charge of something, the entire floor perhaps or maybe a certain number of palace hands.

'I beg your pardon…' he didn't know her name, so he chanced a neutral title '… m'lady, I was just feeling a little ill, so I was getting some fresh Whiterock air into my lungs,' he finished with his hand across his forehead for dramatic effect.

'Well… I wager ye've a fever or something with tat bruise on yer noggin,' she said concerned, her temper after calming down somewhat.

'I'll be alright now… get back to my chores in a moment, I will,' he confirmed.

'The place would come to a standstill without yer participation… I am sure,' she sneered and walked past him, her head high.

He had made it, not as smooth as he would have preferred, but he was alive and ready for phase four.

'Just remember to clean out the linen closet before you leave for the day,' the woman called over her shoulder.

'Of course,' Theo'dor called back and she read the look on his face.

'Are ye new or something, I don't recall yer face?' she questioned.

'Yes… yes that's it, I am new…' he said cheerfully, '…could you remind me again where the linen closet is located… please?' he finished apologetically.

'Should be paid more… I should…' she complained, '…it's the next door on yer left… just right there beside ye… ye can't really miss it even if ye tried,' she called and pointed in the direction in which she had just come from. Theo'dor spotted the door, it was built into the wall next to the last window on the side he had climbed up.

He turned back to thank the woman, but she had already vanished around the far corner, not wanting to be held up again by the newest feather headed palace help.

'*Linen closet, that must be the storage room I was aiming for, but I'm one window out, maybe I should take a look,*' his mind was wondering how he had gotten it wrong and by about six metres, unforgivable.

As he got closer to the closet, he noticed that the door was a lot newer than it should have been. The stones also looked cleaner than those built into the rest of the structure. Then he realised that the room had been built recently, that was why he had missed the storage room by one window, someone had the bright idea to move it, and without telling him first, frightfully rude.

Slowly he creaked open the door and peeked inside the dark room. The light from the hallway was quick to cast shadows everywhere as large shelves filled with blankets and cloths blocked the incoming light source.

He entered the room and looked around for a mounted torch on the walls, he realised then that there were none present because the room was full of very flammable material, it would only take one brave spark trying to escape, landing itself upon a blanket and half the palace would be up in flames.

He noticed a bunch of old portraits stacked vertically against the wall, fascinated by the portrait of a young woman he advanced to gain a closer look. He slid them to the side as he scanned through them, stacking them against the side wall. Then out of nowhere one of the stones moved as the weight of the pictures pushed against it, the stone slid back slowly as if a spring was taking the force, but moving back against the weight, then something clicked behind the wall.

A small narrow passageway revealed itself at his feet as a section of the wall slid backwards, it was dark inside as he tried to peer through the blackness, he saw nothing save a family of spiders that ran scampering out and startled him.

'*Hidden passageway… wonder where it leads,*' he thought to himself.

Being a boy of a certain age, he was compelled to crawl through the gap in the wall.

He was fully inside when his hand met a pressure plate on the ground and the stones slid back into place, trapping him inside his narrow tomb. He didn't know if there was a way to open it again from this side, so he had no choice now but to venture on into the darkness on all fours.

Chapter 11
A Sour Deal

'Won't be long now, birdman, hehe,' Sabat called over to Sparrowhawk.

The Ranger had asked the healer repeatedly not to call him this new name that he was finding so amusing to himself, but Sabat didn't listen.

'Just over the next hill and we'll be there,' Sabat called, head bobbing, pointing to the forest sitting on the rise just in front of them.

Sparrowhawk was new to the area, so he took the word of Sabat, the old man had steered him right all the way, so there was no reason to doubt his navigational skills now. It was Sabat who wanted to travel to Narrow's Crossing with his crate in the first place, so it was proper that the healer knew the shortest route to get there.

The Ranger's mind shot back to Rose, his daughter. She would always be collecting her herbs and flowers at this time of the day. She was a semi-professional healer herself, her mother had shown and thought her all the different benefits for the many diverse flowers, herbs and anything that grew in the wild, including the vegetables that took to the soil near their small home.

He could picture her then, sorting through the leaves and roots in her basket, separating them into jars and wicker pots as she got home, a wide smile plastered on her freckled face. But then she got sick, a fungus had grown on her throat, the healers in Whiterock called it throatrot. It started slowly causing minor discomfort, but as time when on, it grew worse. She always smiled through the pain, but she was entering the later stages of the disease and was confined to bed, he shivered to himself as he pictured her in his mind.

Rogue carried him on the dirt track leading close to, but around the dense forest, Sabat whistling 'The Bards Tale' unsuccessfully.

Best we take the 'Merchants Path,' Sabat breaking his tune to call over to Sparrowhawk.

'Right you be, healer,' Sparrowhawk thought if the old man was not going to use his name, then Sabat would be getting the same treatment as well.

'I'll never get this rotten cart through the "Whispering Forest",' Sabat explained.

'Whispering Forest, sounds like you know the area well?' Sparrowhawk was quick to spot his use of the local names Sabat was employing on the trip.

'Aye birdman, been 'ere a few times, hopefully after today, it'll be me last,' Sabat replied grimly.

They rounded the Whispering Forest in a short time, it was quite a small area and Sparrowhawk was thankful as he was getting tired of the days ride, his belly was moaning for nourishment and he would need to wash soon as his clothes were stinking and wet from the road. His throat was so dry it was beginning to pain him, Sabat had used all their supplies to tend to Long-tooth's wounds and he was starting to think he should let Sabat have another go at the outlaw with that pot, but quickly thought better of it. And anyway, there it was just in front of them, their destination; Narrow's Crossing.

The town looked rather large from his view point on top of Rogue, it seemed to span out at about twenty buildings on each side of the main road. They looked mostly like residential housing, but there was also a number of larger structures dotted in between the mass of homes, probably storage buildings, stores and taverns.

'And here we be,' Sabat called.

'Nice place, this Narrow's Crossing,' Sparrowhawk offered.

'Wait till ye meet the happy townsfolk, that'll change yer tune,' Sabat protested.

They rode into the middle of town, Sparrowhawk noticed that there were no people in the streets, although the road was well used and cut up. It was around midday if the sun was correct, and it usually was. All he saw was a little boy playing with a toy horse standing outside a store front, he had been on the decking as they approached, but some old lady had darted out of the building and dragged the poor fella inside without warning. Other than the kidnapping of the boy, there was not a single person around.

'Quiet town,' Sparrowhawk announced, somewhat nervously.

'Hmm,' Sabat answered suspiciously.

The old man, his two horses and his rocking cart pulled up to the largest building on the street, Long-tooth in the rear, Sparrowhawk checked for good measure.

'Right, ye stay put Ranger, I'll head on in here and settle with me employer,' Sabat said, getting down from the trap slowly.

'Play it safe, old timer,' Sparrowhawk called as he reached the door, he didn't want a repeat of the events at Shallow Water, he only brought a certain number of arrows with him.

Sabat disappeared behind the double swinging bat doors set into the middle of the door frame. Sparrowhawk could see over and under the doors, but all that was looking back at him was the blackness from inside of the room. Laughter came from inside then and he squinted his eyes to gain a better look, but the sun was too bright at his back, reflecting the light off the glass windows from the front of the tavern. He looked all around him instead, trying to piece together how such a large town was so vacant in the middle of a beautiful sunny afternoon.

It appeared to be normal enough; main street from on end to the other as he checked both ends, stores scattered every couple of doors apart and none boarded up, all open for business it seemed. He scratched his head.

Rogue snorted loudly and flung her head back towards Sparrowhawk, something was wrong.

'What is it, girl?' Sparrowhawk leaned forward and rubbed her mane, trying to comfort the horse. Rogue snorted again, she was smelling something, and she didn't like it.

Sparrowhawk checked the street again, but there was no movement, that was it… there was no movement. '*How had the street been so cut up with muck if no one was using it.*' Someone had been in the street and not long ago either, judging by the look of the terrain.

Another fit of laughter came from inside the tavern where Sabat had entered.

Sparrowhawk looked around again, he didn't like this, not one bit. He checked that his bow and girls were within reach, he found them in their usual spot waiting, on his shoulder and back respectively as he looked at the windows of the houses along the street, all the curtains were drawn and there was no movement inside.

His attention was immediately brought back to the tavern as the old healer came tumbling through the doors, leaving them flapping violently behind him as the healer fell to the ground, raising dust into the air.

He had an arrow notched and aimed at the doors, waiting for a target to cross the threshold. A small bulky frame of a man walked out laughing, a clean-shaven face with no hair, he was looking down at Sabat when he exited the tavern, but his gaze shot up to the Ranger as he came out into the sunshine. He raised his hands slowly and stood still, without a word.

Another man came out, the complete opposite of the first, he was tall and skinny, sporting a full beard and long curly hair to his shoulders. He too raised his hands when he saw Sparrowhawk aiming. A third man appeared looking happy to see the Ranger after his initial shock.

'Come in and 'ave you a drink,' the man shouted laughing, it came across as an order and not an invitation.

'Not thirsty,' Sparrowhawk replied, thirstier now than he had been all day.

Sabat was struggling to his feet, almost falling over again as he rubbed his head. The old timer had been hurled headfirst out through the doors and was now feeling the effect timber has when it comes into contact with an unprotected head.

'Keepin' strange company with this 'un,' the third man said to Sparrowhawk, standing between his two comrades, both still with their hands up like they were being robbed.

'We were heading the same way,' Sparrowhawk replied coolly, not allowing the situation to overwhelm his thoughts.

'Do ye be wanting the stuff or not,' Sabat said sourly.

There was a pause, the tension had gotten higher than anyone wanted.

'Sure, we do…' the man said after a moment of thinking '…put yer 'ands down,' he said to the two men with a slap to the back of their heads, they complied.

Sparrowhawk did not loosen the tension on the string.

'C'mon, no need to kill everyone in the street,' he called to Sparrowhawk.

Sabat looked at the Ranger and nodded, Sparrowhawk took this to mean everything was good, so he let the slack out on the string and slid the arrow shaft back inside the quiver.

'Good, good. Hans checked the stock,' the leader called to Hans, the tall skinny man.

'Could kill a man throwing 'em out into the street like that, Chester,' Sabat moaned to the man waiting for Hans to do as he was bid. The horses complained slightly at the extra weight as the stranger climbed into their wagon.

'Aww, you've survived worse than that,' Chester was jeering.

'Boss, we got a problem,' called a voice from the back of the cart, Hans had spoken in shock.

'What is it now. Sabat, you old trickster, did you renege on us with your delivery,' Chester was looking at Sabat, none too pleased.

'It ain't that boss, the stuff's here. It's Long-tooth,' Hans called.

'What in the depts of the Great Harbour trench are you blabbering on about, you… stiff head, Long-tooth is back in Shallow Water?' called Chester.

'I don't think so, maybe you best come see's it for yerself boss,' Hans was clearly not qualified to try to explain this.

Chester shook his head at his henchman and came around to the back of the cart, Hans stood back out of reach of Chester.

'It's Long-tooth,' he called in horror and looked at Sabat.

'It is?' Sabat replied, pretending to be as surprised as anyone.

'You done killed Long-tooth?' Chester asked, frowning.

'Eee ain't dead, pity's about it too, the ugly goat 'erder is just sleeping,' Sabat replied.

Chester took a moment to think, Sparrowhawk slowly bend his arm back in case an arrow was needed in a hurry.

'Sleeping? There's blood everywhere Sabat, people may talk in their sleep, some even walk, but ain't nobody I know's done bleed in their sleep,' he replied, looking for answers.

More silence.

'He works for me, Sabat, touching one hair on his head is like touching one oh' mine,' Chester said. Sparrowhawk notched an arrow, Chester looked up at him, startled.

'Fine with me,' Sparrowhawk spoke calmly and took aim.

'Oh, hold ye' up there stranger, no need to get all worked up now,' Chester called out.

'The Ranger 'ere, captured 'em. Aims to bring 'em to Whiterock for trial or something,' Sabat called to Chester. The man looked at Long-tooth and then at Sparrowhawk, he shrugged his shoulders.

'Fine, take 'em,' Chester said, not seeming too much concerned about the outlaw's future.

Hans started to lift the crate out of the cart, the other man had walked over to lend a helping hand, they had the box down without much effort and were carrying it into the tavern.

Sabat was back at the cart and looking in one of the sacks in the back, he pulled out a small pouch, fiddled around with the contents and popped something into his opened mouth.

'For the pain,' he said, noticing Sparrowhawk looking down at him.

Chester offered for them to come inside, but Sparrowhawk declined the invitation, he was quite happy on Rogue, where he could see all around him, a dark gloomy tavern with a dozen different hiding places for a dozen different men to spring from, was not his idea of playing it safe.

'Fine, suit yerself's, just going to check the stock, Sabat… not that I think ye would be trying a fast one,' Chester said holding up his ten perfectly intact fingers and wriggling them. Of course, he laughed as well, just to rub it in.

Sabat was not impressed by this show of disrespect, not one little bit.

'May the dirt lay thin on yer corpse,' he spat, as soon as Chester had vanished inside.

'Nice friends you got there, old man,' Sparrowhawk said to Sabat as the healer climbed back onto his cart to sit down while they waited.

'Used to be… once,' he replied looking at the Ranger.

'I see, I've enemies that treat me with more courtesy,' Sparrowhawk said, not expecting a reply.

'Brother-in-law… Chester be. Never forgave me for Bianca,' he finished and hung his head.

Sparrowhawk sensed this Bianca was someone important.

'Wife?' he chanced a guess.

'Aye… used to be, long ago now,' he replied sadly.

Just as Sparrowhawk was about to probe further into the healer's past, Chester came laughing through the doors.

'All there Sabat, ye managed to do it in record time this time 'round. Here, catch,' he said and threw a small pouch up to Sabat, who caught it as it landed in his lap.

'Same again next season?' Sabat called down.

'Aye, same again next season,' Chester replied to Sabat, but was looking at the Ranger.

'And you, interested in some work? Could be using a quick hand like ye,' he offered to Sparrowhawk with an ugly grin.

'Just passing through,' was all Sparrowhawk said.

'Shame,' Chester grumbled with a frown and turned his back, he started walking back inside and said no more.

Sabat was lifting the reigns and getting ready to leave when it happened. Three men, one of whom was Hans, came rushing out through the swinging doors, all armed with short steel swords and homemade timber buckler shields.

Sparrowhawk didn't need to think, his instincts shot into third gear and his bow was notched in moments with a razor-sharp, finely sanded arrow shaft.

The men were shouting something that got lost to the wind as an arrow took the nearest man square in the chest, he went down instantly. Without his special brew, Sparrowhawk was slower than he would have liked. The second threat came in the shape of Hans, he was grabbing at Sabat, who to his credit was not giving the bully an easy time. Sabat's left leg swung at breakneck speed and caught Hans in the mouth, the man went down grunting in pain and holding his face as a gush of blood appeared.

Sparrowhawk just loosed as the third attacker was about to grab Rogue's reigns, it wasn't a clear hit as it buried itself in the man's shoulder, Sparrowhawk had to adjust quickly and decided to aim high. He staggered back and fell to his knees, the shaft deep into his shoulder as he had taken it at almost point-blank range, Rogue reared high and came thundering down like a hurricane upon him, ruining his day completely.

Hans was back up and charging at Sabat again, this time Sparrowhawk aimed low and landed a perfectly aimed shaft in the back of Hans right leg, he fell like a bucking mule, screaming in pain, the shaft sticking out at the same distance on either side, about a foot on the front and back.

Sabat quickly lashed the placid horses into action and the cart was off down the street like fork lightning. Sparrowhawk was close on their tails.

The Ranger looked back as men were pouring out of the tavern, he waited for them to run to the stables and retrieve their own horses, to which a chase would soon ensue. But, to his surprise, they just stood there looking at the downed men and after the escapees.

The street was quite long, but they would make it soon enough.

'Nearly there,' shouted Sabat over the pounding hooves of the horses and rickety cart.

Sparrowhawk glance back again.

'Why are they not following us?' he asked confusingly to his partner in crime.

'Who cares… let's just get us outta 'ere,' he called back. Sparrowhawk didn't argue.

Just as they were getting close to the end of the street and the open countryside again, a large group of men came running out from the end of the street, they spread across the exit and seemed to be notching arrows to huge bows. They moved like a military unit, all together with a single purpose. Sparrowhawk squinted to get a better look, they were fully armoured, helmets and everything, and were dressed in black and crimson. 'It's the Kor' Cali,' he thought.

'Stop, turnip heads dead ahead,' he shouted to Sabat and reigned in Rogue, dust flying in all directions.

Sabat heard him, but did not stop. He lashed the reigns harder and the horses upped their speed. Sparrowhawk watched in dismay as the troops loosed a volley of arrows at the cart simultaneously, the effect was staggering.

As the arrows made contact, the horses went down in a hail of blood and dirt, the cart catapulted head long over the downed animals and landed with a splinter breaking thump in front of the dead horses. Dust rose to the heavens and covered the mess of horse's meat and broken timber.

The troops ran forward in unison to digest the damage, some of the men to the flanks had re-notched and kept their arrows trained on Sparrowhawk. He quickly removed his bow and lay it on the ground at his feet, he was not about to take on a regiment of Kor' Cali.

He looked at the cart, the shafts they had used were about double the size of his own, they were much thicker as well and painted all black. He dreaded to think what would happen if one of those caught you in the chest, the damage would be a catastrophe.

'Hold there, don't move,' a soldier said as he approached. He noticed the bow on the ground and realised Sparrowhawk was at their mercy.

'What, by all the gold in the Forever Mountains are the Kor' Cali doing here. They are hundreds of miles away from the war, hundreds of miles behind enemy lines,' Sparrowhawk although not cocky, did consider himself an intelligent man, but this had him stumped.

They stood to attention for the most part, with some soldiers clearing up the street of timbers and dead animals. They were a well-drilled machine of disciplined men that would make any Gala' Mor unit proud, with their black armour and red trims. Most of the foreign soldiers had long hair and clean-shaven faces with rings in their ears, noses, eyebrows and some, for unknown reasons fashioned little metal rings in their lips.

Chester and his posse were coming up the street behind Sparrowhawk, the man who had spoken to Sparrowhawk came forward to meet them as they were closing in on the scene.

'Hang them… hang then now… I demand it…' Chester called and stopped speaking as the soldier held up his hand for silence, Chester obeyed.

'You'll demand nothing, this backwater town is under the control of General Balltimor, I speak for him in his absence,' he called, silencing the local man for only a second, he was clearly an officer and he sported a couple of rings through his right eyebrow.

'Of course, of course… milord, but you…' Chester was cut off again.

'Captain, I am a Captain, not a milord,' the Captain announced.

Chester seemed to frown, either not knowing the difference or not caring that there was any. He opened his mouth again to speak, but this time wasn't quick enough.

'Clear the street, men,' the Captain called and they got straight to it without pause.

'You,' the metal faced Captain addressed Sparrowhawk.

'What is your business here?' he asked politely, but with assertion.

Before Sparrowhawk could answer a shout came from the troops.

'Let me go, ye brigands… I'll have yer 'eads,' Sparrowhawk knew that voice anywhere, even in a backwater town among the wreckage of a destroyed cart with two dead horses, surrounded by invading Kor' Cali troops and an angry mob wanting to hang him, he couldn't mistake the voice of Sabat.

'Captain Hussar?' a soldier shouted, wondering should he run the noisy man through with some sharp northern steel.

'He's with me,' Sparrowhawk announced dryly. The Captain looked at Sparrowhawk, sensing a shaky friendship between the Ranger and old man calling for heads to roll. He nodded sympathetically.

'Bring him here,' the Captain ordered.

Sabat was flung beside Sparrowhawk, who caught him and steadied the old man from falling over. Sparrowhawk checked the man for cuts or bruises, but he appeared unshaved by the crash and volley of huge arrows.

'I told you to stop' hissed the Ranger.

Sabat looked sideways at him.

'I could have made it, had I a proper escort at me back… me thinks,' he answered.

Sparrowhawk scoffed at the old man, a full head below himself.

'So, you are a huntsman, I see,' the Captain addressed Sparrowhawk.

'A Ranger, yes,' Sparrowhawk replied, he knew a huntsman was the term used by the Kor'dorians for a man of his trade.

'I see, then we must but you to death, of course,' the Captain said without emotion.

Sparrowhawk was expecting as much, but thought there might be a sliver of hope, as he was not directly involved in the war, the Captain saw it otherwise. A man working for the King-in-waiting, his enemy, was still working for the King-in-waiting no matter his current employment requirements.

'This one will have to go too,' the Captain said nodding towards Sabat.

Some of the soldiers approached the two men and took them under their charge, bound their hands and started marching them towards one of the buildings.

'What?' Sabat screamed. 'I not be employed by no king, I am a free man,' he protested.

Chester and his boys cheered and clapped, delighted with the justice being handed down.

The soldiers were just reaching one of the houses when Sparrowhawk could see in through the open doorway as the door swung out to greet them. He could make out a dozen or so people inside, standing still with sullen expressions on their faces. It was only then that he spotted the full-length metal bars running parallel down the window, it was the town keep.

'Captain, found another one,' one of the soldiers called as the Captain was discussing something with some other troops, he turned around to see what the new developments were.

'Big man, his hands and feet are tied and he has a small bell wrapped around his ankle,' the soldier replied to the Captain's stares of confusion. They all turned to Sparrowhawk for answers.

'That's Long-tooth, I was taking him to Whiterock, for a trial by the King, he's a wanted murderer, thief, gang leader and who knows what else,' Sparrowhawk explained, one professional to another. If Sparrowhawk was hoping that the Captain would see the honour of capturing a dangerous villain and protecting his homeland, he was mistaken.

The soldiers now had the conscious man on his feet. *'The crash must have woken him up,'* Sparrowhawk thought as he watched Long-tooth look around confused as ever.

'What in the Seven Kingdoms be going on here, who are ye…' Long-tooth started, but when he realised he was surrounded by grim looking Kor' Cali soldiers he held his tongue.

'Let him go, he is one of us,' Chester put in, his men seconded the motion.

The Captain stood there thinking for a moment, not sure if that was a good thing or a bad thing.

'This place is going to see me in the ground,' he said at last shaking his head. His soldiers waited.

'Oh… let the big one go,' he said finally, to the cheers of Chester and his gang. Long-tooth was escorted over to his friends. Friends who just minutes ago, didn't care too much for his safety, but that was minutes ago and they felt it was probably better to be on good terms with the outlaw.

Chapter 12
Dimator's Promotion

Dimator headed the regiment as they were entering the city, he led his unit of tired, angry and subdued recruits. They were a full half day early in their return and the celebrations for them re-entering the city were only half ready.

The city guards on the walls had spotted the approaching group and called out to their superior, who in turn came to check for himself.

'Send an envoy,' he said to the guards on the walls. One of them ran down the ramparts and across the courtyard just behind the main gate. The superior continued to look out, trying to spot if there was anything wrong, it wasn't long after the troops had cleared the trees when he noticed something majorly amiss.

The guard had returned in a few moments and he was standing in the courtyard, looking up.

'Ser, envoy ready,' he called upwards, as soon as the sound hit the superior's ears, he turned down to face the waiting guards. There were eight guards waiting in the small courtyard, all armed and on horseback.

'Good, head out to greet them, quick now,' he called back.

'Right Ser, any trouble?' the guard leading the envoy asked before following his orders.

'Yes, it looks like they are missing a lot of men and some are nursing wounds,' he replied.

The envoy reached Dimator within a few minutes of hard riding.

'You're early... Ser Dimator, where is Captain Titus, stayed behind because the catch was so good, I'll wager?' the guard at the head of the envoy asked laughing.

'Stayed behind because he's dead,' Dimator replied coldly.

The envoy moved aside to let the troops through, they looked at the faces of the young men and frowned. It was not their place to ask and some didn't even want to know, not right now anyway.

'Ride back to the city, cancel the welcome party, something has happened,' the guard leading the envoy said quietly to the man at his side. He took off back the way they had rode out as the remainder of the riders stayed still, watching the recruit's march towards home.

Bringing up the rear was a group of soldiers, marching in a closed formation, circle in shape. It was being led by an officer, he nodded at the envoy as he walked past, they all returned the mark of respect. In the centre of the circle was a small girl, her hands bound to a rope which the soldier at the front of the circle held onto. She looked timid and weak, her face was dirty as were her clothes, they were dumbfounded.

Dimator sat in the chair that was too large for him, he assumed it had been made for a White Rhino's huge frame and not that of a normal sized human. He shifted uncomfortably, but then maybe that was the reason for the chair in the first place, to make the man sitting in it, uncomfortable.

The room was lit by burning torches scattered around the room thoughtfully as they cast enough light to see the faces of every man.

Heading the council was Commander Milian, the most experienced officer in the room, he wore his white tunic that fashioned a huge golden lion's head on the chest.

'Well?' Commander Gladis asked, his face looked like a map of a small rural area, with lines running everywhere resembling the rivers, spots dotted here and there made for excellent trees and a large beak-like nose sticking out like a carrot on a snowman, a large mountain.

'The hunt was going exceptionally well for a time…' Dimator replied, looking around the room at the serious faces staring back at him. The room was full to capacity with Captains, nobles and two of the Kingdoms four Commanders present for the hearing.

Dimator continued, '…we had captured an abundance of food for the King's crowning and morale was high within the troop. Things turned bad once we heard a shrill coming from the west of our position…' he stopped.

'What kind of a shrill?' one of the Commander's asked, interrupting him.

'We did not know at the time what the noise was, however our tracker went to investigate, and soon brought us to a clearing in the forest. The area was open, with many trees after being cut down, maybe ten or so years prior…' Dimator stopped again.

'And you say this clearing was to the west?' a Captain probed, Dimator did not know the man's name or had forgotten it, he wasn't sure.

'Yes Ser, to the west, where the twins meet under the Wandering Bridge,' Dimator replied, giving a full descriptive account of where the regiment had turned into the forest.

'Oh whatever… enough of the petty details… what by the names of the Lost Heroes happened?' called another Captain sitting directly in front of Dimator.

Dimator swallowed hard. 'Of course, Ser,' Dimator cleared his throat.

'After we arrived at the clearing, we found the girl,' he spoke quickly.

'The one you brought through the front gates… yes, yes,' confirmed the same Captain, urging Dimator to hurry up.

'Correct, we were in the process of taking the girl into custody, for her own safety, when she produced a small wooden whistle…' Dimator now produced the same whistle and held it up, all eyes zoomed in on the tiny narrow wooden whistle. The room was silent.

'She blew into the whistle and out of nowhere a flock of hooded crows appeared and circled overhead,' Dimator remember the scene vividly.

'After a second shrill on her whistle the birds…' he froze at the memory.

'What… after the second shrill… what?' the first Commander was shouting, demanding the report quicker than Dimator could get the words out.

'The crows attacked us,' Dimator said through heavy breathing, scarcely believing his own voice as he shivered.

The room fell as silent as a winter's night.

Commander Gladis shot one of the Captains a cold look, Dimator caught it and saw recognition in that look. The Captain downed his eyes after a few seconds, the man shifted in his own chair uneasily, guilt written all over his face.

'Where is the girl now,' Commander Gladis bellowed.

'She is being held in the keep,' one of the men at the table replied, a Captain, judging by his uniform.

Commander Gladis's eyes narrowed at the reply.

Dimator frowned at the Commander *'What is going on?'* his mind was racing.

'She must be sent to the block, and before the boy hears of it,' Commander Gladis announced, standing to his feet, all six foot five of him looking defiantly at his peers.

There were gasps and puffs of air from around the table. The officers all looked at each other, waiting for someone to speak. It was the first Commander who broke the silence.

'To the block without the King's say so, Commander Gladis… you speak too quickly,' the man looked deep into Gladis's staring eyes.

'He is not the King, Commander Milian… not yet,' he paused, allowing his words to sink in. He was of course correct, Armando, would not be king for another three days, and all knew he was not misspoken. But it was an unwritten rule that the block was an official punishment only sentenced by the King.

'True as that may be, Commander, I feel more investigation is required,' Commander Milian looked around the room for support.

'Aye,' came a voice in agreement, it was Corfolk who had spoken, the oldest man in the room by quite some years, nobody knew a man could live so long and nobody really wanted too either.

Commander Gladis was off the mark swiftly as he didn't want a second vote to be cast.

'Now listen here, my friends… this girl took out a third of a whole regiment, recruits as it may be, it is still a vicious attack on the King's Guard, it must be met with equal action. If word should reach the ears of the Kor'dorians that a child has stood against the mighty armies of Gala' Mor and struck such a blow, it will give them pause to consider upping their advance from the Blackwater,' he spoke confidently.

'Aye,' again Corfolk had changed his mind, Commander Milian ignored the senile coot.

'Armando's crowning is but days away, we wait till then, allowing the new king to judge this girl with the whistle,' Commander Milian had announced his decision, and it was final.

The room broke into a collection of conversations as men discussed the problematic conundrum of whether or not they should chop the head off a small girl. In hushed tones they brought up many different arguments both for and against the issue.

'It has been a terrible blow…' a Captain had said, shocked at the loss of life.

'True, but she is only a child, it wasn't her who slew the men, but birds… did she really command the creatures of the skies…' retorted another.

'…and if so, how did she achieve this?' he finished.

The bubble of noise continued for a time, Dimator sat and listened intently, trying to figure out the different alliances building up and more importantly who was the most outspoken in these alliances.

'My friends, nobody can command the birds to attack, it's not possible…' this time a skinny noble had voiced his opinion to the room, shaking his head in disbelief.

'And bears,' Dimator added.

'What… what did you say?' Commander Milian asked as the room heard Dimator's comment.

'After… after the birds had attacked, she blew the whistle again…' Dimator held it up a second time '…and three bears came forward and broke into our ranks, causing chaos and killing men as they swept our recruits aside like straw dummies,' he finished.

'Aye… bears,' Corfolk announced, not really understanding the gravity of the situation.

'That is preposterous,' a new voice added his opinion almost laughing, others were joining him in his scepticism.

'Some of the wounded did have huge claw marks, very similar to a bear's… I saw them myself before I came here,' a voice came from the table.

'Birds and bears… that does it… Commander Gladis, more questions need to be answered, they'll be no block as of yet… do I hear a second?' Commander Milian now had the room glued to his every word.

After a quick glance around the room, most of the men seconded the Commander. And the decision was made to bring the girl in for questioning by the Commanders alone.

The meeting was called to an end and the men started to remove themselves from the room in a noise of chair squeaking and heavy opinions to and for the motion.

Dimator saw the loathing look in Commander Gladis's eyes and he wanted to know more, he wanted to know what the seasoned veteran of the King's service was hiding.

'I request to be present at the questioning,' he shot in quickly to Commander Milian.

'Request denied,' Commander Gladis said as soon as the words had left Dimator's mouth.

'Why?' Commander Milian asked, intrigued.

'I was there when she attacked my men… or the animals attack I mean to say… I have first-hand knowledge of her,' he answered.

'Nonsense,' Commander Gladis grunted and was already speaking in hush tones with the Captain whom he had looked at before upon learning about the whistle.

'No, no Commander… the man has a point, he may have valuable information that we might need when the girl is brought in,' Commander Milian announced calmly.

Commander Gladis frowned at Dimator and then at Commander Milian 'So be it,' he grunted as the Captain at his side was making his way to the door, the last to leave.

The three men sat at the table as the door opened, in strolled a huge White Rhino, ducking as not to collide with the door frame. Behind him came the tiny figure of the girl, her face still dirty almost as much as her ragged clothes and no footwear to protect her soles from the icy cold flagstones.

The Rhino made his way back to the door to join his companion, after he had brought the girl to stand before the men, White Rhinos never travelled alone. They both now stood by the door, they made as much noise as a kitchen full of clumsy workers when they walked, all that armour rattling and clanging, but they stood as silent as a church mouse when they stood to attention.

The girl stood there quiet and calm, she looked from man to man to man and then back again. She was judging who was the most likely to take her side, if any.

Commander Gladis seemed to be appalled at her, he frowned and scoffed.

Commander Milian studied the girl with a keen eye of character evaluation.

Dimator studied Commander Gladis.

'You will be charged with the killing of sixty-three… is that correct?' Commander Milian had begun, but looked to Dimator for confirmation on the final tally.

'Yes Ser… fifty-eight in the field and another five died from their wounds on the journey home,' Dimator said, she was looking directly at him as he spoke, and there was no love in those little emerald eyes.

Commander Milian continued, '…yes, of course… sixty-three dead. You will be sentenced at a trial by the King, you will have nobody to stand council for your crimes, an attack on the King's Guard is considered an attack on the King himself,' he paused for a moment.

'Pleading guilty will do you no use, as the punishment will be the same in each case. You will be sentenced to death when you are found guilty, there are over one hundred witnesses, all trustworthy men, as soon as you accept your destiny, the better for you, I wager.' Commander Milian was a fair man, but under the circumstances, it was hard not to want the girl handed down the maximum penalty.

'Have you anything to say for your actions, any reason as to why you behaved the way you did?' the Commander added.

The girl looked at the man as if he meant nothing, as if he was just another man in the world of stone buildings and stone floors. They all looked at her and she responded.

'Sha woe a mor,' she hollered, first to Commander Gladis, then to Commander Milian and then with all the strength her little frame could muster she roared it at Dimator.

The men drew back from her, their faces a picture of shock, Commander Gladis rose to his feet and was about to move towards the prisoner in a rage when the Rhino's moved forward. He quickly sat back down as he heard them moving.

'Ok…' he called back to them, his hands in the air as a gesture of submission, satisfied he was not going to harm the girl they went back to guard the door, again if you didn't know they were there, you would never know.

The girl looked at the guards, her brain working overtime, she quickly assessed that the huge metal men were not her enemy, they protected her. Then she glanced back to her true enemy, the men at the table, it was these men who wanted to harm her '*What a strange place*,' she thought inwards.

'What is your name?' Commander Milian asked in a fatherly tone.

Silence.

He was going to try again but Dimator spoke first.

'She doesn't speak our tongue, Commander,' Dimator said calmly.

She was looking at Dimator and the Commander spotted it.

'She doesn't seem to like you much, Dimator,' Commander Milian stated.

'The feeling is likewise, Commander. She killed my men,' he answered.

'Not to burst your bubble, but they were not your men, they were Captain Titus's men, if I am not mistake,' he said in a tone where he completely meant for bubbles to be burst.

'True, but I am in command of the regiment now, until a suitable replacement is elected,' Dimator replied.

'We will arrange something… hastily. You are lucky not to be flogged for losing so many young men, it should be you to break the news to each and every one of their families,' Commander Gladis announced, still upset that Dimator was present in the room.

Dimator knew when to keep his mouth shut and this was one of those occasions.

'Dimator…' put in Commander Milian. '…show her the whistle, let's see her reaction.'

As soon as Dimator pulled out the whistle, her gaze fell upon it. Dimator lay it on the table, visible so she could see it but not close enough that she could get to it. Commander Gladis wanted her to go for it, then he would be justified in unsheathing his dagger and preforming his own trial by the King there and then, she did not oblige him.

Dimator saw the sheer hatred in his eyes, he knew it was more than just the killing of the men in the forest that caused it, it went deeper than that he was sure, how could he bring it to light. Then he remembered the look the Commander had thrown across the room at the Captain, a look that said he might have known about the girl, but how.

'Are we finished here, Commander?' Commander Gladis called to his colleague.

'I suppose we are, there is not much point in talking with somebody who cannot talk back,' he finished.

'Guards, take her away,' Commander Gladis ordered, then he corrected himself. 'You may take her away,' this time in a less commanding tone.

The clattering of the metal moved forward and collected the girl in an iron grip, they led her away through the door, but not before she turned on them and shouted again through gritted teeth 'Sha woe a mor,' the sound echoed around the room.

'What by the golden circle in the sky, is she saying?' Commander Milian was asking, as if somebody was going to give him a direct translation.

'Who cares, she'll be dead soon,' Commander Gladis was already making his way across the room to follow the Rhinos.

Dimator was just reaching the door himself when Commander Milian called him back.

'What do you make of it all?' The Commander asked, looking into one of the blazing torches mounted on the nearest wall.

'Me, Ser?' he replied.

'Well… you were there when it happened, were you not? You saw it, did she really have command over the creatures of the forest? And where did she come from?' he asked slowly and sincerely interested in finding out more about the peculiar events of the day.

'I do not know what to make of it all Ser. But, when she blew that whistle, the animals without question attacked, and in battle formation, without care for themselves. Animals do not do that, they survive, that is their natural instinct, but that morning they fought without caution when she told them to do so,' he replied carefully remembering the assault.

Commander Milian held out his hand, Dimator realised he was asking for the whistle, so he dropped it into the waiting palm. The Commander examined it thoroughly, spinning it this way and that, looking suspiciously at the carefully crafted piece of wood. He frowned as he glared at the small weapon of war, he seemed to be remembering something.

'*What are you thinking*' Commander,' Dimator's gears were turning, probably faster than ever before.

'I want you to look into this Captain, find out what you can, you have the full weight of my rank at your disposal. Leave no stone unturned and report only to me, is that one thousand percent clear… only to me?' Commander Milian announced.

'Yes, Ser. Of course, Ser, but you are mistaken… I am not a Captain,' Dimator said respectfully.

Commander Milian's eyes narrowed. 'You are now… and you'll be needing this,' the Commander announced tossing the whistle back to his newest agent.

'Yes Ser, I will do what it takes,' Dimator said proudly.

'See that you do Captain, take this also, if anyone should question your actions just present this to them,' he said and handed Dimator a scroll with a golden wax seal of a lion's head.

Chapter 13
Theo'dor Meets the Prince

Theo'dor crawled slowly through the darkness of the narrow passageway, brushing the cobwebs from his face every couple of feet. It was clear that nobody had used the tiny tunnel in a long time, save for the spiders and the occasional rat that scurried away in the distance, squeaking their protest to their uninvited visitor.

Without any light to see the way, he was not long in getting a little disorientated, he was usually a good judge of direction, but inside the dark narrow tunnel and not having been inside the huge palace before it was impossible to tell where he was heading. One thing he knew for certain, was that the ground was sloping downwards, which made sense as he had climbed to the top floor, so all roads must lead south he gathered.

He had been crawling for over an hour he assumed; however, he had no way of knowing to be exact. He heard muffled voices coming from behind the walls, and as time passed the noises were getting more frequent and ever louder.

As he ventured forth, he had a sense of adventure about him, he was used to reading books and calculating out equations and problems most people had no idea where to even start, this was like a different world to him and he was rightly enjoying his time behind the palace walls.

The thought had occurred to him that he might get stuck, trapped or lost, but he couldn't go back now as the passageway was too small for him to turn around in and it would take a week to shimmy backward up all those slopes and tight corners he had navigated around, he must move forwards.

The steady breeze was making him chilly, but he knew a chill breeze was better than no breeze at all, it meant that there was a constant flow of fresh air getting in somewhere and also if air was getting in, there must be an exit up ahead, he hoped it would be sooner rather than later as his arms and legs were starting to feel the strain, not to mention his back.

A rat squealed as he brushed up against the hairy body of the smelly rodent, Theo'dor received a small gash from the rats' sharp teeth for his reward as he tried to push the creature out of the way. It was only a minor wound, but unwelcomed nonetheless.

Eventually he reached the end, or what he thought was the end anyhow.

A solid stone wall lay emotionless before him, he could only vaguely see it, but his finger told him that it was a solid wall, they were hard to miss really, even in the pitch black.

He was stuck, trapped and lost all at the same time '*Great, this is what happens when you don't stick to your plan, Theo'dor,*' he thought to himself as he decided what to do next.

As far as he was concerned, he had but two options, travel all the way back through the black-cobweb-rat-infested tunnel backwards probably taking him longer than his muscles could manage leaving him forever in his stony tomb or option two, scream for help. Maybe someone on the other side of the walls would hear him and rescue him somehow, although that would lead to questions about what was he doing sneaking around inside the palace walls in the first place, which in turn would lead to his head being sharply removed from the rest of his body, both options none to his liking.

He could hear clattering coming from behind the wall, loud metal on metal clattering. He was not crawling all the way back, anyway he didn't even know if that section of the wall could be moved from this side, so he tried tapping on the wall. Quietly at first, but decided if he was going to be quiet, he may as well not make any noise at all so he ramped up the volume a bit and gave a couple of louder bangs. At first the noise on the other side had stopped, but had now started again. He called out for help and banged again on the cold stone surface.

To his shock and delight a section of the wall pushed forwards and then upwards into the roof of his prison he was now being released from. The light came splashing in and he was forced to squint his eyes as his pupils narrowed to adjust to the brightness.

He slowly made his way out to thank his rescuer, as he came into the room he felt the soft carpet under his hands, the feel was like nothing he had ever felt before, the sheer contrast from the hard cold stones to this new texture was worlds apart, he could not describe it even if he had the chance. He was thrilled to be out of that place and he smiled as he crawled slowly forward into the bright colourful warm room. He only realised then that he had been freezing inside the passageway, the warmth flowed over him and he was content.

'Thank you, my friend… I owe you my live,' he was laughing.

As he entered the room he looked up, staring back at him, behind three drawn halberds were three enormous White Rhinos, he couldn't see their faces behind the heavy helmets they wore, but he assumed that they were not sharing the same amusement.

'Hoo… wrong room,' he coughed as he slowly stuck the gear stick into reverse and was about to make his escape.

'Stay where you are thief, or my guards will dismember you where you stand… em, kneel,' a young male voice corrected himself.

'Thief… I am no thief… I am Theo'dor,' he started to play his trump card, his name. But the voice cut him off sharply.

'Only a thief would sneak around my palace, trying to steal my belongings, it will be your hands that I will be stealing from you,' the voice rasped.

'*Hold on a second…*' Theo'dor thought. '*…my guards? …my palace? Why would he say his guards and his palace,*' Theo'dor looked up and saw the speaker for the second time in his life. The first time he had seen the boy was about a year ago at a wedding just outside the palace grounds, in the square in the upper city.

'What do you have to say for yourself?' the voice came again.
'Nothing… your majesty,' Theo'dor replied, he would have knelt, but he was already on his hands and knees. 'You broke into the King's chambers… you climbed the palace walls… you disguised yourself as a worker… you… you… you,' Anton D'Souza was famous for his short temper and the man was exercising that fact right now in the palace keep '…what were you thinking son? You are lucky to be alive, if the King-in-waiting had not been there in that room at that exact time, and the Rhinos had found you… you… you'd be in a hundred pieces right now…' the man was in a fit, that was certain and Theo'dor knew better than to interrupt him when he got this angry, it was safer to ride it out.

'I have a good mind to expel you from your studies… if the academy has not already done so, and send you to combat school… would that be to your liking… or better still, hand you over to the Rhinos and let those beasts teach you a little discipline…' the man was exhausted, he had been carving a path in the concrete floor for the past half hour walking back and forth, shaking his head and complaining full hilt to his only son and in truth, who could blame him.

'Anton dear… sit down,' his wife called from a safe distance of four meters.

'And… your poor mother has to see you like this…' he was not sitting down and he was not finished his lecture, '…I hope you are proud of yourself, Theo' because the family name will never live this one down… no Ser… not in a century will your latest stunt be forgotten…' he stopped, stood still and panted like a greyhound.

Theo'dor stared out from behind the bars of the tiny cell which had been his home for the past twelve hours. The guards had taken him directly to the keep and locked him in, when asked his name, his parents had been notified and they came as soon as they could, he was only lucky that they were in the city for the upcoming crowning ceremony, otherwise they would have been hundreds of miles to the north-west, looking after their affairs in the mines.

The cell was big enough for him to stretch out his arms on either side, there was no bed, no chair, and no toilet. A silver tray with an empty wooden bowl sat sadly in the corner waiting to be removed. The room was lit by a single torch just outside his cell, it gave little light and no heat whatsoever.

'What were you doing son… the prince is claiming you were trying to rob his room… is it true?' his mother was now by the bars, looking pitifully in at him.

'He wasn't trying to rob the prince's pillows, Bridget… he wasn't trying to rob anything, sure we're wealthier than the prince,' Anton answered for his son.

Bridget may be a small timid woman who lets her husband handle the affairs of the business, but you don't spend twenty-one years married to a man and learn nothing about him.

'What was he doing then… Anton?' she swung her body around and her stern gaze fell on her husband.

He frowned at first, in shock that he was being accused of some ill behaviour, but only at first, you don't spend twenty-one years married to a woman and learn nothing about her.

'He wasn't supposed to get caught,' he whispered in her ear.

'What?… did you put him up to this… Anton, what were you thinking?' she shook with horror.

'Now, that's not true at all…' he answered. '… he wasn't supposed to land himself in the stinking palace bedrooms… now, was he?' he tried to free himself from any blame, her look told him he was still on the stand.

'Look, the palace library contains the trade routes that the ancient D'warfen used to pass through the Forever Mountains… don't you see Bridget?' he was trying to convince her of something she knew nothing about, she shook her head.

'We have to go around the mountains to get to the Northern Realms, if we knew how to go through them, then the continent would be able to trade quicker with our northern neighbours, meaning we could move our produce up to thirty times as fast, Theo'dor did the maths on that one, meaning we would have more weapons and armour thirty times quicker than the Kor'dorians, meaning we could end this wretched war in a matter of days,' he said smiling to a smile-less Bridget.

'If it helps us win the war, why not tell the council, they will grant you access to the library surely,' Bridget was a logical person, but not one up to date on current affairs.

'They can't, only the King or a Commander has say on who can enter his library,' Anton explained.

'Then ask the King… or the prince… or whoever,' Bridget was using logic again.

'We can't tell anybody about the route through the mountains, it would give them a monopoly on the steel, silver and gold trade to the Northern Realms, they would become too powerful. Trade with Gala' Mor would become weakened if they had direct access to the north, our whole continent would collapse. Without the steel to make weapons we would be defenceless. Without the silver to pay for the steel we couldn't get it from anywhere else and without the gold, well wealthy folk wouldn't get to wear their fancy jewellery, there would be anarchy at the highest level, think about it Bridget,' Anton finished.

Bridget saw the dilemma unfold before her, she understood the importance of trade, even if she cared little about the secret dealings that made it all tick.

'I see,' she said puffing out a large breath.

'I'm ok, by the way,' Theo'dor announced to lighten the mood.

'Yes, of course. We are glad you're still in one piece,' Bridget joked.

'So, what happens next?' Theo'dor asked reluctantly.

'There will be a trial, I'm afraid. But it's not all bad, we still have a lot of influence here, nobody will believe you were trying to rob the palace, people are not stupid,' Anton said.

'They can be when it suits them,' Bridget added.

'That is quite true, does anyone benefit from me staying locked here for the rest of my life?' it was a stupid question and he realised it just as the words fell out of his mouth.

'A lot of people, Theo'dor… a lot,' replied his father, you don't get this far up the food chain without stepping on a few big toes along the way, and sore big toes like to kick back.

'So… the plan is?' Theo'dor asked waiting for some master strategy from his parents.

His father looked at his mother and she looked at him, they both shrugged.

'Leave it with us,' Anton replied.

'Ok, not feeling very assured here,' Theo'dor said looking around at his cramped cell.

'Leave it with us,' his father said again this time more confidently, Theo'dor did not share his confidence at all.

They turned to walk away, he watched their backs as they turned the corner, their footsteps now sounded out in dull echoes and they grew more faint. The jailer returned just as he heard the last of his parent's footfalls fade away, he came with a small candle in his right hand and a swinging mace in his left.

'Hehe, well well, looks like daddy isn't getting you out of this mess, fish,' the large toothless man sniggered widely, delighted he had some new meat to harass in his dark pit of despair.

'I will be freed from here by nightfall, you wait and see,' Theo'dor wasn't so sure in truth, but he would not let his captor get the better of him.

'Oh… I see… well well… I'll be sure to have your things ready as the sun goes down, hehe,' he was truly enjoying one so young as Theo'dor pretending to be brave. He had seen it all down here, had the jailer. Tough men came in all talk, putting on a good show for him, but it wasn't long before he had them whimpering like loss children, begging for some mercy, it never came and that was the way he liked it. The world had been cruel to him all his days and it was his turn now to repay the world in kind.

He strolled over to the torch on the wall and blew it out in a barrage of stale breath and spittle, leaving only the small candle as he held the only light source for the whole area.

He banged on Theo'dor's bars with the mace without caution and the noise rang in his ears, causing him to cup his hands over them in case of a second assault.

'Hehe… welcome home fish… we are going to become good friends,' he snorted. 'oh yes… very good friends… indeed,' he muttered as he walked away.

As he was leaving Theo'dor spotted a set of emerald eyes glaring at him. In the cell opposite his own sat a young girl, she looked dirty and wild and she was looking at him with curious eyes, she fingered a small silver pendant which hung loosely around her neck.

Chapter 14
Sparrowhawk's Plan

'Fine mess ye've gotten me into birdman,' Sabat hissed to the timber rafters.

They were tied back-to-back to a heavy upright timber that supported the roof, sitting on the floor of the jailhouse, surrounded by the townsfolk of Narrow's Crossing.

'What?' Sparrowhawk countered, '…it was your idea to come to this place, I was quite happy to escort Long-tooth back to Whiterock, collect my pay and…' he trailed off slowly, thinking about Rose.

'Ah whatever…' Sabat spat back and tried to free his bounds, all he managed to do was receive a scowling look from the Kor' Cali soldier that was stationed in the room to keep law and order, his ears filled with tiny metal loops. Sabat smiled at the frowning man 'No moving, no talking,' he commanded in Sabat's direction.

The room went silent as the soldier moved on to inspect the other prisoners.

'Cut it out or you'll get us all killed,' advised an elderly woman sitting tied to her husband with a gash on the side of his head, close-by.

Sparrowhawk had counted about forty prisoners in the room, that couldn't be the whole populace of a town this size, he gathered that when the Kor' Cali came into town they rounded up a few innocent people, keeping them as insurance and let the rest stay in their homes, knowing their loved ones would be harmed if anyone got clever. But, one thing he couldn't put his finger on was, what were they doing here.

'What's going on 'ere?' Sabat asked the woman low enough so the soldier didn't hear.

'Bloody Kor' Cali, that's what's going on here… you blind?' another voice joined the conversation, this time in the shape of a young man, strong and defiant.

'I can see that, for sure, but why?' Sabat frowned at the obvious answer the man gave.

'How are we supposed to know what they are doing here… why don't you ask them old man?' the man challenged.

'Birdman… ask 'em why they are 'ere,' Sabat called to his partner.

Sparrowhawk remained silent, taking in everything he could about his surroundings '*Only one guard, lightly armed.*'

'Ah, ye're useless,' Sabat retorted.

'They just appeared a few days ago…' the woman offered, '…took some of us in here so the rest of the town would do as they were told,' she said sadly.

'*Two just outside, in view of the rest of the soldiers, could sound the alarm,*' Sparrowhawk was looking for something in the room, he scanned all the faces first, he found the face that stuck out the most, an elderly man dressed in plain clothes with a tiny dent in his earlobe. After a few minutes he found what he was looking for, it was hanging on a nail by the entrance.

'Monsters,' Sabat said, under his breath.

'What are you two doing here?' the younger man asked.

'Business with Chester,' Sabat answered.

'Why you dealing with that low-life no-good cattle-turd?' the man returned.

'He's family,' Sabat said simply.

'Oh… well, I didn't mean any disrespect,' the man quickly replied.

'Why not, he is a low-life no-good cattle-turd,' Sabat said coldly.

'*Back entrance leads to the alley behind the jailhouse, no need for soldiers there, door could be locked, have to risk it,*' Sparrowhawk was getting ready.

'Hey… guard,' Sparrowhawk called to the man pacing around the room. He looked over, not impressed that somebody was talking out loud.

'What are you doing here?' Sparrowhawk called loudly. The room gasped, the old man with the gash on his head closed his eyes, he knew what was coming.

'I will teach you Gala' Mor peasants some manners,' he snarled as he made his way towards Sparrowhawk, unsheathing a small dagger from inside his black tunic.

The soldier was just above Sparrowhawk and was aiming a stab at the Ranger's shoulder. Sparrowhawk quickly ducked low and raised his hands to grab his attacker's neck with both hands as he came down. Sparrowhawk used all his strength to squeeze on the man's throat and the soldier fell to the floor dead as a shadow. It all happened in a split second and Sparrowhawk was on his feet, Sabat looked up.

'Well, it's about time, me backside was starting to go numb sitting on this 'ere cold floor,' he complained, his hands still tied.

Sparrowhawk retrieved his bow and quiver by the entrance and was at the back door before the townsfolk knew what was happening, Sabat among them.

'Hey, birdma… I mean sparrowman… hawkman… whatever, em, could you untie me please?' Sabat pleaded.

Sparrowhawk turned to face the man; it was his fault he was in this mess in the first place. Long-tooth was free and he had a whole battalion of Kor' Cali troops to sneak around, recapture his prey and somehow get out of this backwater town and make it back to Whiterock in one piece.

'Why?' Sparrowhawk asked.

'Well, because we be partners, 'an partners best be stickin' together,' he said with a hopeful smile.

'We were partners until we got to Narrow's Crossing, well, here we are, so our partnership is no longer valid,' Sparrowhawk turned to leave.

'But, what about the rest of us?' the old woman called after him.

'They'll kill us when they get what they want,' the younger man added.

'*They probably will*,' Sparrowhawk thought, it was the most likely of outcomes, why leave a town full of witnesses alive when they left, the people would send word to Whiterock as soon as the Kor' Cali were out of sight, it would be safer to kill the people and burn the town.

Sparrowhawk weighed his options, there were not many.

'Alright, it would be impossible to get everyone out of here without getting caught, there are simply too many of you,' he spoke slowly and clearly.

'Then what do we do?' called a new voice, this time it was the elderly man with the dent in his earlobe, his clothes had not a speck of dirt on them, Sparrowhawk was wondering when the man would make his move.

'We change the guards' clothes with one of you, tie him up and gag him. The new guard, as in one of the townspeople, will report that he had tried to escape and was punished,' Sparrowhawk had them all listening intensively.

'I will go with one of you to Whiterock and let command know that the enemy is here and they will send troops,' Sparrowhawk said, the people were not so sure.

'But that will take too long, we must leave now,' a voice trembled.

'It is the best we can do, trying to get everyone out now would only lead to everyone getting caught and killed,' Sparrowhawk announced in a low voice.

'He is right,' replied the man with the dent in his earlobe. 'I will become the new guard, quickly untie me and we can save these people,' he finished, eager to get his restraints off.

Sparrowhawk had guessed right, he took an arrow from his quiver, notched it and sent it rocketing into the man's chest, he fell over dead.

'What are ye playing…?' Sabat was almost raising his voice to a scream.

'Be quiet, will you?' Sparrowhawk replied, frowning at his ex-partner.

The room looked at Sparrowhawk dumbfounded.

'He was one of them, a soldier in disguise sent among you in case you tried to escape,' Sparrowhawk told them.

'His clothes are too clean; he was too eager and he has a mark in his ear where a ring used to be… how many of you have seen him before the Kor' Cali arrived?' Sparrowhawk questioned them.

The room was thinking, looking at each other for confirmation that somebody knew him, nobody did.

'You're right, only the tribes in the east put holes in themselves, crazy bunch of barbarians,' a man answered.

'Alright, who is going to be our fake guard, he will have to be the same size as the soldier,' Sparrowhawk warned them. A man soon volunteered for the role and Sparrowhawk untied his bonds and helped him arrange the soldier into a position where he appeared to be unconscious. The man was broad and strong, he would fit the part as long as the other soldiers didn't notice the new face among their ranks. He stood there looking at everyone.

'Put a hole in his ear,' someone joked and to Sparrowhawk surprise most of the captives laughed, it was the small sliver of hope that raised their morale.

Another man offered himself as Sparrowhawk's newest companion, he was a thin man with long hair, Sparrowhawk guessed he was in his mid-twenties and he was quite short, he would be a nice adjustment from his previous partner. Speaking of which, Sparrowhawk couldn't help but glance over at the old healer.

Sabat was putting on a fake sulk, hoping to make Sparrowhawk feel sorry for him, it did not have the desired effect as Sparrowhawk nodded to the new man and made his way to the door at the back of the jailhouse.

'Wait… ye're not going to leave me… are ye… bird-hawkie?' he asked, shocked at the betrayal.

Sparrowhawk stopped and thought. '*He's going to be a nuisance… you know he is.*' Sparrowhawk was a reasonable man, but he was no fool. It would make more sense to leave the man where he was, it would also multiply his chances of success by a reasonable margin.

'*He saved Long-tooth you know… and then knocked him out…*' Sparrowhawk had to be fair, Sabat did save Long-tooth from bleeding out back at that town whose name he couldn't remember, and he did stop Long-tooth from recognising him when they stopped for rabbit stew a few days ago. He exhaled, fully convinced he was going to regret his decision.

'Fine,' he exclaimed as he approached Sabat, the man's face lit up with delight.

'I knew ye to be a sensible man, from the moment I seen ye,' he laughed as Sparrowhawk cut his hands free of the rope.

'Just be quiet,' Sparrowhawk shook his head.

Chapter 15
An Important Discovery

The newest Captain of the Kings Guard walked casually down the tunnel like hallway of the Imperial libraries, his footfalls echoing off the timber walls that surrounded him. It was his first time in the huge library and the number of different doors leading to different areas was a bit daunting if he was being honest.

The doors were labelled with all the different sections you could think of, ranging from war history to buffalo grazing, why in all of Gala' Mor an entire room was dedicated to the grazing of livestock, he would never know.

'Lost, are we?' a voice came from behind him, Dimator swivelled round to see a rather serious looking man standing before him, he was holding a tower of books in his outstretched hands, his narrow cheek bones leading up to his slanted eyes resting on the summit of the pile.

'Me?…' Dimator said before realising he was the only other person in the hallway, '…actually, yes I am,' he followed up after the man looked at him with a raised eyebrow.

'Follow me,' the man replied and strolled past the Captain.

Dimator followed the order and walked briskly behind the man, he was unsure as to where the man was leading him as Dimator had not enquired about what section he was interested in looking into.

They seemed to walk for quite a time, going down this hallway and up the next, they passed through a number of doors marked with three or more labels and climbed two staircases until they finally reached a main open area that looked like a reception of sorts.

'This is the reception…' the man said, '…of sorts' as he landed the pile of books onto a huge wide desk with a bang. He then went around to the other side of the deck and faced Dimator.

'Now, how can I be of assistance, Ser?' the man enquired.

'I'm looking for information on the ancient tribes of Gala' Mor, as far back as the time of King Massise,' Dimator asked politely.

'Oh I see, I see…' the man answered curiously '…interesting time period, but unfortunately that information is in the King's private library, only a Commander or White Rhino can be granted access to that area I'm afraid, Ser,' the man replied.

'I am Captain Dimator and Commander Milian has given me his rank to look into this matter,' Dimator replied calmly.

The man stared at Dimator for a moment, making up his mind. He had challenged such a request in the past and almost lost his beloved job because of it.

Dimator handed the clerk the scroll that the Commander had given him.

'Of course, Captain, how presumptuous of me…' the man replied nervously after reading the scroll and returned it safely to its owner. '…if you will but follow me,' the man finished and came around to the front of the desk and walked slowly across the open space towards another door, he was looking around as he walked.

This time when they reached the door the man searched through his pockets for something, he pulled out a single key and slid it carefully into the hole, turned it slowly and gently went to push the door inwards, but he froze suddenly.

'Do not make a sound, let me do all the talking,' he looked sternly into Dimator's eyes.

Dimator nodded, a bit confused.

'I mean it, it could be our lives,' the man was deadly serious.

'Of course, not a word,' Dimator was becoming a bit nervous himself.

When the door opened, the White Rhino standing there about four meters away from them came to attention and lowered his halberd. The man made the room look small, with his huge tower shield and wide metal frame, there was not much room for anything else.

'Password?' the White Rhino boomed.

'The lion on watch, shall never sleep,' the man replied slowly and clearly.

The White Rhino moved aside to produce a door that was hidden behind him, he stood as still as a frosty morning.

The man breathed a sigh of relief as he walked towards the new door, Dimator followed in his footsteps, not saying a word.

When the door was closed behind them the man walked to the side and lit a mounted torch, the flame blasted into light and Dimator could see the start of a shelf in the middle of the room looking back at him. The librarian walked around and lit the remaining torches as Dimator walked over to a shelf which had gotten longer as more torches had been lit, more and more books were now coming into view and he looked around at them all. It wasn't an overly big room, but for one man it might pose a problem if he had to go through all these books by himself.

'Now Ser, all is in order I believe. Anything I can help you find,' the librarian announced happily looking at the neatly packed shelves, he had arranged everything himself and so knew where to find what.

'Could you direct me to the area where I might find out more about the different languages and dialects of the Kingdom,' Dimator asked bewildered at where to start looking.

'Of course, Captain, follow me if you will,' the man replied and made his way over to the end of a narrow shelf fastened to the wall on their left with thick brackets.

'These are all the known tongues of the previous decades, if someone spoke it, it is in these books,' he assured the Captain confidently.

'Excellent,' the Captain replied and picked up the closest book to his hand, he opened the book on a random page and started looking for something. The librarian frowned and watched him. Dimator flicked through the pages, the librarian tilted his head to the side, still watching the Captain search hopelessly.

'Is there any particular linguistic dialect you were looking for exactly?' the man just had to ask.

'I'm not sure… that is the problem,' Dimator responded.

'Ah, do you know any of the words in the dialect you seek?' the librarian asked.

'No, I don't… wait,' the Captain was thinking, '…what did she say?' he remembered the girl had said something, it stuck in his head all day, now he had to recall what it was.

'Yes… do you have something… anything… a passage, a word… anything?' the librarian was getting excited, he prided himself on helping anyone that came to his library, that's how he saw it… his library.

'Sha woe a mor…' he finally managed to get out, '…something like that?' Dimator looked at the librarian, the man was frowning deeply.

'A mor… are you sure?' he repeated slowly, thinking back on something he was now trying to remember himself.

'Yes, I think so, do you know it?' Dimator pleaded.

'A mor…' the man was nodding his head. '…yes, that's it, it means death, or to die… or dead,' he finished unsure of the direct translation.

'Death… why would someone speak this way?' the Captain questioned.

'A mor… it is a northern tongue, of that I am sure…' the librarian said and moved to the very last book on the shelf '…ah here it is, the Complete Guide to the Northern Realms,' he said loudly.

He expertly scanned through the book until he found what he was searching for, the lexicon of words at the back.

'What else did you say, the rest of the passage, what was it again?' the librarian was loving this little puzzle.

'Sha woe a mor' that is what the girl said,' Dimator bit his tongue, he had let it slip out.

'A girl said this, interesting,' the man continued searching the book.

'Here we are, yes. The word Sha, means you or they, depending on the context of the rest of the sentence,' he announced calmly.

'Woe, meaning mother or parent or parents, it might even mean people in some respects,' he said looking at Dimator for his reaction.

'Ok so, we have… death… you or they… and parents or people?' the Captain asked.

'I believe so, the girl also said the word… a, also,' the librarian confirmed. 'a… meaning my or belonging to me,' he finished.

They both thought to themselves for a few quiet minutes, the librarian was first to speak.

'Possibly, she was saying… my people will bring death to you? What way did the girl say this?' he asked.

'She said it with complete contempt, as if she was accusing us of something… something unspeakable,' the Captain answered.

'And did something unspeakable happen to her?' the librarian asked carefully.

'I do not know, we captured her in the woods, on the Kings hunt after she…' Dimator looked at the librarian with a keen judge of character, if he wanted this man to help him, he needed to be honest '…after she killed a third of a regiment.'

The librarian froze, there was no gest in the Captain's eyes, he was dead serious, the librarian swallowed hard before he asked the next question, until that point, he was on the fence, but now he was going to get information that would change his life.

'How could a girl kill so many men in a regiment on her own?' he asked warily.

'Oh, she wasn't on her own… she had bears and crows,' the Captain answered almost beginning to be amused at the sound of it.

'On her own… with bears and crows…' the librarian said and thought to himself.

'Is there anything else about the girl, anything unusual or out of place?' the librarian asked quizzingly.

'Not really, she looks just like any normal girl, long hair, ragged clothing… oh and she does have a silver pendant about her neck, one that is much too large for her size, excellent craftmanship, I only got a glimpse of it, but it looked like it fashioned a wolf's heads,' Dimator replied.

The librarian's eyes widened in recognition, without another word he shot past the Captain and ran to a shelf on the far side of the room. Dimator watched him leave befuddled and stayed put, he assumed the man would return when he was ready.

'Captain, look at this,' he returned in a few minutes holding another book, it was opened on a page and the librarian hurried over to his guest.

'Here and over here,' he pointed to two sections of the opened book and handed it to Dimator.

The Captain stared in astonishment, then he looked at the librarian who was staring back at him. Dimator frowned and read the passages in the book.

'Is this true?' he asked the librarian.

'I have never known a book to spread lies, have you?' the librarian replied.

'No, I have not,' Dimator answered seriously.

He closed the book, tucked it under his arm and thanked the librarian for all his help, Commander Milian needed to see this as soon as possible. He quickly grabbed the first book that they had looked at with the translation and placed that beside the other book under his arm for company.

'The Rhino is under instructions not to allow anyone to take anything from this room, Captain. Not even I can remove books from the King's private library,' he said shaking his head.

Dimator sighed heavily, he would have to resort to plan B.

He opened the books on the appropriate pages and ripped the pages he was after from the sleeves, folded them up, placed them neatly in his pockets and handed the book back to a shocked librarian.

Chapter 16
The Great Escape

The door at the rear of the building was nailed shut, they would make far too much noise in smashing it down. There was however, a window sitting patiently beside the door that was not even locked.

Sabat was last out and he clambered through the small window at the rear of the jailhouse, his left leg got caught on the timber on the left side of the frame and was only rescued from the ground breaking his fall by the local who had volunteered to join the escape.

'Shhh,' Sparrowhawk shot back behind him as the clumsy healer almost gave away their position to a pair of patrolling guards in the adjacent alleyway.

The experienced Ranger hugged the side of the timber wall as he sidestepped down to the back of the building, making as little noise as possible. The other two men tried as best they could to shadow his lead. Then Sabat gasped loudly.

'Shhh, would you,' Sparrowhawk hissed back at him.

'But… look over there,' Sabat said. Sparrowhawk followed his stare as Sabat was mesmerised by something opposite their position.

'It's me supply o' medicine,' he called for joy.

'Great…' Sparrowhawk said sarcastically. '…well, we can't bring it with us, unless you're of a mind to fit the whole crate into your pockets, just leave it be,' Sparrowhawk answered and started to move forward.

He moved a few steps when he noticed something move out of the corner of his eye, it was moving towards the crate.

'You are, you're planning on taking it with you?' the other man said bemused.

'O' course I'm not…' Sabat spat back at him, '…but I can squeeze a vial or two into me belt, fetch me quite a price,' he finished, removed a handful of vials and returned to the mission. Sparrowhawk shook his head and continued on to the end of the ally, already regretting his decision to take the old man with him.

The end of the buildings led to an open area at the back of the town, there was a hundred metres of fresh air now between them and the safety of the trees and overgrowth beyond.

A number of soldiers gathered outside of what looked like a store that sold clay pots and other storage items, the shopfront was facing the open space that they needed to cross.

'*Whistling arrow*,' Sparrowhawk thought, he checked his quiver and found only two remaining inside. It would have to do.

Sabat stuck his head around the corner of the building, in a peek-a-boo style and spotted the soldiers.

'Stinking milk-drinkers,' he called under his breath.

'Move away before they see you,' Sparrowhawk ordered. Sabat obeyed and went back into cover behind their new friend.

'Ok, here's what we're going to do,' Sparrowhawk had their attention.

'I'm going to the other end of the jailhouse to fashion a diversion. I'll draw as many soldiers to the other side of the building as possible, hopefully the ones at that store will go to see what's going on,' Sparrowhawk nodded to make sure they were on the same page, both men confirmed they understood his plan so far.

'When I run back, you two get to those bushes and get down, crawl to the west,' he paused here to point out which way was west, just in case there was a misunderstanding.

'I'll follow you as soon as I lose the soldiers, right?' he asked.

'Right,' replied the newest member to Sparrowhawk's crew.

'Wrong,' replied Sabat.

'What's wrong?' Sparrowhawk quizzed.

'Ye'll not make it to the bushes, it's too far,' Sabat said, eyeing the distance that the Ranger needed to cover before the guards rounded the far corner.

'I have that covered,' Sparrowhawk replied.

'Ye have that covered?' Sabat asked, mystified.

'Just get to the other side of that open area, get down and crawl to the west, I'll take care of the rest,' he finished and sidestepped back towards the window that they had squeezed through, he looked in to see the townsfolks sitting there still tied up and waiting to be rescued. He continued along by the rest of the building; it took him longer than he had realised. He thought about what Sabat had said about the distance, but cleared any doubts out of his head immediately.

As he reached the far end of the alley he checked back at his two companions, they were looking back at him waiting for his signal to move.

'What if the soldiers at the store don't move, Sabat will run straight out into the open right in front of them…' Sparrowhawk removed his bow *'…the plan would fail just moments after it got started…'* he curled his right hand back to his quiver and removed a blue whistling arrow *'…as soon as this arrow leaves this bow the place will be swarming with Kor' Cali soldiers, I don't have enough arrows to take them all, they will catch us and kill us, then they will kill all the townsfolk… then Rose will have nothing to save her from her throatrot… all will be lost.'*

Sparrowhawk aimed the arrow high into the cloudless sky and loosed the whistling arrow.

Without waiting to see what would happen, he turned and ran as fast as his aging legs could carry the rest of his aging body. He saw Sabat and the other man start running also, if the soldiers had not taken the bait they would spot the two men in seconds, seconds passed and no shouts came from the end of the alley, the two men kept running.

Sabat was sweating before he even started to move, halfway across the open space he was panting, fear and adrenaline was flowing through him mixing together, and he smiled at the excitement of it all.

They reached the bushes and dropped down to the soft grassy floor. Sabat looked back and to his shock, Sparrowhawk was gone. Just then a flood of Kor' Cali soldiers rounded the corner at the far end of the alleyway, they had made it unseen, but where was the Ranger.

The townsfolk watched as Sparrowhawk came thumbling back in through the opened window of the jailhouse, he stooped down as low as he heard heavy footsteps get close from outside the window. He had not expected a soldier to check this far away from the sound of the arrow. He hoped the guards at the store would stay away for a bit longer.

He waited for a few never-ending minutes as the people stared at him without a word, they too heard the whistling arrow and knew something was up, best to keep quiet and not to cause any reason for the soldiers to search the jailhouse.

He peeked back out through the window; the coast was now clear. He jumped out through the hole in the wall and sprinted back down to where Sabat had crossed. He checked his pocket for his small bottle, it was only half full. Years ago, a full bottle would get him up to six uses, but with his age he was lucky now to get two or three. This would be his final get out of jail free card, if he had to use it.

He stopped at the end of the alley and peeped around the corner; the three guards were back in front of the store. He could see Sabat and the man lying in the long grass, he was now presented with two choices. Firstly, wave them on and he would have to stay, but would they make it on their own to Whiterock, he seriously doubted it. Secondly, turn the corner with his bow drawn and trust in his abilities to take out the three guards without them sounding the alarm. '*For Rose*' was all he thought and he drained the bottle.

The guards were discussing what the noise could have been, two of them decided it was a strange bird that they had never seen or heard before, the third man was about to call them idiots and put forward his own idea of it being a birthing sow, when a very smooth arrow shaft took him in the chest. The other two soldiers turned to see where the projectile had come from.

Sparrowhawk was facing them with two arrows notched on the bow '*For Rose*' and he loosed the shafts.

Sabat saw both arrows hit their targets and he almost stood up and cheered until he saw a frowning Ranger running directly towards him, waving his hands for both men to move.

'Run,' Sparrowhawk came at them like a released bull and dragged them to their feet.

'Ye told us to crawl,' Sabat was beginning to protest.

'Yes, well, Sabat I did, but that was before I had to leave dead soldiers in the middle of the street, now run,' he called frantically.

They ran for what seemed like a decade, half bend down to avoid being seen, Sparrowhawk and the local man encouraging the old healer as best they could, eventually the strong lad had to carry Sabat piggie-back style for the last three or four years. Sparrowhawk called a halt to their escape when he deemed they were far enough away from the town and within earshot of Rogue.

'Alright… stop, stop here for a moment,' he panted towards the other two men.

'Are ye trying to kill us?' Sabat almost fell to the ground with excitement and fear showing through his wrinkled face. The other man was doubled over, trying to catch his breath and rubbing his back.

'We should be safe here for a while, with a bit of luck they shouldn't find the bodies until the guards change watch,' Sparrowhawk guessed.

'So… we walk the rest of the way?' the man asked confused.

Sparrowhawk took his last whistling arrow from his quiver and send it shooting across the sky.

'Hey… they'll be on us in seconds now… ye sandal-shining half-wit,' Sabat called.

'We're too far from human ears to pick it up, Rogue however, does not have human ears,' Sparrowhawk reassured him.

'Ye're not thinking on yer horse carrying the three of us, are ye?' Sabat asked.

'No… we will ride to Whiterock to raise the alarm about the soldiers in the town while…' Sparrowhawk looked at the man, he still didn't know his name.

'Bernard,' he replied, sensing he was finally being invited to offer.

'…while Bernard here will continue on to the nearest town of…' again Sparrowhawk looked directly at Bernard.

'Potter's Mills… it's about a two-day walk to the north' Bernard was beginning to understand the rules to the game.

'…right, to Potter's Mills. When we…' Sparrowhawk pointed at himself and then at Sabat, so Sabat would not have any follow up questions '…when we get to Whiterock, we inform the palace of the enemy location and tell them there is a man at Potter's Mills…' Sparrowhawk points to Bernard. '…who knows the town and can help the Gala' Mor soldiers to plan an offensive,' Sparrowhawk looked at Sabat for confirmation that it all sank in.

'Wonderful…' Sabat replied. '…but, me thinks ye are forgetting something, no?' Sabat asked.

'Forgetting what?' Sparrowhawk replied.

'Long-tooth… ye let 'em go,' Sabat replied in a shocked tone.

Sparrowhawk scratched his head. 'I let him go… I clearly remember my plan was to bring the bandit to Whiterock, but somebody wanted to make a detour to this place and I clearly remember that same somebody riding like a madman directly at a troop of heavily armed Kor' Cali soldiers with a half dead Long-tooth lying in the back of his shabby old cart,' Sparrowhawk spat back at him.

Sabat frowned and stared at the Ranger 'And ye broke me cart… I'll be wanting at least two ravens for that… and my supply of…' Sparrowhawk cut him off.

'I broke your cart…' he shouted and fired his arms to the heavens. '…if you had listened to me in the first place… if we hadn't come to Narrow's Crossing… if I had left you back in that… that… I can't remember the name of that place… I would be in Whiterock sitting in the sunshine with a bottle of Northern Brew in my hand and…' just as he was about to continue, Rogue darted in from the bushes and almost knocked him over with a hug, well the only way a horse knows how to hug, by rubbing his big head into Sparrowhawk's.

'Ah girl, where have you been,' Sparrowhawk hugged her back, the only way humans can.

Sabat looked on in astonishment at the closeness that man and beast shared.

The ride to Whiterock was a harsh affair indeed. Sabat complained and moaned the entire trip while Sparrowhawk's thoughts went back to the dilemma that he had let Long-tooth slip through his fingers and he was returning empty handed, he thought about his sick daughter Rose and the sunshine was heavier upon his shoulders than usual.

'Can't this thing be moving any faster, I dare say I could overtake it with me own two pegs,' Sabat called in Sparrowhawk's ear as they crossed the Hindlands into Whiterock.

'We're almost there Sabat… but if you would prefer to make the rest of the journey by foot, I can gladly oblige your request,' Sparrowhawk shouted over his shoulder.

There was a pause from Sabat, but not a long one.

'O' well, since we be close by, I suppose I can suffer the rest o,' the ride,' he hollered back.

Whiterock came into view as they cleared the line of trees, the shimmering red sun was sinking behind the hills to the northeast, making the shadows stretch across the field that lay in front of them. It was a truly colossal structure, Sabat had seen it many times before, but the sight of it had always caused him to wonder how man could ever built such a mammoth of a city.

'Takes you back a few notches, doesn't it?' Sparrowhawk announced.

Sabat nodded to himself.

They approached from the south-west across the stony fields and babbling streams that surrounded the high white walls of the city. As they came close to the main road, they noticed that there was a very congested line of people of all shapes and sizes facing in the direction of the central gate.

'Lovely… the city is going to smell of peasant droppings… me thinks,' Sabat scoffed at the crowd of travellers, bobbing his head.

'Fleeing the war, I'd wager. Whiterock can't hold everybody…' Sparrowhawk declared looking at the desperate people '…best we join the queue, and quickly too.'

Sparrowhawk tightened his legs on Rogue in response to her shaking her head. She was trying to tell him something.

'What's wrong girl?' Sparrowhawk asked.

Sabat shook his head. '*Was the fool expecting his dumb animal to speak now?*' He thought to himself.

'Oh, I see,' Sparrowhawk said loudly and sat high on the horse. Sabat shifted uncomfortably.

'What in the bottomless trench, are ye doing?' the healer questioned.

Sparrowhawk sat back down and rubbed Rogue on the neck.

'Good girl,' he said.

'Good girl?' Sabat called from behind, his arms around Sparrowhawk's waist for balance.

'Change of plan, we're heading for the gate,' Sparrowhawk remarked.

'So… the horse be calling the shots now, is it?' Sabat asked.

'Look at the people, they haven't moved a toenail in the time we've been here,' the Ranger replied. Sparrowhawk believed that that amount of information would settle the query.

'And… that be a problem?' Sabat asked.

'Well, it means that they have stopped letting people into the city…' Sparrowhawk answered '…and it means they might not let us into the city. So, yes Sabat… that be a problem.'

Chapter 17
The Not-So-Great Escape

She watched as the small rodent scuttled across the freezing damp floor, keeping itself against the side of the wall to remain out of sight of the three people that were talking across from her cell. One was behind the bars, a young slightly handsome looking boy a couple of years her senior, while the other two, a man and a woman much older than the boy, talked to him from the outside of the cage. They all knew each other well, and by the looks of the boys' facial features he was the cub of the older two.

Meadow busied herself by remaining still and not drawing any attention to herself. She fingered the wound on her neck where the man in the forest had pressed his sharp weapon into her, it had healed over, but stinged slightly.

The light from the single torch was enough for her to see where the guard had hung the set of keys, they were hanging happily on a heavy nail sticking out of the stone wall, about head high for her, and just over his desk.

He sat there with his back to the cell, he was sporting a bald head and a filthy tunic that hadn't seen the rough side of a washing board in a hundred years. The man was working on some papayus, Meadow had no idea what he was doing, nor did she really care, he was in her way and that would not do.

The rat was almost at the desk of the jailer, he wasn't a fit creature by any stretch of the imagination, but he was big and strong, and that would be enough.

The boys' parents were now leaving, they were too high and mighty to even look at her, which was what she welcomed. They strolled past as if she wasn't even there, their focus on speaking to each other about some pressing matter, she didn't care.

The boy however, he was a different story.

She heard footsteps and started counting.

She studied the boy as he watched the man and woman leave, his face betrayed his emotions, he wanted them to return, but said nothing.

The jailer was now back and seemed to be enjoying himself at the torment of the boy. They were speaking and the boy was playing a good game, but she knew he was afraid, she could see it in his eyes.

The jailer walked past her cell and laughed, she stared at the boy in the other cell and he caught her gaze as the bald man walked past her. She then saw something there, in those eyes, it was innocence. He was afraid because he didn't do anything wrong to be caged up like that, he was the same as her. Then the lights went out and they were standing in the darkness facing each other.

The jailers' footsteps were almost back at his desk, she was counting his heavy footfalls on his return trip. When she believed he was right beside where her new friend was waiting, she gave a little whistle.

Next there was a scream and a loud noise as if someone was falling against a chair, the chair fell to the ground with a bang and the screaming continued. The man tried to run towards the door with the rat clinging to his back, biting through his clothes and tearing the skin, blood was now streaming down his back. He shouted something she didn't understand, but it was probably '*Help*,' she thought.

He ran and twisted and turned every which way to get the rat to loosen its grip, but the rodent was all in. The man ran where he thought the door was, instead he had turned himself around one too many times and clattered himself head first straight into a stone wall, knocking himself out cold. He landed with a thump onto the ground and the rat jumped off and sat there, waiting.

The boy in the opposite cell called out, he sounded oddly concerned for his tormentor's welfare.

Meadow gave a second whistle.

The boy called out again, this time he was aiming his words at her. She could tell by the change of his tone, he sounded confused.

Within a few seconds the rat was at her foot, he dropped something from his mouth and it clanged on the hard stone, she bent down on her hunkers and gave the rodent the last bit of food she had saved from earlier.

'Good boy… have this little fellow… you've worked well for it,' she spoke affectionately and rubbed his whiskers, the rat licked her fingers and squeaked softly. After a few more rubs, he took his leave and bounced off back to the crack between the stones in the wall. Meadow stood up, holding the ring of keys in her hand.

She opened the cell door to the sound of metal on metal as the old hinges sang their complaints.

The boy spoke again, nervously.

She walked slowly over to where the jailer was lying on the ground, she felt through his tunic and found a handful of small round metal objects, a piece of cloth that was covered in a slimy-sticky substance and then her fingers ran over a flint.

She walked back towards the mounted torch beside the boy's cell. She struck the flint with the small stone that was attached to it by a small wire, sparks flew to the torch and it was spreading light all across the prison on the first try.

The boy stood there and looked at her, there was fear in his eyes. He then looked at the guard and back to her. He said something, but she didn't understand one word, he sounded like a sick dog barking.

She handed him the keys and gestured for him to follow her, but he remained in his cell, she tried again but there was no movement from him. Did he not understand she was setting him free, what was he doing standing there just looking at her with a confused face. She hadn't got time to dally about, so she left him behind and made her way towards the door, stepping over the jailer on her way out.

She reached for the large metal handle and turned it slowly clockwise, the heavy timber door swung open, the hinges singing in a frightful tone that pierced the ears. The air smelled considerably fresher out in the narrow hallway that lay before her, than in the cages to her back. To her surprise there were no guards to be seen, she had thought she would have to run past whatever waited on the other side of the door, but as luck would have it, the hall was empty.

She walked as softly on the tiled floor as she could, the strange warmness of the tiles felt enjoyable as she scanned the hallway in front of her.

She thought she heard voices and held her breath to listen more intently, someone was coming and they were getting closer with each heartbeat.

She was halfway down the hall, when from around the corner came a handful of guards and with them the man who had captured her outside her home in the woods. He saw her and she saw him, he shouted something and all the men came running towards her. There was nowhere for her to go except back inside the jail, she would fight or die.

The men came thundering down the hall after her, their footfalls bouncing off the walls and some even had their weapons drawn, she had retreated to the opened jail door and she whistled for her friend to join her in battle. As the first guard was about to grab her arm, the rat sprang to her rescue and sank his razor-sharp teeth into his neck, the man fell back onto the ground and his friends kicked at the rat trying to get it off him.

It wasn't long before they had impaled the rat on the end of a sword and the man was holding his neck to stop the blood flow.

The men stood there looking at her, uncertainty plastered on all their faces. She was convinced they would attack any second and she was out of rats.

'No… harm,' the man who had taken her had said in her language, he was looking at a piece of papayus and looking at her with his hand extended towards her, his fingers spread.

He barked to his friends, who backed away and put their weapons on the ground, the injured man hunched over against the wall. He came forward slowly.

There was something different about him this time, he was not raging or looking at her with hatred as he had done before

'*How was he speaking to me,*' she frowned as he spoke again.

'No… harm,' he offered.

'Sha woe a mor,' she hollered.

'No… no,' the man seemed to understand her, but he was lying. They had killed her parents; she was there all those years ago when they came. She only remembered hiding in her small home and looking out through the hole that let in the sunlight, she saw the man-beasts kill them with their shiny sharp weapons.

The man was making a sign with his hand as if he was holding something around his neck, but he had nothing. He was then pointing at her, she frowned.

There was a noise from behind her, she heard footsteps and turned to face them. In the doorway of the jail standing in front of her was a very upset jailer holding his head and frowning, he swung his big fist straight at her eyes, the last thing she heard was the man with the papayus shouting, 'No, harm.'

Chapter 18
Home to Rose

They reached the gate to the gripes and moans of the people standing impatiently in the teeming queue, not at all impressed that these newcomers were skipping ahead to the front of the line.

'Let me do all the talking, Sabat. The guards here will not listen to your ramblings with a kind ear, plus we are in a hurry,' Sparrowhawk shouted over his shoulder.

'Ramblings… what be ye muttering 'bout?' Sabat spat back at the rider.

'That's an order, Sabat… not a word,' the Ranger was dead serious and Sabat sensed the tone.

'Fine,' he replied and muttered something under his breath, a rotten tomato almost smashing into his head as it when flying through the air, thrown by an overweight woman with a hairy face, Sabat grimaced at the sight of her.

'Hey yoooooou there,' called the guard standing to attention at the side of the main entrance. He moved towards the pair as they slowed to a halt.

'You better have an earth shatteringly good reason for cutting the line like this… well go on then, let's hear it?' he looked up at Sparrowhawk as he was sitting at the fore of the horse.

'I am a Ranger in the King's employ and we come from Narrow's Crossing,' Sparrowhawk began.

'Narrow's Crossing eh, know a girl from Narrow's Crossing, I do, pretty little thing she is,' the guard drifted off into his own little dream world for a moment, but Sparrowhawk brought him crashing back down to reality.

'Excellent, well this pretty little thing of yours will be dead if you don't let us through because there is a troop of Kor' Cali soldiers holding the whole town by the sword,' Sparrowhawk articulated quickly.

The guard looked blankly at Sparrowhawk, then he shot his gaze to Sabat.

Sabat remained quiet for once and simply nodded his head, which wasn't against his orders.

'Open the gates,' the guard turned around and shouted up to the gate house that was set high into the boundary wall. The guard then moved to the side to allow room for them to pass into the city without further ado.

Sparrowhawk nodded his thanks as he passed by the guard, his long spear supporting his weight as he watched them leave.

It took a while to get through all the streets that were beyond overcrowded, people were fussing about as if the end of the world was at hand, and to some, maybe it was. Upon reaching their destination they had to wait for what seemed like a lifetime due to all the added security in the palace, in turn due to the ongoing war, but they eventually got an audience with Commander Milian.

They stood side by side in the large room with age old oak for a floor and a high dome shaped roof made from a dark timber and Sabat had never seen such beauty in wood before.

The Commander entered the room flanked by two white Rhinos; the echo of their footsteps boomed all around the two travellers.

Sabat took a step back upon seeing the two monsters walking into the room flanking the Commander, Sabat was standing behind Sparrowhawk before they even got close.

He had heard stories about the palace guards whose sole purpose was to protect the royal family. But he had never seen them in the flesh or rather metal armour before, he was in awe of their size and huge shields that they carried at their left sides. Their right hands held large halberds that looked like they could chop a small house in two. Commander Milian was considered a high enough rank to be granted two of his own White Rhinos while on palace grounds, the top brass needed minding in times of war.

'You have information about the enemy occupying a town to the south-west, I believe?' the Commander announced almost dismissively.

'Yes Ser, a town called Narrow's Crossing,' Sparrowhawk replied respectfully, his face was stone.

'Interesting,' the Commander replied, reading Sparrowhawk he was starting to believe and frowned at the news.

'How many men?' he asked.

'A full troop Ser... I counted at least eighty, but those were only the ones that I saw, there could be more, even double that... I cannot say for certain,' Sparrowhawk answered.

The Commander did not reply for a while, he simply stood there thinking, calculating.

Sparrowhawk felt a nudge from behind him.

He turned around to see Sabat nodding frantically at him. Sparrowhawk scowled his companion.

'Is there something that you have to add?' Commander Milian was speaking to Sabat, he had noticed the healer's actions.

Sabat's eyes darted to Sparrowhawk, his eyebrows raised.

'You may speak now Sabat,' Sparrowhawk said slowly.

'Tell 'em 'bout Bernard,' Sabat said quickly.

Sparrowhawk turned back towards the waiting Commander, who was somewhat amused at the display of the two men before his eyes.

'Oh, of course... there is a man at the nearest town to Narrow's Crossing who can help you, he comes from the area and has a better idea of Kor' Cali numbers, he's a local man with knowledge of the surrounding area,' Sparrowhawk said.

'Very interesting indeed,' Commander Milian expressed his gratitude.

'The town be called Potter's Mills,' Sabat felt the embargo was now lifted and he was allowed to return back to his usual annoying self.

'Excellent. I will call an emergency meeting of the higher council immediately,' the Commander stated and turned to leave the two men alone.

'Great work men, you are excused,' he said before he headed back out the way he had come in just moments before. Both men watched the Commander leave with his bulky escorts.

'Right, well we should leave,' Sparrowhawk said.

'What... that be all,' Sabat replied shocked.

'What did you expect?' Sparrowhawk asked.

'Well, I be expecting a reward... not a run o,' the mill... great work men,' Sabat announced downhearted, trying unsuccessfully to mimic the Commanders accent.

Sparrowhawk couldn't deny that it seemed a rather ungrateful return for all their troubles over the past few days.

'Well, our reward is the safety of the Kingdom,' Sparrowhawk said proudly.

'Bah… safety of the Kingdom me foot,' Sabat replied.

Sparrowhawk was walking back the way they had come while Sabat was continuing to complain about how much money the Kingdom had and if they had saved it, then they were surely intitled to their fair share of the coffers.

'So where do ye go birdman?' Sabat asked as he caught up with him.

'Although there have been many setbacks…' he stopped mid-sentence to look directly at Sabat '…the goal has not changed,' he finished and continued to walk through the doors that led into the narrow hall.

'Aye… too right ye be,' Sabat said nodding his head and then added after a moment's pause. '…and what be the goal again?' he asked.

Sparrowhawk sighed loudly.

'Long-tooth Sabat, I need to find Long-tooth and recapture him,' Sparrowhawk had assumed that was obvious enough.

'Aye… I see, of course… Long-tooth indeed,' Sabat confirmed bobbing his head, it was a good plan.

'First I need to see Rose,' Sparrowhawk added.

'Of course… of course…' Sabat replied, having no idea who Rose was '…and who be this Rose we are going to see?' he asked finally as they had made it back to the main hall at the entrance of the palace. Activity here was at an all-time high, guards hurried about and servants dashed here and there following their many different orders.

'We, are not going to see anybody Sabat,' Sparrowhawk replied over his shoulder as he skipped down the steps leading towards the courtyard in front of the palace. Sabat was slowly coming behind him, forcing his aching bones to obey to the heads instructions, age will do that to a man you know, slow him down.

Sparrowhawk reached the outer gate of the palace that opened up into the Upper Rings where the nobles and merchants resided. It was only a short walk from here back down into the city proper, where the common folk and less fortunate dwelt, squashed tightly together.

The guards had delayed Sparrowhawk's quick escape from Sabat as they were discussing who he was and where he was going, as all palace guards like to do.

Sparrowhawk was explaining his reason for being at the palace and was now requesting the return of his weapons.

'But… where do I go now?' Sabat questioned his partner as he reigned in beside him.

'You can go jump in the Blackwater, Sabat. I hear its extra cold this time of the season,' Sparrowhawk replied and one of the guards sniggered at his insult towards the old man.

'Go ahead,' the guard deemed the pair were of no imminent threat to the safety of the Kingdom and allowed them to leave, handing Sparrowhawk his bow and quiver.

Sparrowhawk made his way down through the Upper Ring, it was a large area with extravagant houses and gardens generously spaced apart from one another. He strolled on, thinking about Rose. He frowned as he realised that he had not calculated in failing to return Long-tooth to the city. He knew deep down in his heart that there was not enough time left for Rose to track Long-tooth again. It was the first time in his life he had failed to catch his quarry, and it was the only time that it truly mattered.

He stopped and rubbed his eyes; they were stinging and they were wet. He had lost her mother and now he was going to lose her too, it was too much to bear any longer. He felt his shoulders starting to shake and then his whole body gave in to the tremors. He half fell to the ground, but someone caught him from hitting the cobbled stone underfoot.

'What be wrong…' Sabat was by his side looking past the tears and past the pain of the sobbing Ranger. '…are ye hurt, where be the wound, show me?' Sabat was genuinely showing concern and was checking Sparrowhawk for an injury.

The Ranger gathered himself and stood straight, Sabat supporting him as best he could, struggling with his own body to get up without falling.

'I am fine…' Sparrowhawk looked at the healer. '…just need to get in out of this heat, it's been a long trip,' he announced and rubbed the tears away. He had never shown this side of him to anyone before, he didn't know it was even there. But every man has it inside of him, weather he wants to admit it or not, and sometimes it just comes out.

Sparrowhawk started off again, Sabat remained where he was. He had nowhere to go, he knew nobody in the city, but the Ranger needed to be alone and Sabat gave him that bit of dignity.

He watched Sparrowhawk leave and wondered what had just happened, what had caused the man to break down like that in the middle of the day, out in the open for all to see. Sparrowhawk turned to face the old man.

'Oh, come on then,' he shouted towards him and waved at Sabat, signalling for the old man to follow him.

An elderly lady with a kind face was sitting on a barrel just outside the front door, leaning against the white washed wall. She was busying herself with a needle and thread, stitching together some garment, long from resembling anything wearable.

'Ah, you are home,' the old lady said with a grin, as she stood to receive Sparrowhawk, clearly glad to see him. She had a young scrawny goat at her side, her big plump hand patted the animal on the head as she was chomping hungrily at some weeds.

'Mena, it is good to see you,' Sparrowhawk offered her a warm greeting.

'Oh, maybe many years ago it was good to see this face, but now… I am not so sure,' she replied happily.

'I see old Milly here is still keeping the place looking modest,' he said nodding to the goat.

'Aye, she is indeed, I'd reckon she might outlive the lot of us, this one,' she replied and rubbed her pet.

'How is Rose?' Sparrowhawk asked seriously, changing the subject.

'She has but a few days to make her peace,' the old woman announced sadly, shaking her head at being the bearer of regrettable news.

Sparrowhawk gave the woman a hug that a bear would be proud of, tears running down the woman's face as Sparrowhawk broke the embrace and looked her in the eyes.

'Thank you for minding her, I am forever in your debt,' he said.

Sabat said nothing as they left the woman outside, Sparrowhawk leading the way past the flaking paintwork of the door and into the stale dank interior.

The house was tiny, dirty and smelled like death itself. The front door was broken and the shabby roof had more holes than a pair of beggar's stockings. Sabat's own shack looked like a palace compared to this place, but he said nothing.

A single small window sat in the north facing wall and was letting in the daylight in a column of faded light and letting out the horrid smell of the one roomed abode.

Sabat spotted the cot in the corner of the room, there was a small figure lying on the bed, old blankets covering her small body in moving lumps as she turned to face the two men.

'Papa?' Rose called to Sparrowhawk and hurled out a fit of uncontrollable coughs.

'No, no… don't try to talk my dear, I am home now,' Sparrowhawk was down beside the girl in a flash, Sabat stood in the middle of the room, saddened to his core at the sight.

He was a man of medicine and he was bloody good at his job too, he knew straight away by the sound of that cough what was troubling the small girl.

'Sleep now, good girl… you try get some sleep, I will take care of everything my dear,' Sparrowhawk lied. He had failed and he was out of time.

Sabat knew what had happened to Sparrowhawk in the Upper Ring now, he remembered his own daughter, dying in his own arms, many seasons ago. He would not let another father lose a daughter that way again, if he could help it.

Sparrowhawk raised himself to his feet, the tears were coming back as the soft sound of steady breathing came from the cot. He turned slowly around to face Sabat.

The old man was reaching inside his cloak and came out with something.

'Here… this be for you,' Sabat announced, extending his arm to Sparrowhawk.

Sparrowhawk looked down at Sabat's outstretched hand, he was holding a small vial.

'What is that?' Sparrowhawk asked, his eyes a waterfall.

'Swallow… I took it from me crate at Narrow's Crossing,' Sabat replied nodding his head slowly.

Sparrowhawk's fingers closed around the small container and he looked into Sabat's soft eyes, a single bead rolling down the man's cheek.

'The crate ye told me not to touch… if me remembers rightly,' Sabat smiled a wide ear to ear, thin lipped smile.

Sparrowhawk looked down again at the vial, he stood in silence, his eyes closed and he smiled back.

'Should be enough there for three grown men… plenty for the wee lass,' Sabat offered.

Sparrowhawk grinned, unable to speak for a moment. He gathered himself, trying to understand the situation.

'Plenty for the wee lass' was all he could say through another wave of tears as they came flooding down.

'Pull yerself together man... call ye'self a Ranger?' Sabat was turning back into Sabat.

Sparrowhawk laughed heartily at the old healer's words and raced back towards the sick girl with the life-saving medicine in his hand.

'Hey, hey... do ye know what yer doing there... move aside birdman...' Sabat called after him and raced over to the bed. '...ye'll probably give 'er the wrong dosage an' kill her outright... let me at it,' he was now giving orders to the Ranger. Sparrowhawk obeyed quickly and stepped aside.

'Hand me a towel,' Sabat said and Sparrowhawk found one quick enough.

'Good... good, now I'll need a basin... in case she needs to cough up some thoatrot, this stuff should soften it up and she'll be needin' to get rid of it, better out than in, you know,' Sabat said, Sparrowhawk obliged.

'Good... good, now the most important part, go out yonder an' catch me a nice juicy rabbit...' he didn't get to finish as Sparrowhawk slapped him across the head and laughed.

Sabat frowned at the attack and then smiled.

It was only a few days later that Rose was able to sit up in bed and talk. Sparrowhawk had told her to stay on the small timber pallet until she had regained all her strength, and only to speak when she needed to. She had started to complain about these restrictions but, when Sabat agreed with her father, she was outnumbered and forced to obey.

Sparrowhawk had not left the house while his daughter fought the illness, Sabat had brought supplies to keep them fed and watered.

Sparrowhawk refused to leave the girl alone in those days and nights, missing out on the diluted celebrations of the crowning of the new king, there was a war after all and the authorities decided it was best not to throw too much of a party as resources were low enough.

They had all stayed in the tiny house for the first couple of nights, but Sabat had found the market one morning before the others were up and had sold most of the vials he had taken from his crate. He now had enough owls to find other accommodation, he felt like an intruder while living with Sparrowhawk and Rose, plus they needed to be alone as a family.

Sabat was walking slowly through the streets one morning, heading to the gardens in the lower town to search for herbs, Rose had told him where to look.

He was closing in on the garden when he overheard a group of men speaking about something.

'You say the whole town was destroyed… by the Seven Kingdoms,' a man was shouting at his friend in disbelief.

'Burned it to the ground they did…' another man replied in a state of shock.

'Should be hung the lot of 'em,' the first man answered.

Sabat did not consider himself a nosey man, but this sounded serious enough for a small imposition.

'Something 'appen?' he asked the men in a curious but friendly tone.

'I'll say… bloody Kor' Cali went and burned down Narrow's Crossing they did. Killing every man, woman and child along with it,' one of the men replied.

'Commander Milian sent out a regiment a few days back, they've returned just this morning with the horrid news. Said the Kor' Cali were nowhere to be found,' the first man put in.

Sabat was speechless.

'You ok… old timer?' one of the men asked as Sabat was staring into space, his face turned a white shade of snow.

'Did you have family there, friends?' a rather chubby man asked cautiously and the group remained quiet, looking at Sabat for information.

'No… no, well yes, but none I cared too much about,' Sabat replied visibly shaken by the update.

He completely forgot about his mission to retrieve the herbs and headed back towards Sparrowhawk's house, he will want to hear about this and best it came from him.

'That'll ramp things up now,' he overheard one of the men saying.

'Sure, it'll be all out war now, whatever truce was on the table is in the dogs house now and…' the voice trailed off as Sabat rounded a corner and heard no more, he didn't need to hear anymore.

'Sabat, did you find anything useful; Rose had a list made up for you…' Sparrowhawk was speaking to him as he entered the house, but stopped when he noticed the look on Sabat's face.

'What's wrong?' Sparrowhawk asked slowly, sensing a terrible thing had unfolded.

'They went an' burned Narrow's Crossing, killed all o,' the people an' disappeared,' Sabat announced. Sparrowhawk froze, his mouth half open.

'Who did, the Kor' Cali?' she asked with a serious face, Sabat had not even noticed her sitting up in her bed, listening intently to the news.

'Oh, never ye be bothering 'bout such things little one… it be…' Sabat was saying when Sparrowhawk interrupted him.

'I've told her everything,' Sparrowhawk said casually.

'What… everything?' Sabat replied, slightly stunned.

'Of course, who did you think is the brains of this operation,' Rose called out smiling.

'Rose, please,' Sparrowhawk said in a very fatherly tone.

She frowned and looked down at the floor, humbled.

The room was silent for a moment while Sparrowhawk allowed his head to process the data.

'They must have found the dead soldiers in the street and punished the town for our escape,' he said dejected.

Sparrowhawk pictured all the faces from the jailhouse that would now haunt his dreams for evermore. The little boy who had been playing with his toy horse, the old couple who were tied up beside him in the jail, all a memory now '…*and it's all your fault,*' his mind was accusing him.

'It lies not with ye…' Sabat comforted him, '…what they did, ye couldn't help it birdman… ye did more than anyone ye could to 'elp those people… me thinks,' Sabat finished, his head bobbing.

'Well, it appears to me that I didn't do nearly enough,' Sparrowhawk replied coldly.

'Bah… ye can't save everybody birdman… people die in war… 'tis a fact…' Sabat offered, '…'tis the whole bloody point to the matter to begin with.'

Sparrowhawk couldn't help but take comfort in those words, although he still felt he had made a mistake in leaving them all behind.

'Where did they go?' Sparrowhawk asked after a few heart-beating seconds.

'Who?' Sabat asked, his eyebrows raised.

'The Kor' Cali, I assume they didn't wait around for the King's Guard to find them twiddling their fingers,' he said annoyed.

'How should I know… I be here with ye,' Sabat retorted, not liking Sparrowhawk's tone, he was after all only the messenger.

Sparrowhawk smiled a half apology and nodded his head slowly to show Sabat that he was not angry with him, just himself.

'Sorry, I do not mean to snap at you, I am just…' Sparrowhawk offered.

'I understand, no need to get all mushy with old Sabat here,' Sabat excepted the half apology and wanted to move on from the moment.

'What can we do?' Sabat asked rhetorically, not expecting or needing a response.

'We can track them, the Kor Cali,' Sparrowhawk said.

'Papa?' Rose shouted from the bed, listening to the whole exchange.

'What in the great trench are ye blabbing 'bout... the King's Guard came back, without finding 'em... me thinks that means they be gone,' Sabat announced with some sense.

Sparrowhawk addressed his daughter first, Sabat was ignored for now.

'My little flower, I know I said that the last job was the last job...' he began.

'Yes, you did and I am getting better now, so there is no need for you to leave, we do not need the owls any longer,' Rose was half out of the bed and she was as stone-faced as the wall behind her.

'I know, I know... you are getting better, thanks to Sabat here, but these men killed a whole town full of innocent people, people with no part in the war... and I fear they will kill again,' he said and looked her in the eye.

She knew her father well, Sparrowhawk was a lot of things but he was a good man and she knew he blamed himself for what had happened at Narrow's Crossing and only wanted to save others from meeting the same end.

She looked at him and sighed.

'Ye will never find 'em...' Sabat said, breaking the tension in the room.

'I can track better than a whole regiment of the King's Guard, besides the Kor Cali would smell that many soldiers coming a hundred miles away. It would be far easier to pursue them on my own,' Sparrowhawk said confidently.

'Ye do make a strong argument,' Sabat admitted.

'Not you too, you can't think this is a good idea?' Rose was looking through Sabat, he shivered at the thought of disappointing the little girl.

'Well, I mean yer father 'ere, does 'ave his wits 'bout 'im when he be on the hunt,' Sabat tried to stay neutral in this as best he could.

'Hmm,' Rose scoffed at his cowardly replied.

'Rose, dear. These men are the enemy of the whole Kingdom, not just here in Gala' Mor, but to all the Seven Kingdoms, they want to bring nothing but death and slavery to the continent,' Sparrowhawk stopped as Rose made her own point of interest.

'Six,' she said defiantly.

'Six, what?' Sabat put in.

'Rose claims that there should only be Six Kingdoms, since Great Harbour has been cut off ever since the earth shaking, all those years ago,' Sparrowhawk answered.

'Well, she may not be wrong there… me thinks,' Sabat returned, nodding his head.

Sparrowhawk was tired of the topic, but let it pass for now, it was not on the table at the moment for discussion, he had more important tasks at hand to deal with.

'Rose, you do understand… don't you… why I have to do this?' Sparrowhawk pleaded with her. It was not something he had wished for, he was home and his daughter was sluggishly on the mend from her throatrot and the last thing he wanted to do was leave her again, but he felt this was very important.

'I do understand,' she said at last.

'You do?' Sparrowhawk asked sorrowfully.

Sabat stood behind him, he felt the love between the two and missed it greatly.

'Of course, it is for the good of Gala' Mor that you go. It would be selfish of me to ask you to stay when people are in danger through no fault of their own… I understand,' she said and he embraced her with open arms.

They hugged for a time and he felt all the tension leave his body, they made eye contact and they both smiled.

'Ye… will be travelling alone… me thinks?' Sabat announced ripping the heart-warming moment up and throwing it out the window.

Sparrowhawk turned slowly away from his daughter to face a nervous looking Sabat. The old healer had had enough of adventuring around the continent to do him for the rest of his days, plus Chester was unlikely to find him in Whiterock, if he was even still alive that is.

'No, you stay here Sabat, rest,' Sparrowhawk confirmed the healers desires.

Sabat smiled widely and was not at all offended that Sparrowhawk didn't require his talents this time.

'Of course, I be rather tired,' he said and bobbed his head up and down. Rose smiled.

Sparrowhawk went to the end of Rose's cot and was pushing in on the wall just at the foot of the sorry excuse for a bed. Sabat tilted slightly to get a better look as to what the Ranger was doing. A second later the wall slid backward into itself and Sparrowhawk reached his arm inside, Sabat frowned at the secret compartment he knew nothing about. Sparrowhawk's arm came out again holding a new quiver, full to the brim with different kinds of arrows packed inside.

Sparrowhawk rose to his feet after sliding the fake wall into place and hiding the hidden compartment from the outside world. Sabat felt privileged that Sparrowhawk had exposed the hiding spot when he was in the room, he felt like part of the family then.

'I shall leave right away, I have an idea where to start searching, somewhere that the King's Guard may have overlooked…' he announced. '…Sabat, drop in once in a while to check on my little flower, won't you?' Sparrowhawk asked kindly.

'Ye couldn't be stopping me if ye tried,' he replied joyfully.

'Thank you, my friend,' he said and turned to say his goodbyes to his sick daughter, but when he turned, he shook with fright.

'You look like you seen a ghost, father,' Rose teased as she was standing by herself.

'You… you can stand,' he said in a whisper.

'Of course, I've been improving greatly ever since the medicine Sabat has given me,' she replied and confirmed he wasn't daydreaming.

'That is excellent news' he,' he said and lifted her up into the air and spun her around, her legs almost catching Sabat on the chin.

'Hey, be minding ye two… could go an' kill a man with that carry on ye could,' he said annoyed.

Sparrowhawk made his way to the door, with a nod to the two of them he was reaching for the brass knob when a loud knock sounded from the other side.

Sabat frowned, it was not a knock from a neighbour calling around to borrow some brown sugar, it had an air of authority about it.

Sparrowhawk opened the door, one hand on his bow.

The man was dressed from head to foot in blue and navy, a king's envoy.

'Sparrowhawk?' the voice commanded.

'Yes, I am he,' Sparrowhawk replied.

'A request for you has been issued…' he spoke especially clearly '…to attend the palace at once,' the messenger announced.

'Of course,' Sparrowhawk replied, his hand moved quickly away from his weapon as he spotted the two king's guards behind the man.

'I will be along as soon as possible,' Sparrowhawk declared.

The man looked at Sparrowhawk and smiled.

'You will be along at once…' the man commanded. '…these two guards will escort you to the palace right away.'

'Of course, right away,' Sparrowhawk stepped out through the door frame as the King's envoy moved back to give the Ranger room and moved towards the guards.

The man stuck his head back inside the room.

'Sabat, I assume,' the man addressed the old, tense looking healer.

'Yeeees…' Sabat replied, shaking a little.

'You are coming too,' the man smiled.

Commander Gladis sat in his hard timber chair and shifted, uncomfortably as he listened to the two rambling fools before him. One was useful enough he thought, a Ranger with a recommendable reputation, a bit on in his years, but of good Gala' Mor stock, that was for sure.

The other man however, he was a different kettle of fish.

'So ye see, yer Sire… we went an' made high tail for Whiterock after that an'…' Sabat was reciting the events that led to the slaughter of the people at Narrow's Crossing, well as best he could anyway.

'Enough… I've heard enough,' the Commander announced and the room fell silent.

The room was full with Captains and nobles, a few of the finer class of merchants and of course the Commander's White Rhinos. It was a tough audience for the two friends to convince that they had no blame in the whole tragedy.

'I believe you… truly I do. But the Kingdom demands somebody take the fall for this catastrophe and unfortunately for you, you two are the number one candidate's,' he said coldly.

'I can find them,' Sparrowhawk spoke up.

'Really, and how do you propose to do that when Captain Hillas here…' Commander Milian pointed to the Captain who had led the men to Narrow's Crossing and found the town in ruins. '…could not locate a single Kor' Cali soul.'

'Because, and I mean no disrespect here, your soldiers looked in the wrong place,' Sparrowhawk looked at the Captain and nodded, a mark of respect.

'Well obviously they looked in the wrong place, because if they looked in the right place, they would have found them,' the Commander had a point.

'Yes, well I assume the Captain here and his soldiers headed south when they reached Narrow's Crossing?' Sparrowhawk glanced over at the Captain.

'Yes, after we reached the destroyed town, we found tracks that led southward, most probably to Water's Edge, where they had landed. We assumed after burning the town they would head back to Kor'dor as they knew we would be coming after them,' the Captain spoke loudly, confident in his actions.

'Exactly...' Sparrowhawk had their attention. '...they knew that you would be coming after them, so they did the opposite to what you thought they would do,' Sparrowhawk announced.

'What do you mean exactly?' the Commander squinted his eyes, intrigued.

'I believe that after they burned the town, they headed further into Gala' Mor,' Sparrowhawk announced.

'What?' the Captain dismissed the notion.

'Why would they do such a thing?' the Commander asked.

'Well, the standoff at the Blacksnake is costing the Kor'dorian's more than it is costing Gala' Mor, think of the supply routes and morale of the Kor' Cali. I believe they are making a move into Gala' Mor because they are getting desperate,' Sparrowhawk replied.

'A few hundred stray Kor' Cali troops won't cause us much trouble, why would they risk it?' Another voice joined the conversation.

'A few hundred stray troops can move without detection more easily, they can go from town to town burning and killing, spreading fear throughout the Kingdom. That is a very useful tool in times of war,' Sparrowhawk announced.

The men in the room started speaking to each other in whispers, looking at the Ranger from time to time, they were taking his evolution of events with some serious consideration.

'Silence,' the Commander roared, and Sabat jumped at the loud eruption.

'You may have a point, Ranger,' Commander Milian said to the grim acceptance of the room.

'We will send a thousand soldiers, our best,' an overdressed man shouted, standing to his feet.

'Really, where will we send them?' Captain Hillas asked calmly.

'I don't know,' the man replied casually, for a second not realising he had put forward a careless motion.

'Then sit down,' the Captain ordered in the same casual tone, the man obeyed.

'Ranger, where do you believe they went?' Commander Milian asked.

'I cannot say for sure, but if I was stationed behind enemy lines to cause the most mayhem and fear, I would lay low for a while, let my enemy think I have left, gone home, let my enemy lower his guard and then strike again,' Sparrowhawk replied.

'We need to find them before this happens again, Commander,' Captain Hillas announced, the Commander nodded.

'I will return to Narrow's Crossing alone, see what I can discover, report back to you when I find the enemy,' Sparrowhawk announced.

The men started discussing matters again amongst themselves, Commander Milian shook his head at them all. Captain Hillas moved over to the Commander and whispered something in his ear, the Commander stood.

'Ranger, return to Narrow's Crossing, find these Kor' Cali butchers and send word of their location, that is an order from the King's Guard,' Commander Milian had just declared Sparrowhawk an official agent under his command.

'Of course, Ser. I will leave at once,' Sparrowhawk offered the men in the room a slight bow, spun about and faced Sabat, who was standing beside him.

'Fare you well,' he said with a nod and turned to leave.

'Glad it be ye an' not…' Sabat was mid-sentence when the Commander called to Sparrowhawk.

'The healer will stay put, of course,' Commander Gladis said and nodded as both of them looked in his direction a little startled.

'Of course, yer Sire em… ship, I had no intentions of leaving this 'ere fine city… none at all,' Sabat smiled.

'Well, I should hope not, seeing that my guards found two vials of something in your accommodation containing substances that require a trade receipt,' the Commander announced and all eyes focused on the surprised healer.

The two friends looked at each other with open mouths and big eyes for a moment.

'Do you possess such documentation?' he finished with one raised eyebrow pointed directly at Sabat. They both turned back to face the voice.

'I… er… well…' Sabat had started.

'I did not think so,' the Commander said calmly.

'Guards, remove this man from the chamber, he should be more comfortable in the keep, I think,' the Commander called to his escort. One of the White Rhinos moved leisurely forward in the direction of Sabat, his heavy footfalls echoing across the silent room.

'Birdman…' Sabat began, but again was not given the courtesy to complete his sentence.

'You will remain there until…' the Commander started with Sabat then turned his gaze swiftly to Sparrowhawk and continued, '…you complete your mission, Ranger. If you are unsuccessful then Sabat here, will face the next king's trial, call him a replacement, seeing how you failed to return the outlaw known only as Long-tooth to us,' he finished with a smile.

Sabat threw Sparrowhawk a pleading glance before the huge frame of the Rhino dragged him effortlessly away by the shoulder.

Chapter 19
A Wealth of Knowledge

She woke to a feeling she had never known before, in a strange place. Her head ached and her nose was throbbing, she flinched as she touched it to check was it still there.

For a few minutes she had to recollect her thoughts, she had no idea where she was, all she knew was that it smelled horrid and it was very dark. She sat up from a lying position and glanced around, trying to get her bearings. A single light flickered on a wall just above a man sitting with his back to her, he was fiddling around with some papayus and a feather, his hand crossing back and forth across the yellow fabric in a rapid motion.

She listened as the tip of the feather made a soft scratching sound and it gave her some comfort.

Meadow spun around on the crate cot she sat on for a bed, her foot made contact with a timber bucket and set the thing clattering across the cell, it banged into the thick metal bars on the far side and the man looked around.

'Oh, well, well, good morning princess,' the man glared.

Meadow frowned at his gibberish, she could not understand that he was insulting her, but she guessed that was exactly what the oaf was doing.

The man reached up and pulled on a rope that was dropping down from the ceiling and stood up. The rope was climbing up through a hole in the timbers and disappeared.

He was walking towards her now; he had a malicious look in his burly eyes and a grin that was thin and hard.

As he got right up beside the bars he stared directly at the girl, it was then that she spotted the tiny teeth marks on his neck and it all came flooding back to her.

He was about to speak when the large wooden door squeaked open, in marched some guards and the man from the forest, he was still holding those same pieces of papayus he had before her lights went out.

The group made their way to where the jailer was standing and he moved to greet them, with a grunt and a nod.

They spoke to each other, the jailer and the man, the ugly one was displeased for some reason, she could not tell.

The soldier approached the cell, the guards stood back and the jailer returned to his desk.

He stood before the girl who had caused so much trouble and he looked into her eyes.

She turned her face away and sat back down upon the bed, her head still paining her from the blow she had received earlier.

'Who… are… they?' he asked through the bars.

Her head spun around rapidly when she recognised the words her parents had thought her. She looked at him, her eyes eating at his, trying to understand what game he was playing.

'…*Who are they?*' she thought, what by all the beasts of the Evergreen was he talking about.

'Na na, who are… you?' He corrected himself and apologised in his own language.

She froze.

She studied his face, the features that made his face his, she took them all in. She read him like a book and he was being genuine, could these beast-men know the meaning of her words, with all their killing and hatred, but here he was standing before her with eyes that wanted to know the truth. She would tell him nothing, not until, she was sure.

'Pour de a tour,' she announced, she was on her feet and defiant.

He paused for just a moment and then looked down at the sheets in his hands, darting over them with great urgency, finally when he was finished, he shook his head.

'I do not understand what she is saying…' he turned to the guards as if asking for them to intervene and offer him a direct translation, instead they just shrugged back at him, '…I don't have those words here,' Dimator finished, frustrated.

'She said, she does not trust you,' a voice came from behind Dimator.

The entire group turned in the direction of the cell, it was a boy in his mid-teens.

'Excuse me?' Dimator announced to the boy.

'The girl, she said she does not trust you,' he repeated.

'And you know this... how?' Dimator questioned him with a serious face.

'I learnt a bit of the old tongues as part of my studies. I'm not sure exactly of the translation of course, but look at her body language. Her straight back, one foot behind the other and staring right through you, oh I'd say she no more trusts you than a stray cat,' he said with a hint of arrogance.

'And you are... exactly?' Dimator asked, sensing the boy did not speak like most of the usual riff-raff that you would find in the keep.

'Theo'dore D'Souza,' the prisoner replied with a smile.

'D'souza... Anton D'Souza?' Dimator was never as confused in his life.

'My father,' Theo'dor said impassively.

'Jailer,' the Captain called down to the man sitting at his desk fiddling with something.

'Aye?' he shouted back, not bothering to turn his head.

'This boy, here... who is he?' Dimator would have the little rascal flogged for lying and impersonating a member of the richest family on the continent.

'Oh, that one... why it be none other than the famous D'Souza scamp, caught sneaking around in the prince's chambers... he was, well the King's chambers now,' the jailer roared back with a crooked grin on his crooked face.

Dimator dismissed the man with a wave, faced Theo'dor and paused for a brief moment, deciding his next move.

'Right... and you can understand her?' Dimator asked.

'A little, I was only studying the linguistical side of things, you know the accents and different dialects when I was thrown in here... a frightful mistake might I add,' Theo'dor answered intelligently.

'Right... so, ask her what her name is and how she can control the animals?' Dimator said with a hint of hope and a lot of excitement in his tone.

'Well, it's not as easy as all that Ser, I mean first I would need to know where in the Northern Realms she hails from and then... did you say controls the animals?' Theo'dor responded with shock.

'She is from the Evergreen, that's where we found her, and it seemed she had lived there for quite some time, judging by the hut we unearthed. Never mind the part about the animals, I misspoke,' Dimator replied, hoping the boy could help.

'But the Evergreen is not in the Northern Realms Ser, unless she moved here a long time ago and never cared to learn our tongue…' Theo'dor correctly concluded. '…or perhaps she has always lived in the forest and learnt to speak from someone from the northern region.'

'Hmm… both scenarios seem quite possible…' Dimator replied and thought for a moment. '…to speak to her, tell me, what do you require?' he asked, a little too eagerly, Theo'dor spotted the Captain's excitement.

'I would need access to the King's library of course, to study the first volume of Ser Nathan Capelan's Dialects of the Foreign Lands. There I think I would find the required chapters to decipher the key points to discovering this girl's native language,' it was a complete shot in the dark, a wild hope against hope, but he had to try.

If he had been any other boy with any other name, Dimator would have seriously questioned the boy's motives and abilities, but he was a D'Souza.

'Fine, I will get you into the King's library,' Dimator said after looking the boy over.

'Jailer, release this one into my custody,' Dimator called.

'You must be drunker than an ox. You think I can just hand over a prisoner to anyone, it's my job and pension you'd be taking with you. There are proper channels that must…' Dimator held up his hand to stop the man mid-rant. He took the scroll out of his inside pocket and showed it to the jailer, who examined it and nodded to Dimator without another word of complaint.

The Kings library was written in big bold capital letters over the entrance of the door. He had heard only rumours about the wealth of knowledge and secrets that the archives held between their covers, he was like a child on his sixth birthday.

The skinny librarian frown at Dimator as they both approached a large desk that was bigger than the cell which had housed Theo'dor for the previous few days.

'Well now, returned to destroy the remaining seventeen thousand perfectly intact books have we… oh and look, you brought a friend. Isn't that just lovely, you can do it in half the time now,' the skinny man was not at all impressed by the Captains presence, and had about as much time for Theo'dor.

'My apologies for before, it was a necessary offence. Here, I've returned the pages,' Dimator offered a very substandard apology, hoping the man would not count them as he had withheld one of the pages for future reference. The librarian took the pages forlornly and scoffed at the treatment of his priceless pages 'All rolled up in a ball, the nerve,' he said.

'We em… need back into that private section again,' Dimator announced.

The man's eyebrows almost went out through the top of his head, and his mouth curled down on either side to touch his chin. There were more wrinkles on his face than a muddy puddle.

'I must say not, surly I am the jester in a play if you believe…' Dimator held up his hand to stop the man, he was liking this wonderful new power.

'I believe I am not asking permission to enter, but for you to step aside quietly or risk a few nights with that unpleasant jailer in the keep,' Dimator announced.

'He has a free cell now, you know,' Theo'dor decided to add to the enjoyment, at the expense of the man.

The horrified librarian breathed out heavily, he knew he had no solid foundation to stand on to launch a protest and he most certainly did not like the sound of the keep, he'd heard awful stories about that place.

'Very well, as you wish… but might I request that you keep the destruction of my library to a minimum, if you don't mind,' he said pleadingly as he led the way to the door that had a hidden White Rhino waiting behind it.

'Of course, we will not harm a page,' Dimator replied smiling, the man did not return the gesture.

'Now, do not say a word when we enter here,' the man cautioned them.

Theo'dor looked at Dimator, Dimator nodded his head in a stern agreement with the librarian.

'He's not joking,' Dimator assured him.

Theo'dor thought it best to comply with these instructions as he stepped into the small room beyond the main library. A White Rhino stood to attention as they entered.

'Password?' the man's voice bounced off the walls.

'The eagle never lands to catch her prey,' the librarian replied.

The guard stood to the side and Theo'dor spotted the door that was hidden behind his huge frame.

The three men entered the small room that was the King's private collection.

'I thought it was something about a lion keeping watch?' Dimator asked the librarian.

'It was, a few hours ago, but they change it at random intervals. They do love their secrecy those lot, well who can blame them, I suppose, they are responsible for the welfare of the royal family,' the librarian replied.

Theo'dor's eyes lit up like a campfire upon seeing the books and manuscripts that few men had ever seen and very few would ever get the chance.

'Right, what did you say you were looking for?' Dimator questioned Theo'dor, forgetting the name of the book and the author.

'Ser Nathan Capelan's Dialects of the Foreign Lands,' the boy replied dryly, his mind was occupied with another matter. He was trying to come up with some way to get a look at all the information on the geography of the Forever Mountains, the real reason he had lied about knowing what the girl in the cell beside him had said earlier.

In truth he had no idea of her strange language, he was playing a ruse on the Captain and hoping to learn enough from the book he had mentioned to the Captain to secure information about her way of speaking, he prided himself on being a fast learner. Then he needed to find plans or maps of the mines and tunnels in the Forever Mountains, to discover where the hidden path was located.

'Ah yes, Ser Nathan Capelan, a citizen of this fine city for a time, many years ago, of course. Why didn't I think of that before?' the librarian had announced, scratching his head as Dimator and Theo'dor listened.

'Came from somewhere to the north I believe, came over the treacherous snow-capped peaks of many mountains and travelled to many lands, I'd wager his writings might be a fitting place to commence,' he assured his two companions as he bent down to a lower shelf and scanned the various volumes.

'Ah, here it is,' the skinny man said triumphantly, struggling to come up with a rather large book that must have contained every piece of information ever recorded.

'Wow,' Dimator said, a bit concerned that the war would be over by the time they had gotten half way through the enormous book.

'I have seen the rest of these in the back room beside the main hallway, I shall go and organise them and you can browse through them when you are finished with this one,' the librarian said and was making his way to the door.

'There's more?' Dimator said flabbergasted.

'Of course, this is just the first tome, there are another seven in the far room. This one must have been more valuable as it's the first edition, hence it's in here,' the skinny man replied as if everyone should have known that.

'So, where do we start?' Dimator asked as Theo'dor was already inspecting the contents of the numerous chapters.

'Ah, got it,' Theo'dor said and smiled at the Captain.

'You… got what?' Dimator asked slowly and quizzingly.

'See here, if you follow the contents at the beginning of the volume it gives you a perfect idea of where all the different vernaculars start and finish in respect to their most spoken areas said casually as if speaking to a baby.'

'If you say so,' Dimator replied.

Theo'dore spend some time flicking through the pages of the tome, stopping here and there and moving on to the next page. The Captain was tapping his foot, growing more impatient by the minute.

'Here we go,' Theo'dore announced proudly after what Dimator considered to be a serious amount of time to be just standing around.

'What, what is it?' the Captain looked on.

'Yes, yes… I see. So, the vowels that we use are reversed, but in a different context,' he said and the Captain nodded in mock agreement.

'She, the girl I mean… speaks with an ancient tongue, not in use for decades, maybe even hundreds of years. She puts a strong emphasis on feeling rather than emotions, that is the reason we cannot understand her, if I can just figure out the code,' Theo'dor said tapping his fingers on the pages in front of him.

'The code?' Dimator asked.

'Yes, there is a way of deciphering all the letters, you see. They are in a pattern of sorts, if I could just find out how to figure it out,' he spoke cunningly.

'How long will this take,' the Captain asked subdued.

'Oh, it could take a few hours or so,' he replied.

Dimator was a man of action, battlefields, training camps and drills were his cup of soup. He was not a man keen on sitting down and spending hours reading books.

'Right, well you stay here and try figure it out, I'll check in on the librarian. Remember, set one foot outside that door with any of these priceless books and you'll be face to face with that ogre,' Dimator warned him and set off to find the nearest toilet.

Theo'dor was delighted, but made no outward show of his fortune. The language conundrum was most interesting and he would soon get his nose stuck into the book in front of him, but for the meantime he must turn his attention back to his primary objective.

Quickly he scanned the labels clearly marking the contents of each shelve, luckily, they had been arranged perfectly in alphabetical order, he found the map section in the crack of a whip.

'Halti Empire... no, islands lost to the Old Salt... no, Great Harbour... no, what... detailed maps of Great Harbour, must be worth a fortune,' Theo'dor thought about slipping this section down his pants, but reality hit him and astutely decided against it.

'Ah... The Forever Mountains,' quickly he searched through the many hundreds of small hand drawn maps and charts, it was easy for a highly educated boy to orientate his way through the varied tunnelways and passages of the snow-covered caves and caverns that connected to each other by underground channels. But that was the problem, they all connected like a huge ant hill, he was looking for one that was aloof from the rest, one that played no part in the main structure of the enormous mine system.

He searched and searched, knowing that sneaking the map out would be a life ending offence if caught, but he had promised his father and that was enough. Time was his enemy now and he would deal with the consequences later, if it came to that.

He sieved through the hundreds of charts and maps, some were ancient and almost crumbled in his hands, the natural oils in his fingers smudging some of the ink in places. Mines and mines and when he had had enough mines to last him a whole other lifetime, he came across more mines. Zigzagging this way and that, writings on the sheets he could not understand, were they in a different language or just plain old and inelegible.

He was uncertain of the lapsed time, but he was convinced it was over an hour since he had been left alone with the secrets of the Kingdom.

He was beginning to believe has task was futile, maybe the secret tunnel was never mapped, and was merely used by a chosen few who had memorised the passage. Worst still, maybe there was no tunnel to begin with. Doubt was sinking deep into his brain.

He heard a noise coming from the outer room, it was a bang of a door closing, the door on the other side where the White Rhino stood guard, someone was returning.

Just as he was tiding up and about to return the book to its snug little home on the shelve, he spotted a drawing of a tunnel that had no side burrows or break away areas, this was no mine, it just went straight. Without thinking he folded the old wrinkled map up in a square small enough to slide up his sleeve, slotted the book of charts into the correct spot and stuck his head into 'Ser Nathan Capelan's Dialects of the Foreign Lands.'

'Well, find anything useful?' Dimator asked hopefully, closing the door behind him.

'Maybe, is there any chance I can take this with me,' he gestured to the Captain.

'If was up to me, sure. But, unfortunately the guard out there, apparently does not allow it,' Dimator replied seriously.

'Ah, I see now why you had a few torn pages and not a full edition when you came to question the girl… you stole them,' Theo'dor smiled accusingly.

'Borrowed them… I returned them this afternoon when I had no more need for it,' Dimator replied coolly.

'Borrowed it, I might just need to use that line myself soon,' Theo'dor thought to himself and accepted the Captain's excuse and went back to reading the tome of languages, using his finger to guide his eyes that were starting to ache at the strain of having looked at so many maps for the past who knew how long.

Dimator looked at the spines of some of the books on a shelve and gasped at some of the titles. 'How to make a gold vein last for months' and 'The art of perfect smithing,' he thought to himself. *'Now I see why there is a guard posted outside, these volumes are worth a lot of coin.'*

'Wait… wait… okay Captain, I think I've just found your code,' Theo'dor laughed loudly.

'What, are you serious? Show me, I want to read it for myself,' Dimator came rushing over like a loose bull.

'Okay, so do you see the consonants here, they are different from our own. Okay, these are the vowels, this dialect contains twelve… astounding,' Theo'dor exclaimed.

'What is?' Dimator replied.

'Well, they use vowels where we use consonants, but not all the time, only when the letters are followed by a singular consonant and not another vowel. However, if the third or fifth vowel in the word is a consonant then the rule, or code, does not apply… unless the second or forth letter is not a vowel, then the…' Dimator held up his hand.

'Can you read the bloody thing… yes or no?' Dimator asked firmly.

'Yes, I might need a few minutes, but yes, I believe I could,' Theo'dor replied, delighted he had achieved something to keep the Captain on his side, he was getting fed up of that cell.

'Can you understand her, if she speaks... just a yes, or no?' Dimator asked.

'Yes,' Theo'dor replied. 'I believe so,' he added quickly as Dimator frowned slightly.

'Right, that's good enough... let's get back over there,' Dimator announced enthusiastically.

They were halfway down the hall when something struck Theo'dor with the weight of a falling oak, he stopped walking and looked at the Captain.

Dimator stopped and looked at him.

'What is it?' He asked nervously.

'Before when she spoke to you, I've just translated it,' he replied.

'What... what did she say,' Dimator gulped.

'She said, "This is my home",' Theo'dor replied baffled.

Dimator's eyes dropped to the floor, he was thinking.

'Why would she say that... Captain?' Theo'dor asked not expecting an honest answer, he wasn't even sure if the Captain knew the answer.

The Captain was still thinking.

'You will speak only to me about the girl, utter a single word of it to an ear that is not attached to my head and you'll be for the block, I do not care who your father is... are we clear?' Dimator was a good-hearted man and an honourable soldier, but more than anything he was a patriot and he meant every word of what he had just said.

'Of course,' Theo'dor swallowed hard and his shocked face watched the Captain continue on down the stone hallway for a few seconds and he followed close behind.

They walked on in silence for a time, both men thinking to themselves, trying to figure it all out.

A group of soldiers stood together, huddled like a bunch of elderly ladies at the market gossiping about the latest scandal.

'What's all this, nothing better to do with the King's coin, how about you all head down to the drill fields first thing in the morning for some extra lessons on discipline,' Dimator called to them in a tone that captured their attention. He was already in an irritable mood, soldiers on duty engaging in idle chit-chat was something he scowled with pleasure.

'Ser, sorry. Ser, it's just the news of Willows Pass, that's got us all worked up, won't happen again, Ser,' one of the soldiers replied and started to return to his post before the Captain could confirm his punishment in concrete.

'Hold up,' Dimator commanded the man who had spoken, the rest were glad to escape.

'What is this news you speak of… Willow's Pass, you said?' the Captain was curious.

'You haven't heard Ser?' the youngish looking soldier replied.

'Well, let's just say, I'd love to hear your take on the subject,' Dimator said sarcastically.

'Oh, well… the Kor' Cali have burned it to cinders, Ser, just two days past,' the man replied.

Dimator froze on the spot like a six-foot-tall icicle.

'Ser?' The soldier said puzzled.

'Get back to your station,' Theo'dore ordered.

The man went quickly on his way and Theo'dore liked the new him. He started to smile, but dropped the foolish looking grin as Dimator stared at him.

'Narrow's Crossing is in Marshaven while Willow's Pass is located in the north-east of Gala' Mor, do you realise what this means?' he questioned his tag along companion.

'Am… they can fly?' Theo'dor mistakenly jested.

'This is serious, it means that there is more than one unit of enemy troops in Gala' Mor,' Dimator announced.

Chapter 20
Sparrowhawk Meets His Match

Rogue was pushed to a level she had never witnessed before, and she was not impressed with the heavy task her master was asking of her.

Her legs were aching, her head was throbbing in the baking heat and she had not had the sweat brushed from her hair in days, it was starting to clump together in long wiry braids. *'He's pulling on the reigns, what does that mean again… oh right, stop,'* and she did.

Sparrowhawk was almost propelled over the head of Rogue, barely saving himself in time from meeting the rough ground with his head rather than his preferred, time tested feet first approach.

'Easy girl… easy now,' he called into her ear, rubbing her head and noticing his hand returned covered in sweat and long course horse hairs.

'I am sorry girl… I will make it up to you, I promise,' he said softly as Rogue neighed her distrust. She was a horse, but she was no fool, she knew there would soon be a return trip and she neighed again in protest.

'Alright… alright, we shall rest a while,' Sparrowhawk said sensing his mounts discomfort.

He had pushed on with all he had as soon as he had left Whiterock, stopping only for food and rest, of which he got little. He knew it was wrong to force Rogue as such a pace, but it was necessary to save lives.

He smelled the scorched earth miles before he saw the town, or what was left of it. The King's Guard soldiers had done little in a clean-up effort, but they too had no time to waste, they needed to search for the Kor' Cali responsible for the atrocity before his eyes.

'By the Seven Kingdoms,' he exclaimed looking at the scene that was something from his childhood nightmares.

He slid down from Rogue and allowed himself a chew from the rations of dried meat and a few precious mouthfuls of two-day old water from his sheepskin water sachet. Rogue snorted loudly at the sight.

'I know… I know,' he said assuringly, leading the horse to the well in the middle of the town, his head down, not wanting to see more than he needed to.

After Rogue was satisfied, Sparrowhawk started with the men that he had despatched during their escape, the three soldiers at the rear of the town, behind the alleyway. It was a shot in the dark as surely the Kor' Cali would have removed their men and not left them where they had been killed, but he had to start somewhere and that was a good a place as any.

To his amazement they were still there, lying on the ground with the arrow shafts still penetrating their bodies. Sparrowhawk bend down beside them and noticed a few irregularities. Firstly, as they were common soldiers, somebody in their unit would have taken their drinking and gambling owls, but Sparrowhawk found all men carrying a small, but modest number of coins.

Secondly, the men's tokens were missing, small cloths that hung around soldier's necks, usually given to the men from loved ones to remember them by while on campaign. The men had been left there on purpose.

Sparrowhawk stood and looked around, to the south and then to the north, nothing but open land and far away hills.

He heard the sound of a bowstring snap and threw his body to the ground in an instant, his reflexes kicking in against his aging bones. He landed with a heavy thud and rolled to the side. He quickly threw back a deep swig of his special brew and came back up onto his knees bow drawn and arrow notched facing east. Standing beside a tree in the opposite side of the open area was his target, Sparrowhawk loosed and the shaft pounded into the bark of the tree, waving back and forth for a few seconds before coming to a dead stop.

The man fully dressed in black was behind the tree before the arrow landed, he moved almost as fast as the speeding shaft, Sparrowhawk notched again, not taking his eyes from the enemy position, behind the trunk of the tree.

In three seconds, he would advance, keeping the razor-sharp arrow trained on that bloody tree. 'One… two….'

A sharp pain exploded from his left side and he fell down, lying close to the earth, blood seeping from the shaft half buried in his thigh.

'*There's more than one… blast*,' Sparrowhawk's tactical cogs were working overtime and he was struggling to come up with a solid plan. He grabbed at the shaft, breaking it off near his body, leaving an inch sticking out instead of trying to remove it completely.

'*Get up... move,*' so he did.

He was out in the open, injured and now it appeared also surrounded by highly trained archers like himself. He swung his attention to where the second arrow had come from, there was nothing there only a burned-out store facing him.

'*Get to cover... but where... the buildings?*' Water was gathering in his eyes as he calculated out his next move, the pain in his side was increasing every time he took a breath.

He levelled his bow in a semi-circle to cover the tree and the burned-out store.

In a flash his bow was taken out of his grasp from behind in one swift movement, Sparrowhawk turned but was kicked to the ground with a strong right foot square in the chest, he sprawled out across the dirt, his side causing him all sorts of trouble.

He looked up at the man dressed all in black from his head to his strong right foot. His face was covered also, only the eyes could be seen, dark and unforgiving. The unnamed man was holding a long narrow blade in his left hand. Sparrowhawk's gaze fell upon the weapon and he stared in wonder. The sword was curved and wavy, it shone a brilliant black, he had never seen a blade of its type before, it glistened in the sunlight as the man stood over him, shining with a blinding glow as the beams of light from the sun seemed to be attracted by the swords perfect surface.

'*Well... I guess this is it...*' his mind racing, his burning side on fire and his vision blurring more and more.

'At least I was able to save Rose... the rest of the world can sort itself out...' he said loudly and laughed. '...you, tell Sabat... he's alright in my book and Rogue, ha, you may as well take her,' he announced to the man standing over him.

He didn't know how it would come or how he would take it, well know he knew. At least he wasn't begging or crying like so many do in their final moments. He was Sparrowhawk and he would go out like a King's Ranger.

'Sabat...' the man said in a muffled tone as his voice was struggling to get through the black scarf covering his mouth and neck, '...where is he?' The man finished, his eyes not shifting from Sparrowhawk's.

Sparrowhawk looked into those eyes and saw recognition at his friend's name being mentioned. *'Does he know Sabat?'*

'Sabat must die, where I find him?' His eyes narrowed to slits.

'Ah, he does know Sabat, anyone that knew the old healer usually wanted the man dead,' Sparrowhawk smiled at the thought.

'Or you must die?' The man spoke in a foreign accent Sparrowhawk could not place.

Then his head began to feel very light, his eyes started to close and opened compulsively slowly, the world around him was going dark, he was out cold before his head hit the ground.

It was dark and cold. He was tied to the ground with stakes and ropes, spread out in a giant human sized X, staring up into the starry sky. His arms were stiff and his wrists were extremely sore as the ropes stretched them for a time longer than comfort had allowed.

'You sleep long,' the muffled voice announced.

Sparrowhawk moaned, his head throbbing from a lack of hydration.

'This Sabat you speak of, you are not him?' the man asked, sitting beside Sparrowhawk's head, looking down at his captive.

'Me, no. Sabat is a friend,' Sparrowhawk realised that if the man wanted to find Sabat, then a breathing Sparrowhawk would be more useful than a Sparrowhawk that was not breathing.

'Friend, eh…' the man lolled over the word. '…no such person where I come from,' the man said while sliding a whetstone down the length of his wavy sword, the sound echoing off in the distance.

The stars twinkled above him, it was a cloudless sky so there were hundreds of the burning little dots, laughing at him from millions of miles away.

'Then what do you called the others at the ambush you set for me, the ones that shot arrows at me?' Sparrowhawk quickly recalled the arrow that had struck his side, he glanced down and saw a bandage wrapped around the wound. Funnily enough, he felt no pain.

'That was I…' the man replied. '…I work alone,' he followed.

'Alone, but you couldn't have been in all three positions at once?' Sparrowhawk questioned.

'Of course not… I moved,' the man said casually as if it was a stupid question.

'You moved…' Sparrowhawk was thinking back. '…but nobody can move that quickly?' he said, convinced the man was lying.

'Hmm' was all the man in black replied and turned his attention back to sharpening his sword. Sparrowhawk then noticed the bow strung over his right shoulder, then he realised that the man had held his sword in his left hand before, could it be that there was only one of him.

Rogue came over and sniffed at Sparrowhawk's face, Sparrowhawk ordered the animal back as she licked at his cheeks.

'My horse like you?' the masked man asked.

'I am sorry to disappoint you, but that horse belongs to me,' Sparrowhawk was really in no position to argue with the man, but he did anyway.

'You give horse to me, before you sleep,' the man rightfully recollected.

Sparrowhawk thought for a moment.

'True, but that was when I thought you were going to kill me,' Sparrowhawk argued his point like a pro debater and smiled.

'I am going to kill you,' the man said calmly, sliding the sword back into the sheath on his hip.

Sparrowhawk swallowed hard.

'Then why did you patch up my wound, it doesn't add up to heal a man then kill that same man?' Sparrowhawk asked.

'You said you know Sabat, I want to find Sabat, I keep you alive until you tell me where I find Sabat,' the man replied logically.

'But what if I do not tell you where he is, then you cannot kill me,' Sparrowhawk was a rational man, so he tried that approach.

'So then, it is settled, you do know where Sabat is,' the man said wisely.

Sparrowhawk thought for a moment '*Wait, did he just trick me?*' he looked up at a shooting star.

His wrists called out for mercy as the tight ropes cut deeper into his skin, red marks turning a dark shaded blue.

'Why, you here?' The man questioned.

'Me, I'm trying to save the Kingdom,' Sparrowhawk joked. With half the mans faced covered it was impossible to tell whether or not he saw the funny side, Sparrowhawk doubted it.

'Save the Kingdom, how you do this when you cannot save yourself?' he asked curiously.

'Oh, I'll think of something,' Sparrowhawk knew the blade would be coming for him soon, he might as well enjoy his last moments of fresh air.

'I know of your kind…' the man said after a few minutes of thought. '…the bow you carry, the horse, she is bred for endurance, not a warhorse,' the man was now standing and rubbing Rogues mane.

'Beautiful beast…' he commented with an air of knowledge about horses present in his muffled tone. '…you are hunter or mercenary or something,' the man was looking down at Sparrowhawk, his head tilted to one side.

Sparrowhawk did not see the need to deceive his captor.

'A Ranger, yes' he confessed.

'Then you are not here by chance, you too look for someone or something… yes?' The man asked, coming down beside the sprawled-out Ranger.

Sparrowhawk knew the man was not Kor' Cali, or someone who just happened to be passing through, he might as well be open about everything, maybe he might bring some information with him to the grave, he took a deep breath.

'Yes, I've been sent here to find the men responsible for burning the town…' Sparrowhawk announced to the inquisitive ears of the man in black. '…we believe they are still in Gala' Mor, and are going to do the same to the next town to cause devastation among the people, hoping to gain an advantage in the war,' Sparrowhawk spoke as clearly as he could.

'It would be a good tactic,' the man replied carelessly.

'Indeed, it would, if hundreds of innocent people didn't have to die,' Sparrowhawk spat at the man's tone.

'People die in war,' the man said, repeating what Sabat had said before. Sparrowhawk had time to reflect on this.

'Not like this they shouldn't,' Sparrowhawk said with bitterness in his voice.

'True,' the man replied after looking around at the buildings, some still smouldering.

The man looked at Sparrowhawk for a long moment, as the Ranger tried to shift his weight slightly to the left, his body was complaining against the prolonged unnatural position of his muscles.

'The men you seek are to the north, make camp in large wooded area,' the man offered.

Sparrowhawk looked into his eyes and saw something resembling sympathy there, deep into the centre of his dark pupils.

Sparrowhawk thought about the layout of the land and decided that the largest forest north of their position was in the Boro Hills, a range of high hills covered mainly with trees and valleys, it would be the perfect place for an enemy force to stay concealed.

'Boro Hills,' he said softly.

His kidnapper frown at him, he seemed not to care, but then why say anything *'he has given me information that is extremely important to my mission and the safety of the Gala' Mor people,'* Sparrowhawk's lack of water and aching bones were acting as a barrier to his thoughts, maybe that is what the man had wanted.

'Sabat… where I find?' the man announced in an equable tone.

'Why did you tell me where the Kor' Cali are hiding, what good does it do you, what good will it do me, tied to the ground?' Sparrowhawk returned.

'First… Sabat?' the man answered.

Sparrowhawk breathed slowly, thinking quickly *'what does he want with Sabat? Nothing good I am sure of it.'* But in all truth, he didn't know.

'He had no reason to tell me where the Kor' Cali were if he didn't plan to let me go, but maybe he wanted me to think that,' Sparrowhawk could not read the situation, something just didn't add up. *'If I tell him where Sabat is, I have failed my friend, my friend who saved my daughter, but if I say nothing, he will leave me here to die.'*

'Whiterock, Sabat is in Whiterock,' Sparrowhawk said quickly, not wanting to over think the dilemma he found himself in. Sabat was after all imprisoned in the keep, protected by the King's Guard, he would be safe there.

'The Walled City,' the man replied and looked to the east. Sparrowhawk could tell that the man was calculating the journey in his mind, evaluating his next move. Next, the man would ask where in the city, Sparrowhawk would not give him that.

The masked man slid the curved sword out of the sheath in one swift movement, the metallic sound hissed in the cold night air *'Oh, maybe he won't ask where in the city after all,'* Sparrowhawk swallowed hard as the sword came into full view.

The sword was raised high into the air onto a backdrop of shining stars, it came down so quickly that Sparrowhawk did not see it or hear it cutting through the mist.

'Take this,' the man said and dropped a full waterskin down beside Sparrowhawk, it landed with a thud on the solid ground, sending dust and tiny stones in all directions.

Sparrowhawk sat up and rubbed his wrists, they were terribly painful, but he was never so acceptable of pain in all his life, pain was after all, the greatest reminder that you were still alive.

Sparrowhawk grabbed the waterskin and drank a few mouthfuls of water, forcing himself not to take too much too quickly. The man whistled loudly; he was already walking away before Sparrowhawk had finished swigging the water.

'Thank you,' he called to the man as a thunder of footsteps came from somewhere beyond the treeline. A tall black horse with a full white face exploded into the clearing in a few seconds and the man leaped onto it in one very impressive passage of footwork and summersaults, almost like it was nothing.

Without another word or acknowledgment of Sparrowhawk's presence, he was gone into the night, heading east to Whiterock.

When morning came it brought with it a beautiful sun and a cloudless sky. Sparrowhawk had hoped for a little less magnificent day, he had just about enough of the blistering heat and was not looking to the long journey ahead of him with anticipation.

He had rested the previous night for one reason only, he needed to. He would not have gotten far in that state and that would not do anybody any good to end up collapsing in the middle of the night and falling from Rogue's back. Better he rested and gain some strength for the journey back to Whiterock or he was likely to risk exhausting himself out.

He filled the waterskin in the well in the centre of the burned-out town, tied it to Rogue's saddle and mounted slowly. His muscles were still much the worse for wears after being tied up for such a long period, his wrists too, caused immense discomfort. His side where he had stopped the arrow, was somehow only causing him minor pain, the man had covered the wound with a sticky yellow paste, it smelled something awful, but it worked a treat.

Rogue shook her head violently from side to side.

'What is it, girl?' he asked looking around. He saw and heard nothing. Deciding she was just being awkward and still angry with him for pushing her so hard, he whispered some words of encouragement to her and she responded with a shake of the head, then he listened, more carefully as Rogue stood like a statue.

'Voices, heavy footfalls, from the south,' quickly he lowered himself from the horse and led her into the nearest bit of cover he could find, a half-scorched building to his left, he closed the door behind him.

He examined his hiding spot with caution, although the store was seriously damaged, the front was intact enough to conceal both him and his mount. The roof was completely gone, as were most of the inside walls, the only remaining part of the structure was the front wall, although that too was severely damaged above the door level, how it still remained standing was a mystery.

Sparrowhawk put his finger over his mouth while looking at Rogue, the horse nodded ever so slightly to confirm she understood the command.

Then they waited.

'Whooooo eeee, went an' done a fine bitta work 'ere... those turnip heads did, eh?' Sparrowhawk heard a voice coming from just up the street, he frowned at that voice.

'Sure did... bloody butchers... the lot o' 'em,' came a deep voice that Sparrowhawk thought he recognised.

'Best we be not staying 'round 'ere too long... King's Guard may just be coming back,' the first man said.

Sparrowhawk looked at Rogue squinting his small blue eyes and Rogue looked back at Sparrowhawk with her big brown eyes, if she knew something, she wasn't talking.

'Ain't nothing 'ere for us,' the second voice shouted, now just out in front of the store Sparrowhawk was hiding behind.

'Ye be right there Long-tooth, best we be heading back to the boys,' his friend replied.

Rogue nodded her head slowly as if she knew all the time, maybe she did.

'Long-tooth and Chester, the two idiots had probably come back to scavenge anything they could from the destroyed town... the Kor'dorian's must have let them leave before burning the place,' Sparrowhawk thought to himself as he realised that there might be a bit of good fortune here after all.

Quickly he glanced out through a hole in the wall of the collapsing building and verified his belief that it was in fact, his two old foes that had strolled back into town, and there they were, walking their horses up the main street like they owned the place.

He needed Long-tooth alive so he removed a green tipped arrow from the middle compartment of his quiver, checked it was the correct colour and returned it safely back inside, for Chester a regular arrow would suffice, the world could do without a man of his talents. Sparrowhawk took the bow from his back and removed the required arrow. Next, he played it safe and took a small swig out of his special brew, you can never be too careful when dealing with back-stabbing low-lives after all.

Watching for a moment when both men were facing away from his hiding position he slowly and quietly crept towards the door, placing his hand with the arrow on the handle gently.

'S'pose we best get on outta 'ere,' Long-tooth advised, looking around.

'Sure, ain't nothing but ash and rotting corpses anyhow,' Chester replied not too concerned about his fallen townsfolk.

They were both about to climb back onto their mounts when Sparrowhawk came bursting out onto the street with his bow drawn and aimed at the two men.

''Hold up there a second,' Sparrowhawk announced.

The two men turned to face him, when they realised who had surprised them, their faces turned from shock to distain in a heartbeat.

'Yoooooouu,' Long-tooth cried.

Chester's mouth was open but nothing came out, he could have swallowed a house.

'Don't move,' Sparrowhawk commanded, they complied.

'Now, now… let's not get carried away here,' Chester finally found his voice.

He started to advance on Sparrowhawk, slowly.

'There's no need to be pointing that thing at us, now is there,' he said in a calm tone as his feet inched forward.

'We are all businessmen here,' he called to Sparrowhawk with his hands held out by his sides to show he meant no threat, slowly evaporating the distance between himself and the armed Ranger by the second.

Sparrowhawk listened and watched the man's hands for movement.

'I'm sure we can all come to some kind of an agreement if we just put our weapons down and engage in friendly conversation,' he smiled at Sparrowhawk, his hands back down beside his body, his fingers dancing, he was merely a few meters away from the Ranger.

Long-tooth glanced at Chester's lower back, just for a split second, but Sparrowhawk spotted it and released his fingers on the feathers as Chester went for something behind him.

The shaft took Chester in the chest and sent him hurdling back across the main street, crash landing right beside Long-tooth with a scattering of dust, face down in the dirt. A concealed blade was tied to his back, the sheath was about eight inches long with a wooden handle visible now that the man was down.

Long-tooth kicked Chester onto his back and looked down at his dead comrade, the arrow buried feathers deep right where is heart used to beat, he looked up at Sparrowhawk.

'No… not agh…' he shouted pleadingly as a cloud of green powder enveloped his upper body, seconds later, Chester was joined by his colleague.

Sparrowhawk was back in business. The pain in his wrists and bones did not seem anywhere as intrusive as they had been when Sparrowhawk did not have a wanted outlaw tied to the back of Rogue.

There was however one small issue that had to be resolved before Sparrowhawk could make the return trip to Whiterock. With the extra weight, Rogue would need to rest more often and not be able to maintain her usual high speed, that would cost him time and time was not on his side.

Gathering that the turnip heads would more than likely be keeping a low profile for a while, after the burning of Narrow's Crossing there were extra patrols sent out to the region. Sparrowhawk felt they would stay hidden until the patrols were cancelled before they moved on to their next target. Time would prove him right.

The ride back to Whiterock was slow, so Sparrowhawk decided to cross the 'Long Grass' to save some time. It was named fittingly as the vast area between the Boro' Hills and the great city of Whiterock was lush and beautiful, its only fault were the roaming tribes who, depending on which tribe you happened upon, could be friend or foe. It was a valid reason to skip the area completely whenever possible, so Sparrowhawk always travelled through the Hindlands in the past. He had diverted south on the way to Narrow's Crossing, but now with the labouring pace of Rogue, he felt he could make up the time with a more direct route back. Time would prove him wrong.

The warriors on the hills looked peaceful enough, that was until they sent a volley of arrow heads in his direction, they had misjudged the wind and their attempt had fallen short. Sparrowhawk dug in his heels and he had to push Rogue on harder than the animal had ever been pushed, he hated to do it, but it was necessary if the trio wanted to return with their limbs intact.

Removing an arrow, he let fly at the approaching enemy, the Hitaloop, he thought judging by their red garb and angry yelps as the chase began. A fierce tribe that was swallowing up all the lesser tribes and purchasing a monopoly with their killing sprees. Their desire was to convert all native Gala' Mor tribesmen to their tribe, one way or another, Sparrowhawk had chosen not to join voluntarily.

There had been eight at the start of the chase, but the advancing enemy was down to five as Sparrowhawk's third arrow struck its target sending another bold warrior to the green carpet below, three out of three, not bad for a retiring Ranger. He had drunk the remainder of the liquid his daughter had made and he was making good use of it.

The war party came to a halt when they had lost their third member, they seemed to be discussing if continuing on with the hunt was worth the effort, they decided to let the trespasser go, Sparrowhawk smiled to himself, *'another close call to add to the list.'*

He arrived at the gates of Whiterock where the crowd seeking access to the safety of her walls had gotten larger and angrier at not been admitted entry. Sparrowhawk marched Rogue straight past them all and was thanked with a shower of rotten fruit for his troubles.

First, he headed towards the keep to unload his cargo.

The jailer took the man into his 'theatre of misery,' as he liked to call it and handed Sparrowhawk the coin in a small black velvet sack.

'Took out Markos's cut,' the jailer told him and Sparrowhawk nodded. Sparrowhawk didn't count it, he casually dropped it into a hidden pocket on the inside of his long coat.

'When's he going to come 'round?' The man with the ugly smile asked.

'A day or two…' Sparrowhawk replied. '…and he's going to be quite hungry when he does, not to mention mighty upset.'

The jailer had menacingly laughed at that.

'Where is my friend, I'll be taking him too,' Sparrowhawk asked.

'The old grumpy one, please do, he's being giving me a blasted headache ever since he got here with all his blasted singing,' the jailer replied and told Sparrowhawk that Sabat was housed at the far end of the keep, away from his own ears.

On his way out of the prison Sparrowhawk noticed a young girl in the cell close to the jailer's desk. She was dirty and had a face that would turn milk sour, the only thing that was noticeable about her was a pendant that hung loosely about her neck, it looked like a wolfs head, but Sparrowhawk could not be sure.

His audience with the Commander had been short and not very sweet.

After confiding to the man all he knew about the whereabouts of the enemy Kor' Cali troops, he was asked if anything else had happened on his venture. Sparrowhawk had thought it best not to mention the man in black who had briefly captured him or about the near misses with the Hitaloop tribes crossing the 'Long Grass,' and replied that the journey had been uneventful.

Back at his small home he relayed all that had happened to him on his excursion, leaving nothing to the wind. Rose and Sabat listened intensively.

'Glad I packed a brew for you,' Rose stated thankfully.

'Indeed, my aim is not as it once was my dear,' he replied.

'I be meaning to ask 'bout that?' Sabat put in, he had seen the strange little flask the Ranger had kept close to his person at all times, he was waiting for the right time to bring it up.

'It's a concoction, my mother had been working on it when she took the path, she was close to finishing it, but over calculated the ratio of wilther flowers required to nullify the adrenaline flow caused by the hempo weeds,' Rose replied.

'Hempo weeds canna be regulated,' Sabat shouted in sheer bewilderment.

'Well, with extreme care and manipulation, and only by someone well-trained in the use of daphar plants. Yes, it can be regulated,' she answered calmly.

Sabat's mouth was open, he had no idea he was in a room with a mind far more advanced in the homeopathic field than himself, she was after all a child. He looked at Sparrowhawk.

'Hey, don't look at me, I only shoot my bow at who needs to be shot. She picks all the flowers and makes the trinkets,' he replied to the invisible question.

'Astounding… I be sure,' Sabat replied and looked at the girl in wonder.

'Do you know who that man in black might be?' Sparrowhawk snapped him out of it.

'I know not this man, nor why he seeks me,' Sabat answered.

'Perhaps hired by Chester to play out his vengeance on you?' Sparrowhawk thought it was unlikely, but it was a possibility.

'Bah, not his way. He be having trouble with you, he be the one to make the kill… but I guess he be not killing anymore,' Sabat announced with little sympathy.

Rose was working at the table and Sparrowhawk looked at her and was forever grateful to Sabat for his generosity. She had improved to almost full health by the time he had returned from his trip and he smiled as he watched his daughter mixing and crushing more ingredients for his next batch of brew.

'I am sorry my friend… for giving away your location,' Sparrowhawk apologised, eyeing the man.

'Never ye be minding 'bout that…' Sabat waved his hand. '…t'was what needed to be done at the time. Ye needed to save yer own skin to get back 'ere…,' Sabat replied. '…I would a done the same meself,' he finished with an uncontrollable nod.

'We'll be ready for him if he appears here, do not fear that,' Sparrowhawk said confidently.

Sabat did not reply.

Chapter 21
A Breath of Fresh Air

She was sitting on the pallet cot when they came towards her cell, she did not stand to greet them, in fact if there had been anything to throw at them, she would have.

She had been moved to the cell that the boy had been locked up in and the sleeping man that looked more like Koda, than an actual beast-man was silently snoozing in her previous accommodation.

The boy looked down at the sleeping bear as he came beside the desk, the one that had captured her never took his eye off her since the moment he had entered the keep until the jailer asked him a question.

The boy, not that much older than she was, lifted some parchment from the table and a thin feather.

'Why is she in my cell?' Theo'dor questioned the guard as he spotted the girl staring at them.

'You want it back?' Dimator inquired.

'No, no. She is welcome to it as long as she wants,' Theo'dor replied, his hands held up.

'No bloody rat runs in that cell, is there?' The jailer replied pointing to the huge hole in the wall just beside Long-tooth's stretched out feet.

'What?' Theo'dor replied.

'She can control animals,' the Captain said seriously.

Theo'dor looked at him like he had a second nose in the middle of his forehead.

'Excuse me, Ser, but what?' Theo'dor asked.

'Well, is it that difficult to believe?' Dimator replied.

'Ah, yes,' Theo'dor answered the question like there couldn't possibly be another option.

'Trust me, I was there,' the Captain said and walked straight to her cell, Theo'dor was left standing just outside Long-tooth's cell with no idea what the Captain was talking about.

Dimator stopped at the girl's cell and he was sizing her up.

'You were where, exactly?' Theo'dor felt he was already knee deep into this mess, whatever it was, so he might as well go all in.

'The Evergreen Massacre...' he replied. '...that's what they're calling it,' Dimator did not take his eye of the girl behind the bars.

'I've heard of it, sure. It was on the King's hunt... you were there?' Theo'dor noticed the Captain's face was stern and focused.

'I was there...' he repeated coldly '...and I saw birds and bears fight for her... killing my soldier's,' he shook his head.

'But, how can that be?' Theo'dor was a very educated boy, but had never heard of anything of this nature before and he had studied every battle and tactic that was ever recorded.

'With this,' Dimator replied and held up a small timber whistle. It was a homemade piece of whittling, but was crafted with great care and looked sturdy and durable.

The imprisoned girl shot up from the bed when she saw the whistle, she stared at it.

'Be a more tat,' she commanded.

They both glared at her, and she at them.

'What did she say?' Dimator asked quickly. Theo'dor scribbled something down on the piece of papyus, and scribbled again.

'Be a more tat?' she bellowed again.

'Am, emmm... she want's that back... says it belongs to her,' Theo'dor translated.

The girl looked at him.

'Find out who she is... a name... something,' Dimator requested.

The boy scribbled again as she watched him closely.

'Tour say a she?' he asked and looked up, her face transformed from one of murderous rage to one that was calm and placid as he spoke.

'Mea'dow,' she said to him, almost in tears.

'What did she say?' Dimator demanded.

'Meadow,' Theo'dor repeated.

'Meadow,' the Captain tried to pronounce it correctly, he looked at Theo'dor.

He then fiddled around with his feather and papayus, looked up and asked her where she was from.

She answered and again he wrote it down and jumbled around the letters, trying to decipher her words into his own, making sure his suspicions were correct.

'Pour de a tour,' she said, looking at Theo'dor, he thought he spotted desperation in her eyes, she wanted to communicate, days locked up will have strange effects on someone who all her life had been free to do as she pleased.

'There, she said that before, what by the wild beasts of Halti is she talking about?' Dimator demanded.

'Pour de a tour,' Theo'dor repeated 'Home here, I come from… I think she is saying she is from here,' Theo'dor confirmed his translation from before.

'Gala' Mor… you mean the Evergreen, we know this…' he was saying when Theo'dor cut him off.

'No, she is saying here… as in Whiterock,' Theo'dor corrected him.

'What, it can't be… her hut in the Evergreen has been lived in for years,' Dimator replied.

Theo'dor turned to her again and asked a question, Dimator stood back and listened.

This time the girl said many things, it was like she had started into a rant, waving her hands about the place and making all kinds of facial expressions that the Captain did not like the look of.

'What by the depts of the Old Salt was that?' Dimator asked when she had eventually finished.

Theo'dor had been writing as she was rambling on, he was still writing and moving letters around, then he froze.

'No, that can't be right… hold on, I'll try that again,' he said and Dimator frowned.

After he had completed a second run of scribbles, he looked up at Dimator.

'What?' Dimator pleaded.

'She says she is from the palace,' Theo'dor replied and smiled.

Dimator froze, but he did not appear shocked, a brush of relief had washed over his face and Theo'dor smelled a rat, and not the one nibbling at Long-tooth's boots either.

'So, it is true, follow me,' Dimator said.

The girl shouted something at them as they were about to leave.

'What now?' Dimator asked.

Again, Theo'dor produced the papayus and feather, his hand working frantically to translate the latest passage.

'I think she said… outside?' he replied to the waiting Captain.

'Outside… what do you mean, outside?' Dimator interrogated him as if he was a prisoner, well actually he was, but he was hoping the Captain would forget about that after all the help he was providing.

'She wants to go outside,' Theo'dor replied.

There was a pause for a moment as nobody spoke, the only noise in the room was the snoring of the wanted outlaw in the opposite cell.

'I suppose the girl just wants a bit of fresh air, how long has she been in here?' Theo'dor put in.

'Jailer, how long has the girl been here?' Dimator shouted at the desk.

'Not long enough, you ask me,' he replied.

'Good grief, that man is as useless as a blind archer with one arm,' Dimator snorted.

'Couldn't hurt?' Theo'dor took pity on the poor little thing, he remembered that she had tried to help him when he was in her position behind those same bars.

'And if you think about it, the girl has probably never been indoors for this long in her life, she must be feeling mighty ill' Theo dor added to aid the girl's case.

'Right, blast it, let her out,' Dimator commanded to the jailer. Dimator was a strict man and even harsh when he needed to be, but he was not cruel.

The three of them walked through the heavy keep door, down the narrow hallway until they reached the stone steps that led up and out into the grand city of Whiterock.

Dimator's arm was chained to her left arm and Theo'dor's to her right.

'Keep your eyes opens,' Dimator warned his unlikely new partner as he scanned every inch of the path in front of them, looking behind and all around, covering all the angles.

Theo'dor frowned and looked around him, who exactly was he keeping his eyes open for, the girl was miles from her home with no known friends in the world, he felt the Captain was being a touch over cautious.

Up they climbed, Dimator walked past all the doors that led outside as he led the small group further up the hard stone steps.

'Am, where exactly are we going, to the moon?' Theo'dor asked.

'Almost...' Dimator replied. '...to the roof,' he finished with a nod.

'The roof?' Theo'dor asked, uncertain as to why all the mountaineering was necessary.

'So, she can't run,' Dimator replied harshly enough for Theo'dor not to ask any more questions and just enjoy the rest of the climb as best as he could.

The golden sunlight washed over them as they entered through the small doorway that opened out on the high roof of the keep. Dimator had to duck low under the lintel as he passed through.

The girl held up her hands as best she could, the restrains not allowing her full freedom to relish the moment. Her eyes hurt a little at first, but soon she became accustomed to the welcoming brightness. She felt alive again for the first time in a long time.

'Maybe a bath next?' Theo'dor commented.

'Don't push your luck,' Dimator replied.

'Me?' Theo'dor acted the victim.

'Don't pretend you didn't argue for her back in the cell?' Dimator threw him a knowing glance.

'Well, I feel that the happier she is, the easier she might give us the information we are looking for, whatever that is,' Theo'dor answered.

'True,' Dimator conceded.

Meadow made her way towards the edge of the roof, as she got closer, she observed the scene before her. At this height they were high enough to see a panoramic view of the huge city. The only taller buildings were the palace itself and the monument that was in the centre market, build for the remembrance of the lost soldiers in the bygone war against the Halti Empire.

She took it all in, the different sized structures all around, the vast lands and mountains that surrounded the boundary walls, the huge line of people waiting outside the main gates pleading for access and all the people within going about their daily lives.

She was stopped from moving any closer by the chains, she frowned at such things, designed for holding people against their will, bending them to do the will of others. She would break such things, one day.

The smells and the sounds encompassed her and she felt strange, not well even. It was not the way nature had intended for man to live. So cluttered and tightly packed together, she could see houses on top of houses with no area in front or behind to run in, or to catch food, what did they eat, she speculated.

She saw no animals in the streets, save a stray dog rutting through some metal bins full of rubbish and broken timber planks. There was a lone bird flying high in the sky, circling around.

Then it hit her, there were so little trees inside the huge walls that surrounded the blocks and blocks of buildings, how did all these people breathe she wondered.

She missed her home, she missed the lakes and the morning smells and sounds of the forest, she must get home as soon as possible.

'I think that's long enough,' Dimator announced and began to move. He jolted to a stop as the girl stayed still, looking over the landscape. The chain straightened and Dimator frowned.

'Let me talk to her,' Theo'dor offered. Dimator was still frowning.

He scribbled something down and looked at it, turned the papayus sideways and then back upright.

Theo'dor went to stand in front of the girl, her hair matted and her face marked with filth.

Dimator heard it, but had no idea what was being said, he then realised '*What if he is not being honest with me,*' Dimator made a mental note to test the boy at some stage, and soon.

Theo'dor nodded to the Captain and the girl turned willingly back towards the small timber door which they had entered minutes before.

'What did you say to her?' Dimator asked astounded.

'Am… well, I promised that if she left now, she can come back tomorrow,' Theo'dor made a face.

'What?' Dimator roared and they all stopped.

'Look, keep her happy and we… I mean you, get what you want,' Theo'dor reasoned with the man.

Dimator did not like being given stale information after the fact, but he agreed with Theo'dor and then led the girl inside.

'We put her back in that stinking keep and we go see Commander Milian right away, he'll want to know what we've learnt,' Dimator declared.

Just as she disappeared into the strange building, an eagle swooped low and gave out a cry of disapproval. The gliding bird had one broken leg and a twisted beak, now he was heading back to his home.

The Commander was smaller than Theo'dor had imagined he would be.

'What news do you bring, Captain?' He questioned Dimator.

'We have identified the girl, Ser,' Dimator replied.

'We have?' Theo dor was as shocked as the Commander.

'We?' The Commander said and looked at Theo'dor.

'This is Theo'dor D'Souza, son to Anton D'Souza, the merchant general. He has been a vital associate in discovering the girl's true identity,' he introduced the boy.

'Excellent, who is she then boy, tell me everything you know,' the Commander smiled.

'Err… I don't rightly… maybe the good Captain here should be the one to divulge the information… I mean to say…' Theo'dor started but was saved by the Captain.

'She is the daughter of Lousia, Ser,' Dimator said rather quietly.

'Lousia, Lousia who?' the Commander asked.

'Princess Lousia Ser, sister to the late King Matais, Ser,' he replied.

'Princess Lousia,' the Commander said, barely a whisper.

Theo'dor's mind was racing, he had remembered something about a Princess Lousia many years ago, but nobody had ever talked about her much. Ran off to the Northern Realms or some such, he couldn't fully recall her story.

'You have undeniable proof, Captain?' the Commander asked shrewdly.

Dimator removed a piece of papayus from his pocket and handed it to the Commander, his eyebrows went up and he perched his lips. Theo'dor could not see from his position so he stepped in beside the Commander to gain a better vantage point. He felt a huge hand rest upon his shoulder and squeeze ever so slightly.

'He is alright, I do not guess Theo'dor here is much of a threat,' the Commander said to the White Rhino behind him.

Theo'dor looked at the papayus, instead of a page full of words he beheld a picture of a couple, a tall broad man with a much slender woman on his arm. The woman held a bundle of blankets, resting on her arm, a tiny face peeping out from underneath the warm cocoon. They were dressed in royal attire and standing elegantly at the foot of the palace steps with much flowers and greenery around them. They looked so happy and content with the world and the woman wore a shining pendant loosely about her neck.

'It's the girl's pendant,' Theo'dor announced, looking at Dimator.

'Yes, it was specially made by the D'warfen in the mountains at the request of her father, one of a kind, priceless too,' the Commander spoke affectionately.

'And the girl looks exactly like the woman, I can see the man in her too, those eyes are unmistakable,' Theo'dor confirmed.

'Well, well, good day to all,' Commander Gladis had just entered the room and was making his way towards the group.

'The soldiers we sent west have reported that they have found a camp in the Boro' Hills where the enemy had been hiding,' Commander Gladis spoke loudly.

'And…' the other Commander asked for more information.

'And… nothing. They are gone, and it's been quite some time, so I expect that they are gone home. That Ranger must have been mistaken,' Gladis said with an uneasy confidence.

'But, a second town has been destroyed, hundreds perished, there can be no mistake there,' Milian said, looking at Gladis with suspicious eyes.

'Of course, there is no mistake there, we have sent out another regiment to investigate that area too, we should hear back from them any day now,' he replied feeling threatened.

'So, you would have us wait while our land is being burned, sit at the Blackwater and hope Balltimor retreats back into Kor' dor,' Milian asked mockingly.

'We wait until we know where the enemy is Commander, you would have us cross the Blackwater, think of all the lives that would be forfeit as the trumpets die off into the breeze,' Gladis knew he was right and sounded as much.

They were at a stalemate at the Blackwater and they had to wait until they could discover the enemy troops in their own land before they could plan a counter offensive.

'Alright, we should not discuss this without the other members of the war council present,' Milian announced, holding up his hands for peace.

'Exactly right, we wait for news of their whereabouts before any plans are drawn out. What is that you have there?' Commander Gladis said while spotting the piece of papayus in Milian's hand.

Commander Milian was considering concealing the picture behind his back but had forgotten it was even there during the debate and now it was too late, the man had seen it as clear as day.

'Nothing, we were trying to get to the bottom of something, it does not concern the war effort, just a trivial matter,' Milian was many things, but he was not a seasoned liar and Commander Gladis approached, it was now his turn to be suspicious.

'What's all the secrecy about, may I intrude?' the Commander was not asking.

He came close, Theo'dor and Dimator stepped back a few feet to give way to the Commander and his own twin bodyguards.

'Princess Lousia and that northern fool?' Gladis scowled as Commander Milian had handed him the picture.

'Where have I seen that…' Commander Gladis was about to refer to the pendant, so his peer jumped in and asked that the White Rhino's remain outside for a few moments.

Theo'dor stiffened at this move, he knew something was not fitting into place here, why were the Rhinos asked to step outside, as scary as they were, he felt Commander Gladis was somebody to truly fear.

With the palace guards out of the room Commander Milian explained the situation.

Commander Gladis's face turned every colour of the rainbow before he demanded an audience with the girl.

'And what is it you wish to discuss with her?' the smaller of the two Commanders asked.

'Oh, my sword will do all the discussing that needs to be done,' he sneered at the men.

'Do not forget, Gladis, that she is a member of the royal family, like it or not. Harming her will only be met with retaliation from the Rhino's should they discover your actions, you do not want that,' Commander Milian advised.

Theo'dor was now on board as to why the Rhinos were asked to leave the room before Commander Gladis was told about the girl's identity.

'Hmm, your right. Rhinos, can't get a whisper past that lot,' Commander Gladis announced, not happy but he understood he would have no power over the Rhinos in such a circumstance. He thought for a moment.

'I have it, you Captain… em?' he was looking at Dimator.

'Dimator… Ser,' Dimator replied coldly.

'Right, of course… you take this girl out of the city and remove her head from the rest of her and bury her where no one will think to find her, I don't care where, just make it happen, this very minute,' he shouted the last of his speech to emphasise the importance of his words as he walked away, leaving the three men to look at each other in disbelief.

Commander Gladis knocked on the door as the White Rhinos flanked him on either side.

'Enter,' the voice called from deep inside the room, Gladis lifted the heavy circular knob and rotated it clockwise a half turn, the door hinges sprang into action and the solid oak door swung easily open. Gladis instructed his escorts to remain out in the hallway.

'Commander,' the man in the poorly lit room stood to attention as he saw his visitor cross the doorway. If it wasn't for the small window in the centre of the outside wall, the room would have been in utter darkness.

Gladis closed the door gently and moved closer to the man.

'Need something taken care of,' Gladis said.

'With pleasure,' he replied, offering the Commander a nod. The man's face was stern and his hands were clasped behind his back. He stood straight and had the face of complete determination.

'I need you to follow this… Captain Dimator, make sure he kills the girl in his company and returns here at once,' Gladis ordered.

'It shall be done…' the dutiful servant replied. '…and should he not carry through with his instructions?' he asked.

'Then the Kingdom will no longer require the new Captain's services, if you understand me, Captain Hillas,' Gladis announced.

'Completely, Ser,' he replied.

Chapter 22
Man of the Mountains

The treacherous journey east had not been planned when he left the safety of The Two Glens all those weeks ago, he had been on an adventure, that was for sure.

At first the D'warfen folk that had practically kidnapped him, had not taken well to the bard. But, as time went on, he slowly won them over. They enjoyed his singing and even more so, they enjoyed making him the punchline of many of their jokes.

It was not long before the first of two reasons for his addition to the party was revealed. Zaltan told him that he was needed to carry the extra baggage due to the seventh member of the group taking too many knocks the night before at the brawl in the tavern. The poor man was bed ridden for at least a week and was unfit for the journey.

'A pack mule, you're using me as a pack mule?' Gormley replied aghast upon learning the information.

'Aye?' Zaltan had said, wondering why Gormley was not impressed with the honour.

'I've spent four years training at the bard's university in Whiterock and toured the continent for more than a decade, entertaining the world, not to mention a brief audience with Cronan, the High King of the Hindlands and…' Zaltan cut in to stop his ranting.

'We'll be paying ye an Eagle for yer troubles, laddie,' he had announced.

With that Gormley's mood changed on a six-pence. An Eagle was more than he could make singing the taverns and palaces of Gala' Mor in half a lifetime.

'Have I ever told you that pack-mulein' was an old hobby of mine, been meaning to get back into it,' he replied and Zaltan threw him a sideways grin.

Travelling through the mountains was never easy for the D'warfen, their height was an issue when trying to climb over obstacles that normal sized men had little difficulty with.

Of course, what they lacked in height they more than made up for in sheer strength and determination. Gormley had been impressed with their will to carry on when unplanned incidents occurred, like the time the youngest of the group, Haltan, had fallen and damaged his leg. Without thinking the others moved in to aid his walking and, on many occasions, they had to carry the man over slippery ice and uneven surfaces, and they did it all without a single complaint. They may have been a vertically challenged and grumpy race, but one thing was certain, they were united.

The first few days for Gormley had been a nightmare, not being accustomed to walking over such rough and cold terrain he was always asking for help and every question seemed to agitate his captors, for that was how he saw them.

They camped under trees the first night, lit a heartly looking fire and sat around it on stones and fallen debris. Their food was a humble helping of piping hot potato and leek soup, that one of the men had carried from the inn back at Winter's Peak, it wasn't much but it was food and more importantly, it warmed the blood.

As days turned to nights and weeks followed weeks, he adapted to life on the trail. Still, he missed his horse. He could see now how the D'warfen people had become so strong and ill tempered, anybody living this life couldn't help but be as such. Besides, he would have no use for a big animal up on the ridges of these mountains, some passes so narrow, he could scarcely find a safe footing on occasions.

'Not long now, laddie,' Zaltan said over his shoulder.

Gormely realised that he had not been told where their destination lies, and had given up inquiring as to how long the trek would take. He was kept in the dark to any kind of navigational information.

'Glad to hear it,' Gormley replied, excited to be reaching the end, although the fact that he had been given this same update for the past couple of days, lessened his enthusiasm.

'Be seeing the peak over yonder?' Zaltan announced while pointing to a rise that looked impossible to scale.

'Unfortunately, I do. I mean you can't miss it Zaltan, where does it lead to… the sky?' Gormley had learnt to answer their questions with wit, the trip became more tolerable than letting them get the better of him at every turn, Gormley believed the D'warfen appreciated this.

'Ha, if we were meant to fly, we wouldda been born with wings and not these strong little arms,' Zaltan joked, flapping his arms to see could he take to the air, it didn't work.

On they walked, through the passes and up the slopes.

When they got to a point where the ledge became so icy it was frightening to step upon, they tied a long rope to the entire group, slipping the rope through notches on each man's belt. It was a life-threatening moment when Gormley slipped and was taken over the edge by his own weight, he dangled freely for what seemed like a lifetime, helplessly swinging left and right, suspended over the jagged rocks hundreds of meters below, calling to him to come and join them, but the other's managed to pull him back over the ledge. He thanked them all profusely for their efforts.

He had started to wonder as to the true reason for his inclusion into the party, the D'warfen appeared capable of making the trip without him, his pack only contained blankets and extra clothes for the missing D'warfen for night time use, the only addition he made was at night when he sang the ages old D'warfen tales and stories by the campfire. They all revelled in his presents then, singing themselves, in rough voices and adding their own names to the heroes of old.

The climb up that final peak had not been enjoyable, but he was rewarded with a view that only a few eyes have ever set gaze upon. He wasn't sure if it was the forty degrees below or the sight before him that took his breath away. He stood and took it all in.

'Won't see that at The Two Glens, eh laddie?' Zaltan had called to him.

'It is incredible,' Gormley agreed.

It was only then that he spotted the huge round tower scraping the floor of the sky to the east. Towering high out of the mountains it was a structure so out of place he had to rub his eyes to make sure it was not an illusion. The top of the tower had a flat platform build into the stonework, there was something sitting on the top, it looked like a massive ballista that was pointing towards the east.

'Winter's Watch,' Zaltan announced seriously.

'That's where we're going?' Gormley asked.

'Aye, seems there's been activity 'cross the trench,' he replied and walked off, following his kinfolk down the far side of the peak they had just conquered.

'What... you can see into Great Harbour?' Gormley asked doubtfully.

'Aye, bout twenty miles into the belly of the wicked realm' another man answered, looking back at Gormley, Timot was his name.

'I thought nobody has seen inside there for decades, wait till I sing the tales of such an…' they all stopped and threw arrows at him with their eyes. Their forehead became ploughed fields full of wrinkles, their mouths thin hard lines and more than a few reached for their weapons.

'Okay, I see, I see… no songs it is,' Gormley quickly corrected his err before he was left in the cold on the side of a mountain where he would never be found again.

They were much quicker to descend the Widow's Friend, the name that the D'warfen had honoured the mountain with, 'not every mountain has a name ye know, only the fiercest,' Zaltan had revealed to him.

The tower was colossal at the base, made from huge flat grey stones cut form the mountain itself. Snow and ice covered the surrounding area as well as camouflaging the tower, it was why Gormley had not spotted the turret right off the bat, it blended perfectly into the white and grey scenery.

'How did you build such a thing?' Gormley queried, craning his neck to see the summit, it was impossible to locate as there was a heavy mist covering the tower from about the half way point.

'With these bare hands,' one of the D'warfen announced, holding his shaking hands up for Gormley to witness in case there was any doubt running through him that the man was jesting.

Gormley looked up at the structure and noticed that there were no windows, well none on the west side of the tower at least, if there were some higher up, he could not tell from the ground. Then he realised they were all standing there, just looking at the tower.

Gormley rubbed his hands and blew into them to fight off the bitter cold, he looked around again, now he noticed that there was no door. The D'warfen just stood there.

'Am, is there nobody home?' Gormley asked.

'Shhh,' one of the men replied. Faltan, he was a grumpy sort and Gormley obeyed immediately, not wanting to taste the quickness of the man's tongue again.

A stone moving slowly against stone scraping sounded from somewhere inside the tower, Gormley inspected the area that he believed the noise had originated. He was at the foot of the building while the others stood back.

'I think there's something moving inside here, can you hear it?' He called to them.

'Aye,' one of them answered, he looked at their grim faces but, he wasn't sure which one had spoken.

The noise got louder and Gormley felt the huge stones of the tower, considering that a secret opening would soon present itself, he was getting excited.

'It's definitely getting louder,' he announced as the D'warfen folk still remained at a distance and looked up, directly over his head.

'What… is… that?' a voice came from above him.

Gormley strained his neck and was met by a stranger standing on a ledge not ten feet from him. The new D'warfen was looking straight at Gormley, but was clearly addressing the other folk of the same kin.

Gormley had guessed correctly about there being a secret opening, although calculated wrongly as to where it might appear.

'Hello there,' he called up from the ground to the man on the ledge.

'Had to improvise, Saltan got into a spot of trouble the night 'fore we left Winter's Peak,' Zaltan replied to the man's question.

'I'll bet… did mead and singing have any part to play in his spot of trouble, eh?' the man replied knowingly.

'You know us too well, Rurin,' Zaltan laughed and the others joined in.

'World's fallen to sow dropping in a saucepan and you fine fellows think only of fillin' yer bellies with mead,' Rurin said beneath his breath.

'Can we be coming in sometime today?' Faltan hollered up to the man '…freezin' our sorry little scuts off in this frost,' he frowned, rubbing his hands against the cold.

'Aye, aye… don't get yer knickers in a twist,' the man returned.

A ladder came crashing down into the soft snow from the new entrance, almost catching Gormley in the leg.

'Ah, missed,' the man shouted from on high. The other D'warfen laughed at the attempted attack.

They climbed the steps inside the tower and it wasn't long before Gormley was feeling the strain. His legs had just carried him over snowy mountains and now he was expected to scale this monstrosity of a tower, without so much as a well-deserved nap or a cup of hot soup.

'How long to the top?' he assumed that was where they were heading, nobody took the time to inform him.

'Tried counting the steps a number of times laddie, got lost around the four thousand mark more than once,' Rurin called back to him.

'Four thousand steps,' Gormley announced flabbergasted.

'Aye, that be only 'bout halfway, I'll be thinking,' he finished with a sneer.

Gormley doubted he could make it that distance without a strong drink and a two-day rest in between.

Out of breath they scaled the final few steps and were greeted by a number of fully armoured D'warfen waiting for them at the end of the flight of steps. They were armed with bows, instead of the usual hammers and mallets that the small warriors had been accustomed to wielding. Gormley could not remember ever hearing of D'warfen using bows before, the large weapons were taller than their holders and looked oddly out of place in their hands.

'Took yer time,' one of the men greeted them.

'The tall one 'ere slowed us down something terrible,' Rurin commented and walked past the group of soldiers without another word. He opened the only door in the room, only to be met with a howling burst of wind and the entire room shivered in its presence.

The light flooded inside and Rurin crossed the threshold, the room slowly emptied and Gormley felt it best he joined the queue of exiting men. Outside the gale force wind almost knocked him over, he was now standing on the top platform of Winter's Watch. A huge ballista was sitting all alone and facing the eastern lands of Great Harbour.

They were huddled close together in the centre, which helped them to hear each other as they spoke.

'When were they sighted?' Zaltan enquired.

'Round about a month ago. Just to the west of that hill over there,' one of the men answered, Gormley did not see which one had spoken, but he followed all the men's gaze as they looked at a large hill covered with dead trees. He had never seen over the trench before, he thought nobody had, but somehow these D'warfen had built a lookout right into the abandoned lands of Great Harbour.

'Then we have orders?' Zaltan asked.

'Aye, we keep watch, for now. But anymore sightings and we breach and investigate without further delay,' the voice replied.

Chapter 23
Stranger in the Night

The moon was slowly ascending across the starless heavens as he sat on an upturned bucket beside the door of his small home. In his hands he played with a small vial, it contained a ruby red liquid that resembled more of a paste than a beverage. His thoughts went back to the fight at the Golden axe, all those weeks ago. The men he had killed and the ones he had not. He shook his head at all the troubles in the world as he remembered the band of outlaws had just robbed and more than likely killed an unnamed person or persons, to obtain all the coins that they were counting on the table in front of them, he was sick of it all.

'Nice night,' Sabat came strolling by.

'I prefer the stars; I see no beauty in the moon,' Sparrowhawk replied a little too frostily.

'Something vexing?' Sabat said cautiously.

'Forgive me, my friend. My mind is on far away matters,' Sparrowhawk apologised.

'It be a demanding few weeks, ye be causing me no ill will,' Sabat was a realist, he was not a people person, but he did enjoy Sparrowhawk's company and tried to keep that bond open.

'Still, we survived, didn't we?' Sparrowhawk tried to lighten the mood.

'Aye, supposing we did,' Sabat replied, and threw a fake smile to sweeten the deal.

Sparrowhawk did not notice the man was putting on a brave face. Sabat was concerned about the masked man in black that had managed to outwit his Ranger friend, and Sabat had never known a man to be as quick with his bow or his mind before. But this stranger who had captured him at Narrow's Crossing had done it with ease and that was something to think about.

'I have been thinking,' Sparrowhawk broke the heavy silence. 'I must track this man that seeks you,' he finished as if reading the man's thoughts without knowing it, with a nod to the skinny healer who had sat down on the ground beside him.

'Bah... ye be doing no such nonsense,' Sabat announced.

'We get him before he can get to you,' Sparrowhawk explained the logical tactic behind his idea.

'And how ye be tracking this man... tell me?' Sabat confronted him.

'I will ride back to the burned town and look for clues, he must have left tracks or something. If he did, I will discover them,' Sparrowhawk said with poise.

'Bah... a man like that be leaving nothing behind. Tracks... bah, ye be wasting yer time,' Sabat replied.

'I must try Sabat, why do you resist...' Sparrowhawk had not yet finished, but stopped as Rose had exited the house and greeted them warmly.

'I thought I heard voices, welcome Sabat... I will have soup, bread and dates ready in a few minutes, it is good to see you as always,' she said cheerfully.

When she returned back inside Sabat looked at Sparrowhawk with more seriousness than Sparrowhawk thought he possessed.

'That is why ye not be bothering 'bout old Sabat. This bugger, whoever he be, has saw fit to leave ye be, he has no interest in a washed-up Ranger, he hunts me,' Sabat said.

'I see,' Sparrowhawk replied.

'Aye... I will not be responsible for that girl losing her last parent, I could not live with it. So, no, birdman, I will face this man, not ye... ye would probably get in my way anyways,' Sabat replied with a rue smile.

Sparrowhawk returned the smile and said no more of it. Although, he had heard the words with his ears, he had felt them with his heart.

Sabat eased himself up and patted the Ranger on the top of the head. He started to walk away, back to his own lodgings.

'I just be hoping he don't come tonight, got me some work to finish afore morn, the bugger,' Sabat said and strolled off.

'Good night to you, may the moon stay still and light your path home,' Sparrowhawk called to him.

Sparrowhawk lifted himself up and went inside, the door rattling on the hinges as he closed it slowly.

'Where is Sabat?' Rose questioned her father.

'Said he can't stand your soup, so he snuck off before you had it ready,' he teased.

'No, he did not,' Rose laughed and looked at him with crossed arms and a crooked smile.

'Has an early start in the morning, gone to get some shut-eye,' Sparrowhawk replied honestly.

'Oh, well that's a more believable tale than the first one...' she replied. '...not like my soup, indeed,' she shook her head at the cheeky remark.

'Smells good,' he said, whiffing the air as the mixture of aromas pleasantly glided up his nostrils.

'Of course,' she replied with a hint of puzzlement.

'Looks good,' Sparrowhawk said as he sat on the wooden bench, looking into the deep bowl of a thick orange broth with flecks of greens and purples swimming across the surface.

'Of course,' she replied, a little mystified that it needed to be said.

She joined him on the bench and they both started to eat.

'What did Sabat want?' She asked astutely.

'I think he is concerned about the man at Narrow's Crossing. The one that got the jump on me,' he replied.

'And should he be?' she asked concerned. Sparrowhawk did not reply for a few minutes, he was deep in thought and Rose spooned a few more gulps in and let him ponder on the question.

'Maybe,' he said between mouthfuls.

They sat in silence for a time and Sparrowhawk pulled up his shirt to check the wound where the man had shot him with the arrow. It was completely healed.

'Have you ever known medicine to work so fast?' He asked his daughter.

'No, it is remarkable that you could ride all the way home from Narrow's Crossing after taking such an injury,' she replied, genuinely amazed at the masked man's healing abilities.

Another silence lasted for a time as they ate their late-night meal.

'You think that man can find Sabat?' Rose asked anxiously.

'Yes, I think he can,' Sparrowhawk replied woefully.

Sabat made it home after the long walk from Sparrowhawk's home to his own accommodation above a tavern. Two men, obviously after spending their wages sitting on a high stool, staggered out the door as he was just coming up to it.

'Cheat… ee, I never did…' the first man called to his mate.

'I saw yee with me own two eyes Daxos… sure yee went an' spilled have the third tankard all over the floor… yee donkey's breath yee,' his friend alleged.

'Lies… ee never spilled a drop… ee didn't,' the man was horrified at the accusations.

Sabat had to step to the side to allow the men past.

'Ser, I apologise… but did ye see ee spill a drop,' Daxos asked Sabat as he wobbled back and forth like a flagpole on a windy day.

'That's right… we have a witness… now,' the second man declared, he had a full bushy beard and no hair on his head although he was quite young. Sabat frowned at the pair and just wanted to get past them and go to bed.

'I didn't see ye spill anything,' Sabat replied honestly and walked slowly past the two men.

Daxos let out a triumphant roar with his hands punching the evening air.

The other man was deflated but conceded defeat and said something about beating Daxos the next time.

Sabat closed the door behind him and walked across the hardwood floorboards on his way to the door on the far side, stepping over a huge puddle on his way. The tavern was near empty with just the usual nobodies sitting in their usual places, looking glum and miserable. He greeted the barkeep with a nod and disappeared behind the inner door that led to a hall, at the end of the hall was the old rickety stairs that led to the upper bedroom.

Sabat guessed the stairs was twice his own age, every step was an adventure, as he clung on to the wobbly handrail for dear life, he was sure it would choose this moment when he was just nearing the top to collapse. Luckily, he made it and the steps remained intact, for another while at least.

His room was the only one upstairs, the rest were on the ground floor. It was not a big room, so it was cheap and besides, he didn't need much space to make his potions and elixirs. He fell down upon the chair at his table which was just under the window, the window itself was set in the west facing wall so the moonlight came flooding in and cast enough light for him to work with.

Sabat had entered the market the day after he arrived in Whiterock and sniffed out where the city healers sold their wares. He struck a deal with a man, after much haggling, telling him he could make everything on his table for a fraction of the price. The mam at first was sceptical as was his way, but Sabat had told him that he would make the medicines and take only a small fee for himself, he wanted to get his foot in the door and the large bearded gent agreed to give Sabat a trial run. The deadline was in the morning.

Mixing the last of the herbs in his mortar and pestle, he relaxed against the back of the chair, he did not see the man standing in the shadows in the corner of the room.

Sabat ground up the mixture into a paste and added some water to the bowl, he finished by pouring the contents into a vial that was waiting patiently on his table. He popped the cork lid into place and lay the full vial beside the others, he had produced thirty in all, that was the target the healer in the market had set, he barely reached it, but it was done.

Slowly he raised himself to his feet satisfied at his work, he knew the trader would be delighted with his efforts, his own product was far superior to the ones he had for sale, and at the new lower price, they would both benefit from their business arrangement.

He climbed into the bed without thinking and rested easily on the straw pillow, he closed his eyes, confident things were finally looking up.

The man in black had waited for a few minutes until Sabat had settled himself into a light sleep, it was then he approached the bed and silently slid the sword with the black blade out of its scabbard. Raising it above Sabat he was poised to strike, just as he was about to lower the sword into his target a very smooth arrow thudded into his chest, right where his heart used to beat. He looked at the doorway and saw the Ranger from Narrow's Crossing, then he saw nothing.

Sabat rose like a rattlesnake as the body hit the creaky floorboards, he looked at the dead man lying on the ground beside his bed and noticed the shaft, he recognised the feathers.

Looking towards the door he found Sparrowhawk with a serious demeanour plastered upon his face, and immediately realised what had happened.

'Ye could o' knocked…' Sabat frowned, '…waking a man with such a racket,' he shook his head.

'Get in your way, would I?' Sparrowhawk grinned, he wasn't expecting a thank you or anything of the likes. He strolled slowly into the room and went to inspect the assassin.

Sparrowhawk bend down to get a closer look, removing his mask, Sabat gasped as he spotted the strange tattoo on the man's chin and cheeks.

'Friend of yours?' Sparrowhawk quizzed.

'Knight of Alchemy,' Sabat replied soberly.

'Knight of who?' Sparrowhawk pressed for more information.

'The Alchemy Circle...' Sabat began. '...they be the keepers of the secrets of all healers,' Sabat announced.

'There is such a thing?' Sparrowhawk asked.

'Of course, there be such a thing, although their influence has not yet reached Gala' Mor, they preside mainly throughout the Halti Empire, they take their matters very seriously,' he finished very seriously.

'So, why do they seek to kill you?' Sparrowhawk looked suspiciously at the man.

Sabat froze for a moment, seemingly gathering his thoughts.

'The blade,' Sabat said finally.

Sparrowhawk picked it up, twisted it around in his hand to inspect the craftmanship. From a distance it appeared beautiful and deadly, up close and personal, it proved flawless.

'What is it?' Sparrowhawk asked, intrigued by its mesmerising hold over him.

'Obsidian...' Sabat replied. '...one of a kind, seven times sharper than yer own steel, an,' it be twice as strong.'

'That's why this Knight of... alchemy, was after you?' Sparrowhawk asked.

'It would appear so, Ranger, looks like the Circle be tying up some loose ends, getting rid of anyone that knows about it,' Sabat replied.

'And how do you know about it?' Sparrowhawk asked in a friendly tone.

'I was there when it was made, I helped with the crafting...' Sabat stopped '...or rather Bianca did, she knew about such things, she did,' Sabat fought back the tears at her memory.

They both looked at each other, neither knew what they should say.

'How did ye know he be here?' Sabat asked to break the silence.

'I didn't really, I was returning this vial, Rose finished her medicine, she thought you may want it back. When I got here, I noticed a tall black horse with a full white face outside,' Sparrowhawk said as if Sabat knew what that was supposed to mean.

'Hehe, t'was me vial that saved her and t'was her giving me back the vial what saved me in return, we can call it even, me thinks,' Sabat bobbed his head up and down and smiled.

Chapter 24
Meadow's Home

'What, by all the fish in the Old Salt are we going to do now?' Theo'dor said to the Captain as they walked back towards the keep.

'*Princess… how did she survive all this time alone?*' His mind was pulling in too many directions all at once.

'We can't kill her… can we?' Theo'dor asked, and again he was ignored.

'*The forest kept her alive, her parents must have taught her to survive, but where are they… dead, she said we killed them,*' Dimator was trying to solve this riddle and by the Seven Kingdoms, he would work it out.

'I mean, killing her would mean our own heads resting on the block, wouldn't it?' Theo'dor had accepted the fact the Captain was in another world, but he too was dealing with their situation the best way he knew how.

'*Who killed her parents… she said we did, does she mean soldiers, our soldiers? Why?*' He didn't know what to think.

'I have it, we replace her with a double, a decoy. Then we shall have our own royal puppet in the palace,' Theo'dor was of course speaking without thinking, just running his mouth, after all nobody was listening.

The heavy outer door to the keep was strangely locked, so Dimator knocked loudly.

'State your business?' The jailer's voice shouted out at them.

'What?' Dimator shouted back, baffled.

'What do you want?' The jailer raised his tone impatiently.

'Come to collect prisoner for relocation,' Dimator replied.

'Which prisoner and state your name and rank?' The jailer called.

'Are you serious?' Dimator replied.

'Look, ever since the attempted escape of an inmate, the King's Guard has decided to implement these new precautionary measures. So, who are you and who do you want?' The jailer's answer came with a hint of frustration.

'Captain Dimator and we've come for the girl who can't speak,' he replied, raising an eyebrow to Theo'dor.

'Which girl who can't speak?' The jailer returned.

'How many blooming girls have you got in there that can't speak,' Dimator was getting annoyed.

'Oh… right,' the voice replied.

The heavy wooden door with iron bars running vertically through it opened slowly.

'Well, you can take her, sooner the better I say,' the big jailer said as the two men walked past him into the prison, the bridge of his nose slightly off centre after his kiss with the wall.

'Ah look who's up…' Theo'dor said as they passed by Long-tooth's cell.

'Who ye be setting those eyes upon?' He called a useless threat at them.

'Be setting these eyes on you soon, watching that ugly head bounce all the way down from the scaffolds come your time at the King's court,' the jailer called to Long-tooth and started into a fit of laughs.

'Tell her that we're bringing her for a little trip,' Dimator said directly to Theo'dor.

After an extensive exchange with the tone getting a little too heated at times, Theo'dor said she agreed to go.

They passed through the overflowing city on horseback as people were in a state of panic at the news of more towns inside their borders being attacked and some even destroyed. People had family in those towns and were not happy about the lack of action from the palace. Many lined the streets with pitchforks and old weapons ready to march towards the upper town and straight for the palace itself, looking for answers. The city was in a chaotic state and Dimator did not blame them.

When they finally snail paced their way to the main gate it took an age to pass through, the area immediately outside the city walls was ten times worse than inside. Hundreds upon hundreds, had made camp under the shadow of the great city, pleading for entry before the Kor' Cali arrived on their doorstep.

'We ride east,' Dimator announced to Theo'dor over the shouting of the throngs of peasants, many grabbing at them as they kicked their way through the mob.

They were a couple of hundred meters out of view of the city when Theo'dor noticed an eagle flying overhead, it was unusual but he thought the bird was watching them and even keeping pace with them. He kept this to himself, no need to get an already disgruntled Dimator, even more disgruntled, he had enough on his plate at the moment.

Meadow was tied to Theo'dor's horse in a sitting position, she found it easy to balance herself on the hefty animal as Theo'dor ran her across the valley.

She knew they were heading east, that would bring her back to her forest, her home. But she doubted that they would make it that far, she guessed they would be stopping somewhere along the way, and she guessed the reason as she noticed the one in charge was wearing a sword again, he had not worn it at any other time she had seen him inside the city. Was he expecting trouble or would he be using it to rid himself of a certain small problem he had kidnapped not long ago?

It was getting past midday as the sun gave away the time.

They reached a small grove, just off from the main road into the next small town, Dimator forgot the name. It was a shaded area and offered a few fallen trees to rest upon, it was as good a place as any to get it over with. He had used this spot before; it was not far from the Evergreen and was an ideal spot to set up camp when away from the Walled City.

They dismounted their horses and took the girl down, her hands still bound, she stood looking at them through clumps of hazel hair that flowed down over her face.

Theo'dor had dreaded this moment, but he knew the Captain would follow the orders given to him by his superior. Dimator was a career soldier and didn't care much for the girl to begin with, he was probably looking forward to ending her.

'Tell her to go home, never to return. Tell her if she does not stay in the Evergreen, I will hunt her down myself and redden my blade with her lifeblood,' Dimator didn't look at either of them, he was focused on something in the distance.

Theo'dor didn't ask any questions; he scribbled for a time and then spoke to the girl. Another altercation ensued, but finally Dimator heard her light footsteps, getting fainter and fainter.

'Probably for the best,' Theo'dor announced trying to comfort the Captain as best he could.

'Killing the only surviving cousin of the King, boy or not, might hold a heavy cost if it was ever discovered she was killed like a lamb to the chopping board...,' Theo'dor used common sense to convince Dimator the correct course of action was chosen '...and, I heard the Rhinos have their spies everywhere. I mean who wants to live their lives constantly looking over their shoulder,' he added.

'We ride, let's move,' Dimator announced and darted over to his horse. Theo'dor followed suit and they were heading after the girl in a heartbeat.

After a while it dawned on Theo'dor what might be happening, he was a genius in the classroom, give him a forgotten language to translate and he'd be in his element, but war games and survival in the wild, well, he was still just a novice and only learning the trade.

'Are we being followed?' He shouted to Dimator.

'I am afraid so,' the Captain replied.

Theo'dor looked back, but could see nobody on the horizon, not even the eagle that had been tailing them ever since they left Whiterock.

'We need to protect the girl; I have a feeling the old Commander didn't quite trust us to complete our mission,' Dimator called.

'The cheek,' Theo'dor answered, highly insulted.

It wasn't long before they caught up on Meadow, she had heard them coming and was standing beside a low stone wall. Theo'dor explained the situation as best he could without the time to jot down every word he needed and she seemed to understand, although did not look happy about it.

Then he saw them, coming over the rise, the blue sky at their backs.

'Maybe ten or twelve, we will lose them in the Evergreen, it's not far,' Dimator announced.

They rode hard with the pursuers not giving up the chase as they crossed over a stream and up another slope, the forest was just in view.

'Ha, we're going to make it, the trees will make for an excellent hiding place,' Theo'dor called, reassuring himself more than anything.

The men chasing them had gained much ground and were only about thirty meters behind. They would have made the forest only for the Kor' Cali troops that had appeared out from the treeline directly in front of them.

'Turnip heads?' Theo'dor called.

'Must be a hundred of them,' Dimator answered.

Dimator looked back at the men coming up the rear, they were getting too close, he knew what they had in mind and was pretty sure the unit of highly armed soldiers in front would be of a similar deposition. Any doubt was wiped away as the troops standing just outside the forest quickly stepped into formation and readied their long bows. At this distance however, Dimator was sure they were out of range.

'Best take our chances with the Commander's men, it means certain dead to get any closer to the woods,' Dimator announced.

Theo'dor looked around, he was calculating the distance, wind speed, high elevation and the pace of their horses.

'No, ride straight for them, they'll miss,' Theo'dor replied.

'Excuse me?' Dimator replied, with a look as if Theo'dor had just exploded into a million pieces.

'I've done the research, trust me,' and he took off towards the waiting archers. Dimator saw who was chasing them, it was the Captain from the meeting that had looked oddly at Commander Gladis, quickly he followed Theo'dor heading for the enemy soldiers.

As Dimator reigned in beside the two on the other horse, he called to Theo'dor 'I hope you know what you are doing' and took the lead.

The volley of arrows came rocketing towards them, Dimator looked up and saw the tiny streaks flying through the air, soring high and then curving to come thundering down upon them from the heavens without mercy.

He lowered his head just as the shafts were about to hit, but nothing pierced through his chest and sent him thumbling to the hard speeding ground. He looked behind and saw ten or twelve horses and men lying dead in the dirt, riddled with the long shafts.

'They missed,' Dimator announced.

Theo'dor had not doubted it for a second and threw him a boastful smile.

The archers were reloading.

'We only get lucky once, they'll adjust to our speed, cut to the left as soon as they let fly,' Theo'dor advised, Dimator had passed command over to him without a word and nodded his compliance.

The arrows left the bows and immediately both horses darted effortlessly to the left, they were aiming to cut into the trees before the enemy came marching after them.

The shafts landed pitifully into the ground as the riders entered the treeline, out of range of the firing squad.

It wasn't long before they had to dismount as the forest was too thick and overgrown for the horses to get through comfortably.

'Leave them…' Dimator, resuming charge, ordered. '…we'll make more ground on-foot, they will be looking for us, now they know we are here.'

They dismounted quickly and slapped the horses away, hopefully they would return to Whiterock and the guards at the gates would recognise them as soldier's horses, though he doubted they would get that far, someone waiting outside the city was sure to take them.

'Which way?' Theo'dor called looking about the trees as if each direction could lead to their escape or capture.

'Head into the trees for now, we must get as much distance between us and the turnip heads as possible,' Dimator replied. 'And good work back there, with the archers, I mean,' Dimator offered. '*Seems the boy can be trusted after all*,' he thought.

'All in a day's work,' Theo'dor replied.

Dimator led them hastily through the trees as Theo'dor took up the rear, keeping the girl between them at all times. Her hands no longer bound, they were all in the same boat now, plus it would make for a slower escape if she was restricted in any way.

'What are they doing here?' Dimator asked to nobody in particular.

'Balltimor sent regiments into Gala' Mor, so our army would look for them, that's why they burned the towns, hoping the main force at the Blackwater would thin out and leave their position. Giving them a huge advantage to take the Blackwater,' Theo'dor replied.

Dimator looked at him aghast.

'It would be easy to slip men behind the lines because our main focus was on holding the river, we wouldn't expect a move such as this and more so, we would not be prepared to deal with it in time,' Theo'dor added.

'Makes sense…' he confirmed. '…but, in time for what?' Dimator asked.

'Stands to reason with our numbers dwindling at the Blackwater, we will have to fall back to Whiterock, it's the city that controls the Kingdom. I think Balltimor is pushing for a move on the capital and with his men this close… it looks to be coming soon,' Theo'dor said grimly.

Dimator shook his head at the news and wondered why he hadn't considered it before.

They moved deeper in to the trees; the girl did not speak or make any signs that she wanted to escape. They ate berries and roots that Meadow indicated were safe to consume.

It would be getting dark soon, Dimator was on the lookout for a place to camp, just as he was checking the sturdiness of a fallen tree a soldier dressed all in black came rushing at him from behind some thick bushes.

'Get back,' he called to Theo'dor.

The man came with his sword drawn and was raising it for a swing at Dimator's head, but the Captain saw it coming and ducked under the attempt and came up with an uppercut to the man's chin. It knocked him back momentarily, but he was a big lad, so he shook it off and came again. Dimator unsheathed his own blade and met the man steel on steel, a hiss ran through the trees as the blades slipped apart.

They circled each other for a moment, then the soldier came in again, swiping low twice, but Dimator was equal to the man and parried him easily. Dimator heard the footsteps of another soldier, but did not look up as it would give his present enemy a few seconds to get another swing in, instead Dimator moved forward ignoring the footsteps and quickly lunged at his attacker, catching him in the shoulder, quickly he retracted his blade and the man fell to his knees.

The second man was in the fray before Dimator could finish the first, he came quickly but mistimed his blow and Dimator ducked to his right, the man had swung too wildly and his momentum spun him around in a wide circle, Dimator spotted the mistake and quickly moved in to the man's left side and sliced low to rip a long gash across his stomach, he fell grasping at the open wound.

'Move,' Dimator called to his companions.

A third man came from the other side and Dimator moved to meet him, sword in hand.

The man was eager and attacked first, Dimator stepped back with the blade missing his face by inches. The soldier swung the blade in a reverse attempt, hoping to catch Dimator off-guard, but the captain had trained too long and too hard over the years to fall prey to such a move and parried the steel with his own, giving him enough time to step inside the soldiers reach and took him cleanly in the chest with a quick lunge, using only half the normal pressure to puncture the heart. The man dropped dead into the ivy below.

He caught up to Theo'dor and Meadow in a few moments, stepping over two new dead soldiers on the way.

'What happened?' Dimator asked stunned, referring to the dead soldiers.

'Alsamat, happened' Theo'dor announced.

'What's an Alsamat?' Dimator asked panting while looking constantly around him for his next assailant.

'My tutor, he taught me poetry, arithmetic and Lu po' Theo'dor replied calmly.

'Okay fine, let's just Lu po out of here and we'll discuss those two dead soldiers later,' Dimator said and started to move.

'Captain?' Theo'dor hissed.

'What?' Dimator replied, turning around to see what the problem was now.

'She's pointing that way,' Theo'dor indicated the girl, Dimator looked down.

Meadow had a stone-cold face and was pointing to the south of the forest.

Dimator thought for a second.

'It's her forest, Ser,' Theo'dor said thinking the girl might have a plan.

'Your hut…?' Dimator said to Meadow. '…ask her,' Dimator said to Theo'dor.

'She says we will be safer there,' Theo'dor nodded as he replied when finished speaking with the girl.

'Hey, I didn't require the feather, I'm getting the hang of this,' he said proudly.

Dimator remembered his last visit to the clearing where the girl lived and had no desire to return to that place *'She only attacked us because we posed a threat to her… it's the Kor' Cali that are the enemy now,'* he realised.

'Ok, we follow her,' Dimator moved aside to allow the girl to pass him and show them the way.

They could hear footsteps coming from all directions and voices called to where the three were heading, the soldiers were homing in on their prey.

The clearing was just past the next few trees when another soldier caught up to them. The man had an eight-foot spear and small buckler shield. Meadow jumped to the side as Dimator came forward to greet the man with his sword. The soldier had the greater reach and used it to his advantage, he had steadied himself with his feet apart and was hunched down to make himself a smaller target, his spear came poking at Dimator in a flurry of rapid darts.

Dimator had turned his body sideways to make himself a more difficult target, it was easier to dodge the oncoming attacks as he stepped from side to side. Although he was avoiding the soldier's lunges, he had no way to safely advance on the man without risking taking that shiny spear in the side. They danced around in a circle for a time, the soldier coming close once too many. Without warning Theo'dor was behind the soldier and slipped inside the man's reach, grabbed him around the neck and the soldier fell to the ground three seconds later, unmoving.

Dimator looked astounded at Theo'dor who was standing over the body of the soldier.

'Lu po,' Theo'dor announced to the stunned Captain.

Meadow darted out from behind the tree she was hiding behind as a group of soldiers came running at them, she ran between the men who were still staring at each other and headed into the clearing.

'Too many, run, follow the girl,' Dimator called and they made their way into the spot where Dimator had first met the girl.

Soldiers were closing in from all directions, shouting instructions at each other to encircle them.

It wasn't long before they were the honey in the sweet-roll, completely surrounded on all sides. Their shiny weapons were drawn and it would only be a matter of time before they closed the ring. They sported mean faces, it must have been a tough trek through the forest for them, for they had travelled through the entire Evergreen to get this far west into Gala' Mor, they were tired, angry and ready to fight.

'There is no escape,' a voice boomed at them as the tall officer stepped forward.

'Escape? We were not trying to escape,' Dimator called back to the man wearing the metal helmet that sported a small sphere that sloped into a point sticking upwards towards the sky, resembling an upside-down turnip.

'Ha, running away like scared children, cowards. Kor' Cali do not flee the battlefield; they stand to the last man,' the officer spread his arms wide to show the great strength of his men.

'When we are finished with you, we will topple the great Walled City, bah,' he scoffed at the mention of the name.

With all the troops now facing the trio in the centre, nobody spotted the bear among the trees, watching them and listening.

'And you bring a girl with you to battle, ha. Fools one and all, you coward Gala' Mor peasants, you're not fit to stain my blade,' he laughed and his men joined in on the joke.

'It is not us who brings the girl to battle, but the girl who brings us,' Dimator announced to the entire forest and handed her the whistle.

The officer stared in delighted wonder at the girl as she held the small timber object to her lips and blew a single loud shrill. He cupped his ear with his hands to block out the eerie sound and laughed heartly when the sound died off in the distance. They all laughed and let their guard down as they believe they were in no danger.

With all their attention on the unlikely trio, nobody thought there was a threat from behind, but as the huge bear hit the rear of the troops, mass confusion set in.

The livid animal came thundering into their ranks with ferocious speed and power, he sent troops collapsing to the floor with his strong claws and body, they panicked and began to fall out of line, embracing a kind of 'every man for himself' stance.

The bear roared and rose up on two legs, towering above them, the whole troop of men seemed to be frozen in place looking up at the frenzied animal, their eyes wide and their mouths gaping. The bear dropped down on all fours and charged at a man who brought his shield into play too late as a huge claw took him in the chest and sent him head over heels into his friends, knocking a number of them aside, the bear continued into the heart of the troop looking for his next victim.

The officer was quick to react, after the initial shock wore off, he was ordering troops back into position, calling at them to encircle the creature, they were quick to comply and it wasn't long before the bear was surrounded and being attacked on all sides. The soldiers had formed a shield wall encircling the bear and their spears were levelled, punching holes in his thick fur.

More troops had fallen in behind the men with the shields to add their own spears over their comrades' shoulders which made the shields more stable with the second and third rows coming in to add their strength.

Within a few more moments the bear was down and the soldiers were cheering their victory. The officer gasped for breath and wondered where the creature had come from, then he realised what had happened '*The girl with the whistle,*' he thought. He spun around to where the three people he was chasing were standing, they were gone.

'Find them… spread out, I want them alive,' the officer called.

The troops were just catching their breath and gathering themselves together after the strange battle. There would be no time for trophies today.

The men were starting to obey the officer's command when another soldier approached him.

'Ser, permission to speak?' The man said, somewhat nervously.

'Speak, Logan,' the officer replied.

'We are already behind after looking for them all day, the other units will be nearing Whiterock as we speak, do we have time to search this wretched forest for three strays?' Logan asked respectfully.

The officer looked at his dead and wounded troops, he wanted to capture those three more than anything, but Logan had made a valid point, if they delayed any longer, he risked arriving too late at the Walled City with his unit and Balltimor would not be impressed with him. On second thoughts, he valued his life more than catching the three fugitives.

'Form up, we move to Whiterock,' he called to his men and nodded his thanks to Logan.

The Kor' Cali had moved on; the forest was still and the girl along with her two companions climbed out of the hut that she once called home. In her hands she held a small rabbit with two perfectly good ears, he darted away as she let the creature down.

They watched her walk slowly through the bodies, not paying them any heed. She only stopped when she came close to the bear.

Dimator looked around at the clearing that he had been to once before, not too long ago. He had harboured different feelings about the girl then. The enemy had left their dead behind, like he had done, he wondered would they come to collect them when they had time like his own people had done with their fallen soldiers or just leave them here for the animals.

Theo'dor who had been closer to the girl now approached Dimator.

'His name was Koda,' he said referring to the bear.

'She named them?' Dimator replied perplexed.

'They were her family, they protected her…' Theo'dor said sadly. '…and they protected us,' he finished with a nod of his head.

The girl rose with tears streaming down her face, she looked around and gathered it all in. All the death and destruction these beast-men had brought to her home, her parents had warned her of this *'The day would come when they will come for you... be ready my little wolf,'* her father had told her.

'What now?' Theo'dor whispered to Dimator.

The girl turned to face them, they looked at her and for the first time they saw in her eyes something that had not been there before. It was a determination of will that no small girl should have in her.

'Har ala tour,' she said with a sheer resolve that no man would stand against as she walked on towards the trees, stepping over bodies and weapons.

'What did she say?' Dimator asked.

'She said she is going home,' Theo'dor replied.

'She is home,' Dimator said slightly puzzled looking around at the forest.

'No, she does not call this place home. Remember, she called Whiterock her home,' Theo'dor explained.

Chapter 25
Enemy at the Gates

It had been four days since all the soldiers stationed at the Blackwater had been called home, three days had passed since the city had been opened to let all the people inside the safety of her high walls and two days ago the Kor' Cali had come to the gates of Whiterock.

'A bold move…' the Commander announced. '…I'll give them that,' he finished as he stood before the High Council. They had listened to him explain the situation and the lead up to the siege of Whiterock, but what they really desired was options.

All six members were present, as too was the King, his Commanders and all their Captains, except for four, who were spread out throughout the Kingdom investigating the enemy units that were burning entire towns to the ground, now they all knew what was behind it.

'Indeed Gladis, but what do we have in the way of retaliation, we mean to end this siege before these blaggards start to think they can take this city,' one of the council members barked.

'They'll not set a toe inside our walls, let alone take anything,' the Commander replied.

'We have enough food to last three months, the underground well has been opened and our archers can keep them back for as long as it takes for them to get sick of waiting on their behinds,' a very finely dressed man sitting at the council called.

'We have enough food for three months, but only with normal capacity, we have taken in hundreds of extra people in the last few days that will eat into our stock pile and rapidly reduce that time frame to about two months if we are lucky and enforce strict rations,' a Captain with long shoulder length hair commented.

Sparrowhawk stood in the room and took in all the information that was going back and forth. He still did not understand as to why he had been summoned to the palace for the emergency council meeting, he was after all the lowest ranking man in the room, but then that would be easy as he had no rank to begin with.

'Our archers will only be effective for a short time; the enemy has begun chopping down the trees in the forests and are manufacturing siege weapons and large tunnel shields to get them within range for their own archers' another anxious voice added.

'And, I heard reports coming in that they are manufacturing a battering ram of sorts' another voice added.

'What are our numbers, Commander?' The first council member asked.

'Well Mr D'Souza, we have about twelve thousand standing troops inside the walls, most of whom are battle tested and ready to deploy in a moment's notice. The archers on the walls come in at about eight hundred and fifty and our count of trainee recruits is at a strong three hundred,' Milian announced perfectly, he had made a note of the numbers before entering the room.

'And Balltimor?' the merchant inquired.

'We cannot say for certain… more units arrive every day, but at the moment we count, somewhere between seven to eight thousand troops, mostly heavily armed infantry. No horse whatsoever and only lightly armoured archers,' Milian was proud of his attention to detail.

'Then we outnumber them, that's a positive at least,' Anton D'Souza said with a hint of hope shining in his voice.

'It is for now, but our walls are our best defence at the moment. Walking out there with our blood up might just be our undoing, we play it safe until we know more,' Commander Gladis called loudly.

The room was in agreement with the tall Commander save a few anxious Captains who believe they should attack at dawn. Milian turned towards the King, who had remained silent since he had entered the room.

'Your majesty, I propose we see what the enemy's plans are before we make any of our own to attack,' Milian said, Armando nodded his consent.

'It is decided then, we wait, for as long as possible…' Milian announced and the motion was carried. '…keep your men on constant stand-by Captains, we may need them at the drop of a pin if Balltimor launches an attack without warning, double… no treble alert to all soldiers inside the walls,' Milian ordered.

'What of our men outside the walls, the ones that were looking for these units, what news do we have of them?' A small tubby council member inquired.

'We have no contact with them as the Kor' Cali have blocked all information coming in and out of the city. No doubt they will have heard of the siege and will be lying in wait to see how events unfold,' Milian replied.

'How many men were outside when the turnip heads showed up?' The stubby man asked.

'Four units with fifty men each, a good number of capable men to be without, when the time comes,' Milian replied coldly.

'If we could get word to them somehow?' Anton D'Souza said.

'That is exactly what we propose to achieve,' Milian replied.

'Ranger, step forward,' he called and all eyes landed on the ageing man in the back of the room, more than a few grey flecks appearing in his charcoal hair, who nobody had paid much attention to.

'Ser?' Sparrowhawk said and came slowly to the front of the room where everybody who mattered in the city could inspect him, most were unimpressed.

'Ranger, you have succeeded us in the past, you will do so again…' Milian started confidently. '…there is a passage under the palace, an emergency escape tunnel built at the time of the palace's construction for extracting the royal family if the need ever came,' Milian looked at the young king.

'It is with permission from his majesty that the tunnel be used now…' looking around the room he continued, '…Sparrowhawk, you will traverse this tunnel that leads under the city walls and beyond the Kor' Cali. You will find our troops and inform them of our situation. You will tell them to watch the skies above the city, when they see a blue flag being hoisted from the palace's east tower, it will be the signal to attack. The Kor' Cali will not be expecting a charge from the rear, it is most likely that their archers will be at this position, take them out and continue on through their ranks until there is nobody left to fight,' the Commander spoke clearly.

'Ser, it will be done,' Sparrowhawk replied.

'We cannot rest the cities hopes on this man's shoulders, I will send one of my own men, they will not fail,' Gladis interrupted.

'This man knows the land, he knows how to find people, we have all seen that, Commander Gladis. He is our best hope to locate our troops,' Milian defended his choice.

'Bah, he will likely show the turnip heads the entrance to the tunnel for a handful of quick owls, all his kind think only of themselves,' Gladis retorted.

'He will do no such thing; this man can be trusted,' Milian's voice had raised to a commanding level. The rest of the room was beginning to take sides in the debate.

'Trusted, I wouldn't trust my dog with him, my men are trained for this kind of endeavour, they remain our best hope. I for one am a man of…' Gladis was cut off.

'Sparrowhawk will go,' the King announced loudly, but without emotion. The room fell silent and Gladis was uncharacteristically at a loss for words, his disliking for the Ranger was evident, but the King had made a decision, there was nothing he could do.

'You leave now,' Armando called to Sparrowhawk.

The Ranger gave the King a bow and left the room, followed by one of the King's Rhino's as Armando gestured for the guard to go with him.

'I call an end to this meeting; we recess until this time tomorrow,' Milian announced clearly and the meeting promptly broke up with much discussion and chatter.

Sparrowhawk was led down to the basement of the palace where a series of large rooms of Rhinos were stationed. There must have been a few hundred of them and Sparrowhawk was in awe of the huge guards. They looked like they were preparing themselves for something, but he couldn't guess what.

It was a lengthy walk down all the narrow corridors and hallways, he never knew a building could be so massive.

As he was ushered into the back of a room, some Rhino's stepped out of his path as he came forward. The one who had accompanied Sparrowhawk bent down and slid a rug out of the way, Sparrowhawk had not even noticed the rug before as it was the exact same colour as the floor underneath, there was also a timber design on the rug that tied in perfectly with the hardwood floorboards.

A heavy looking ring pull was embedded into the timber as not to be noticed from under the rug, the Rhino grabbed the metal handle and pulled a section of the floor up into the room. It was on hinges and some kind of spring mechanism, leaving a gaping hole in the floor.

A freezing gust of wind came swirling up through the dark hole in the floor and a foul damp smell soon followed into the room.

Sparrowhawk looked into the hole and saw a flight of stairs leading down into the darkness.

'Take this' one of the Rhino's said and handed him a torch, where he got it from, Sparrowhawk did not see. He took the lit torch from the guard and nodded his thanks.

'Go straight all the way, do not deviate from the path,' the Rhino advised.

'Straight, okay I understand,' Sparrowhawk replied.

'See that you do, the other paths are full of traps… very… sharp… traps,' the Rhino said seriously.

'Very sharp traps in a very dark tunnel… that lead somewhere, excellent,' Sparrowhawk replied and took the steps leading downwards into the underground.

It was a long walk before he reached the other end of the tunnel, he was exhausted and hungry by the time he heard what sounded like water falling in great gushes. Then as he got closer, he realised that the exit to the tunnel was hidden behind a thundering waterfall.

There were pictures drawn on the stones just inside the entrance, probably drawn by a child years ago and a small toy soldier carved from the bark of a tree was sitting patiently for his 'Captain' to come back. Sparrowhawk hoped his owner had not ventured down one of the side tunnels, looking for adventure.

From the inside of the tunnel, he could not see clearly what lay on the other side nor could he tell how far the drop into the pool below was, he would have to risk all and jump, hoping that the engineers of the secret escape route had consider that whomever was using the tunnel would realise that a jump would be required and a safe distance was calculated into its construction.

The slash of the water falling sounded like there was not too much distance left to reach the pool, but it was a leap of faith whichever way he looked at it, so he jumped.

He knew that by over jumping he might clear the deep pool below and land in shallower waters, so he stepped out easily and came down with the falling water, he hit the pool in a matter of seconds, he had guessed correctly and the exit to the tunnel was only a few feet above the deepest part of the water. He did not notice that something slipped out of his pocket as he hit the water below, the small vial sank to the bottom of the pool.

He allowed the water to slowly carry him down stream and swam to the shore as soon as the bank was low enough to scale. He was lucky in the sense that the water was clear and fresh. As he pulled himself up the bank, aided by the roots of a tree that were waiting for him, he looked around and listened for a few moments. He was in an area covered with dense trees, the sky above was covered with branches and leaves and the usual sounds of the woods greeted him kindly.

It wasn't long before he was picking berries and tearing leaves from the foliage to quiet his belly groans and regenerate some energy into his bones and muscles, without Rogue to aid him, he would need all the help that nature had to offer.

The waterfall had been an unexpected hazard he had to deal with, unfortunately he was now soaking wet with no proper means to dry his seeping clothes. This would not be too much of a setback during the day, but as night rolled in, it would bring with it the colder air. The brilliant sun was overhead and the air was warm, this would be especially helpful to dry out the wet clothes, he doubted there was much risk freezing to death.

The wooded region he had found himself in was a small overgrown patch just south of Whiterock, he could see the Kor' Cali army from his position in the trees, they were a bit off, but he stayed back inside the safety of cover in case their scouts were in the vicinity.

He now knew his position; next he would need to decide where the missing troops were stationed. They must be close, waiting for something to happen, he knew they would be ready when the time came. They knew the land far better than the Kor' Cali, so they would be able to remain hidden while keeping an eye on the city.

'*But where?*' he thought to himself. '*…somewhere close, somewhere concealed, a place where food was available… the nearest town… no, that was the first place the enemy would have invaded for resources*,' he looked around for inspiration.

A rider wearing the all-black armour with red trims of the Kor' Cali rode past, close to his location, but was not paying much attention to the trees. He rode a dark bay and was scanning the open area between himself and his own men '*an enemy scout.*'

'*The most advantageous location to lay in wait would be one of the hundreds of wooded areas, just like this one*,' Sparrowhawk realised such a place would offer cover and food. The Kor' Cali could not check every forest in the area without seriously weaking their presence at Whiterock. A strong force attendance in view of the city would be essential to show strength, they could ill afford to send half their troops into the forest looking for men that may or may not be there.

'The biggest and the closest forest is a couple of miles east, the Evergreen,' he thought as he remembered the layout of the land, that is where they would be.

After his lengthy walk through the tunnel, he decided to rest for a time where he had exited the dark underground. It would not do anybody any good if he didn't have the energy required to make the trip to the Evergreen. He also wanted to wait until nightfall, the cover of darkness presented the most likely percentage of success, if he was to travel cross country in an enemy occupied land.

He had carefully chosen a bush with wide leaves and stuffed the leaves between the layers of his clothes to help dry them out as much as possible, it provided some relief, but the clothes were still quite damp.

He caught a hare with his bow, washed it in the river and skinned it with his hunting knife, cleaning it as he went. He lit a small fire, constantly fanning the smoke so it didn't ascend out of the trees in a meandering stream. The meat was delicious and he could feel his energy building back up. Then he rested among the bushes.

The sounds of the forest at the dead of night differ greatly than those of the brightness of day, he knew them well from his travels over the years and knew the ones to be cautious of.

There was a couple of scouts riding around in the darkness with torches, but none posed much trouble for him, he slipped through their net as easily as a fish through the hands of a novice fisherman.

He had spent a few nights travelling, crossing the open fields that led to the Evergreen. The days he spent in the safety of overgrown areas and once he hid in an abandoned farmhouse. The moon and the stars guided him to his destination with ease and he entered the great forest as the night air bit at his skin. The high ground was his best bet, it would be further into the forest, but it was the most appropriate spot for his countrymen to be positioned.

The pace was slowed greatly as he navigated around trees and overgrowth, stepping over briars and ducking low under fallen trunks, kept off the ground by supporting trees. The moss provided a slippery challenge from time to time as he scrambled over the bigger stones.

He had found an old work coat in the farmhouse and it offered some welcomed relief against the cold, it was a life saver as he travelled at night.

Often, he took a low-lying branch in the shoulder or the head, he ducked under the ones he could see, but the shadows were difficult to distinguish from what was actually there.

With his arm out in front of him he made slow progress, but it was progress and he must go on, he must find them.

He was three hours at least walking through the maze of trees and bushes in the bitter night cold, when somebody found him. He felt something pressed close against his back while two shadows moved towards him.

Someone said something to him in Kor'dorian and Sparrowhawk slowly reached for his knife, he would take as many of them as he could.

'He's a Ranger,' the man who had the sword against Sparrowhawk's back declared and lowered his blade.

'You're sure?' one of the shadows asked.

'Yes, no turnip head carries a bow like that,' the man replied.

Sparrowhawk took his hand off his hunting knife and relaxed, they were his countrymen.

'What are you doing here old man?' If the man had not been standing directly in front of him, Sparrowhawk would have assumed he was speaking to somebody else, but reality hit him and he understood that he was indeed 'the old man.'

'I bring orders from Commander Milian,' he said and he felt them straighten up.

'From the Commander? How is this so?' the soldier in front asked.

'I came from the palace, there is a secret tunnel underground that leads out, I was ordered to find you, and relay your instructions, take me to whoever is in charge,' Sparrowhawk replied.

'Good job I didn't run you through then, isn't it?' The man behind laughed and slapped him on the shoulder.

'Yes, I am quite happy about that too,' Sparrowhawk replied.

Chapter 26
The Third Army

'What's she doing now?' Dimator asked nervously.

'For the last time, I don't know Captain,' Theo'dor quietly replied.

They had been her guest over the previous few days while she prowled through the Evergreen, sleeping among the trees and eating the wild berries and herbs. She roamed from one area to another, crossing streams and climbing steep slopes, gathering her followers as she went.

Theo'dor had enjoyed his time, he was learning all the wonders of the forest, Dimator on the other hand had wanted to get back to Whiterock to help with the defence of the city. He was restless and concerned about how effective this young girl could actually be.

The two men stood still as the small girl disappeared into the mouth of a stone cave that had bones and small animal carcasses scattered all about the entrance. Flies filled the air while feasting on the remains, as maggots squirmed by the hundreds all over the dead meat. The smell was almost nauseating, they had to cover their nose and mouths to remain from throwing up.

One of the bears stood so close to Dimator that he could hear it breathing, he glanced at the huge creature with the corner of his eyes and remained as quite as a mouse. The bear scratched at the ground, looking for something.

'You're the one with the sword,' Theo'dor added after a long pause.

Dimator stared at his younger companion.

'And what would you like me to do with it?' he hissed back rhetorically.

Theo'dor smiled, either through fear or acceptance that they would probably be ending up on the ground beside those remains.

One of the bears roared from behind them and they both turned instinctively on their heels.

The one closest to Dimator turned also and called back, what seemed like an order to the bear that had spoken out of turn.

'Is that more coming?' Theo'dor asked quietly.

'I think so,' Dimator replied.

'So... how many is it altogether?' Theo'dor wasn't sure if he wanted to know.

'I count about forty,' Dimator replied, amazed at the army of huge animals just waiting on all fours behind them.

They looked so peaceful, with their big heads swaying from side to side, every now and again one of the bears would butt his neighbour and get a butt back, it was almost like they were playing.

'How is this even possible?' Theo'dor asked, knowing the Captain had no idea, but it seemed like an honest question.

'The bears?' Dimator replied.

'The bears, the eagles... the everything. I mean how can she do this, talk to wild beasts like this?' Theo'dor bafflingly inquired.

'How should I know. Like you said before, they are her family, I guess. She grew up here, with the animals, they seem to have established some kind of unique bond with each other,' Dimator gave the most reasonable answer he could think of.

They turned back to face the cave as they heard the girl coming out, she was walking backward out into the brilliant daylight and was talking to someone or something as she slowly exited the cave. She held her hands up as if trying to calm something down, she was speaking slowly and then she looked over to where they were standing.

'Is she looking at us?' Theo'dor asked timidly.

The bear beside Dimator moved forward a few giant steps and stood up on his back legs, the men's eyes went up with the bear as he rose. It was the biggest living thing they had ever seen.

She called something to the bear and he dropped down on all fours, she shouted at it angrily, and the bear lowered his head, snorted and shook it from side to side.

Satisfied, she motioned for whatever was in the cave to come out.

Dimator and Theo'dor jumped backwards into the waiting bears when the largest wolf they had ever seen strolled out of the cave and into the light. They quickly moved forward fearing the bears may have taken this as a sign of aggression.

The wolf looked at the girl and licked his teeth, he then looked at the bear that was closest to him and approached. The wolf rubbed up against the bear and the girl smiled and said something.

'What did she say?' Dimator asked.

'Something about peace and then she mentioned a great battle was coming, and that they were not enemies, peace must be… I missed the last part, sorry' Theodor replied.

'Tour a war,' she said as she walked past, not even looking at either of them.

'Battle for home… em, I think she means, they… as in the animals, will fight for their home,' Theo'dor told Dimator.

'Of course, when the bears and the birds attacked us before, she thought her home here in the forest was at risk, so she attacked our men,' Dimator replied, Theo'dor nodded.

'Now that she knows Whiterock is under attack, which she also calls her home, she is gathering her own army to attack the Kor' Cali,' Dimator concluded.

'Which also means that she no longer sees us as an enemy, right?' Theo'dor was not convinced, but just put the idea out there.

'It would make sense…' Dimator was saying '…but, only for now, as long as we don't give her another reason to think we are a threat, we are safe,' Theo'dor finished for the Captain.

The bears started to move and were following the girl.

'I agree, as long as we do not threaten her home or her animals, she will not attack us,' Dimator said confidently.

'So, we stay on her good side, good idea,' Theo'dor announced.

'I think we should leave, and right now,' Dimator hurried past Theo'dor and followed the bears marching north.

'Why so…' Theo'dor stopped as he saw a large hungry looking pack of wolves exiting the cave and walking straight at him, he decided that maybe some of them didn't realise that they were now all on the same side, you know how wolves can be.

Chapter 27
Attack of the City

The Kor' Cali had been stationed outside the walls of Whiterock for over two weeks now and were growing impatient, he could tell even from the safety of the trees a couple hundred yards away. That number of soldiers would take a lot of feeding and they would need to launch an assault before they had emptied the countryside of all the wildlife. A supply route back to Kor' dor was not an option as they had not yet established a proper outpost.

After years of fighting with the Gala' Mor soldiers in the field, winning this battle and losing that battle, the war was dragging on longer than anybody could have imagined. Balltimor's invasion plan had worked perfectly, now he wanted a quick victory over Whiterock and he was never this close to seizing it.

Sparrowhawk had guided the men he had located in the Evergreen to the nearest safe spot closest to Whiterock, it was a densely covered forest that lay within sight of the main Kor' Cali force.

His eyes were on the palace, there was no raised flag to be seen at the moment, but he knew commander Milian would not wait much longer to test the invading army at his doorstep. They would have to attack the besieging foe sooner or later, they could not wait this one out forever, but Sparrowhawk did agree that keeping the wall between the two forces was the best option for his people for the time being.

'Why don't you sneak in there and kill Balltimor, Ranger?' someone from behind him whispered.

'Aye, arrow in the face and we all go home, I say' another man put in.

'Too many soldiers, nobody could get past them all. Anyway, Balltimor isn't here,' Sparrowhawk answered.

'You sure?' The second man asked, he was a clean-shaven man with high cheek bones and a square jaw, he resembled more of a noble lord than an archer with the King's Guard.

'Positive, he wouldn't risk his seat just yet, there's inhouse fighting back at Kor' dor, if Balltimor came here with his army, win or lose, he'd be returning home to someone else's backside sitting on his throne,' Sparrowhawk announced.

'Too right,' the first man said.

'Hold up... something's happening,' Sparrowhawk announced as he saw the enemy troops all fall into a strange formation.

'What are they doing?' The handsome man asked.

They were too far away to make a proper assessment of what was going on, but heavily armoured troops were falling into lines, while others to the rear were readying their bows.

'They're getting ready to attack, report to your Captain, get your men ready to hit the rear of those archers,' Sparrowhawk called to the men who were sent with him to keep tabs on the enemy. Both men took off at a running start to muster up the regiment of troops hiding in the trees.

'When I give the order, you hit that front gate, Chief. Take your men straight for the target and secure the position, understood?' The Field Captain sitting proudly on his chestnut mare called to one of the tribal Chiefs, he forgot the man's name, but it didn't matter as he would never see the old warrior again.

He was a stout man who had seen many battles and was more at home on the field, commanding his troops than anywhere else, he had two scars across his aging face and a large nose ring that he fingered when he was nervous, but right now he was confident.

'No fail,' the chief replied, banging his chest like an angry gorilla and rallied his men, who returned the chest banging with even more enthusiasm than their chief. They were mercenaries from Gala' less, barbarians who wielded large clubs and dressed from head to foot in animal fur.

'You're sending the hired help first, Ser?' Captain Hussar asked, usually that honour was given to the First Knights, the Kor' Cali's leading unit of decorated soldiers.

'Of course, they'll distract the guards on the walls, it will keep them busy killing the chief's men while our soldiers focus on the tower. That's where their weakness lies, Captain. The ramparts at the top are too narrow to support more than one archer at a time, there we will break them,' he answered.

'Ladders to the rear?' Hussar bellowed to the troops, he read the situation like a picture book.

'Exactly, if our man behind the walls comes through for us, there shall be as little guards as possible to the left of the main gate. Send our main force there, support their charge with all archers,' the Field Captain announced to his first officer.

'All archers, Ser. That will leave all our other units unprotected?' Hussar asked, maybe he had misheard.

'Yes, it will,' the Captain replied coldly.

The sun was beating down upon the grim-faced soldiers of Kor' dor when the drums began to beat. They knew that beat and what it meant, they waited for when they would charge on the famous 'Walled City' that had never been taken. Well, today that would change and the entire world would remember this day was won by the Kor' Cali.

'Ser, they have started their drums,' a Captain came thundering in through the doors, almost sending a half dozen nobles to the ground in the process.

'Ready the archers,' Commander Milian announced as the room gasped at the news.

'Ser, right away, Ser,' the man replied.

'Hold on a moment…' Commander Gladis held up his hand to stop the Captain from leaving the meeting room '…we must consider their attack patterns first. My spies inform me that when the Kor' Cali attack a fortress, they concentrate all their force to the right side of the main gate, we have no reason to think they will change their tactic with us,' Gladis announced to the room.

'It would give them a better chance of success to do so, they would get more ladders and more men on those ladders if they directed all the men to one area,' a noble wearing a bright green gown offered.

Commander Milan nodded his agreement and the Captain left the room.

'Sire, you must enact the Rhinos last stand protocol,' Commander Milian called to his king.

'It's a bit early for that…' Commander Gladis shot in and was offering his advice.

'The Rhinos have been briefed on their orders and they will follow them,' King Armando announced to a stunned room.

'You've already given the Rhino's orders for the incoming attack?' Gladis asked slowly.

'Indeed,' the King replied and looked at the Commander with a gaze that he had never seen before. The Commander looked away as Armando, surrounded by his escorts left the room. The two Commanders noticed that their own bodyguards left with the King, without a word.

'To the ramparts men, the rest of you take cover in your homes until this battle is won,' Commander Milian shouted at everyone, and the council room was emptied as officer's hurried to their positions and nobles to their families.

Hussar watched the strange barbarians charge at the main gate, following their chief without any consideration for their own safety whatsoever. Their small shields were light and made of ash, they were circler and had a small wooden handle for an easier grip with various designs painted on the front the day before. Their weak fur armour was more for the look than serving as an actual barrier, it was practically useless against the plummeting arrows that were destined to mow them down like cattle to the slaughter, never the less, on they ran.

The chief had seen an eagle in the sky that morning, closely followed by another, then wonder of wonders, a third had flown over just moments later, it was a sign of victory and he had no doubt in his mind that his people would see these huge gates fall.

He roared to his men as they were getting closer to their target, they answered him with their war cry. He glanced around and saw the rest of the Kor' Cali army just sitting there, waiting for him and his brave warriors to clear a path into the Walled City, a rush of blood went to his head and he believed himself invincible at that moment.

His men ran in a loose formation, no structure, no discipline, just wild and fearsome. He could see his enemy high on the walls as he approached, he called to them, boldly taunting them to stop him. He knew he was inside their archer's range, but they did not fire, he thought it was through fear.

He heard the drums coming from behind just as they were coming up to the gates, he looked back and saw the main body of the army moving forward, today was the day he and his men would be honoured beside the great Kor' Cali.

The men on the walls moved into position, poised and ready.

'Single volley… ready…' a call came from inside the walls. '…loose,' the voice shouted.

The chief saw hundreds of tiny black dots coming towards him from the top of the ramparts and from the many slits build into the stonework of the walls. He had to blink to regain his vision. He felt many sharp thuds banging into his whole body and he was driven backward as he looked down and saw three or four shafts pinned into his body. He went to his knees and noticed that all his men were on the ground, some dead and more moaning as they were littered with arrows and bleeding from every point of entry.

He could hear thunder from behind, the ground was shaking and he struggled to turn and face the sound. A line of heavily armoured soldiers was marching right for him, huge shields covering most of their bodies with only their pointy black helmets visible over the charging wall of shields. They were a sight to behold.

It was just over half of the entire force that had been trusted with taking the city, while the remainder of the army waited at a safe distance, ready to take their comrades place should they somehow, not succeed.

'Gave us enough time to get our lines past their first controlled volley,' Hussar noticed.

'Indeed, the chief has served his purpose, plus we won't have to pay him for his efforts, it's a win-win for us Captain,' his superior noted.

The advancing Kor' Cali did not have time to go around the dying Gala' less warriors, so they effortlessly marched straight over them, crushing any survivors underfoot with their heavy boots as they hurried to the left side of the gate.

Archers from the walls and window slits were now firing at will, picking out men below with accuracy. Their arrows were not as effective as a controlled single volley, but some of the more experienced archers were adding to their account slowly.

'Keep firing, keep firing,' the officer bellowed at them.

The runners inside the walls were working double time to resupply the archers with fresh bundles of shafts from the store rooms. There were thousands of shafts in storage, but there were also thousands of enemy troops outside with metal plated armour and tower shields, soon enough they would run out.

'Keep those shields up,' an officer shouted at anyone thinking about lowering their shield to get a bit of rest. The heavy shields weighed about twelve kilogrammes and were not so easy to keep in position for a very long time with one arm.

'Switch shields in twenty seconds,' he added after seeing that most of his men were ready to break formation. Switching shields was unfortunately unavoidable. Each shield was designed to protect three soldiers when held overhead, it allowed the other two men to shoot arrows back at the enemy from a kneeling position. Switching shields meant that the man to the holders left would change places with the current holder, it would leave them vulnerable and give the enemy a free shot as the shields were being changed.

'Ten seconds,' the man called.

Arrows were raining down on the Kor' Cali, bouncing off their protective cover as the archers on the walls fired hopelessly down. They were coming in dribs and drabs and in all the excitement the attackers on the ground did not notice that the arrows were coming more slowly over time, the archers on the walls were waiting for something.

'Switch shields,' the officer roared, the practiced manoeuvre took about four seconds to complete in perfect conditions, these however, were far from perfect conditions. The very moment the men holding the shields dropped them to the ground a concentrated volley of shafts came from above, it took out about a quarter of the soldiers on the ground. They fell to the mud, holding arrows sticking out of their bodies, crying out in agony while others lay dead.

Quickly the remaining soldiers had their cover back in place before another volley came. The archers had been waiting for the switch and half of them had held their bows notched while the others send down arrows constantly.

'Ladders, where are my ladders?' The Field Captain bellowed after witnessing the blow.

'On it, Field Captain Bartus,' Hussar replied and ran over to a group of soldiers waiting for orders.

The men with the ladders were of course being picked off by the archers on the walls, they were easy targets as they had to use both hands to carry the huge ladders to scale the walls.

Many ladders lay on the ground unattended due to the carriers being shot from above.

There were four men per ladder and eight ladders in total, it was not a desirable job to carry a ladder unprotected, so nobody bothered to pick them up again.

'Soldiers, we need those ladders up front now or we lose this war,' Hussar ordered some of the reserves to get the job done. Reluctantly a group of men ran forward.

'Get the archers into position to support our men on the left, Captain. When they are in position send in a unit to the right of the gate, distract their archers from our main attack point before the ladders get up there,' Bartus called, not wanting the enemy to wonder why all the ladders were going to only one location before he could give them proper covering fire with his own archers.

'Ser, of course Ser,' Hussar answered and ran to the archers to relay the command.

The archers moved quickly; they carried barricades with them as they advanced towards the walls. The barricades were constructed of felled trees and held together with heavy ropes. The shelters were about eight feet in height and ten feet long, it took every man that was using the cover to carry it forward. Two healthy looking stands were fastened to either end of the shelter, permitting it to stand freely. It would offer great support for the archers, allowing them to remain protected against the archers on the walls, but they could also fire over and to the sides of the makeshift shelters to provide covering fire for their own troops.

'Soldiers at the gates,' Captain Samus called to his unit of King's Guard.

His men moved into position behind the heavy main gate of Whiterock and awaited further instructions.

'When that gate comes down... we hold this court,' he bellowed.

The Kor' Cali were just on the other side of the timber gate, they were using a battering ram to try knock the gate inwards, so far, the strong timber had held, but it would only be a matter of time.

They were in a tight phalanx formation, twelve wide and twenty-four deep. Heavy metal shields locked into position with three layers of spears overlapping the first line. They stood back about ten feet from the gate to allow it to swing in when it finally gave.

With every loud bang the enemy were making with their ram the gate shook and the hinges moaned loudly against the assault. They were ready to repel whatever came through.

The archers had scored a great victory with the switch over of shields against the enemy, but since then they had not caused any serious damage that looked like fending off the advancing foe. The Kor' Cali were now moving their own archers into a position on the right side of the city, soon they would know what it was like to be the victim of enemy projectiles.

'Ladders… concentrate all fire on those ladders,' an officer shouted as he spotted enemy troops coming forward with the ladders.

The archers took aim to fire at the men carrying the long ladders, just as they were about to fire, a volley of enemy shafts came thundering across the sky and landed perfectly into the archers on the walls. Many shafts struck and bounced uselessly off the stone cover, but many more got through and sent men down from the ramparts to the waiting ground beneath.

'Return fire,' the officer who had escaped the onslaught by the skin of his teeth, demanded.

'Archers or ladders?' One of the trained archers replied, stooping down below the cover of the toothed wall.

Another volley struck their position, killing more men and scaring the lives out of the rest.

'Archers… their archers,' the officer shouted.

'Red arrows to the archers on the ground,' the man shouted to his fellow marksmen. They discarded the normal shaft and picked up special arrows that had tar and straw on the ends, just below the tip of the arrow head. One of the runners came forward with a torch and quickly ran across the rampart setting light to all the archers red arrows.

'Light up the archer's shelters,' the man roared and they all rose together and sent flaming arrows across the sky down into the enemy shelters, as the targets were so big, no one missed.

The men behind the shelters retreated as their timber covers were ablaze. The archers on the walls picked them off as they tried to run back out of range to their waiting army.

'That'll teach 'em,' a shout went up from the wall.

The celebrations were cut short however, as a spear took the man in the chest. The man beside him looked confused, nobody could throw a spear that distance. It was then he realised that the spear had not been thrown, it had come from an enemy soldier from the other side of the wall. The Kor' Cali soldier climbed over the wall and took the second man in the leg with his now drawn short sword. The nearest archer killed the man with a shaft as another enemy came over the wall, he was grabbing at the archer who had killed his friend when a shaft struck into his back.

'Ladders, they're coming up the ladders,' the officer shouted. In all the commotion with the enemy archers, the enemy had hoisted up the ladders and were now flooding over the walls. The archers on the walls retreated and a huge roar came up from the enemy outside as they saw their own men storm over the city walls.

'Full attack,' Field Captain Bartus shouted at his men. They would no longer be under threat from enemy fire, so an all-out frontal charge was the order of the day.

All the reserve units came thundering forward, most of them remaining in formation, but a few eager soldiers broke rank to get into the action quicker. All that lingered behind were his personal bodyguard of thirty soldiers and the young men with the drums.

'The day is yours, Field Captain,' Hussar announced contentedly.

'Not yet Hussar, the battle is not over until we have the boy-king,' Bartus carefully reminded his officer.

'Indeed, Ser,' Hussar replied, realising he had spoken too soon.

All the ladders had men climbing up and scaling the walls, the battering ram at the front gate was about to shatter it to splinters and his advancing men would soon flood the city.

He looked down as he heard something hit the ground to his left, it was Hussar, and he had a very smooth looking arrow shaft sticking out of his back.

Bartus instinctively spun around on his horse. Just a couple hundred metres away dashing forwards were an advancing unit of Gala' Mor King's Guard. He had known that not all his enemy would be in the city, it was the reason they had attacked when they did. But he had no idea they were so close; they had probably been watching all this time he thought.

'Drums,' he called to the men holding the big animal skin drums beside him.

Quickly they beat in perfect unison a series of bangs and booms that sounded a light retreat.

The reserve troops that had just left to join the attacked stopped suddenly and turned to see the advancing unit of enemy coming from the trees, they quickly ran back to their waiting Field Captain and moved into position in front of him, to face the oncoming attack.

'Their coming over the walls, Down-side,' his fellow soldier roared in dismay as the enemy were fighting their way across the high ramparts, the defending archers had retreated and the King's Guard were climbing up to meet the attackers with swords and spears.

'What the blazes do we do now, you great oaf,' Daxos shouted over the noises of war.

Down-side looked around; he saw his fellow soldiers forming lines to defend the gate when it broke. He also saw the troops defending the walls with their lives.

'Run,' he shouted to Daxos.

'Run where…' Daxos replied. '…they'll take the city and skin us alive, or our men will send them back over the walls and home to Kor'dor, in which event our own men will skin us alive,' Daxos's logic was not pretty, but it was the truth.

'And how do we not get skinned alive, let's do that,' Down-side responded.

An arrow came over the walls and landed two inches from Daxos's foot, plodding into the mud, it was big and black.

'Kill them all,' Daxos announced and drew his sword that was never used before, unless you count splitting melons.

'Agreed…' Down-side replied. '…walls or gate?' He added.

'You two half-wits, defend the walls,' someone shouted, they did not know the man, but he looked like he knew what he was doing as many more King's guards followed him to the gate.

'Walls, it is,' Daxos said rather calmly.

'Indeed, my friend, may we both drink to this after the last soldiers have fallen' Down-side called out as he ran towards his position, Daxos followed but was not too sure they would.

'Not sure this is a good idea, Ranger,' one of the men called to Sparrowhawk as they came out of the tree line, it was the man who had the sword at his back the night he found them.

'We fight for the King, men… we fight for our home and our way of life… but, most of all we fight for our loved ones trapped in that city,' the officer of the missing unit cried.

'They outnumber us about a million to one,' one of the men replied formally.

'Well, I'm going to have to borrow some of their arrows then,' Sparrowhawk replied and the men within earshot laughed nervously.

'Captain, may I suggest we head straight for their officers,' Sparrowhawk offered his advice.

'Indeed, listen up men…' he shouted to gain their full attention. '…there are more of them than there are of us. They have our capital city under siege and they look to be gaining the upper hand. But they have not calculated us into their formula for victory, which is why they will not have it…' he paused as the men shouted their agreement. '…we head straight for their command; we start with that cowardly looking gentleman on the horse…' he said in a fancy tone and his men laughed. '…and we take back our city this day from those who would take it from us,' he roared the final part and was rewarded with an enormous roar from his unit.

Sparrowhawk checked the sky above the city and there, flapping violently in the strong wind was a blue flag, right over the palace. The sign to attack had been issued, he did not see it being risen, so had no idea how long it had been flying.

The enemy was so busy with the battle in front of them it was unbelievable that his unit of King's Guard had gotten so close out in the open to the rear of the enemy.

Sparrowhawk checked his pocket for his special brew, but noticed it was gone. He would have to rely on himself to see this one through.

'Ranger,' the officer called to him.

Sparrowhawk notched an arrow, stepped to the side and stood still. He controlled his breathing and let his mind take the arrow to his target, then he fired at the man on the horse. He missed.

The unit continued running, about two hundred men in all, with their weapons drawn, well-trained but only about two hundred. They had solid armour on and medium grade shields with them, in a skirmish they would hold their own, but against that many Kor' Cali, it was a David vs Goliath affair.

The surprise attack was now over as the enemy was facing them with all the force they could spare.

'Shield wall,' the officer shouted and the men complied. The enemy did likewise and advanced slowly. The invaders had spread out on both flanks and the Gala' Mor soldiers got an idea of what they were up against now. From the safety of the trees, they looked a lot smaller, both in number and in size. But, the Kor' Cali were neither. Their shields were locked tight, their spears came forward and the earth seemed to shake as they came closer and closer.

'Hold,' the officer shouted and his men held. They did not break or run, they were fighting for their home and their way of life, they were out flanked, outnumbered and out of time, but they would give everything.

Sparrowhawk joined them from the rear. There was nothing he could do to aid them now, he was not a disciplined soldier, he was a Ranger. A few arrows over the top would do nothing to slow down the marching enemy. The day was almost theirs and they came on like a raging storm. Feet pounding the ground and the rhythmic beat of the troops banging their spears against their shields caused the very air between the two forces to become heavy.

The enemy flanks were curving in around the small group of soldiers, nearly encompassing the King's Guard.

'Hold,' the officer repeated.

The enemy stopped their advance. The air was silent, not a sound could be heard as the Kor' Cali waited for the order from behind to come.

Suddenly a long howling came from the north of the open area where the two armies stood, a slight rise leaning back towards the forest that would have made for a pleasant green picnic area had there not been a war raging under the cloudless sky.

Sparrowhawk turned to where the noise had originated.

There sitting about half way up the slope was an estranged collection of animals and three human figures standing among the beasts. He was not sure how many there were in total, but guessed their number at around three hundred. He saw bears and wolfs facing them on the ground, and oddly they seemed to be arranging themselves in some kind of battle formation as they slowly came down the incline.

'Prepare to brace… it's the girl,' a shout came up from Bartus, for he had seen first-hand what devastation was in store.

'*Brace for what?*' Sparrowhawk thought as he watched the scene unfold before him. The rest of his countrymen had also witnessed this peculiar event and stood ready for whatever was coming.

The turnip heads turned their entire force to face the animals that were coming at them, shields up and spears ready. Sparrowhawk realised that they had made their whole flank open to attack from his side.

'Captain?' He shouted.

'I see it, prepare to attacked their right flank,' he roared back, his men heard the call and poised themselves to charge at the unusual opportunity that had just presented itself.

A shrill came from the animal army and in a heartbeat the beasts of the forest came running down the slope, they ran in a controlled wave, the wolves leading the charge and the Kor' Cali braced for the moment of impact.

'Sir, do we brace?' one of the men shouted, confused as anyone.

'No, that is Captain Dimator with them,' he replied.

There was a pause within his ranks.

'So, the animals are on our side?' the man responded bewildered.

'It would seem so…' the Captain grinned. '…ready men to hit them on the flank when those wolves hit their shield wall.'

The wolves ran at a high speed down the slope and were just about to reach the enemy's shields, the bears a bit slower; came a fair distance behind their fanged friends. The Kor' Cali were ready to meet the wolves head on, but the pack of about two hundred angry wolves had a different plan.

As they were about to clash into the metal wall, the line of wolves leaped into the air simultaneously and right over the first lines of enemy soldiers. The grey and black wolves landed into the men on the third ranks and went wild, the soldiers were not ready for such a tactic, they had their twelve-foot spears in hand, expecting to fight at a safe distance behind their shields.

The wolves ripped into the exposed legs and sank angry teeth into unprotected arms, sending troops to the ground, injured and unable to function, but mostly still alive.

'Draw your swords, loose the spears, you fools,' Bartus called to his frightened men.

It was at that moment that the right unprotected flank was hit by the King's Front Guard. The effect was devastating, the well-trained soldiers had come unannounced like a battering ram into the enemy's side. The Kor' Cali had lost sixty men before they could organise and muster up a defence of shields to stop the butchering.

The wolves were causing mayhem among their force, each animal taking down three or four before they were outnumbered and slayed with the curved swords of the Kor' Cali.

Their shields were holding back the spears of the King's Guard, but they were still taking losses on the right and inflicting no damage in return, they were concentrating on holding the line.

The wolves continue their attack into the enemy ranks and were running riot among the now disordered troops who were panicking in a frail attempt to subdue the ravaging wolves. A man was an easy enough foe, you could predict to a certain degree what he might do, but a wolf whose only ambition was to main and kill was a completely different proposition. Howling was coming from everywhere inside the unit, once a tightly knitted outfit, the men were starting to break file as the enemy wolves were causing terror.

'They're just dogs… hold together, form lines, do not break,' Bartus was roaring at his unit. 'Shields up, lock and push…' another seasoned soldier roared '…swords levelled, advance,' and the men followed his instructions. Soldiers were forming up side by side and locking their shields together, the wolves had no way through such a defence. The four-legged beasts needed room in order to build up speed to jump, but that space was beginning to be cut off. The soldiers came forward in numbers and jabbed advancingly with their swords, cutting at the bodies and heads of the wolves. More howling could be heard across the land as the wolves were almost spent, the soldiers were surrounding and hacking them down.

'Support the right flank,' Bartus called seeing the hole that the King's Guard had punched into his force. Men were dying as the main body of his unit was dealing with the wolf threat, now that the creatures had been dealt with, he needed to strengthen up that flank and repel the enemy there. His men heard the call and were moving to answer the command, it was at this moment that the huge bears arrived, about seventy to eighty in total, he hadn't time to count.

Bartus had been focused on the wolves and the Gala' Mor King's Guard threat, the bears had been too far away when he last saw them, now they were killing his men.

'The bears, by all the gold in the Forever Mountains… the bears,' he called, but it was too late to get his men into a proper defensive position as most of them were now busy with the King's Guard on the right.

The soldiers had been ordered to lose their spears and only had short swords to fend off the roaring bears, which gave the animals a huge advantage over their two-legged enemies. Claws tore into flesh as the overpowering animals inflicted immeasurable casualties into the enemy.

Bartus sat on his horse, fingering his nose ring as he wondered how to fix the bloody mess he was stuck in the middle of. All his years of training and wargames could not provide him with an answer. The right flank was holding, but morale within his troops was rapidly diminishing.

'Spears, pick up the spears… you fools,' he called, but the fools could not hear him as they were fully engaged in being mauled and it was rapidly causing a state of panic among his men. Soldiers were breaking rank and running out into the open and fleeing the battlefield, Bartus was taking mental notes of who the men were, for they would need a whipping later.

His only advantage now, was his overwhelming numbers, his men were taking a beaten, but they were also bringing down bears slowly, they were being instructed by those who had fought the bear in the Evergreen days ago. Although without the conveniency of the long spears it was nowhere near as effective. Bears were roaring and grabbing men, mauling them and roaring again, it was a terrifying scene that no man should have to witness.

'Surround them, attack from all sides as one,' a shout came up from someone who had been in the Evergreen. The men were running out of men, so they did as requested. The bears could not deal with being assaulted from different angles all at once and soon the soldiers, although exhausted and deflated they were not defeated, and now they were gradually gaining the upper hand. The strategy was working and the bears were beginning to succumb to the blades of the Kor' Cali. More than half were out of action and the remaining wolves were being dealt with.

Bartus surveyed his unit, he had less than a quarter of his original five thousand still standing, as the ground was littered with dead and wounded men, a few hundred or so had taken to the safety of the countryside, causing the remaining men to doubt their own resolve. It was an epic disaster in the eyes of any officer of Kor' dor.

Bartus was becoming desperate when another loud shrill came from just outside of the killing zone, he looked and saw the three people still standing there. The girl had blown the whistle again, what now. Suddenly, he noticed that the bears were leaving, retreating, he had won, if you could call it a victory.

A roar went up from the Kor' Cali as the bears left the fray, they had beaten them back.

'Spears,' Bartus called again, wanting his men to be properly armed for the Gala' Mor King's Guard to his right, this time all his men found a stray spear lying discarded on the ground and quickly picked one up. He had lost a lot of men, been outdone by a small girl and a few animals, he would not allow the King's Guard to survive this day if it was the last thing he ever did.

Sparrowhawk watched the whole battle taking place with amazement in his eyes. The bears had now retreated and the enemy was preparing for another frontal assault towards him and the unit of King's Guard.

'Brace,' the Captain shouted. The Kor' Cali had taken a heavy blow and lost a huge number of their men, but they still had more than his own band, and they would be mad with rage after suffering such a loss due to the animal attack.

Just as he felt the call was going to come, another shrill came from where captain Dimator was standing with the girl and another young male.

The Kor' Cali stopped their advance and nervously looked in the direction of Captain Dimator. Sparrowhawk looked to the Kor' Cali officer on the horse, he was scanning the area frantically, then the sun grew dark.

Over the heads of the three companions on the slope came a cloud of blackness, it was not one single entity, but thousands of flapping black birds. It came as quick as if it had always been there and the black cloud roared across the empty space to where the Kor' Cali waited.

'Shields high,' the man on the horse bellowed as the black swarm clattered into the unit of soldiers, causing the men to duck low under the safety of their metal shields. Knocking him off his fine mare and into his men below. Those without shields got engulfed by hundreds of flapping birds and the screams of the men as they fell about the place waving their arms helplessly sounded sickening to the ear. Men falling lifelessly from bleeding heads into the lush summer grass, birds pecking at their eyes.

'Lose the spears… you fools,' came the call from within their ranks and swords were drawn again as the spears fell to the blood-soaked ground.

Sparrowhawk watched as the enemy was being battered by the birds, his own unit although a mere twenty yards away remained unscratched by their sharp claws and pecking beaks.

The soldiers were now starting to retaliate by swinging their swords into the air, chopping down the winged foe by the bucket load. They began to rise from their stooped position as the threat seemed to lessen and were now in a position to organise themselves into a functional unit again. Shields were locked and swords were slicing through the small airborne attackers.

It wasn't long before the unit had the situation under control, the birds were starting to return back in the direction from where they had come.

Bartus rose to his feet, his beautiful mare had taken off when the birds had pecked and scratched at her head and body, she was now gone and Bartus was not in the mood to go and look for her.

Blood was streaming from his nose as he had broken it in the fall, he looked around as his unit and saw disarray, he had no idea what his number had been brought down to now after that last assault, but he was about to inflict at least three casualties into the enemy before whatever else was going to come for them.

'The girl… take the girl,' he roared.

'Ser, the King's Guard?' Someone foolishly called, worst still the man was standing right beside the Field Captain. He was a casual soldier, no rank to talk about and no one would miss him. Bartus plunged his sword into the man's chest and retracted it in an almost fluid motion, the man dropped dead.

'The girl,' he bellowed the loudest he had bellowed all day, nobody else questioned his bellowing.

The unit turned to face the three people on the rise and started to move forward. A few held shields towards the King's Guard and walked backwards, just in case they tried to intervene, it would not have been out of the question at this rate if they did.

Bartus and his unit were slowly making their way up the incline, rage in his eyes and anger boiling in his heart. His campaign into Gala' Mor could still be won, he had breached the walls and his men were ransacking the city this very minute. He would just need to chop the girls head off, figure out how that bloody whistle worked and returned to Balltimor victorious. All would be right in the world again.

The King's Guard were following the Kor' Cali from behind, matching their pace, their own shields and spears ready for who knows what was to happen.

Without warning, a huge cheer when up from within the city walls, everybody froze as both sets of soldiers looked back towards the city. Who had cheered, did it mean the city had fallen or somehow did the defenders manage to repel the enemy. The answer was quick in coming.

The Kor' Cali were coming back over the walls, many soldiers pushing and shoving others out of their way and over the high walls to their deaths as they hurried to secure a place on the ladders.

The huge gates open from the inside and the enemy soldiers wanting to get inside the city turned on their heels and ran. They were dropping their weapons and shields to lighten their load as speed was their most important defence now, they ran in all directions to get out of the way of something coming out of the gates. It was then that the sound came, it was a thundering noise and Sparrowhawk even checked the skies for signs of a storm brewing, but the beautiful sun had wiped that theory away in a flash. He looked back at the gates and the fleeing enemy.

Bursting out from the opened gates came a huge wall of charging White Rhinos, their shining tower shields five foot high and their enormous halberds levelled at anyone or anything stupid enough to stand in their way. Some enemy soldiers were too slow to move and were either trampled over or bounced to the side, they ran in perfect unison and seemed to be coming straight for the Kor' Cali unit advancing on the girl.

The Kor' Cali archers that remained fired a volley at the Rhinos, but the arrows had no effect on their heavy armour, they did however manage to kill a few of their own fleeing troops not expecting the assault.

Bartus was quick to assess the new developments, and logic told him in a heartbeat that his men had failed and were not ransacking anything.

'Retreat…' Bartus bawled and his men gladly complied with the command. The Gala' Mor archers were back on the walls, picking off any enemy soldier within range.

The flood of Rhinos kept on coming out of the gates, there must have been four or five hundred of them. The sound of their march echoed around the land and the ground seemed to shake as they came closer.

Bartus stood meters away from the three he sought, and there she was staring at him with those little emerald eyes. His men had fled the field and were making their way east, the King's Guard had no way to detain or pursue them, so they had no choice but to let them leave.

Bartus stood there contemplating his options, of which there were two. Return to Balltimor and lose his head for failure or option two, he looked at the girl, it was an easy choice.

Quickly he drew his sword and lunged at the girl. Dimator stepped forward and drew his weapon, but was too slow. The Captain had his sword out, but Bartus's blade was coming forward for Meadow's chest. Meadow did not move.

Just as his curved sword was about to pierce her heart, Bartus fell to the ground, unmoving.

Dimator and Theo'dor looked with shock at the very smooth arrow shaft sticking out of his back, right where his heart used to beat.

Both men found the source of the shaft, a Ranger standing beside the King's Guard about four hundred meters away, it was an impossible shot. The Ranger nodded to them and they returned the gesture, stunned at the man's skills with the bow, the girl looked blankly at him.

The unit Sparrowhawk was with let out a roar of complete triumph, he witnessed fully bearded grown men weeping freely and no one judged them.

The enemy had retreated to the east and were heading home before the Rhino charge. The Captain of the victorious unit, looked fearful as the Rhinos got closer to his men. But, as they came up the rise, the palace guards turned to march up the hill to where Captain Dimator stood with his companions.

The powerful charge stopped right in front of the waiting trio, the bears and remaining wolves had disappeared back into the forest, Sparrowhawk saw the last of them return to the safety of the trees.

'Captain Dimator?' one of the Rhinos asked.

Dimator stepped forward and nodded.

'We have been asked to bring the King's cousin into the city,' he looked at Meadow.

Dimator looked at Meadow and then his attention went to Theo'dor.

'I'll ask,' the young man said ruefully and faced the girl.

Dimator took in the Rhinos before him and a shiver ran up his spine, he was glad to be on their side.

'She says she will return to the Evergreen,' Theo'dor announced, Dimator swallowed hard as he had never seen anybody refuse a request from a Rhino before.

'So be it, the King offers her welcome and an investigation into her parent's death will begin as soon as safety allows. We will send word to the daughter of Princess Lousia when results are forthcoming,' a different Rhino said.

Dimator did not know which huge man to respond to or even if a response was required.

'How?' Dimator said in a confused tone.

'King Armando send us to protect his cousin, under the advice of commander Milian, he felt it best to detain Commander Gladis in the keep until an inquisition can be arranged,' a third Rhino replied.

'Commander Gladis, I had a funny feeling about that man,' Theo'dor announced, shaking his head.

'Indeed, the King had suspected someone was working with the enemy. They knew too much information, they seemed to roam freely across our land without detection,' a different Rhino added to the conversation.

'But, the Commander?' Dimator was a naturally sceptical person.

'Yes, the Commanders received two Rhino escorts not for their protection but to keep an eye on them. We have been investigating them for a time now, Commander Milian was true, unfortunately Commander Gladis was not and he will be judged accordingly,' the first Rhino announced.

No more was said between the men, the Rhinos turned around and the ones at the other end of the column led the return charge back into the city.

Sparrowhawk came forward to the three companions.

'Captain Dimator?' he said.

'Indeed, nice shot,' Dimator said referring to the shot in which Sparrowhawk had killed Bartus with.

'Not my first day,' he smiled.

Theo'dor introduced himself and Sparrowhawk knew the name of the merchant family.

'And this is?' Sparrowhawk asked about the girl.

'Meadow,' Theo'dor answered.

'Mea' dow,' the girl interrupted.

Theo'dor looked at the girl and said something Sparrowhawk did not understand.

Theo'dor's face lit up with realisation.

'Her name is Mea' dow,' he looked at the two men.

'What's the difference?' Dimator asked carefully.

'Mea' dow is in her own tongue, it means "little wolf" when translated,' he replied.

Chapter 28
The Aftermath

Sparrowhawk walked slowly under the stone arch of the main gate; he noticed the massive timber door was hanging on by the hinges with its last breath. It was riddled with arrows and damaged beyond repair with a gaping hole in the centre where the battering ram had made short work of it.

Men were dying in the streets as others ran about in a haphazard fashion trying to bring a bit of organisation among the people. Most of those present were soldiers aiding their injured brothers in arms, however, there were others who were patrolling the scene, searching for any remaining Kor' Cali troops. Sparrowhawk saw three soldiers drag one of them out of a house and carry him off in the distance to deliver their own style of justice, he did not relish the enemy soldier.

The common people were starting to resurface from wherever they could find shelter during the assault. Most of them were a mish mash of emotions, clearly overjoyed that the enemy had been repelled, but there was also the devastation that had come with the attack, they all looked exhausted.

Two soldiers walked past him and he overheard them discussing who was buying the first round after their valiant performance at the ramparts. The one with the bald head was convinced it was his bravery that had stricken so much fear into the hearts of the Kor Cali, that the turnip heads just turned around and legged it, the other man was convinced it might have had something more to do with the White Rhinos charge.

He made his way to his own house where Rose would be waiting. He hurried back as the enemy had scaled the walls and were inside the city, no one was safe until they were all taken care of.

There was a group of children playing 'see who can loot the most bodies before we get caught' running freely around the courtyard, before a soldier chased them off saying he knew their fathers and there would be trouble when he informed them of the children's behaviour, Sparrowhawk hoped they would receive the beating rather than be told that their fathers had given his lives so they could be free.

The dead and wounded were thinning out as he progressed off the main road leading to the palace and passed down through the narrower streets preceding to the poorer regions of the city. Women were peeking out through windows to see what was happening, obviously too scared to venture out into the unknown. Sparrowhawk informed all he saw of the good news that the enemy had been beaten to the yelps and cheers of all he spoke to.

His house was coming into view and he saw what looked like the body of a woman on the ground just a few meters from his house, a large gash on her back, standing over the corpse was a scrawny goat, chewing at the woman's hair.

'Mena…' he said softly when he discovered who it was, he bent down and released her grip on the goat's lead. '…seems the old fellow has outlived you after all,' he finished with a nod and walked slowly back towards the old battered house.

Theo'dor and Dimator returned to the city. Many soldiers and commoners cheered the two as they entered through the main gate, Theo'dor smiled, soaking in the applause while Dimator roared at the soldiers, ordering them to get back to work with the huge clean-up effort that was underway.

They walked together towards the Upper Ring, Theo'dor to his family's estate, Dimator to the palace to report to Commander Milian. As they approached the keep, they noticed a lot of activity, Dimator called to one of the on-duty guards.

'What has happened here?' He said in a commanding tone.

'Bloody Kor' Cali breached the keep, freed all the bloody prisoners, didn't they,' the guard replied annoyed. Dimator frown, looking around, maybe he expected to see all the escaped convicts just hanging around waiting to be recaptured, he was not to be so lucky.

'Speaking of which?' Theo'dor looked at the Captain sheepishly.

'Oh right,' Dimator had completely forgotten where he had met the boy.

'Well, we can't be locking up a hero of the Kingdom now, can we?' He replied calmly, there were other, more pressing matters that needed his attention.

'Then I will make my way to my father,' Theo'dor replied and nodded to the Captain.

'Of course, mind yourself while you go, there may be enemy soldiers still inside the walls,' Dimator called after him.

'I'll manage,' Theo'dor smiled and Dimator remembered the boys hidden talent he had witnessed in the forest.

Theo'dor arrived at the door of his parent's home in the Upper Ring. The private security allowed him access without question. His mother hugged him until his father had to pry her away, who could blame her with recent events. Both his parents expressed their concern for the boy as they had no idea of his whereabouts, they feared he had been killed by the raiders. Tears of joy were flowing freely from all three sets of eyes, even the servants who were present, felt overjoyed at his safety.

When he produced the map of the tunnels through the Forever Mountains he had 'borrowed' from the King's library, it was his mother who had to pry his father off Theo'dor.

Sparrowhawk tied Milly to the door frame as the door swung easily open and the light beamed inside and lit up the small room.

Sparrowhawk went for his bow, but the man was quicker with his blade.

'Drop it,' he said, a ring pierced through his lip at each corner.

Sparrowhawk did as instructed, the man's blade was pressed close against Rose's side, his other hand held tightly onto her shoulder.

'Easy now,' Sparrowhawk threw his weapon onto the rotten floorboards with a bang and spread his hands out, hoping the Kor Cali soldier would not see him as a threat.

'What were you going to do with that...' the soldier indicated Sparrowhawk's bow on the floor. '...you don't have any arrows left...' he said and Sparrowhawk realised that his quiver was concealed behind his back, he had the element of surprise and that at least gave him a chance.

'Probably killed all my friends with them, did you... eh old man?' the man spat angrily.

'*Need to calm him down*,' Sparrowhawk thought.

'I was not defending the walls,' he said honestly.

'Bah,' the soldier said, eyeing the Ranger with a dubious stare.

'Look at me, would you put me on the walls,' Sparrowhawk was playing the age card, he knew he did not resemble the young fine archers of the King's Guard and was hoping the soldier knew it too.

'True, you probably wouldn't hit a horse in a stable,' the man joked.

'Rabbits,' Sparrowhawk said quickly.

'Eh?' The soldier replied, not loosening his grip on Rose.

'I hunt rabbits,' Sparrowhawk answered, somewhat honestly, he did hunt rabbits.

The soldier appeared to be buying Sparrowhawk's cover story, for now.

'Move over there, into the corner, out of the doorway,' he spat at the Ranger, Sparrowhawk obeyed and slowly sidestepped over to the corner of the small room, not taking his eyes off the invader.

'You want out of the city,' Sparrowhawk was not asking, but gently leading the man into planning his next move.

'Aye,' the soldier replied. Despite his mean appearance and sharp sword, the soldier was quite young and more than likely not a hardened killer, his own safety was the first thing on his mind and Sparrowhawk read him effortlessly.

'Let her go and I will get you out of the city,' Sparrowhawk said in a commanding tone.

'Bah, I cannot do that,' the soldier replied defiantly.

'If you do not let her go; you will die here today,' Sparrowhawk assured him. Rose shook at the mention of somebody dying and the man tightened his grip on her, she squirmed for a moment, but calmed down as her father's eyes met her own.

'She will die first,' he shouted back.

'That may be so, but so will you,' Sparrowhawk told him in no uncertain terms. The man heard his words and understood them, Sparrowhawk was in charge of the situation and he knew it.

'Ok… you win, how do you get me out of this place, there are guards everywhere?' The man said quickly, he felt his time was running out and he needed an escape plan ten minutes ago.

'First, you must remove those rings in your mouth,' Sparrowhawk said to him.

'I cannot, I do not have the tools, they need to be numbed first,' the man replied.

'Well, I'm afraid it's the block or you remove them without the numbing,' Sparrowhawk said.

The soldier stared at Sparrowhawk; it was a look of desperation. He stood still for a few moments, thinking over his options, of which there were few.

'Ok… you win, what then?' The man asked after a while, concerned.

'Then, I will give you my clothes and you can walk out of here,' Sparrowhawk knew that he would not get past the King's Guard that easy and was hoping the man was not thinking straight enough to land on the same assumption.

'Ok, what now,' the man replied, his eyes darting around nervously.

'Now, you let her go,' Sparrowhawk said calmly.

To his surprise the soldier released his grip on Rose, she ran over and threw her arms around her father. As her hands swung around to the back of him, she hit into the quiver that was sitting low on his back and knocked out a number of arrows that landed on the floor, rattling for a few seconds and then coming to a rest.

The already agitated soldier spotted the incident as soon as it happened and felt immediately threatened by the sharp arrowheads. His mind was racing with rage as Sparrowhawk quickly stepped in front of Rose and held out his hands again, showing the man he meant no harm. But the Kor Cali soldier now came to the conclusion that he could just kill the two of them and be on his way, leaving no witnesses to his presence.

He lunged his weapon straight for Sparrowhawk and the Ranger managed to step out of the way just in time, the blade missing him by a quarter of an inch.

Sparrowhawk's right hand instinctively went up to connect with the man's face and he heard a shattering noise, the soldiers nose a bloody mess. He was forced back for a second but came forward quicker than Sparrowhawk thought possible.

The soldier was trained well and pain was only a trivial matter in times of life and death, he sprung forward and sliced high through the warm air of the room and Sparrowhawk was forced to duck to the floor to avoid the slash. His hand found something smooth, without looking he knew what it was and came up with as much speed his age allowed and sunk the arrow shaft into the soldier's neck, the sword fell with a clatter.

There was a moment of eye contact between the living and the dead, the soldier blinked twice and fell to the floor holding the arrow, breaking some of the timber underneath as he landed with a lifeless bang.

Rose darted over to her father and threw her arms around him, thankful he was alive, she sobbed uncontrollably for a time as he just held her, looking at the soldier on the floor.

Rose was safe now, he had stayed with her for a while until she gathered her composure again, the attack had rattled her and she didn't want to let him out of her sight.

'We must go to the palace to report that there are enemy soldiers still in the city,' he said to her, she smiled as she had been invited to tag along, he didn't want to leave her alone, not yet.

'People will be edgy and suspicious throughout the city, especially the soldiers we cross, and they have a right to be so. But we will be safe, do you understand?' He asked.

'Of course, Papa,' she replied seriously.

She donned her coat and they both headed out the door into the scenes of death. Milly called out to them as they passed her in the door way, Rose told the old goat not to be afraid and that they would return before long.

They passed all the petrified people, although the battle was over, many wondered about the streets looking for loved ones, others sat and wept openly as word came back that they had lost sons and fathers to the fighting.

Sparrowhawk tried to protect her from the aftershock, covering her view from the most gruesome scenes and trying to distract her, but he could do only so much.

The guards at the palace outer walls recognised him and let him through with a nod, respecting him as one of their own.

He entered into the palace and there were many guards and soldiers rushing about the place, he approached the main doors that led to the military section of the building. Rose looked up at all the huge sketches hung around the walls, with the faces and busts of many decorated Kings and Commanders from bygone eras, glaring proudly down at the people they would never know.

'Hold there,' a soldier called to him as he neared the door.

'I am Sparrowhawk, I've come to report in with Commander Milian, there are Kor' Cali troops inside the walls,' the Ranger offered.

'I know who you are, Ser. I've been instructed to escort you to the council hall, and don't concern yourself with the enemy troops, we have everyone in the King's Guard searching the city for them, follow me,' the soldier replied and headed through the doors.

Sparrowhawk and Rose followed the man closely, taking in the excitement of the people around them.

'Ah, come in, come,' Commander Milian announced when he saw them enter the room.

Sparrowhawk walked to the centre of the room with Rose only a few inches behind him.

'I can see that you have once again succeeded in your latest mission. When we raised the blue flag, we were uncertain that you would come through for us, but you did,' Commander Milian nodded and smiled a wide grin. The room erupted with a chorus of applause and some men cheered the Ranger loudly for his success.

'The King's Guard are stripping the city bare in search of any remaining enemy troops and we will soon have a regiment on stand-by to track down those fleeing turnip heads,' he announced to the entire room, again they applauded and cheered.

'It was more than I who stood outside the walls, Commander,' Sparrowhawk replied to the Commander when the noise calmed down.

'Yes, we saw them from the walls, the King's cousin and Captain Dimator, what a sight, all those animals fighting alongside the brave King's Guard,' Commander Milian shook his head, astounded at the turn of events over the last couple of hours.

'It was unusual, to be sure,' Sparrowhawk agreed.

'Indeed, there is one last thing Ranger,' the Commander said as he spotted Sparrowhawk beginning to make his way towards the door, clearly the man was not comfortable in a room full of nobles and high-ranking officers.

'Of course, Ser,' Sparrowhawk announced.

'It is the matter of the breach in the keep,' Commander Milian cleared his throat.

'A breach in the keep?' Sparrowhawk responded in haste.

'Indeed, it would appear that some of the enemy troops got as far as the prison and released all of the inmates, the place is as bare as a pig's backside,' Milian said with a heavy heart.

'That is terrible,' Sparrowhawk replied.

'Indeed, it is…' Commander Milian said. '…That is why we need you; you must track down two of the escapees for us,' he finished and the room clapped as if the fugitives had already been apprehended.

'First, you will hunt down Commander Gladis, he is wanted for conspiring with the enemy, a most serious crime,' he announced loudly to a chorus of boos and hissing.

'Then, once you have the Commander in custody, you will retrieve the outlaw known only as Long-tooth,' he finished with a nod, as if Sparrowhawk had no say in the matter. Sparrowhawk felt something poke him in the back; he turned around to see a certain young lady frowning up at him.

Stars of the Story

ANTON D'SOUZA
Father to Theo'dor, he is the wealthiest man in Gala' Mor. He owns the largest share of the mines in the Forever Mountains and trades his metals with the Northern Realms and to all parts of Gala' Mor, he is strong headed and loving towards his family.

ARMANDO
At just eleven years old, Armando, prince to the Gala' Mor Kingdom has found himself on the throne. His father Matias 'the Peacemaker' has died in his sleep. believed to be of natural causes. Armando is given the customary position of king. The boy-king is surrounded by advisers and Commanders, he has two younger brothers, twins, Raynard and Roland (7), and baby sister Tilly (3).

CHESTER
A fast-talking criminal that lives in Narrow's Crossing, specialises in ripping people off and instilling fear in those around him, friend or foe.

COMMANDER GLADIS
Commander in the King's Guard. He tends to be a grumpy old man with a short temper. He has seen many battles and has a past that he wants to keep buried.

COMMANDER MILIAN
A long serving Commander in the Kings Guard. Generally liked by his fellow Commanders and everyone under him for his natural righteousness and firm, but fair assessment of any situation. Married with eight soldier sons and a single daughter, Neadielo, she has just become he first girl to join the Command Academy.

DIMATOR
Ser Dimator is an officer in the King's Guard. Serious man with excellent leadership skills. Patriot and loyal to the Gala' Mor Kingdom.

LONG-TOOTH
An oversized outlaw that has a bounty on his head. He is a hot-tempered man that will do anything to stay on the lamb.

ROSE
Rose is the daughter of Sparrowhawk; she is dying of an illness and her father must capture outlaws to pay for her medicine. She is a talented herbalist and makes her fathers 'special brew' and also helps to craft his weapons.

SABAT
Sabat is an old healer from Marshaven, and has lost all his family to the Halti Empire when they invaded Marshaven twenty years ago. He lost himself in his work to make medicines and ointments for the local people.

SPARROWHAWK
Sparrowhawk is a Ranger in the Kingdom of Gala' Mor, a land so vast it is said no man has ever crossed its reaches in a single lifetime.
His wife died about four years ago, now he will do what it takes to save his daughter Rose.

THEO' DOR
Theo'dor D'Souza, the only child of the merchant Anton D'Souza, is an overly intelligent boy who excels in mathematics and physics. His yearning to learn as much as he could cause his father to notice his talents. Not too strong or tall, Theo'dore quickly stored all his eggs in the brains department. His father hired private tutors for him, the boy although not bulky, soon understood the arts of hand-to-hand combat by theory and applied his skills by calculation. He became an expert in single hand to hand fighting, though he only used this in extreme cases, most of the time he waited for the right time to exact his abilities to gain a greater advantage.

Read the First Chapter in Book 2

Kingdom of Heroes

Army of the Night

Chapter 1
Gormley Learns to Fly

He was dreaming of home, the beautiful green hills and valleys where he had lived all his life. It was where Marley waited for him to return. Her round little face and long dark hair was all he longed to see again. The Two Glens was a picturesque slice of earthly heaven, that any man would be glad to call home.

'Get yer lazy tender backside up,' shouted a rough voice that was accompanied by a pale of icy cold water.

Shaking the water off his head and out of his ears he sat up on the floor, his straw mattress and his coat pillow soaked through.

'Alright, alright, have your kind never heard of easing someone gently out of their sleep?' He asked and was expecting to be ignored, he was correct.

'Up to the roof,' the man commanded as he exited the room and left the door ajar for Gormley to follow.

'Blasted… half-sized impatient people, no manners whatsoever,' he whispered to himself.

The day was bright, but so cold he had to shiver as he stepped outside where the others were gathered, this far north, that was about the best weather you could ask for.

'Movement again this morning,' one of the men said to him as he came to stand with them in a huddle. It had been weeks since the D'warfen had brought him to the great tower they called 'Winters Watch' and he was about to discover the primary reason for his kidnapping.

'Prepare the anchor,' Rurin shouted and some of the men ran into position behind the ballista that was stationed on the roof beside them. One thing about the D'warfen, they were disciplined workers, they fiddled around with the large timber catapult for a few moments and signalled that everything was in place.

'Gormley, it is time,' Zaltan said to him seriously, more serious than the small bearded man had ever spoke before.

'Time, time for what... to go home, good. I was getting a little fed up being here to be honest, I was thinking we could stop by maiden Treasa's store on the way, pick up something nice for Marley, see if she is still talking to me,' he smiled, but the stone-cold stare he got indicated that he was not going home just yet.

'Gormley, do ye know what is beyond dat trench?' Zaltan asked.

'Nothing. The earthshakers killed everything beyond it many years ago. They caused great holes in the earth and released some kind of poison on the people of Great Harbour, killing every living thing east of the blasted thing,' Gormley pointed to the enormous trench that had appeared all those years ago, shutting off the north-east of the continent. He was just repeating what he had learnt from stories and tales be had been told.

'Then tell me what de ye see, just over there?' Zaltan asked and pointed across the trench.

Gormley looked, expecting to find the dead trees and loose stones that had always been there, instead he was greeted with a sight that no man could explain. There, right in the middle of the open expanse, was a herd of horses, searching through the snow in a bid to find some grass underneath. They were casually strolling through the dead earth, as if they had no respect whatsoever for the tales and stories told in the taverns around Gala' Mor.

'It cannot be,' Gormley swung around to meet the gaze of Zaltan.

'Oh, but it be,' Zaltan replied.

'Nothing can survive in there?' he said, turning to all the men at his side.

'Tit would appear something can, laddie,' a voice came from behind, it was Faltan.

'Who else knows about this, we must inform King... what's his name?' Gormley announced.

'We must inform nobody until we can evaluate what exactly is going on for ourselves,' Zaltan responded.

'But the King should surely be informed of any...' Faltan cut him off.

'The King would merely send his entire army here, they would fret 'bout de place like lost puppies an' no doubt kill themselves trying ta cross the trench, just ta kill those innocent horses,' he sighed.

'So, ye see, by not telling the King, we are saving lives' Timot stated.

'Anchor away,' someone shouted and the man hit a level on the ballista with a heavy mallet.

A second later the machine vibrated as a huge metal ball came thundering across the sky attached to a heavy rope that Gormley had not seen until now. The rope shot into the air and followed the metal ball across the skyline and curved as it fell in a long looping descent, landing on the far side of the trench with a barely audible thud. The other end of the heavy rope was attached to the ballista and now made a bridge across the wide trench.

'What do you intent to do, exactly?' Gormley looked around at them and would soon come to regret his question.

'We investigate, or rather send someone else to investigate,' Zaltan announced and they all looked at Gormley.

'Woa, woa, hold onto your scruffy little beards for just one moment, send who and how?' Gormley asked in a panicked tone, his eyes darting around at all the different faces that to him looked the same.

'You of course, laddie,' Zaltan replied softly.

'Me?' Gormley announced in a squeaky voice, then he cleared his throat.

'It's simple really, you just use this device…' and someone came forward holding a hanger made of wire and fabric and handed it to Gormley. '…to swing yourself down the rope and take a look around when you are on the other side of the trench,' the small man spoke like he was ordering breakfast.

Gormley approached the rope and looked down, he could barely see the bottom of the tower through all the clouds. He swallowed hard.

'And, might I ask, as to why none of you fine fellows wish to risk sliding down the rope of death, over an endless hole in the ground and into a place that nobody knows anything about?' Gormley made a good point he felt.

'We are afraid of heights' Timot responded flatly.

'Excuse me?' Gormley announced.

'Why de ye think we stay in de middle here all stuck together like a bunch o' sisses,' Faltan replied.

'I see,' Gormley said shaking his head from side to side at his situation.

'Look laddie, it's easy really. Just slide down the rope and if there is trouble or anything amiss, fire these arrows into the sky…' Zaltan said and handed him a quiver and a bow. '…And we'll call the King and his army to come kill whatever is over there,' Zaltan finished with a trusting nod.

Gormley wasn't too sure about the idea in the least, he was about to throw the bow to the floor and make his escape when Timot spoke again.

'Think of all the songs you could write about your adventure into Great Harbour... think of all the stories de people will tell of... of... Gormley the Great,' he announced.

'Gormley de Great,' Zaltan bellowed and his men joined in the chant.

Gormley thought about it, and the more he thought, the more he liked the sound of it. It would be him who had made peace with whatever wild tribes were across the trench and him who saved the Kingdom from whatever imaginary threat they posed, it would be him who tamed the wild horses and scaled the unscalable mountains, the songs would be about him this time and it sounded good in his head.

'Alright, I'll do it,' he said without thinking.

A cheer went up from the platform on the high tower.

Gormley swung the quiver and bow around his shoulders, a man came forward and gave him a bag of supplies, which was also swung over his shoulder on the bow side.

He approached the rope as the D'warfen watched eagerly.

Gormley placed the hanger into position, it locked in with a click and he checked it to judge whether it was secure by leaning all his weight on it, the hanger was well made and would see him safely across to the other side. The drop down was far, if he fell, he would not have to be concerned about being injured, it was death that waited for him below and death would have to wait a bit longer he told himself.

'Remember, fire an arrow into de sky if something happens, there will always be someone on watch,' Zaltan bellowed to him. Gormley nodded, he wasn't stupid after all.

With a count to three, he rocked himself forward as he counted 'One... two... three,' he shouted and launched himself out into the open air, just his hanger holding him hundreds of meters above the freezing hard ground. He was sliding down at blistering speed when a thought occurred to him; he shouted back over his shoulder, 'Hey, how do I get back?'